The
Glovemaker's
Daughter

BOOKS BY SHARI J. RYAN

The Bookseller of Dachau

The Doctor's Daughter

The Lieutenant's Girl

The Maid's Secret

The Stolen Twins

The Homemaker

LAST WORDS

The Girl with the Diary

The Prison Child

The Soldier's Letters

SHARI J. RYAN

The
Glovemaker's
Daughter

bookouture

Published by Bookouture in 2023

An imprint of Storyfire Ltd.
Carmelite House
50 Victoria Embankment
London EC4Y 0DZ

www.bookouture.com

ISBN: 978-1-83790-677-2
eBook ISBN: 978-1-83790-681-9

This book is a work of fiction. Whilst some characters and circumstances portrayed by the author are based on real people and historical fact, references to real people, events, establishments, organizations or locales are intended only to provide a sense of authenticity and are used fictitiously. All other characters and all incidents and dialogue are drawn from the author's imagination and are not to be construed as real.

To Bretts
The memories spanning five generations from my family's shop
will forever be a part of my life's story.

PROLOGUE

RAYA, PRESENT DAY, OCTOBER 1943

Ravensbrück, Germany

I should have left Paris years ago. I should have gone to Zurich with Alix, but there was no way of knowing what was coming, just like it is now.

Pain is all I know now—a constant companion of this war. Our hearts suffer from loss, but our bodies endure brutal encounters. Through excessive lashes across the back and face, a fist to the stomach, and other unthinkable assaults, I've learned that the worst type of agony is not knowing what's becoming of me.

I search around the grim shadows between the narrow light beams filtering in through crevices along the enclosing walls. The tears trickling down sullen faces and the tension pinching everyone's foreheads make me wonder where the other women came from and if they are here for similar reasons.

The stench of cow manure, stale breath, musty skin oil, and sweat fills the air like a dense gas. My arms are pinned between two other sets of arms, grease gliding between us all as we dance like rag dolls in harmony with the momentum of the speeding train. Questions percolate in my head, only to repeat in a cycle without an answer.

What could I have done differently?

What might I never get to do again?

Who will I leave behind?

The love branded onto my heart inflicts a shroud of darkness that will consume me even if I find a way out. A way out. It suggests there must have been an initial way in, but I ended up in this cattle car without a choice.

After what must be a full day of traveling, the train screeches to an abrupt stop without warning.

Then we wait.

German soldiers shout orders from the outside, acting as though they aren't aware of how many of us are crammed into one container. The suspense while waiting to find what awaits us on the other side of the door is twisting my stomach into cramping knots.

The heavy metal locks unclasp, the sound much louder than the secure locks I released each morning before opening my shop. When the door slides open, the metal grinding against rust, sunshine pours in like a spotlight, blinding us as we gasp for a taste of the chilled, untainted air. We pour out of the cattle car like milk spilling out of a tipped jug, flooding onto the platform with no perception of where we are.

Orders roar through the air, but I'm unsure if they are for those of us trying to see through the blinding daylight after being confined to darkness for so long. We're pushed and shoved into some semblance of formation, a messy line containing limp bodies, tired and weak from standing upright in one spot all day.

The sky is icy blue here without a cloud in the sky, but the temperature is colder, brisker, and biting. With so many of us lined up like the cars of the train we were on, there isn't much to see except a sign that says Ravensbrück. I've never heard of the location, but I assume I'm about to find out more than I want to know about this place.

I notice others have belongings with them, but I have nothing. The Gestapo only gave me a second to consider what I would have to leave behind.

The most unthinkable sacrifice a person can make is to give up their life hoping to save another. There's no way of knowing if I made the right choice or if I'll make it back home, but somehow, I must try to find a way to reclaim what will only ever be mine.

ONE

RAYA

LAST YEAR, MAY 1942

Paris, France

The bulky brass metal locks unclasp one by one as I release the choke hold on the shop's front entrance. Ten years ago, I might not have remembered to lock every one of my doors but now I can't sleep unless every door in my building is secure with a deadbolt. I flip the closed sign so it faces me instead of the locals on the street.

Until two years ago, when Germany invaded our country, Notre Dame's bells would ring out in the distance, rattling the light fixtures ever so gently. I sometimes wondered if my life revolved like a clock because of the fifteen-minute intervals I was so aware of, but then they stopped, silencing the city with grief as we lost hold of what should be ours. Even though it's been two years, the church bells continue to play in my head, keeping my life in sync until they someday, hopefully, return for all to hear again.

I straighten the disorderly array of wallets and belts perched on the shelf along the back wall. I've gotten into a good habit of straightening up after closing the shop at night, but I sometimes forget. When we were children, Mère and Papa assigned my brother, Alix, and I different tasks. I would keep track of inventory and Alix would straighten up the products to ensure their displays were perfect for opening hours the next day. We maintained these tasks long after Papa passed away, then Mère too. But when I convinced Alix to move to Zurich two years ago to obtain a college degree, I had to add his responsibilities to my already full plate. I've carried on fine but there are days some tasks slip my mind.

The flower-filled resin-globe paperweight next to the cash register pins the small stack of custom-order slips. I also forgot to organize these for Charlette last night. I sort through each one, separating simple tasks such as stitching repairs to the more time-consuming leather embossing orders. Charlette prefers to work through the challenges in the morning and end her workday on a lighter note. I can't say I blame her. She wasn't always so particular and organized. When we first became friends in grade school, I remember her frenzied moments of digging through her knapsack searching for a homework assignment. The papers were usually crinkled when she found them, but she always handed them in on time. In grade school, we were determined to achieve the best marks possible, thinking it would give us a better chance of a lavish future in fashion design. We dreamed of having our own clothing-line and becoming known as inspiring, successful women in Paris.

We haven't talked about our visions these last few years. Not since they floated out of reach.

When Mère passed away, my future became a blur between what I wanted and what I needed. There was no way I would give up on the family business that had put food on our table for generations. In support, and as evidence of our unbreakable friendship, even at just seventeen, Charlette clung to my side when I needed her and promised wherever we went in life, we'd be together. She has stood by me and helped to keep the shop running ever since the day the world fell on my shoulders.

I was too young to know what I would do for the rest of my life. In different circumstances I'm not sure I would have chosen to stay in Paris to help Mère run the shop, but with her and Papa gone, I can't imagine being anywhere else. This is where I'm meant to be, carrying on our family name and selling the leather goods for which we've been known for more than a hundred years. These walls embrace everything my family has ever been, keeping them alive and with me every day.

Though I'm sure of the time, I glance up at the old grandfather clock between the storefront windows. Usually, Charlette would be here by now. She even has her own set of keys because she sometimes arrives an hour before the shop opens. Occasionally, she'll come upstairs and join me for a quick breakfast unless she has too much work to complete down here. When we were kids, the shop was on her way to school so if she left home early, she would come upstairs and have a second breakfast with us before it was time to leave. Like me, Charlette is never late.

I think we owe that trait to our mothers. They spent many evenings playing gin rummy in the shop after it closed for the day. Charlette and I were always curious to know what they were chatting about, so we would put a glass against the stairwell wall behind the shop and eavesdrop. We overheard them exchanging motherly advice, sharing secrets, stories, and, if we were lucky, gossip. One night, they were talking about something so secretive, we were only able to hear every other word until Mère said: "That's what she gets for being late. I've told Raya time and time again; the world will never wait for you."

"What does that even mean?" Charlette had whispered to me. I shrugged because I hadn't the faintest idea, but those words seem to replay in my head whenever I consider taking an extra moment to powder my nose.

Despite my lack of desire to poke my head outside the front

door, I feel the need to check as worry blossoms within me. The door squeals and screams, reminding me to grease the hinges. I wouldn't be able to sneak out of the shop without drawing the attention of any passerby. Although the quiet has taken over the streets these last few years and there aren't nearly as many people strolling by the shops as there used to be. The German soldiers and the collaborating French police have scared most Parisians into staying inside their homes unless it's necessary to leave.

Not much appears out of the ordinary. Monsieur Croix is in his usual spot, ringing up patrons paying for the daily paper they've taken from his wooden newsstand wagon. He's there, rain or shine, hot or cold, Monday through Saturday from sunrise to sunset.

"Salut, Monsieur Croix," I holler to him over the chatter.

"Salut, chérie." He waves quickly but barely twists his head around enough to see me. He yearns to give each customer his full attention for the brief few seconds they interact in the mornings.

I slip my key from my sweater and lock the shop's door. I don't want to turn the sign back around to say we're closed because it will send return customers the wrong message with so many other shops closing lately.

While turning away from the door, I spot a young man fussing with a stack of newspapers at Monsieur Croix's newsstand. He's clearly in a rush with whatever he's doing, his hands trembling ever so slightly as a newspaper slips out of his grip.

I stop to help, unable to determine whether I recognize him as the rim of his black beret curves sharply over his eyes. "Are you all right?" I hand him the fallen paper as he steadies the remaining pile in his hands.

"Pardon me, please. Thank you," the man says, finally glancing up to reveal his unfamiliar face. He replaces the newspapers on the rack, lining them up to look untouched. Except, the newspapers he's straightening are from *Vraie Nouvelle*, a local French paper. The German papers are supposed to have priority in visibility.

"What are you doing, monsieur?"

"Fixing the faux pas," he concedes with a sigh.

"You'll get Monsieur Croix in trouble if a German soldier spots what you've done," I explain, wondering why I should be explaining what we should all be used to by now. Our country has been taken over, making the French secondary to Germans, even with something minute like shelf space for newspapers.

"No, you see," he begins, pulling the first newspaper away from the rest, "the others are German. This way, it looks like a patron was looking through the papers before placing it back down. Everyone knows Monsieur Croix wouldn't mix up his perfectly curated stacks." A sly smile stretches to one corner of his mouth, exposing a dimple encircled by faint freckles. His eyes are the shade of ripe blueberries with a hint of purple. He's quite handsome, dressed for work, perhaps in a shop or an office based on his attire: a white collared shirt, wool tie, tan trousers, and matching coat.

"Don't get him in trouble. He's a good man," I warn.

"You're the woman who works in Pascal Maroquinerie over there, aren't you?" he asks, smiling with charm and confidence.

"I'm the woman who *owns* the shop over there, yes," I correct him. "And you are?" He lifts his hand, fist curled, to check his watch. I notice ink stains and lead smudged along the side of his hand. "Other than a left-handed man who works with ink." I feel the need to add the last bit so he knows it's been noticed in case Monsieur Croix ends up in trouble because of him.

"I'm late for work," he says. "Nicolas Bardot. I'm a journalist at *Vraie Nouvelle*." He reaches for my hand, and though I should hesitate, I offer it to him. He politely kisses my knuckles and releases my fingers. "It was a pleasure to meet you, Woman-Who-Owns-The-Shop-Over-There."

His wit earns him a quiet chuckle, but I must stop this nonsense and move along to find out where Charlette is. I glance down at my wristwatch, noting it's fifteen minutes before the hour, which means something must be wrong.

"I'm Raya. My name may be easier to remember," I say, smirking. "Enchantée, Monsieur Bardot." My heel catches between two cobblestones, and I thankfully wiggle it loose before losing my balance and making a fool of myself. My cheeks burn as I make my way down the curb. There is no time for handsome strangers, especially a witty and charming one.

Charlette lives only a few blocks from the shop, but the walk is long enough to notice another regression of familiar sounds. This city has lost its heart. So many people left their homes because of the German occupation that it's now more common to hear boots marching down the street than children playing with a ball and squealing with laughter. There are few shoppers along the streets; the musicians and artists who used to spend their days entertaining others have packed up their belongings to become invisible like the rest of us.

My fellow Parisians and I ponder if life will return to normal, but each day this occupation lasts, the less hope we have. At least the oil-spill-colored pigeons are still croaking among themselves, and the flowers are still blooming in window garden beds. The air still smells the same—a mixture of baked goods and floral essence.

Right before I reach the next block, a man on a bicycle sweeps past me, his wheels clunking from rusty springs. It seems bicycles have gotten older or louder lately, but it might be that there was never enough silence before to hear the metal gears grinding.

I step into the front entrance of the building. Charlette and her parents live in a flat on the third floor. The war changed her plans to move out and live on her own by the age of twenty-four, forcing another dream to wait.

I hope she isn't sick. We both had our fair share of common colds throughout the past winter, but it's spring now, so that should be behind us.

I rap my knuckles gently against their door, hoping not to startle anyone if they are still asleep. "Charlette, it's me, Raya. I'm worried about you."

A thump from something falling to the floor on the other side of the door startles me. Feet scuffle around inside before a long wave of silence creates a distinct pause before the lock becomes unlatched, and the door creeps away from the threshold, enough to see Charlette's eyes peeking out beneath the chain-link lock.

"Are you alone?" she asks, breathless.

"Yes, of course. Who would be with me?" Her question is so absurd it's almost funny. Charlette and I have each other and, aside from her parents, that's enough for us. We've been best friends since the third grade and though other friends have come and gone, nothing will tear us apart.

She unlocks the door, and the chain falls loose, jangling as she creates an opening large enough to pull me through. No sooner than I'm inside her flat does she secure the doors again.

"What in the world is going on?" I ask.

"Keep your voice down," she whispers, her words huffing with exasperation.

I scan the open layout of the flat and spot her parents sitting on their royal-blue velvet sofa with melon-green taffeta accent pillows. Long room-darkening drapes cover the large window off to the right. Usually, Charlette's mother, Rose, would have them pulled to the sides, allowing the sunlight to spill in. The open kitchen to my left is tidy, but there's a pile of pots and pans on top of the oven. It's unlike Rose to have disarray anywhere in her home. What's worse is how she and

Monsieur look as they sit on the sofa, their knees pinned together, their posture straighter than arrows. With stares of disbelief, they sit in front of the coffee table as if they're afraid of what an inanimate object might do to them. They don't even seem to be aware that I've joined them in their home. I notice their hands interwoven between their hips. I step in further, wishing someone would tell me what's happening.

An unfolded letter sits in the center of the coffee table. I can only wonder if it might be the reason for their silence and the apprehension I can feel through every cell in my body.

Charlette doesn't stop me from approaching her parents or the coffee table, and no one tells me to stop when I reach for the paper that might as well be burning a hole through their teak table.

It's as if I've forgotten how to read as I focus on the German words. I'm not entirely fluent, but I've been keeping myself versed for the last few years. Though never did I consider it would be to read a letter such as this.

"By the end of next week, we will be branded as Jews of Paris. We already know what's happening in other European regions. Denial can't keep us safe forever," Charlette speaks on behalf of her parents from behind my shoulder.

My heart swells while listening to the woman I call my sister speak words that no human should ever have to murmur.

"It isn't just the stars we must wear," Charlette's father, Jacques, utters. "The letter also says the ownership of our building will be transferred to German authority by the end of the week. All Jewish residents must evacuate before then. They're barricading us within the borders. Even if we were to run, there's nowhere to go. I'm not sure what they expect from us." Jacques was a lawyer before the Jewish people lost their eligibility for high-paying positions. Without a choice, he joined a factory line in an old mill on the outskirts of the city. He works twelve hours a day, but they are mostly surviving off Charlette's income.

Rose hasn't blinked her long dark lashes in over a minute. She's staring through me as if I'm nothing more than a foggy mist. "Where else is there to go?" she asks her husband.

"I have space," I offer, before thinking through the commitment. In truth, it isn't something I need to ponder. Charlette and her parents are nothing less than family and have treated me like a daughter and Alix like a son, especially after losing Mère.

"We won't all fit in your flat," Rose says, staring at her fidgeting fingers.

"I have storage space where I keep inventory. The ceiling height is low, but I can clear it out. You'll be comfortable and it's hidden well. I only learned how to access the space from my mère a year before she passed away." It was certainly a well-kept secret. *The space kept my grandparents safe during the Franco-Prussian war*, my mother had said.

I'm not sure my comment eases their minds, but it's an option that doesn't require running away from the city.

Charlette wraps her arms around mine, resting her cheek on my shoulder.

"You have access to the tunnels under the shop, too, right?" Jacques asks.

"Indirectly, yes. The sewer line beneath the shop leads to a tunnel entrance."

Jacques presses his hands against his knees before standing up from the couch. He walks over to me and cups his hand against my cheek. His poor skin feels like rough cement from all his work, and a hint of machinery grease emits from his body—a smell that must not come out of the canvas jumpsuit he wears to work.

"Raya, if we were to stay in your flat above the shop, we would endanger you. The German officials were clear in the letter, all locals should report any Jewish family not residing in a Jewish neighborhood. We won't consider risking your safety. I wouldn't do that to your parents."

I shake my head, but his hands remain firm on my cheeks. "No, they would protect you. I know they would." He can't argue. Mère would be the first to take someone in if they looked hungry or cold. Never mind our dear friends.

"What other choice do we have, Jacques?" Rose cries out. "La Marais and the small area of Montmartre are already overflowing with Jewish families. There is no space for us. We must go somewhere else."

Jacques's eyes soften, and his brows furrow as he accepts his wife's words. "I know the other two Jewish neighborhoods are too far from here," Jacques digresses, weaving his fingers through his hair. "I suppose—just for now—it'll be best for us to stay with you. We will help however we can with the shop. Charlette says you never have a shortage of orders. We can all help. It will be the least we can do."

I would take care of them even if they had never done a thing for me. I love them, and that's what we do for those we cherish. "You don't need to worry about anything. It will be nice knowing I'm not alone at night in the building. Ever since Alix left, I fall asleep to a symphony of creaks and croaks moaning through the walls and my imagination gets the best of me sometimes."

I suppose I didn't realize before how lucky I am to be Catholic, even if Parisians are no longer wanted in our own city. I've seen how the Germans have treated the Jewish citizens here and it's frightening to imagine being in that situation. At the same time, I wouldn't be able to live with myself, knowing I didn't do everything possible to help the three of them. They would take me in if need be. I know they would. I don't see my neighbors often and if the Levis stay out of sight, there won't be a risk of anyone reporting us to authorities. I must do what's right for them despite the danger.

Jacques pulls me into his chest and wraps his burly hand around the back of my head. "You are just like your mère. She and your papa would be proud of the woman you've become."

Charlette embraces us both. "This is a good plan, Papa."

"I agree," Rose says, joining us. "I'll gather some belongings, but only what we need."

We all step back and study each other momentarily, likely worrying about different aspects. Regardless, my offer remains. "We'll set everything up for you tonight," I reply.

"I'm so sorry for not showing up at the shop this morning," Charlette says. "I couldn't—"

"Nonsense. Take your time and help your mère. You're welcome to come in whenever you're ready."

Rose crosses her aging hands against her chest; the swollen veins are prominently purple and blue beneath her pale skin. "We are so grateful."

"I feel the same about you. I should get back to the shop, but come by tonight. I'll stay downstairs to wait for your arrival."

TWO
NICOLAS
LAST YEAR, JUNE 1942

Paris, France

There is usually no easing into the day with casual chatter, except today, with the lovely young lady who scolded me at the paper stand. *Woman-Who-Owns-The-Shop-Over-There*. I'm not sure the blushing cheeks of many women have distracted me as much as hers did this morning, not after being woken by the sound of explosives down the street from my flat.

I feel as if I've been awake for hours following my early morning search around the city blocks to gather information on what had occurred. Even worse, once I gathered the news, I came to realize I would be unable to write about the events that had unfolded.

"What do you have for me?"

People don't greet each other with morning salutations here. Paul Dubois, editor in chief of the *Vraie Nouvelle* daily paper, doesn't believe in small talk. The short, stocky, middle-aged man with a t-shaped receding hairline and a thin dark mustache that stretches from the edge of his top lip to the other, hasn't shown an ounce of enthusiasm in the five years I've been working for him. By one quick look, I can see that he and his wife must have had an argument last night because his pale-yellow button-down shirt is wrinkled—the collar is hardly folded down in place. I think Paul would starve to death if his wife stopped taking care of him. One might think it would stop him from ticking off his old lady, but I guess not.

I've been jotting down notes for a half hour but crossed it all out seconds after the ink from my pen dried.

"All Jewish citizens of France have received a written notice, demanding they wear the Star of David badge on their clothing to identify them. This goes into effect next week, June 7th. Is that what you're looking for?" I already know what he's going to say... *We always remain neutral. We will not pick a side, but at the end of the day, we are in France.* Every day, it's the same statement. He has nothing else to reply with.

"We remain neutral—"

"Paul, with all due respect, we are not neutral. The French don't hate the Jewish people, nor are we okay with the Germans playing tug of war with us using barbed wire. What is the purpose of staying complacent? Our paper is hidden behind the stacks of German ones anyhow."

Paul inhales sharply and pulls a box of cigarettes out of his shirt pocket and plucks out a stick. I toss him the box of matches I have sitting on top of a stack of old papers.

"Look, I understand where you're coming from, but if we speak out we'll get shut down. Then we'll be out of jobs. You know this. Our options are to play nice or go hungry."

Playing nice isn't in the cards for anyone. It never has been. Father used to tell me that people will say "the less we know, the better off we are", but it's a lie—the worst lie anyone should believe. The truth is what will keep us on guard. He told me that being one step ahead of the others with knowledge was the only reason he made it home from the first war alive. I didn't grasp the meaning of what he meant until this war begun.

"Write the piece but be neutral. Got it?"

I shouldn't have suggested the topic. There's no way to sound impartial about the laws affecting Jewish people. They're our neighbors, Parisians, no different from myself or anyone else aside from their faith. It's unfathomable.

I scan the room and its scattered metal desks, seeing nothing but clouds of smoke puffing out around everyone's heads as they most likely stare through their paper the same way I have been. "If we don't have anything to write about, we aren't going to have a paper to print," I remind him.

"Make something up then. I don't care what you do, just write something," he says, huffing a mouthful of smoke into my face.

"Why don't you write about what you've been up to at night for the last few weeks?" one of the other guys says, chuckling from his desk.

I knew when I ran into Lou the other night, he'd go flapping his lips in the wind. I crumple a page of scratched out notes and throw it at Lou's head. "I should ask you the same question." He was out looking for late night company. I had other things on my mind.

"By the look on your face, I don't want to know anything about what you've been up to when you're not in this office. You have two hours to get something written and on my desk, or I'm cutting you from the paper this week." Paul slugs away with his cigarette burning between his pinched fingers. He wants news but not news that makes the French look weak or the Germans appear strong. We've been writing articles about the upcoming Mother's Day holiday all week, but I'm not sure how many of the readers have an interest in what the typical mother does at home all day and why it's important to stop and celebrate a life many find dull in comparison to a man's. People want to know what to expect tomorrow—what information is being swept under a rug, or ideas on how to remain safe during a time when our country is being taken over by mongrels.

I can't sit around and be complacent. I can follow rules and still do what I've devoted my adult life to. I bring my notepad in closer and press the tip of my pen against the paper once more. My pulse rattles as I scribble out the headline.

Explosion in Paris Cafe, Two Dead

The memories from this morning are still fresh. With the number of unbelievable scenes I've witnessed these last few years, I've yet to become numb to the unnecessary causalities. I'm not sure what I was expecting when I walked up to the curb outside the disintegrating cafe, waving my hand back and forth through the lingering smoke and dust. Then I heard someone say there were *only* two deaths. Only. It's a hard fact to face, knowing we're not supposed to worry about others anymore.

> Two *unknown* men set up a young boy to carry a suitcase, secured with an explosive, into the café early this Monday morning. The boy fled from the café just before the explosion set off, rattling the bones of the street. The damage to the café is significant.

I've never written an article so quickly or kept one this short. It lacks detail, description, and emotion, but any further hints would explicitly draw a scene of Nazis tricking a young child into blowing up a café before he then watched the destruction from the street...body parts flying, blood covering every surface, screams and cries he will never forget. Forever, he will know what he did and will likely hold the blame for listening to two "strange" men. I shove my chair away from my desk, my heart in my throat, clenching my jaw.

I slap the paper on Paul's desk and toss my cap onto my

head. "Here you go, guts and gore like you prefer. Oh, and no mention of evil German murders. If no one knows, no one will ever guess, right?" I'm asking to be fired right here on the spot and, frankly, I'm not sure I care much now. I'm a journalist without the power to speak the truth. What's the purpose?

"Nicolas, I told you—"

"Take it or leave it, sir."

"Now wait a minute," he shouts after me. "Don't walk out while I'm reading your article."

"You'll toss it in the can. There's no need for me to watch." I make it halfway across the open warehouse full of tables and personal desks before Paul calls for me again. I twist my head over my shoulder, finding him waving at me to come back. I sigh silently, wanting to grumble out loud, but scuff my heels as I turn to comply with his demand. "Yes, sir?"

"I like what you did, keeping the criminals nameless. It could be anyone who did this."

"It wasn't," I say to him.

Paul places the paper on his desk and tugs at his tie, loosening it from around his neck. "I know. I walked past the scene this morning too. They didn't even try to hide what they were responsible for. They were proud."

"Well, maybe they'd prefer to be named in our paper after all," I tell him.

"No, no. We stay under the radar, and this is as high as we fly. Impactful, unfortunate story. Keep up the good work, Nicolas."

I should feel proud of the rare compliment, but I feel as dirty as I did this morning while ashes from the smoke and debris from the building powdered over me like thick snow. In less than a hundred words, I summed up the untimely end of two lives. There's more I can be doing than this.

* * *

"Do you want to chew your food before swallowing it whole? You're going to choke."

At some point I'm going to have to break the news to my mère that I'm a grown man and no longer the young child she had to remind to chew with my mouth closed, never mind chewing altogether. I wish I could see her as young as she was when I was a child, but this war has been leaving its marks on her in the form of aging lines and dark circles beneath her eyes. Her hair has become dark gray, mixed with threads of white, and her dresses are all worn, the patterns fading, the original colors in the fabric almost unrecognizable.

The small casserole dish steams from the center of our little pine table, a space never large enough to entertain more than one or two others at a time. Mère makes a vegetable and legume casserole on most Monday nights. Although there seem to be fewer legumes as of late with the price increase and ration allowance decrease. I've tried hard to forget about the meals she used to have the privilege of cooking. She used to say she was put on this earth to feed the men she loves—my father and me. I miss the taste of meat and poultry, but we aren't privy to such delectable food unless we are of German descent.

"I'm meeting a friend this evening. I won't be back until late, so don't wait up for me," I tell her, scooping the last bite into my mouth.

"Nicolas, what do you mean by late? They blew up a café a few blocks away this morning. The streets are not safe."

"I'll be fine, Mère. You don't need to worry."

"I will worry until the day I die. You are my son," she scolds me with a bent finger pointing between my eyes. "Besides, you must be home by nine or the German officers will arrest you. I've heard some terrible stories of what those soldiers are doing to Parisians who are caught out past curfew." She shivers and pulls her shawl tighter over her shoulders.

"You don't need to worry. I won't break any absurd German

laws," I say, crossing my fingers behind my back. What she doesn't need to know is that I won't get *caught* doing so.

"Where are you going? Won't you at least tell me that?"

I used to think quicker when conjuring a lie, but it seems I've been coming up with so many of them lately I'm having trouble keeping up with the last one I told. "Lou asked for help. He has a broken pipe and isn't handy with tools."

"Lou? From the paper?"

I guess I've used his name before.

"Yes, him."

"You are just like your father, you know that? You can't sit still."

I hate to reply with the reminder that that's all Father was able to do after he was injured in the First World War, so I stay quiet.

She groans and rolls her eyes, maybe realizing the same thing I'm thinking. "Please, be back before nine, Nicolas, or I will come looking for you myself."

Mère pushes her chair away from the table and I follow her into the narrow galley kitchen separated from our dining space by a waist-high wall that serves as a cooling counter for Mère's baked goods. I place our empty glasses on the counter and give her a kiss on the cheek.

"Dinner was wonderful, thank you. But, Mère, must I remind you, I'm a grown man, here to love and protect you from the evil outside of that door?"

She shoos her hand at me. "Grown man," she hisses. "You're twenty-five. That's nothing on my fifty-seven years. You should listen to your mother, Nicolas."

I understand her frustration that I won't stay put at night, but no matter how often I leave, I always come back. She should take comfort knowing this, and that what I do when I leave here is something that will benefit our safety and well-being. I just can't tell her that.

THREE
RAYA
PRESENT DAY, OCTOBER 1943

Ravensbrück, Germany

No sooner than we've shuffled through the foreboding parallel iron gates are we swept into a landscape surrounded by thick forests lined with rows of identical wood-and-brick shallow buildings. We're led into the opening of a tall stone edifice with barred windows. I walk through the foreboding entrance where the long line I'm in continues. From me at the back of the room it spirals toward each barren white wall, between the sides, and up to the front where we are all waiting to go without knowing what we are waiting for. There are no windows, the ceilings are unusually high, and the concrete floors make for an enclosure that is made to feel like the confinement of a prison cell.

Some women in the line have children by their side, even some with babies—bundles in blankets they tirelessly rock side to side. There isn't much talk among anyone in the line, but the sighs, groans, and mild grumbles speak loud enough to verbalize each internal thought.

I try to count the minutes passing, wishing it would distract me from terror-filled eyes, crying children, sniffles, coughs, and heavy breaths. I've lost count several times, but I guess I've been standing between the same people here for at least two hours when I notice ahead, perched on a raised platform, a long table in front of SS guards questioning every woman before sending her through a set of doors.

A whistle was my command to come forward. Like an obedient dog, I shuffle my tired legs up to the table, cringing at the curved cap covering the guard's head and concealing his eyes.

"Name?" he asks with the tone of a demand.

"Raya Pascal," I say, finding mostly air escaping my dry throat. I clear my throat and repeat myself, "Raya Pascal."

"Age?" he continues, holding his pen above a box on his paper.

"Twenty-six years old," I say as he simultaneously scribbles down the answer within the small box.

"Nationality?" I would think everyone who stepped off the train is from France, but I shouldn't assume that means they are of French nationality.

"French," I utter.

"Speak up!"

"French," I say sharply, staring into the man's bloodshot eyes as I try to control the shiver of fear running down my spine.

"Religion?"

"Catholic." I'd like to ask what difference my religion makes, but unfortunately I know the truth. Yet, I'm not sure being Catholic rather than Jewish is enough to keep me alive at this point.

"Are you married?" Yet another Nazi asking me this question. I wish to say yes, wondering if it would spare me from the turmoil I've already endured for appearing "available."

"No," I respond.

"Profession?" If they knew enough about me to arrest me,

why ask all the questions they must already know the answers to.

"I own a leather shop supplying custom-made goods."

The guard peers up at me, flashing his beady eyes for a brief second before jotting down his notes. "Politische Zugehörigkeit?" he scolds.

I'm unsure of his German. I only understand the word political, and I don't want to answer unless I know exactly what he's asking.

My brief pause forces him to repeat himself so I can understand. "Political affiliation?" He must have been testing me to see if I understood him.

"None," I say, honestly.

"Okay then, Fräulein Pascal, what is your reason for being arrested?"

His question is clearer than day but my answer will be far less so.

"I don't know. I've done nothing wrong." I press my hand to my chest and stare up at the unforgiving eyes of a monster. "I've done nothing more than follow every bestowed regulation, and yet here I am. Please, I beg of you to see this is a mistake. I shouldn't be here."

"Enough," he says, holding up his hand in front of my face. "You were supporting the French resistance, correct?"

"No," I deny. "No, I did—didn't do anything. I'm innocent." But I'm not, and worse, I'm not a good liar. He must see right through me. But I didn't hurt anyone. I've supported my fellow Parisian citizens and that shouldn't be a crime. The Nazis are the ones who have committed the unthinkable crimes.

"You sound like all the other liars." He inks a large x over a box on his paper and hands me a piece of blood-red cloth, shaped as a triangle. "Political prisoner. Take this into the next room."

Before I take the symbolic, branding scrap of cloth, the guard whistles for the next person in line.

The adjacent room is as large as the first, but also full to the brim with a maze of people, weaving in and out between table stations. Everyone past the first table is naked, from head to toe, not a stitch of clothing left on their body.

I hold my arms around my chest, dreading the next command. I've always been modest and private, never willing to flaunt what someone else isn't privy to seeing, but I seem to have lost that control now.

"Get undressed!" an SS guard shouts.

I said no. I begged for him to stop. Even a scream won't work. They will still take what they want.

I see what stands before me, others stripped of their clothes and rights, bearing their soul to the enemy in the most vulnerable way a human could do. My blood runs cold as the memory of the last time my clothes were torn from my body brings me back to the moment ice-cold hands were all over me, stabbing me like knives. I can't live through that—this—again. I can't do this. *Please, God, spare me. Please.* My integrity, need for privacy, and unwillingness to bare my flesh has no place in this new cruel world and I want to run and escape. If I don't comply though, I will feel that thug's hands on me again—the hands that haunt me every night when I close my eyes. I might as well peel off my flesh and hand it over along with my clothes because there is nothing else left to take.

My chest threatens to cave in as I will myself not to show an ounce of care, but they know. They can see what they are doing to us all with their entitlement over humanity.

I quiver with each movement, slipping off each article of clothing I've been wearing for what must be three days now. A guard seizes my shoes, stockings, skirt, undergarments, blouse, scarf, coat, and gloves from my hands as he points me in the direction of the line I have been in since arriving here.

There is a buzzing sound, like a swarm of bees, rumbling from the next station and it takes only a minute to figure out what I'm listening to as each woman at the station walks away with a shaved head. My mouth falls open with disgrace as I watch the process of what I can only consider to be dehumanization. What else will they want from us? Will I still know my name when I leave this room?

I run my fingers through my hair, feeling the dirt coating my strands from going so long without a shower or the ability to wash my hair. My hair hasn't been shorter than chin-length since I was a young girl, and it was only once when I had a bad haircut. I refused to ever cut it that short again, but a refusal won't get me anywhere here.

With everything I have endured so far, it isn't until the shaving razor drags across my scalp that tears fall from my closed eyes. I hope I don't have to see myself in a mirror. I'll struggle to recognize the stranger I'm becoming.

To add insult to injury, I'm forced to stand with my feet spread apart and my arms out to the side at the next station, where I'm sprayed down with a burning liquid that I assumed was water. The burn against my scalp could be mistaken for a fire on top of my head.

I'm examined by a doctor, poked, and prodded several times before being given the all-clear to attend the last station in this room. There sits a prisoner with hollow eyes in a striped uniform with a number badge sewn to her chest. In her hand she holds what looks like a thick pen, except the tip is a needle. She's inking numbers onto each woman's forearm.

She wipes the forearm with alcohol, then jabs her instrument against the skin, carving a new set of numbers, over and over. I watch, my stomach churning into knots from nausea, hunger, and disgust, until I'm in the seat, awaiting the evident pain I witnessed on every woman's face before me.

The number means I'm not going home. I'm not going to be

released no matter how hard I try to convince someone, anyone, that I haven't done anything wrong. The number will likely replace my name when added to the list of perished prisoners. There is no exit to this hell. I can see that much from here. This torment is what I was trying to protect Charlette and her parents from. This is why I told Alix not to come home, or even try. I knew he was safer in Zurich. He didn't want me to be alone, but I was sure I could take care of myself. Not once did I stop to think I would need someone to protect me too.

FOUR
RAYA

Paris, France

Not a day in my life have I broken a rule, let alone a law, not until yesterday when I took Charlette and her parents into my home. So far, the soldiers have had little interest in the shop, and I pray it remains that way. They have no need for leather goods when they have access to whatever it is their hearts desire, whenever they please. The life of needing for nothing is something they will stop all of us in Paris from ever having again most likely.

In the kitchen I've sealed off the window with a curtain, and I've also pinned layers of newspaper to the fabric for extra concealment. I fear the thought of someone spotting more than one shadow up here. There is only one person registered to this address and I'd be a fool to think the Germans aren't aware of every inhabitable square of this city.

Jacques helped me set up an extra set of small bells upstairs to act as an echo to those at the front of the shop. They're connected by a thin thread woven through the upstairs floorboards, down through the ceiling of the shop, and secured to the back wall where I cover the register throughout the day. I'll chime these bells along with the other if a German soldier enters the shop during the day. It will be a discreet warning to Charlette and her parents to make their way into the hidden room where they sleep at night.

"I'm going to have to find a way to secure food rations," Rose says, tapping her fingernails against the tabletop where the four of us sit, staring at one another. I had enough food to feed the four of us pasta with butter, but I won't be able to acquire enough food for us all on a regular basis.

"Are there other ways to access this building?" Jacques asks, his forehead glistening with sweat.

"There is a back door that branches between this space and the jeweler next door, but the main back exit will leave you on a street just as busy as the one in front. There are always soldiers lurking around there too. The only other option is the sewer line." I knew we needed to make sure the Germans didn't spot the Levis coming or going from the shop, but I hadn't considered the challenges involved with acquiring enough food.

"That's right," Jacques says. "That won't help in this situation."

"I will take Charlette's identification card and pick up the food."

The three of them gawk at me like I have two heads.

"We're only allowed to buy food at locations designated for Jewish people. You would have to wear a star, dress in all black, and try to conceal your face. It would be putting you in danger and I can't have that," Rose says. "The authorities are watching every move we make, and they know they are evicting us. They'll wonder where we're living."

"There aren't many other options," I explain.

"You should not be punished like we are," Charlette says, standing from the table as if to make a motion to stop all this chatter. "You are protecting us. We will find a way to replenish our food. Please, don't worry about us."

Charlette's emotions are getting in the way of the facts. They can either hide here or remain Jewish citizens of this city and go back home to then be evicted and forced to move to one of the Jewish enclaves. There isn't a middle ground.

"We always said if one of us was going to be a secret spy somewhere, it would be me, right?" I nudge my elbow into her waist now she's standing beside me.

"This isn't the same thing, and assuming our home is taken over by a German soldier, they will question the address on my identification card."

"From what I've heard, the German authorities are telling Jewish people to leave their homes, not the city, so everyone has to go somewhere, and your identification card wouldn't change if you're staying with others for the time being." I'm aware my plan is not foolproof but there are no other options I can think of right now. "I will be fine. You will not go hungry. That's all there is to it."

"First, it's our home, then it's our ability to leave this building," she mutters. Charlette's inky thick curls flop around on her back as she shoots exasperation out of her swinging arms. She takes each of our plates, stacking them one on top of the other and brings them to a shallow counter next to the sink. "What did we ever do to deserve this?" I know she isn't asking us this question, but muttering to herself like she often does when she's mad. "Someone should take all the Germans' homes away and see how they feel. It's obvious no one taught them how to act appropriately as a young child."

"Charlette, enough," Jacques says, his voice calm but stern.

The reprimand was enough to break the dam of tears. With her back to us, she holds her hands up to her mouth, shaking her head as if she refuses to believe what's happening.

I stand and meet her at the sink, taking one of her hands in mine. "We're like sisters. Sisters protect each other, climb mountains and cross rivers for each other. I can pick up food for you. You won't be trapped here forever." I shouldn't say things I can't support with facts, but I couldn't bear someone telling me I'll never go outside again.

Charlette wraps her arms around me and rests her cheek on my shoulder, facing the newspaper-covered curtain. "You used yesterday's newspaper?" she says with a sputter.

We both let out a chuckle.

"Does it matter?" I ask.

"The news was stale yesterday," Charlette says.

"I resent that statement," Rose adds. "I think it's lovely that there have been so many articles about mothers for Mother's Day."

I didn't mean to drop my gaze to the ground. I've gotten used to hearing someone say the word mother. I don't enjoy the holiday much, but people should while they can.

"Oh dear, Raya, I—"

I shake my head because I don't want Rose to feel like she's said something she shouldn't have. "I visited Mère's grave yesterday and left a handful of wildflowers. That's where I was in the morning."

Jacques lifts his glass from the table. "I think it's time to call it a night." He gives his family a stern look, making it known they should follow suit. "Allow us to clean the dishes, dear, then we'll see ourselves upstairs. You don't need to tend to us again tonight."

I might have argued under normal circumstances, but I know they feel indebted to me. I wish they didn't have to endure that, especially with this being out of their control. While they're cleaning up, I make my way to the far end of the flat and remove the tall mirror off the wall. As I place the heavy glass down and lean it up against the wall to the side, I clearly hear Mère's words play through my head: "A mirror's reflection will often hide what resides on the other side."

When she eventually shared the family secret of the room on the other side of the wall, she told me the mirror was the perfect illusion to conceal a hiding place from anyone since most people will only ever see their reflection rather than the small opening that leads into the spare room. I always thought the saying was silly, but I didn't understand the true meaning of the words until recently.

I climb in through the hole and poke my head into the angular space, finding Rose has done all she can to make do while also adding a touch of warmth with beds made of blankets, and neatly folded piles of clothes for the three of them. I lent them some extra blankets, candles, and books, which add a splash of color to the bare wooden walls. It's not so bad. There's no window and therefore no form of natural light, but it's safer that way. We can only hope that France will step up and reclaim what belongs to us, so we don't have to live under Germany's thumb forever. Although a day feels like forever now. Who knows what will become of us next week.

The instant I step out of the hole in the wall and spot the three of them drying the plates we used for dinner, a rumble quakes through the flat. The pictures on the wall rattle and my heart tumbles into the pit of my stomach.

"What was that?" Charlette cries out.

"We shouldn't be near this window. Move into the room right away. Raya, you too." Jacques ushers us into the concealed room, and closes us in as if I truly am a part of their family. "It must have been another explosion. That's the second one in two days," he says. "I'm sure you all heard about the café."

"I'm scared," I utter, ashamed to be speaking these words out loud to a family who has far more to be fearful of than I do, but the reality of what's happening on our streets is searing through me, injecting me with a type of fear I've done my best to shield myself from. It feels like this war is closing in on us, no matter who we are, no matter what our religion is. The Germans don't want any of us in Paris, not just the Jewish population, and it's being made perfectly clear that their government plans to eliminate us all, slowly, and most likely painfully.

FIVE
NICOLAS
LAST YEAR, JUNE 1942

Paris, France

While slinking down the dark streets through wisps of fog that glide along the damp stones, I debate my objective, as I do most nights. To weigh the basis of my decision with Mère on one shoulder and Father on the other makes it easy to feel torn. The imbalance is dangerous and might get me and others killed, but I have a hard time believing we don't all feel the same way. Not one of us is or was an experienced criminal. Most of us have never used a weapon, or gotten into a physical altercation, but now we spend our nights training our bodies and minds to be fit for whatever might stand in our path while correcting our country's wrongs.

Father would tell me to forget about everything else and focus on the goal as well as the reliance others unknowingly have on me. Mère would wring my neck if she knew what I've been up to, especially after all she'd endured with Father. Therein lies the heaviest form of guilt. I'm all she has left. Yet, thirteen years ago when Father passed away, he left the status of his nobility in my hands, wishing for his life to not be forsaken. That's why I retrace my steps each night.

* * *

The older I become, the more I wonder about Father. At twelve, I ponder what he's thinking, why he stares at the barren wall all day. He made Mère take down the portraits that were hung years ago. She said he doesn't want to be reminded of the life he once had. It doesn't make much sense to me since he was much better off. "I brought you a croissant and coffee," I mumble, wondering what mood he might be in this morning. Father doesn't shift his gaze from the wall to me. He doesn't acknowledge that I've said a word. "I'll place it down here. I'll be late for school if I don't leave now." I set the breakfast tray on his nightstand between the empty glasses of cognac, each with cigar ash floating along the bottom.

"You don't need school," he says, his throat coated with mucus. "I went to school. A lot of good that did me." Father coughs to clear his throat but holds his stare on the wall. "We live our life searching for a purpose, Nicolas. My purpose was to protect this country during the war, and I failed to do so. That's why I will be bedridden for the remainder of my life. I'm useless to the world without my legs, never mind having only one good eye. It was all for nothing, wasn't it?"

Father says the same thing to me most mornings. He's like a broken record, playing the same notes over and over each time we place the needle onto the spinning vinyl.

"It wasn't for nothing. You're a war hero. I idolize you for your bravery and sacrifice."

"A sacrifice must be worth something in the end. Otherwise it was a waste."

I've checked the meaning of sacrifice so many times, wondering if I'm misunderstanding what he's trying to tell me, but him fighting for our country was nothing but a sacrifice. "Our country won the war," I remind him.

"Most of us lost in the end though, didn't we?" he asks, peering down at his quilt-covered body.

Mère says he suffers from shell shock, symptoms of post war fatigue, but it's been twelve years since he was sent home, and I don't understand how he can still be tired from fighting in the war. I wish I knew him before he enlisted. Mère also said I'm beginning to look like him and I have his same wit and humor, but to me, it sounds like she's talking about a man I've never known. I was born two months before he was injured, four months before the end of the war. This vision of him, lying in bed all day, is all I know of him.

I shrug in response to his question because there is nothing I can say. "I love you, Father. I'll be home after school."

"Nicolas," he says, shifting his gaze to my face, "Promise me you will always stand up for the innocent. I want you to be braver than me and accomplish what I didn't. Never let something bigger than you get in the way of what you want to be remembered for. This world needs love and compassion, and far less hate."

"I promise, Father."

He lifts his hand to cup his long fingers around the side of my face. "That's my boy." As I lift the needle off the record, he refocuses on the wall and sinks back into his pillow, his mind having left the bedroom.

* * *

The unlit street, once filled with crowds spilling out of pubs late into the night, offers an echo from each step I take, the gravel crunching between the treads of my boots' soles. The windows are boarded up on the lower level of the brick building, a sign of neglect when most of our cafés and pubs were forced to close because of the economic drought Germany enforced.

I amble down the few stone steps that once led to the cellar of Maison de la Bière, and glance in every direction though there is little visibility in the darkness. The air traveling to and from my lungs is the only sound I hear. I tap out four knocks, with a pause between each, against the black painted door. Seconds pass before I hear six finger taps from the other side of the door, three quick and three slow. I knock four more times, three quick and one slow.

The door opens enough for me to squeeze through, and I walk until I spot a thread of light guiding me to a blocked-off room surrounded by wooden shelves packed with crates. I move a stack of the freestanding crates to one side and enter the meeting space with Hugo following at my heels. The meeting appears to have started without me even though we'd all planned to arrive at different times. Once we're all together it's hard to keep thoughts or stories to ourselves. We're bursting at the seams all day, waiting to talk to another person who thinks the same way. It's hard to predict whether a neighbor under-stands what it means to be an active participant; to being an upstanding citizen of France. We're all the same here.

"What did I miss?" There are fifteen of us now, cramming into a space that used to comfortably hold eight of us.

"We need more space," Hugo says, summarizing what they must have been chatting about when I arrived.

"Where will we find that?"

"There are other groups like ours forming in the sewers and quarries and they're having an easier time covering their foot-steps and acquiring information. Plus, with the explosion in the café, we think it's best to find a better location to meet," Bette, Hugo's sister, says, standing from her crate to pace back and forth between the circle we've formed around one single lantern.

"We've talked about this. There isn't a readily available map of the underground tunnels but we'll need one if we're going to locate an accessible entrance that hasn't been blockaded."

"We need to make our own map then," another one of the guys shouts from the corner, throwing his arms up with exasperation.

I have the urge to tell him one doesn't just make a map. We'd need to find access before considering a plan.

"We should all be on the search for a possible entrance. It won't be easy, but I believe we'll be able to find a way down there. In the meantime, I'll see about contacting a fella I know. He's part of the maquis and they collaborate underground," Hugo says.

The maquis are violent, with an agenda to kill the German soldiers and police. It's not something any of us are opposed to but those missions are the most dangerous and with the little fighting experience we have, we've remained vigilant in assisting the resistance with delivering communication instead.

"Did anyone collect any intelligence today?" I ask.

"Aside from you gabbing on about the beautiful woman who tripped over herself in your presence?" Hugo glances in my direction and chuckles.

"Very funny," I chide. That wasn't exactly how I worded my brief story to him, but he hears what he wants to hear.

"You should have seen the smitten look on Nicolas's face this morning," he tells everyone.

"I'm going to avoid your family's bakery on the way to work from now on." My threat is impossible since he's next door to my office.

"You'd starve all day so that's unlikely," he whips back.

Hugo and I have always been the worst at being friends, but that's what makes our camaraderie so unique. We're more like siblings who pick on each other, although Bette would argue that she has it worse than I do.

"Slow day, I guess. Bette, do you have more bulletins prepared?" I ask.

Bette is the most nervous of the bunch, her fear visible in her round, deer-like golden eyes. She's only here to support Hugo, though she's an asset to us. With the nimblest fingers, she types faster than any of us so she's the one who transcribes the information we've acquired and need to share with members in other groups of the resistance.

Bette returns to the crate she was sitting on and lifts it to pull out a stack of papers. Hugo reaches for them and divides them between everyone to place around the city before we meet again in two nights.

"These have been updated with the new law about the badges all Jewish people are being forced to wear starting next week, right?" I ask.

"Yes," Bette squeaks. "Now we should all be going. It's nearly nine."

No one says much when she makes this same announcement at the end of each meeting. None of us want to abide by the mandatory curfew.

Over the course of thirty minutes, we disperse one by one. I'm the last to leave tonight, responsible for ensuring the door is secure on the way out. The back alleyways are the safest route to avoid German soldiers on the prowl for people breaking their imposed rules, their next victims. The French citizens tempt their luck nightly, despite knowing what will become of them if they're caught.

No sooner than I reach the road leading to my flat I hear another explosion, the second one today. I can't go running after it this time because I'll become the target of what might be another ploy to weed out the resisting locals. Shouts echo in the distance, Germans screaming "Halt," with a long string of obscenities I can't translate as quickly as they speak.

The journalist in me needs to know what's happening.

Others should be warned and given proper news. Despite my good common sense, I run toward the commotion, stopping short at the corner of a building where a closed café intersects a split road, facing an old stone church. German vehicles are stopped ahead, trapping whatever their target might be. They use their doors as shields so I can't see who they're fighting, but from the sound of an old machine gun, I can assume a resistance group took a chance on an attack. They're cornered now without the same protection as the Germans.

Shots are fired from both directions. I have nothing on me to help but if I did, I'd have the perfect shot at the back of one soldier's head. I hate to question if I should stay or go. I know what I should do.

SIX

RAYA

Ravensbrück, Germany

In the middle of the night, the first night of being a prisoner in this confinement, I try to force myself to sleep, knowing there will be no forgiveness for exhaustion in the morning. The wooden plank I'm resting on between several other women is beneath two bunk tiers, and there is another one below. There's only enough space to roll from side to side. The disquiet among us all is palpable as bodies squirm, thin wool blankets catch on splinters, and fingernails scratch against skin. I hear groans, whimpers, and restless snores.

Outside of our wooden barrack, there are distant shouts and the sound of gunfire. I wish I was imagining the cries I'm sure I hear, echoing like the wind between a wooded forest. Planes fly overhead and I wish they were searching for people to rescue rather than heading toward their next battle.

My life flashes beneath my eyelids every time I close them, picturing the moments I once considered difficult, the times when I should have appreciated more than I did, days when I had everything and more, but still dreamt of what else was possible. Even at my worst, I used to be able to find a source of light, but now there's nothing but darkness no matter the direction I search.

"Here," the woman beside me says, handing me a scrap of paper and a dull chewed pencil. "Write to someone. Even if you can't send it to them, it helps."

"Thank you," I whisper. My gratitude is less about the paper and more for the fact that she's the first person to speak a word to me since I arrived.

She doesn't reply. She flips onto her side, her bald head a fingertip length away from the tip of my nose.

A slight glow from the lamppost outside seeps in through the small window across from my bunk, allowing me to stare at the paper in my hand and prop myself on my elbows. I don't need to consider who to write to, or what to say. The words come on their own.

My Dearest,

Forgive me for promising you I would be back, and for leaving you the way I did. If I knew how we would end up, there is so much I would have done differently, but the worst part is, I'm not sure the outcome would have changed.

We should be together, forever. This isn't the way our lives were supposed to go. I am eternally sorry and hope you know how much I will always love you no matter what might become of me.

I slip the scrap of paper into my pocket and place the pencil down between my body and the woman beside me. I'm sure she'll want it back. I imagine pencils are hard to come by here.

Though my skin is covered down to my knees by the smock-like striped pajamas, the sensation of small spiders crawling up the backs of my legs keeps me scratching as I wonder if it's my mind playing tricks on me or if there are truly bugs crawling up my legs. I bury my face between my arms, willing myself to sleep. When I wake, maybe this will all be over.

SEVEN
RAYA
LAST YEAR, JUNE 1942

Paris, France

My hands tremble as I unlock the shop door, my arms weak from shaking all night. What if the world beyond this door is gone? The shots and blasts that started after dinner went on and on, but where and between who, I'm not sure. I hold my breath until I spot Monsieur Croix in his usual spot, lining up stacks of newspapers. I peer in both directions, finding the surrounding buildings still erect. I wish there was a way to convince myself it was a bad dream, but I'm sure if I walk just a few blocks in either direction I will find that to be a tale I've told myself.

"Salut!" Monsieur Croix greets me. "What is it, mademoiselle? Are you not well?"

I don't know what might have given him the idea that something is wrong, but I know for sure my hair is a mess and I didn't sleep for more than an hour. I'm also sure we aren't the only ones who heard all the explosions last night.

"There was a lot of rumbling last night. Have you heard anything about what happened?"

Monsieur Croix shakes his head and drops his gaze. "No, I

don't know," he says, tugging off his beret to scratch at the bald patch on top of his head.

I've interrupted him from lining up the newspapers. If something was important enough to make a headline, normally he would have already been made aware, but not much is published for the public's knowledge now. The Germans interfere as much as possible, preventing us from knowing the truth of our surroundings.

"Air raids. Thirty-six British aircraft were shot down between here and Cologne." A man's voice comes from the back of the newspaper stand.

Air raids? I suppose that might explain the rumbling, but there were snapping blasts and they sounded far too close to be happening anywhere outside of this city.

"There is your reputable source for information," Monsieur Croix says, pointing to where I clearly can't see. I take a few steps toward the back of the newsstand, and find the same man I encountered here two mornings ago, doing the same peculiar task he's doing right now—switching around the German and French newspapers.

"You know this man is reorganizing your papers, Monsieur Croix?" I ask, surprised to see the blatant disrespect shown by this man.

"Yes, yes, but it's better if I turn my back to him. He knows I'd rather not be a witness to what he's doing."

"What exactly are you doing?" I pin my hands on my hips, tapping my toe with irritation.

The man, Nicolas Bardot, I believe he said his name was, smiles sinuously and continues shuffling the papers around. "The people of our city must know the real news, don't you agree?"

"What are those papers you're slipping in between the pages?" I press up on my toes to catch a glimpse of what he's inserting, but he places the last one before I can see the head-line. "Helpful information."

"Helpful information," Monsieur Croix repeats, belly laughs erupting through his elderly body. "Sometimes it's best to be blind to a reality no one wants to see. Surely you agree with that?"

"Yes, he's correct. We're already living in so much fear. What more do we need to know?" I question as a gust of wind blows my chin-length hair across my face—mother nature blinding me in response.

"Weren't you the one who left your shop seeking informa-tion about what happened last night?"

I close my mouth, feeling caught in the same malicious act I was accusing someone of doing.

"Fear can be worse when it accompanies curiosity."

"Well, I'd like to buy one of those newspapers you slipped a leaflet into," I say, holding out my hand.

He takes a paper from the front of the pile and passes it over.

"You didn't put a leaflet in that paper."

"How do you know I didn't add one before you stepped out of your shop?"

I take the paper and flip through the few pages, finding them bare of any leaflet. I instinctively narrow my eyes, but his response is a snickering laugh accompanying a witty smile. He switches out my newspaper for another and I flip through the pages again, this time spotting the extra page. "That wasn't so hard, was it?" I ask, raising a brow to emphasize my question.

"Raya. Did I remember your name correctly? Or was it, Woman-Who-Owns-The-Shop-Over-There?"

I curl my windblown strands behind my ear and leave his joke dangling while I make my way to Monsieur Croix to pay for the paper. "It's Raya."

"He's a pleasant young man," Monsieur Croix says, raising his brows before offering a sly wink.

"I am," Nicolas agrees.

"I'm sure you are," I say, walking back toward the shop, trying my best to fight the smile pressing into my cheeks.

"Well, hold on a second. Seeing as you want to read my paper, might I be able to convince you to join me for a walk after work so we can discuss your thoughts on the piece I've added?"

Monsieur Croix clucks his tongue. "How thoughtful. Raya, dear, you should go with the nice young man," he says, adding gusto to his words to ensure they carry over the rustling leaves in the trees.

"You should," Nicolas replies.

My cheeks burn as I run out of responses.

Before I have the chance to wrap my hand around the shop's door handle, Nicolas follows his statement. "I'll meet you here at five unless you say otherwise."

I should say *otherwise*. I can be cheeky.

"Oh, Raya," Monsieur Croix stops me from going inside. "I meant to ask if you heard from your brother this week?" Monsieur Croix checks in about Alix regularly, like a worried father. He's known us both for most of our lives and watched us grow up in this shop, then saw our lives fall to pieces when both Papa and Mère passed away.

"Yes, he's doing very well, but worried about us all here. He mentioned coming home for a holiday, but I asked him to stay put."

Monsieur Croix shakes his head and waves his hands in front of his face. "No, no, no. He shouldn't come home. You were right to tell him to stay there, as much as I'm sure you'd like to see him. I miss the kid too. He ought to know he's the lucky one though. God bless him."

I'm so caught up in the pileup of thoughts of Alix wanting

to come home for a visit and reasons why I shouldn't go for a walk with that man that I manage to make it back into the shop without saying another word to either of them. I debate poking my head back out the door to apologize for being rude, but I have a suspicion Nicolas will still show up here at five tonight.

I haven't always run away from men. There was a time when I was ready to begin the search for that next part of my life, especially after spending so much time focusing on the shop or Alix. When he left for school, we made an agreement: he would take the opportunity of a lifetime and fulfill his desires if I promised to focus on myself here and find what would make me happy in life. He should have known I already had what makes me happy here. The shop is my life and is important to both of us. Alix needs his home to come back to when he's finished and I will do whatever it takes to keep our shop up and running. I just need to make sure our city's intruders stay away.

* * *

I'm not a mother. I'm hardly an adult. But as I stare at Alix scraping up the last of his eggs with the crispy edge of his toast, I question if I've done right by my brother since he became my sole responsibility when our mother died three years ago. It feels like an eternity has come and gone since then. Alix was hardly fourteen at the time. I was only seventeen. I stopped attending classes to tend to the family business full-time. Neither of us deserved to lose our parents before adulthood, but I would spare him more grief than necessary if I stepped up into a motherly role—into Mère's shoes.

Today is Alix's last day of secondary education, leaving us at the next crossroads.

"Do you have a minute to talk before you leave for school?" I prepared his breakfast a few minutes earlier this morning so that he wouldn't have the chance to say no.

He dabs a napkin across his lips as worry pierces his teal eyes, ones that mirror mine. "Yes, I have time. Is everything okay?" I'm not sure when he stopped looking like a boy and I don't know how I didn't acknowledge the milestone when it happened, but I guess we all change over the course of time. It all happens so slowly we don't always notice until something makes us take a deeper look. His strawberry blonde hair is no longer in messy curls, but short and slicked back, and his cheeks aren't pinchable like they once were. His limbs have filled out with muscle, and steel-like edges define his facial features. With a full head of height on me, people tend to confuse who is older.

I take his empty plate to the porcelain sink in the corner of our tiny kitchen. The glass plate clinks in the hollow basin, and my heart pounds while I work up the courage to answer the question I provoked. I hardly slept a wink last night, dreading this moment—wondering how it would go.

I pull open the rickety drawer next to the refrigerator where I keep essential letters and papers, and pull out the envelope, prestigiously scripted to Monsieur Alix Pascal. I have been holding on to this for the last couple of days with anticipation. "I know we discussed the possibility of you attending the University of Zurich to further your education."

"Spoke of, yes. It was a passing conversation, nothing to stir over," he responds with haste while wiping his mouth again with the napkin. It doesn't take long before his gaze locks on the envelope. "What is that in your hand?"

"You can be furious with me if you like, but I went ahead and filled out an application on your behalf. Your teacher was kind enough to write you a lovely letter of recommendation and your transcript—well, we both know it should be framed and hung on the wall." Alix has always been a good student, much better than I ever was. He enjoys learning and wants to become a teacher. With his cheerful personality and the ability to make an entire room laugh with few words, children would be grateful to learn from him.

"Raya, you applied to the university on my behalf without speaking a word to me?"

"You wouldn't have done so on your own. You won't leave here unless I force you to go. You're a good brother, Alix, a wonderful, bright young man, and you deserve so much more than what resides in our flat above the family shop."

"No, no. We aren't discussing this possibility. What about you? You've given up your education, youth, and ability to do what you might want to do, and you have done so for me. How could I leave you now? I can finally work the same number of hours as you, giving you more time to do those other things. That was our plan. You can't just change our plan now."

"It was no one's plan. We shouldn't have become orphans, but this is where we are, and there is a chance for you," I say, holding up the envelope as if it is a ticket to his future. The art of steaming envelope glue to peek inside is unlawful, but I couldn't surprise him with the fact that I'd filled out the application on his behalf and then unknowingly give him a rejection letter. "I won't let you pass it up. I won't."

"You're speaking as if you already know what the letter says." His golden eyebrows arch over his shocked eyes.

I open my mouth to speak, but words don't form quickly enough.

"Raya, you are such a nuisance, you know that?" He lunges from his seat to snatch the envelope from me.

I wring my hands, squeezing as he tears open the flap and pulls out the cream-colored parchment paper, a red wax emblem stamped on the top right.

Alix's hands shake as he reads the first few lines. "I was accepted?" he says, surprised, the words catching.

My throat tightens as I try to form words. I wonder if this is how a mother feels when her son receives life-changing news. My chest aches with pride, but also at the impending days of loneliness without him. "I knew you would be," I tell him with tears in my eyes. He's been through so much and continued to persevere.

"I can't believe what I'm reading." His pupils grow as he stares past the letter briefly before returning his focus to the words he's trying to digest. It's a true pinch-me moment that might leave him with bruises. He lowers the letter, and his head falls to the side, weary and torn, a furious fight igniting in his eyes. "I can't leave you. You shouldn't be here all alone in this big city."

"I have Charlette and the Levis. They are always around to help if I need anything." I'm not alone, not as he's making it out to be.

"You have an answer to everything, don't you?"

"You can't argue with the truth," I say.

I've thought this through carefully, concluding I've done the right thing. I will miss him more than I can stand to imagine, but I can't stand in the way of his future. I won't...no matter how much it hurts to let him go.

My little, big brother envelops me in his arms and presses his forehead into my shoulder. "You are the best sister a person could have. Mark my words...once I acquire my degree, I will return home and take care of you in every way I can. I promise you. But, Raya, you must promise me that while I'm gone, you will make time for yourself and find what will make you happy in life, and I don't mean the labor of running our family's shop. Is it a deal?"

"Of course," I agree without much thought. Promises can be tricky when we become aware of how little we control.

* * *

I tried to find something that could make me happy outside of the shop, but I feel more lost than found. Even if I had time to take part in ordinary activities like going for a walk, no one does that for pleasure much these days because it seems as if we're just looking for trouble with the German authorities.

The newspaper Nicolas gave me crinkles in my grip and I drop it on the front counter, eager to pull out the leaflet inside, but a clatter upstairs pulls me away from the front desk.

Without a need to worry about sounds from within in this building before, I never focused on how noticeable the creeks and whines are from the floorboards above. I consider my options for masking the noise.

We used to have a radio in the shop, but the French stations don't come in too clearly now and I refuse to play German music. I wish I had more records to spin but the repeating songs will be better than worrying about the obvious movement from upstairs among the silence down here. I tend to the gramophone in the back corner of the store and set down the needle on the Debussy vinyl.

The shop door opens, and the single bell chimes. If a German soldier has walked in, I will have missed my opportunity to ring the upstairs bell to warn the Levis. I clasp my hands behind my back, squeezing so tightly my fingernails pinch my skin. I try to act casual as I meander to the front desk, wondering why no one has entered the shop yet.

"Bienvenue!" I state. *Please don't be a Nazi.* I poke my head around the corner of a product display to see the front door and my shoulders fall, finding Nicolas standing in the entrance gazing around the shop. "Can I help you?" I spout with more confidence than my welcoming salutation.

"This shop is beautiful," he says, narrowing his eyes at a display of leather wallets, hand stitched by Charlette. They shine as if they are made from glass. He moves slowly through the narrow paths between displays, his dress shoes popping and crackling over gravel on the stone floor.

"Are they custom-made?" Nicolas asks, lifting one of the

wallets to inspect. He inhales sharply. "I love this smell—rich, fine leather."

"Yes," I say, keeping my answer short to avoid going into detail about the seamstress being Charlette, a Jewish woman who is working for pay, unlike most women in Europe. "Everything in the shop is custom-made."

"I'm not sure I've ever been inside a leather goods shop before." He moves his gaze from the wallet and scans the space around him. "It's quite welcoming in here." He runs his hand down an exposed beam reaching from the wall in an angle up to the ceiling. The wood is so old the texture feels like silk. He continues touring the shop, stopping just before the back wall where I have a display of framed photographs. "Who are all these people?"

"My parents, grandparents, and great grandparents. They all ran the shop before me. I hope to pass it down to my children someday too but I suppose that all depends on how long I'm able to carry this business on my shoulders through the duration of this occupation."

"A family business...I don't blame you for wanting to keep this shop alive," he says. "Not everyone has the opportunity to walk around the inside of an heirloom quite like this." He appears enamored by every product and apparently every structural beam as he runs his fingers across each as he passes by. It's as if he's exploring a museum rather than an old family shop. "Custom gloves too. Very nice," he says. "And belts."

"We have many options," I say, sounding as if I've been holding my breath for an entire minute.

"Debussy," he says, passing the gramophone. "I can't think of a more inviting sound. Although the soldiers out there might not agree."

"They don't seem very interested in leather goods."

"I would consider myself lucky in that regard."

I make my way back behind the counter and place the

newspaper on the shelf beneath the register. He takes his time inspecting every product we sell before approaching the front desk. "Would you be able to tell me what size gloves I might need?" he asks, holding out his hand.

His question flusters me, and I step in to take a closer look at his hand, the one with black ink marks along the side of his palm. My elbow knocks over the stack of orders next to the register and they fly off the counter.

"I'm so sorry," Nicolas says. "Let me get those."

"No, no, it's fine. I can get them."

As easily as I ignored him, he ignores my rejection of help and we're both on our hands and knees peeling notes off the dusty floor. I should have swept last night. He might smell the leather, but dust tickles my nose as I scoop up the papers.

He manages to gather the rest in one swoop, quicker than I do, and hands them to me as we both rise to our feet. "Those were probably in some sort of order, weren't they?"

"I can sort them." They were in perfect order, so Charlette knew which to tend to first, but I've dated everything and added a priority number to the top of the slip.

"If you tell me how to sort them, I don't mind," he offers.

"You don't honestly want gloves, do you?" I question while placing the papers on the counter.

"I might, but it's June and there's no sense in buying gloves as of now," he says, smirking. "I'll be honest with you and say I wanted to confirm if your silence outside was a form of agreement to take a walk with me tonight."

"You did say you would be here unless I said, 'otherwise,' and as you said yourself, I didn't say anything at all." I'm proud of myself for holding on to the last bit of wit I seem to have inside of me currently.

"Wonderful. Not only will I have something to write about today, but possibly tomorrow too."

"You can't write about me," I tell him.

"I didn't say I was going to. That's quite presumptuous of you."

Despite another wave of embarrassment flushing through me, I notice a hint of blush blooming through his cheeks too.

"Have a good day, monsieur."

"And you, mademoiselle." He removes his beret and bows toward me before spinning on his heels and disappearing like a passing breeze.

The instant the door closes, another creak from upstairs strikes my pulse up a notch. I can hear the sound clearly, even over the record playing. What will I say if someone comes into the shop and questions who is upstairs? And what will happen if I don't have a good enough answer?

EIGHT
NICOLAS
LAST YEAR, JUNE 1942

Paris, France

Paul rejected my article about the air-raids even though I kept the piece short and lacking in detail. I ended up handing in a story about the diminishing number of artists setting up easels in Montmartre, but left out the part about them hiding from the German soldiers who pace the streets all day. They're suffocating the heart of our city, which is precisely their intention.

The distance between *Vraie Nouvelle* and Pascal Maroquinerie is shorter than a five-minute walk, and I am early for meeting Raya at the end of the workday. To be a man of my word, I spot a bench to the side of the shop window beneath a pink chestnut tree and take a seat. The sun bleeds brilliant golden hues, which warms the dull atmospheric ambiance. After being stuck inside all day, I inhale the floral laced breeze and embrace the early summer heat against my skin. If I squeeze my eyes shut, I can visualize a glorious day at the south shore. I miss the days of dropping down onto a bench with my notepad and waiting for a story to fall on my lap. A dog on the loose, or an act of heroism when someone trips on a curb, or a child separated from their mother are the stories that would fill my pages. I was responsible for giving people a reason to smile while reading the paper. Now, I feel responsible for ensuring our city is aware of the truth and facts of what surrounds us, but suppression is the law we must abide by. It seems impossible to write anything uplifting when we're all in a state of despair.

The thud of boots scuffling nearby pulls me from my daydream and I watch as the German soldiers pass, exchanging words and laughter between each other, living a life we all once knew. In the same moment, a man and woman step out of Raya's shop, releasing the melody of Debussy in the faint flurry of air. The thuds from the boots pause and my heart patters as I peer over my shoulder toward the soldiers. They're pointing at the shop and exchange brief words before pivoting toward it.

I barely know Raya, but the thought of any French person having to deal with these hounds makes me mad to the bone. Once they're inside, I follow them through the door, hoping they aren't walking in to start trouble with the nice young lady.

"What is this music airing out of your shop and polluting the city street?" one of the officers says.

Raya doesn't answer, she only hustles to the back of the shop and lifts the needle off the record before I have time to take my next breath.

"Are you unaware of the German regulations?"

"It—it was j-just an orchestra, I did-didn't think—"

"There are plenty of German composers to honor— Beethoven, Bach, d'Albert, and Stavenhagen. There's no need for the nursery sounds of Debussy."

"Of course," Raya replies. "Understood."

"Ja, good. Don't let us catch you disregarding the German culture again. Good day, Fräulein." The German officers share a glance with each other, and as if called into formation, stiffen their posture and stride, with what appears to be purpose, out the door.

Just as the door closes, Raya flees to its window and flips the shop sign from open to closed, then draws a thick drape across to conceal the inside from the street. She does the same for the storefront windows.

It's been a while since I've tried to pursue a woman for purposes outside of the complicated life I seem to be cycling through each day. Everyone in this city feels more like a stranger than a neighbor. We're all known for our questioning looks and our small talk has digressed to whispers, or we remain silent. No one knows who to trust or who thinks alike. It's clear most of us are afraid of our hostage situation, but there are only two ways to live in fear—compliance or resistance—and one can endanger the other, which makes us all a unique mystery.

I'm standing in the middle of Raya's shop and I'm starting to ponder if she realizes I'm in here with her, but she doesn't strike me as the type who misses a beat of anything that's happening around her. She reopens the door and gestures for me to step out before her, still without exchanging a word. Maybe I've made too big an assumption by coming back here tonight.

Outside, Raya spins around and locks the door before turning to face me. It's now that I notice she looks a bit different than she did this morning, or even the other morning for that matter. She has a glow and there's less tension pinching her expression, which is saying a lot considering her recent encounter. It even seems she might have spent time preparing for our walk seeing that she's also dressed differently than she was earlier. Her long cream-colored skirt is affixed with a matching leather belt and topped by a short-sleeve royal-blue sweater. Her chin-length golden blonde hair is in loose curls, one curl dangling over her radiant emerald eyes. My chest tightens at the sight of the luminous rays highlighting her features. I'm not sure how I got lucky enough for a woman this beautiful to agree to go on a walk with me, but I'll count my blessings.

"So, where are we going, Monsieur Bardot?"

"Please, call me Nicolas," I say, dipping my hands into the pockets of my navy-blue slacks. "Are you all right? You seemed unaffected by the presence of those men, but I'm no stranger to concealing the tar-like fear that sits at the bottom of my stomach whenever I must interact with them."

"I'm fine," she says. "They were right. I should have chosen a German composer."

"They're all bastards. I much prefer Debussy myself."

"It's their city and their rules now, right?"

"No. It's not right."

Raya props the strap of her purse up over her shoulder and clasps her hands in front of her waist. "Where are we taking this walk, Mons—Nicolas?"

I wish there was something to say that might ease the remnants of her worries, but her reaction is typical. We must remain brave even though we are all breaking inside. "Well, unless you have a preference, I was thinking we should walk along the Seine since it's a lovely night."

Raya's gaze darts around the city block as if she's taking inventory of what's around her. "Do people still casually stroll along the river these days? It seems everyone has given in to the fear of enjoying life in their city."

Her mention of giving into fear confirms my assumption that she is not supportive of the rules we live by, rather than simply having a preference for orchestral composers. It seems obvious that I'm not taking a stroll with a Nazi sympathizer, but it's hard to tell who is who these days. It's appalling how many locals have fallen into their hypnotic delusions of control.

"Some locals still take in the beauty of the city at night but not as many as before."

"The Nazis swarm that area, don't they?" she asks inquisitively.

I take it she must not wander out too often.

"They do, but if you aren't Jewish and are abiding by their regulations, they'll most likely only ask to see our identification papers. It's more of a nuisance than anything else."

"It's almost as if we're looking for trouble then?" Her question is innocent and understandable. Through the eyes of a journalist, I've refused to give in to avoidance. Being asked to see my papers feels normal now too.

"I don't see it that way."

"What about Jewish people? What do they do if they cross their paths?"

I truly want to ask her how many times she's ventured away from her block in the last two years, but it would be insulting. I know many people who stay close to home for the sake of their safety and well-being.

"They have their own set of restrictions and curfews. The Nazis and police are usually belligerent to them, trying to scare them into not stepping out of their homes again—for those who still have their homes, that is." I glance over at Raya, noticing her jaw tense and the lines on her forehead deepen between her eyebrows. "Are you Jewish?" It's a ridiculous question. She wouldn't be allowed to run a business if she was, but people have pulled the wool over German eyes before.

"No, no, I was just curious. Do you think all Jewish people will be forced out of their homes soon?"

"Unfortunately, yes."

She draws in a deep breath, puffing out her chest as if she's struggling to collect enough air in her lungs. "Oh, mon dieu," she mutters.

"Did I say something to offend you?" I ask.

"No, of course not." She forces a tight-lipped smile. "These aren't your rules." Her statement comes off as more of question. She may be pondering if I'm German, trying to fool her into thinking I'm French.

"I've lived toward the center of Petit-Montrouge my entire

life, so not too far from your shop. What about you? Did you grow up here?"

"Yes, above the shop. I've lived there my entire life. At first, I was with my parents and brother, but it's only me—" Her statement ends abruptly as she stops to face her reflection in the short row of empty storefront windows along the curb. "They're all gone. They were open for business just a few weeks ago. Even the café..." Her hand clutches her neck as faint pink welts climb up to her chin.

"It's a disappointing sight," I agree. "Terrible."

"I suppose it's just a matter of time for us all," she says, taking a slow step back in the direction we were traveling.

"I'd like to hope that we won't all be affected. We can't let go of our faith. It's all we have."

"Yes," she says, her mind seemingly floating into the distance.

"So, you said your parents and brother no longer live with you. You live alone in this big city?" I ask, feeling more concerned than curious.

"Don't you?"

I shake my head. "I live with my mother. My father passed away twelve years ago and I'm an only child." I haven't had the need to tell anyone about my father in years. An ache burns through my chest, just as it has so often over the last thirteen years. I usually avoid the topic, knowing most will ask how he died and very few people know how to respond when I say he chose to take his own life, but I've come to an understanding over time—or maybe I've just pushed away the grief by telling myself I can imagine life from his perspective.

Raya's posture stiffens as she twists her head to look at me, her gaze cutting to mine as if I've captured her attention. "I'm so sorry," she says, studying my expression. "There's nothing worse than losing a parent."

I would usually look away from someone offering me

sympathy. I don't desire that form of attention as I don't want to feel sorry for myself again, like I did for far too long. However, I sense there's a reason she might know there is no worse feeling. "You speak the truth."

Her breath spilled out softly from between her lips. "I lost my father too, and my mother a few years later. My brother is studying to be a teacher in Zurich."

"So you're holed up in a city full of your memories that you refuse to leave behind?" I ask with a wry smile.

"I guess I'm not the only one," she says.

Our conversation flows effortlessly after the initial life woes tick by and we're already approaching the wrought-iron gates enveloping the Luxembourg gardens. At this time of the year, the masquerading trees weave between the ornate floral décor along the black posts and cement pillars. Though it's impossible to see into the gardens from where we are, Raya still peers through the grates, maybe trying to catch a glimpse of the concealed beauty on the other side.

"So as a journalist, do you spend your days lurking around corners in search of your next story?"

I laugh at the idea of lurking around corners like Sherlock Holmes with a magnifying glass in my hand. "I suppose I do."

"Then, what do you do in your free time?"

I can't think of an answer because I spend my nights under the pub planning how to push the Germans out of our city, and she might run if I tell her this.

"Search the city for beautiful women like yourself." It's not a bad line for escaping the truth.

"Is that so? Do you find many of them?" she asks, peering off into the distance toward Notre Dame. A rouge hue flourishes along her cheeks, and it seems she's fighting a smile.

"You're the first in quite a long time." My heart rises into my throat, making me realize I'm not spouting off riddles to capture her attention. It's all the truth. Except the part where I go around looking for beautiful women every night.

"But there are so many women in this city," she says, peering toward me and tilting her head to the side.

"I suppose I've only noticed you."

She drops her head, staring at the stone we're crossing. "You're certainly one with your words, but I suppose that shouldn't be surprising given your occupation."

Perhaps I am coming off too poetic to convince her I'm attracted to the woman who made me smile twice in the same week.

"When you see certain people walking around, do you ever feel like you're living in a different world from them, even though you're merely a few steps across the road?" I ask.

"All the time," she says.

"To be honest, I haven't given much thought to meeting someone special, at least not over the last couple of years. Before that I was finishing up university and didn't have a lot of free time. Even with the few dates I've been on, I haven't quite made a connection with anyone because I'm more concerned about what they might think of me, or if they are someone I shouldn't trust. It's an unsettling feeling deep in the bottom of my gut, and no matter how many people I talk to, it's rare to find myself at ease."

Raya nods with a sense of understanding. "I've had a couple of short-term relationships over the last few years, but everyone scattered when the Germans arrived and the thought of finding someone to settle down with at that point became daunting for similar reasons to yours, I suppose." She wraps her arms around her waist again and squeezes her fingers together.

Our conversation seems to come to a stop when we reach the steps leading down to the riverside. I lean over the rail to make sure there aren't any police or soldiers in the small crook beneath. There's no one down there at all, something Parisians wouldn't dream of two years ago.

"Are you sure this is okay?" she asks, glancing in each direction as if we're breaking the rules.

"It's not blockaded. It's fine."

We take a seat on the ledge over the river and Raya leans back on her hands, allowing the dipping sun to warm her face. She closes her eyes and a small smile blossoms across her cheeks.

"At what point of the night were you going to confess to being a part of the—"

I place my hand on her knee and squeeze gently. "Please don't finish your question," I whisper. If there's one thing I know not to do, it's to say incriminating words between stone walls. She might suspect I have an angular opinion on the war since I'm a journalist and she knows about the leaflets I dropped into the papers this morning. Most aren't so forward with asking anyone if they take part in such acts of rebellion. Although I'm coming to learn she isn't most people. There is a world of wonder living inside her head that she may never share with anyone, but if she does, I would hope it to be only with me.

Raya opens her eyes and straightens her posture suddenly, staring out across the river. I remove my hand from her knee, hoping that wasn't part of the reason for her look of shock. Though I might prefer that to whatever she might be thinking about me.

"I'm not a criminal," I whisper so softly I'm not sure she hears my words.

"Doesn't that depend on who you ask?" she replies.

"To whom it matters, I'm not. I'm a man of allegiance and nobility, willing to protect what's important to me." When I speak these words, I wish sweat wouldn't form at the top of my forehead or the back of my neck, but I'd be a fool to disregard the dangers of what I'm committed to.

"You're a good man," she utters, keeping her voice to a whisper. She swings her head to the side and leans forward to glimpse the walkway lining the river on the other side of the shallow inlet above us. "Germans," she says without sound.

"Stay calm. They smell fear. We're not doing anything wrong. We're walking home." I can see Raya has trouble portraying the act of being calm by the warm splotches on her chest and neck returning, contrasting vividly across her pale skin.

I take her by the hand and pull her up to her feet so we can leave. She squeezes against my grip, and we move toward the stone steps that lead up to the road. She's trying to move faster than I am and I'm doing my best to keep her walking at a common pace. "If they think you're running from them, they will run after us. They're like wild animals," I whisper into her ear, placing my other hand over our intertwined ones. "This is our city, not theirs. Remember that."

"I wish it was the truth," she replies solemnly.

The welts haven't dissipated, and I'm worried she might be in a frenzy, which is completely my fault. I take a casual glance over my shoulder to see if we were spotted. We were, and there is a soldier walking at the same speed but a block away. "Follow my lead."

My directions cause her to squeeze my hand tighter. The heat between our palms is enough to start a fire, and I want to enjoy the sensation rather than muster the words I'll need to speak as soon as this soldier comes any closer.

"I'm scared," she says breathlessly.

"I won't let anything happen to you."

"Papiere!" the soldier shouts.

"He wants our papers?" Raya asks, a frozen gape forming across her face.

"Ja, natürlich. Wir haben sie hier," I say to the soldier who is stopping us from going any further. "Raya, pull out your papers."

Raya's hand shivers as she reaches into the pocket of her skirt to retrieve her identification. Her nerves are on display, and I can tell this soldier is going to have his way with verbally torturing her. It's always the young ones who are bored from guarding the streets all day.

"Was ist los mit ihr?"

He can't be so dense as to ask what's wrong with her, as if they don't know they make most Parisians feel this way. "Sie ist nicht der Typ, der Ärger macht." Raya glances at me from the corner of her eye. I'm not sure if she understands what I said.

"Sind Sie sich da sicher?"

"Ja."

The soldier takes our papers and inspects them both thoroughly before staring coldly at Raya, who keeps her gaze pinned to the gravel beneath us.

The soldier lets out a chuckle. "In Ordnung. Weitergehen."

"Ja, natürlich. Guten Abend."

The soldier studies us for a long minute, purposely using intimidation for effect. It's never safe to move too fast or not fast enough. When my gut tells me to do so, I retrieve our papers from his hand and tug Raya away from him.

We're two blocks away before she pulls in a sharp shuddering inhale and glances over her shoulder. I do the same to make sure he's not still watching us. Thankfully, he's moved along too.

"What did he want?" Raya asks.

"He wanted to know what was wrong. He thought you looked bothered by something, but I told him we weren't looking for any trouble and you were fine. That's when he told us to keep moving."

Her hand unclenches but she doesn't release me. "I don't understand why the soldiers feel the need to parade these streets, flagging down Parisians to check if we are French citizens when they are the intruders. And why do they seem to find pleasure by inciting trepidation in us?"

"Because we scare easily sometimes, and it must make them feel more powerful."

"I wish I had spit in his face," Raya says.

Her statement shocks me, and I tug her hand to stop her from continuing forward. "What was that?" I can't help the quiet laughter that rumbles in my throat.

"I wish I had the nerve to spit in his face," she repeats.

"I'm going to advise you not to do that, ever, but the fact that you feel that way makes you even more beautiful than what I can see on the outside."

Adrenaline must be powering through her body as she glances back in the direction we came from. "They'll get what's coming to them. They will. I can feel it in my bones."

"Okay, let's take a deep breath," I tell her, reaching for her other hand so she looks at me instead of down the road.

Her eyes glisten as she peers up at me. There's a wild look flashing between her lashes and I can't help but smile. "I knew we had something in common."

"I'm not sure if that's a good thing," she says, pulling her hands out of mine.

NINE

RAYA

PRESENT DAY, OCTOBER 1943

Ravensbrück, Germany

There is no mistaking the cry of a siren as it grows in volume, reaching the level of a howling tornado before subsiding enough to highlight the beginning of the next cycle. I had always thought of sirens as a warning system, but here they are used to infiltrate our nerves with terror.

"Get up. Get up," a woman shouts. "Everyone up. Roll call." She's someone from the barrack, but no one who has spoken up in the day I've been here.

Everyone snaps out of their sleep, if they were able to fall that far into an unconscious state throughout the night. I watch as they all scurry off the bunks, straightening their smock uniforms, and securing their shoes. There is no sunlight shining in through the small windows, confirming my suspicion that it must be before dawn. I follow the lead of the others, slipping my feet into my black loafers and straightening the seams of the uniform across my shoulders. We all flee out of the barrack toward an open courtyard. The sky is gray, and the air is thick with a chilling moisture. Clouds seem to rest on top of the surrounding buildings as if they're ready to watch whatever scene is about to unfold.

The tired and ragged women move into several straight rows, switching from spot to spot when another person arrives. I make my way up to the next open space in the center of the newest formed row and glance around to see what others are doing to prepare for what's coming next.

"You're in the wrong spot," a woman, who must look like me without hair, a pale complexion, and a smock that's far too large for her frame, says. "We are to be in order by number. You're going to be two rows up with the other Fs." She points to my tattoo; five numbers follow the F on my arm and on a badge on my chest.

I want to ask if she knows what the F means, but I'm sure I'll find out soon enough. I sneak through the rows to make my way forward, stopping when I spot other badges that start with the letter F. A couple of them whisper in French and with the variety of languages I've heard since arriving, I'm going to assume that's what the F stands for. The dirt beneath our feet billows around our ankles, the sand-like particles sticking to my damp skin.

"We'll be waiting for hours this morning," one of the women in my row says. "If they would give advisement on what they expect rather than hoping everyone follows one another—"

"That would be making things easy for us," another woman responds.

"Shh," says the woman on my right. "They're coming."

I'm not sure if I noticed when the siren stopped whirling around us, but there's a ringing in my ears as its replacement.

A guard steps in front of the rows we're in and begins shouting numbers. Each number is followed by a woman replying with "Hier," to claim they are here. I don't want to question what would happen if someone was not here. I stare down at my arm, still unfamiliar with the number I wish to disassociate from.

"P-2310," the guard shouts a second time. He lifts his head, breaking his gaze with the list he holds and moves toward the rows. Two women step to the side, leaving a gap between them to show where the missing woman should be.

"Hier!" a voice yells from the back row. We're shoved to the side, then shifting around to allow the woman forward.

"Nein," the guard responds. "You were not here on time."

"Yes, but I'm here now—" The woman attempts to argue with the guard. She's disheveled, her smock misbuttoned, and the short hair she has is matted down every which way.

The guard pulls her out of the row and up in front where he yanks a whip out of the holder on his belt, then tells her to turn around. "Let's all count to twenty-five."

No, no. She was less than a minute late. I want to pretend as if I don't know what we will be counting, but the breaking sound of the air against the leather, followed by a startling thin slap, is what we will all watch the poor woman endure twenty-four more times for being a moment too late. Her cries howl against the wind, blood splatters, and I wonder if she was wrongly arrested and brought here. If she left a family or loved ones behind, they're lucky not knowing what she's enduring here. I force myself to watch the evolving look of despair warping her face. I want to save her and yet I've never met her. It's the human thing to do. But if I move, I will be next in line for a lashing. That's why no one is moving from their spot.

By the end, acidity rises into my throat and the woman is unconscious, face-down on the ground.

My entire life I have viewed leather as a beautiful material, luxurious, and of high quality—something my family and I have used to make wonderful, long-lasting items. Before today, I never considered the idea of leather being used as a form of punishment, torture, and turmoil—a smooth finish among the lacerations bleeding through the back of her smock.

TEN

RAYA

Paris, France

I drop the stack of leather scraps we'll need for orders today on top of Alix's bed, imagining doing this while he was still lying in bed being lazy on a day that he didn't have school. He wasn't one to wake up on his own so I did what any good sister would do and woke him up with a face full of scraps. I'm the only one who found humor in those moments, but I would do it again if he was still here and asleep at this late hour.

As I hand Charlette the pending orders, I notice a paleness has taken over her face, accenting her puffy pink eyelids. Her smile, full and broad, is hardly believable, but she doesn't want me to know she's been crying. When she notices my inquisitive stare, she lowers her head as if it will hide what I already know.

Charlette spends more time trying to convince me of her bravery than anything else. I don't see a need when she has every right to be afraid and worried. She has always been the braver one of us, or maybe even the stronger one. Charlette never stumbles when life spins us in circles. When Mère died, she held me upright, spent more time here helping me with Alix and the shop than she did at home. She never asked if I needed help, she was just there giving me what she could. I used to feel guilty, thinking she had been a better friend to me than I had been to her. Charlette's life might have seemed simpler at one time but it took a nosedive when antisemitism began to rise. I promised I would protect her however possible. I just hope that is what I'm doing by keeping her here.

"Don't forget about the bells in case a German enters the shop," she says, reminding me as she has been the last few mornings.

I was so caught off guard last night when the two officers piled in just before closing that I didn't ring the bell upstairs. I've kept the news of their visit and threat to myself for the sake of not giving her something more to worry about.

"I won't forget," I tell her, suppressing the guilt rising as acid in my stomach. I take a seat on the edge of Alix's bed, facing Charlette, who is seated at the sewing machine we moved into this room.

"Are you going to tell me about your night with the gentleman?" she asks, unwinding a tangle in the spool of thread. I can't tell if she's asking to be polite or if she truly wants details. If I were in her shoes, I might not ask, knowing how unfair it is that one of us has the freedom to walk the streets while the other doesn't, never mind spending time with a man for pleasure.

"It was nothing. We walked to the river and came back," I say, lifting the pile of leather scraps onto my lap.

"It was nothing, and yet you're blushing and won't look at me," she teases. Charlette tears the piece of thread she can't untangle and drops the spool into place on top of the machine.

"We had a nice talk," I say, making eye contact with her this time.

"Is he good looking?" she presses.

I shrug, trying to hide the smile threatening to unfurl across my lips.

"Come on, Raya, you must give me something. If I must live vicariously through you, you need to do a better job at giving details." Charlette sweeps her hair off her shoulders and winds her curls into a loose knot, then snags a pencil from the table and jabs it through the bulk of her hair.

"Yes, he's very handsome. He also has a wit about him and a way with words—quite easy to open up to. He was also demure when we were stopped by a German officer last night and asked for our papers. I was about to faint from how fast my heart was pounding, but he stayed calm and handled it with such poise."

Charlette's shoulders slump forward. "You were questioned?" she asks. "What for?"

"The soldier wanted to know what we were doing and where we were going. It's precisely why I haven't gone too far out of our district. There's a risk walking around these surrounding blocks. Never mind crossing half the city to the river."

Charlette shakes her head and huffs. "You're not Jewish. You should be able to walk wherever you want."

Her words strike a nerve. I don't want to feel lucky that I'm not Jewish—it's a terrible thought. "You should be able to walk anywhere just as much as I should."

"Well, we both know that doesn't matter."

"It does matter to me. I feel shame knowing I can take a chance on stepping outside these doors and you can't. There is no difference between us and yet it's like we're seen as two different species. I shouldn't be able to enjoy sporadic moments in the day if you can't. It's not fair to you."

"These rules aren't yours to feel bad about. You're protecting us and for that you deserve some moments of happiness."

I set the stack of leather back down on the bed and lean over the sewing machine to loop my arms around her neck. "You are my happiness. We're in this together, always."

"Okay then. If I am your happiness and you are mine, please tell me more about my—your—date last night." She giggles and her smile is believable now. "Are you going to see him again?"

I fold my arms across my chest, protecting the thoughts I tried to avoid last night in bed, staring at the ceiling with a giddy smile until I fell asleep. "We didn't make plans, so I guess we'll see what happens."

"You've spent so long caring about everyone else. Don't deny yourself the chance of someone doing the same for you."

With a deep breath I allow her words to sit with me before I snap out of my daze. "Okay, I need to open the shop. Do you have everything you need?"

"I do. Go on," she says, taking the top order note from the pile.

I spin around before going downstairs and spot the sweater I left in here yesterday when digging through Alix's closet. The only upside to living here alone was the extra closet space I'd gained.

"You dropped something," Charlette says, leaning to the side. She unfolds the piece of paper before I reach for it. "What is this?"

I'd forgotten what was in my pocket until she flips around the yellow-tinted paper toward me. Two French flags are crossed on the top above the bold printed text that is addressed to every innocent resident of this country.

To all of France:

We might have lost a fight, but there is still a war to win.

We refuse to give up our pride or hope.

Join us in our act of bravery and stop allowing

THE FORCES TO TAKE AWAY OUR RIGHTS AND FREEDOM.
WHERE THERE IS UNITY, THERE WILL BE SUCCESS.
TOGETHER, WE WILL REACH OUR VICTORY!
LONG LIVE FRANCE!

Blood rushes through my cheeks as I step toward her to take the paper. "It was just in the newspaper. I—I'm not sure." I leave out the part that Nicolas was the one who had slipped it in.

"You kept it?" she questions as concern weighs heavily over her dark eyebrows.

"I didn't want anyone to find it."

The tilt of her head voices her thought, she knows I'm not being truthful. "I'm sure plenty of them have been passed around in various locations throughout the city, and I'm sure the Germans have come across them. So why would anyone think anything if they found one?"

Charlette's right. Persuasion to work against the Vichy government, who blatantly collaborate with Germany, has been in effect for the last two years. Most people aren't advocates for what has happened—is happening. But I would be terrified if a German thought I wasn't in agreement with the government, and the consequence would be detrimental to not only me, but the Levis and the shop that's supporting us all.

"A German officer or soldier would, so I wanted to make sure it wasn't floating around in the shop anywhere."

"Good point." Charlette tears the paper into scraps and tosses them into the trash bin to the side of the bed.

"I'll check on you around noon," I tell her before leaving more abruptly than I normally would.

I wanted to ask Nicolas last night if the leaflet was something he was responsible for or if he was handling a task assigned by his boss at the newspaper. He stopped me midway through my question. After witnessing his easy submission to the German officer's demands last night, I didn't pursue the thought that he might be part of a group soliciting for volunteers to join in force against the government. From what I've heard, most people who are a part of those groups wouldn't have surrendered so easily to a German the way he did last night.

Of course, if I'm wrong, I'd be jeopardizing my safety, Charlette's, and her parents by being around him. I can't let this go any further until I find out for sure. That is, if I see him again. Which, I hope I do.

* * *

As soon as the shop is unlocked and open for business, the door swings open, revealing two familiar faces I haven't seen in a while. They're frequent patrons, two gentlemen who were friendly with Papa.

"Salut, ma petite chérie!" They greet me at the same time. They have never stopped referring to me as little even though I've grown up and become the woman who runs this shop.

"Salut, messieurs! How are you both doing this morning?"

Monsieur Faure shuffles up to the counter and places his old, worn black belt on it without a word of explanation. The recurring tear seems to occur at least once every three months. I'm not sure how he manages to tear it because Charlette's stitches are tighter than nails, just like Papa's and Mère's were when they were the ones stitching. He's never questioned whether it's something we did wrong during the repair, therefore I see it as a "do not ask if he doesn't ask" situation.

Come to think of it, I've only ever seen him wearing brown slacks, and his brown belt. Maybe this beat up old piece of leather belongs to one of his sons. He doesn't mention them, but I remember meeting them many years ago. Monsieur Faure turns away from the counter to meet up with Monsieur Caron, who has never made a purchase in this shop during the time I've been old enough to work here, but he might be the best window shopper I've ever met. I admire restraint in a person. He's also much quieter than Monsieur Faure, who seems to do most of the talking on behalf of them both when they're here.

"How is your brother doing? Have you heard from Alix lately?" Monsieur Faure asks, tending to the shelf of fitted gloves displayed next to Monsieur Caron.

Alix. We write to each other frequently, but my letters to him are subdued to keep him from worrying about me. He must focus on his education. Most of Alix's letters are updates about his daily life and questions about mine that I rarely answer in kind.

"Alix is doing quite well, acing his studies, and enjoying his time in Zurich. In fact, I just received a letter from him yesterday." I pull the folded paper out of my dress pocket and hold it up like it's my treasure.

"What did the young man have to say for himself? We should all be so lucky to live vicariously through him right now," Monsieur Faure says, nodding toward the letter.

"I couldn't agree more." I open it and straighten the creases. "Well, he says..."

My dear sister,

The warm air has finally arrived here and I'm writing to you from the cement flowerbeds in the promenade overlooking the crystal clear Limmat River. Everyone is extra cheerful for the bout of seasonable weather. I've begun work for the summer school program, assisting another teacher with a group of twenty grade school children who need a bit of help after this last year. After all this time sitting through classes of my own, learning how to become a teacher, it feels wonderful to have a chance to use my skills and hopefully help these young minds.

Your last letter sounded a bit grimmer than normal, and

I've been worrying, as usual, about what life must be like at home right now. I can read between your words of positive remarks and the headlines of most newspapers. I pray for you every night before I go to sleep, Raya, and I hope you are being vigilant and keeping safe.

As mentioned in my last letter, I'm going to try to come home in a few weeks, so you won't be able to hide anything from me then. And, yes, I received your reply telling me to stay put, but I'm afraid you have no say over what I do now. Sorry for the disappointment.

Anyway, I miss you dearly, sister. Take care of yourself.

With love,

Alix

"He's a lucky kid, being away from the mess of this city," Monsieur Faure responds. "Why didn't you go with him when he left?"

Although I know the answer to this question, I still get caught asking myself the same thing sometimes. "Who would run this shop?" I ask him with a pain-filled smile. In truth, if I left this shop, I would be leaving Mère and Papa behind—everything they worked for. Their souls run through these walls, and I won't walk away from the only connection I have to them. Though even if the shop wasn't a permanent fixture in my life, I couldn't afford to leave Paris when Alix did. The cost of moving to Zurich without a secured source of income would have ruined Alix's education and my well-being.

"Listen, Raya, I'm not sure if you're aware but Alix won't be able to get across the border to come home any time soon. I'm sorry if I'm the bearer of bad news, but from what I've heard, no one is getting through without a miracle."

"I've told Alix this many times, but he's persistent in thinking he'll eventually find a way."

"I'm not sure that's something he should want to do so badly. He's much safer there."

"I've told him," I reply.

"It's a wonder the shop is still open. I'm sure he must know that." It is. Most of the small shops have had to close due to the draining economy but we've been taking in more repairs than needing to purchase inventory so the business has remained fairly balanced.

"I'm grateful for the business," I tell him, trying to change the downward slope of this conversation. I prefer to see the light in Alix's letters and move about knowing he's safe and happy.

"In any case"—Monsieur Faure sighs—"these gloves are beautiful." He whistles while inspecting one of the two from edge to edge. "Fine job, young lady."

Charlette and I have been able to make the gloves from scrap pieces of leather we've accumulated throughout the years.

"Merci. I can have this belt fixed up for you by the end of the week," I say while writing the repair slip. As soon as Charlette sees his name, she'll know exactly what to do even if I don't write what is needed.

A creak from the floor upstairs startles me into smudging the tip of my pen across the paper. I force myself to keep writing, to act as if I didn't hear anything.

"Do you have someone working upstairs?" Monsieur Faure asks, staring up at the ceiling as if he can see right through it.

"No, it's just me," I say, taking the stack of order slips and straightening them out to keep my fidgeting hands busy. It's no wonder we need leaflets to remind us of the corruption being fed to us. I can't even pay Charlette the credit she deserves for her hard work.

"Good for you," he says, tapping his knuckles on the

counter. "Well, we'll leave you to it and I'll be by on Friday to pick up the belt. Take care, ma petite chérie!"

"Salut," I say as the two men leave the shop.

A minute doesn't pass before the door opens again. I whip my head to the side, scrutinizing who's walking through the door in case I need to pull the string behind my back.

"Bienven—" I begin to say before Nicolas appears through the sun's glare.

"I'm not worthy of a full welcome?" he asks, removing his beret from his slicked dark hair. A wry grin dons his cleanly shaven face.

"Bienvenue, Nicolas," I correct myself, feeling my dimples deepen along the corners of my lips.

"I don't know how you like your coffee, nor was I able to find an open café this morning, but I was able to find this in a garden I probably shouldn't have been passing through." He lowers his right hand from behind his back and hands me a handful of stems fringed with lavender flowers.

I touch my fingers to my chest, taken aback by the sweet gesture. "Lavender is my favorite." I hold them up to my nose, reveling in the soothing aroma. A scent different from leather is always welcome in my life.

Nicolas drops his free hand into his pocket and lifts his shoulders as if he has something he wants to say but isn't sure whether he should. "I enjoyed our time together last night and I'm hoping we can do it again sometime soon...if you feel the same way, of course."

I can't contain the smile growing along my lips as I feather my fingertip along the fuzzy stem between the small flowers. "I was hoping you might say that."

My heart spoke before my mind. I'd told myself I needed to know more about what he does in his free time before this goes any further, but at some point, between that internal debate and now, the thought of spending more time with him blocked out my concern.

He dips his head and presses his hand to his chest. "I had myself convinced you were too good to be true."

I place the flowers on the front counter and fiddle with the thin bracelet dangling from my wrist. "And why is that?" I ask, biting on the side of my bottom lip.

Nicolas rubs the back of his neck and huffs a quiet laugh. "It isn't often I find a woman with the strength and determination to hold her life together the way you have. I'm not sure I'd be able to run a business on my own and be successful at doing so. I'm enamored by you."

I twist my lips to one side, relishing in the compliment I rarely hear. Running this shop alone has been anything but easy, but I wouldn't give up on it either. It's my family, a part of me.

"There's something stirring in those pretty eyes of yours," he says, taking a step toward me.

There's a lot whirring around in my head, but I'm not sure which thought he's inquiring about. I hum, warning him that I have something to follow his analysis of me. "You say you don't think you could run a business on your own, but you still take risks in life, don't you?"

"Risks?" He glances at the flowers lying on the counter. "Assuming you like lavender was quite a risk, I suppose."

I can't help the unexpected bout of laughter rumbling through me. He's quick on his toes. "That's not what I meant." I take a step toward him, trying to show a brave face before asking him what I'd like the answer to.

"Oh," he mutters beneath his breath. He clears his throat and straightens his posture.

With another small step, I'm standing in a position to look up at him. I lower my voice. "Did someone ask you to place those leaflets in the newspapers, or did you do so of your own accord?"

He fidgets with his beret, twisting it between his fingers, between our bodies. With a long inhale, he sets his sights over the top of my head before answering. "Someone asked me to."

I'm not sure what answer I was hoping for, but I let out a sigh of relief. My question only determines who was leading the action.

"To be fair, though," he says, pausing for a beat, "I would have done it even if someone didn't ask. Is—um—is that what you were afraid to hear?" His eyes soften and his brows furrow. "Being a proud citizen of France doesn't shouldn't really be defined as a risk."

"I couldn't agree more," I say, dropping my gaze to the ground between us. "But I must know...are you part of a group that—"

"I—I can't deny nor confirm. I believe we feel the same about the corrupt power over our country though, or did I misunderstand?"

"I am entirely against the German occupation and what our government is complying to, but I'm one person and not brave enough to make a stand against something I have no control over. I do know how many people have been tortured and killed for rebellious behavior though."

Nicolas wraps his other hand around his hat and holds it tighter against his waist. "I'm not any braver than you and I don't see devotion to the people of our country to be an act of defiance. If a leaflet can bring more of us like-minded people together, we gain hope of becoming stronger than the German force. I can promise you I'm not a bad person, Raya."

I clutch my hand over my chest. "That—that's not—not what I meant. The Germans terrify me but when I think of my safety, I know my rage and resentment aren't enough protection. I guess, I'm the one who hides in the face of danger."

Hearing my words out loud makes me sound like a terrible person—a selfish, terrible person.

Nicolas reaches his hand out for mine and I comply. "I don't want to make you uncomfortable."

"I can't take part in anything like that..." Or anything that stands up for what I believe to be right. I hate to wonder if my father would be disappointed in me, but I know Mère would agree with my actions to stay out of sight.

"Then, don't. It doesn't have to be a part of our conversations. My feelings on supporting rights have nothing to do with how much I enjoyed every minute of our time together last night, and truthfully, I would give up my freedom to whoever asked for it if it meant seeing you again."

"After just one night, you would give up your freedom to spend more time with me?" I wonder if the expression on my face tells him I think he's crazy.

"Maybe not all of my freedom..."

I laugh and drop my gaze to our intertwined hands. "I don't want to know any more than I do, but I hope you aren't hunting the enemy with weapons."

"My mother would kill me before I had the chance to pull a trigger, and she'd do so with a frying pan or a rolling pin. It's not worth the mess."

"Your mother is in the dark about your secrets too?"

"I never said I had secrets. I said I wouldn't mention my feelings on supporting our rights." Nicolas touches his hand to my cheek. "I told you last night I wouldn't let anything happen to you, and that's the one thing I'll say about my feelings on the matter."

The warmth of his touch weakens my internal battle. I would be angry with myself for telling him to go away and never come back, especially after the way he left me in a clouded haze last night.

"The shop is so quiet, I can hear how hard you're breathing," he whispers. "You don't hide your feelings too well."

The grandfather clock on the wall chimes to the hour and Nicolas's eyes widen. "I have completely lost track of time and my editor is going to kill me before my mother can. Tomorrow night I'll come by the shop, and we can stand right here and talk, or go for a walk where you feel safe. Would that be okay?"

I purse my lips, forging the hint of thinking through the proposal.

He leans down and brushes his lips against my cheek. "Please?"

"Okay," I agree.

Nicolas releases a lungful of air and presses his palm to his chest. "You're good at making me nervous. I kind of like that. I'll see you tomorrow night, ma chérie."

"Be safe, please."

His gaze falls to my lips. Hesitation holds him hostage briefly until he steps in closer toward me. He sweeps my hair behind my ear then lowers his hand to the back of my neck. The muscles in my stomach tighten and I close my eyes just as he brushes the tip of his nose against mine. My heart convulses as I touch my hands to his chest, finding his heart is dancing to the same rhythm as mine. His free arm loops around my back to close the small gap between us.

As if the sun is rising in my chest, every part of me melts.

Maybe it's been a minute, or three, but he pulls away to catch his breath. Enamored by his mouth, I noticed I've stained his lips. I reach up between us and run the pad of my thumb across them. "Lipstick," I say, biting down on my bottom lip.

He takes my hand and curls it within his. "You have stolen all of the air from my lungs and now I must figure out how to make my way to work when it would be safer for me to stay here for a while longer."

If only our safety was defined so simply. I've gotten used to saying goodbye to those I care about—my parents and brother—making it difficult to remember that not everyone will just step out of my life, whether forever or just long enough to wonder if I'll see them again. Aside from Charlette, even my other friends have fled Paris. Staying here during this occupation isn't the option many chose.

ELEVEN
NICOLAS
LAST YEAR, JULY 1942

Paris, France

"You don't have to go," Raya says, like she has every night for the last month, taking a break from her nightly product maintenance checklist to grab a hold of my arm. She spins herself into my torso and pulls me to dance as we listen to the classical records echoing between the shop walls, the music much louder now as she pulled the muffling rag out of the gramophone's horn after closing the store to the public. It's nice to be immersed in pleasant sounds, even if they're composed by German musicians. It's better than the German chatter along the streets or German folk music playing in many local shops.

"I wish I didn't have to go, but I promised—them—I would be there, and I didn't show up once last week because you were a bit too good at convincing me not to leave." I wrap my arms around her and kiss her cheek, wishing I didn't have to go. I'm a man of my word though and it's important to tend to my commitments.

"I can appreciate your loyalty, I suppose," she sighs.

I respond with a groan because she makes it impossible to

just walk away. Even if she didn't say a word, I'd still have to force myself out the door. I twist her around and cup my hands on her warm cheeks, stealing a kiss for the road. She loops her arms around my neck and I'm lost somewhere outside of this world again. It's like a dream, but dreams always end with a cold burst of reality. It's the worst feeling.

"Be careful," she murmurs against my lips.

"You have nothing to worry about," I insist. "I'll see you first thing in the morning with your daily dose of fresh lavender." I kiss her cheek once more and slide my hands across her shoulders and down the length of her arms, taking in the warmth of her smile before I turn for the door.

* * *

I'm leading a double life. It's the only way to describe this separation of light and dark I glide between. Each night after work I make my way to Raya's shop just before closing, so she can shut me in with her. I help with the mundane tasks of tracking inventory and straightening products, but once the work is done, she's in my arms, and I can't think of anything else happening in the world around me until I have to leave.

The streets of Montmartre are the epitome of the night's shadow, especially when I recall how many vibrant lights used to color these cobblestones. There is no French life after nine now. With nothing but darkness among each step over uneven paths. I'm tempted to light a match, but we've been warned not to, and have agreed to silence and obscurity when approaching the back door of an abandoned church on the outskirts of Montmartre. We've had to move the location of our resistance meetings twice due to the growing number of German soldiers crowding the streets. They're making it near impossible for anyone to walk from one point to another without being noticed in some capacity.

This will be the third time we've met in this location atop one of the steepest hills in Paris, with overgrown vines and branches camouflaging road corners. We've been finding our way by measures of our average walking speed and the duration of time each road takes to travel. I continue counting out the seconds, reaching the last turn onto a narrow, vacant road, lined with moss covered fragments of stone while I seek the coin-sized spot of untarnished metal, shimmering against the moon's reflection, along the church's rusty gate.

The surrounding trees seem to speak to each other through the wind, leaves rustling, branches crackling—they are the real spies watching over Paris. My chest tightens as I climb over the gate, being cautious not to slip or scrape the bottom of my boot too loudly against the decaying facade. I jump from the top into the overgrown grass below, steadying myself following a body length's leap. I should be one of the first after Hugo and Bette tonight according to our agenda from earlier in the week.

After the ritual of quiet knocks against the door, I'm inside the church, a faint glow from the sky highlighting parts of the glass cathedral. I follow Hugo four steps to the right, ten steps forward and another six steps to the right before catching the door he's opened. Not until the door has closed can we safely light a match, knowing light won't carry any further than the stairwell.

"We can't keep this up. Not only are we sinning in a time when we need prayers answered but someone is going to end up breaking their neck getting here," Hugo says as we enter the lantern-lit space of the cement-clad cellar.

"What other choice do we have?" I ask.

"We might have a few. I've acquired some information on unsecured entrances to the tunnels."

We are still searching for secluded entry points to the underground tunnels. We've come to find that accessible sewer holes are visible to anyone passing by.

"Where did you get this information?"

"I attended a meeting in Lyon after waking up to a sealed letter under my front door the other morning. It was a call for leaders of resistance groups to gather and exchange up-to-date information. The meetings will become more regular, and I'll have continuous insight for ongoing larger scale plans." Hugo's tired eyes stare through my forehead as he explains what he's done to gain this information. He looks like he's been on the run all day, his oily hair pushed back to appear neat when it's not, and the sweat stains on his undershirt can't be attributed to the trek here an hour after the sun has gone down.

"Why didn't you mention you were going?"

He turns his back to me, facing his sister instead. "You've been a bit preoccupied, brother."

I should have expected this comment to come sooner than tonight. Until now he's been quiet about my growing distance this last month as I've stuck to assignments rather than standing up to take more initiative like I used to do. "I'm here, aren't I?"

"Are you?" he counters.

The one thing Hugo isn't good at is hiding his apprehension, but he'll never confess to succumbing to his nerves. The act of holding on to friends lately is almost as impossible as finding a like-minded woman in this torn city. Fortunately, Hugo and I have known each other since long before the war began. We went to school together for nearly ten years and live only two blocks from each other. Our paths always seem to cross and after one conversation about our disdain for the government's actions, we agreed to do something about it. A year later, here we are. We're partners, supposed to be heading up this group, Lions Rebelles, together.

But there's a fine line between devoting myself to the resistance and maintaining well-being at all other hours of the day. My involvement with Hugo and the other Lions Rebelles could endanger my mother, and now Raya as well. While keeping up with my promise to be quiet about my triweekly evening activities, with each passing day it becomes more difficult to maintain the separation, especially with the overwhelming desire to spend more and more time with her. Not only can I not seem to stop thinking about Raya every waking minute, but those feelings come with the need to protect her too.

"How's the future wife?" Hugo asks, his voice dropping an octave, a clear indication he's switching topics. He spins back around to face me. "Oh, by the way, you—ah—have a bit of lipstick," he says, brushing his finger to the side of his mouth. "I guess that should answer my question." His eyebrows waggle.

"We haven't discussed marriage. We've only known each other for a bit over a month." It feels like much longer.

"I think I see little glowing hearts in your eyes," he teases. "And the hair, it's always combed so nicely now. That and the lipstick all over your face, I'd say this city of wilting lights still holds a little bit of power over you."

I rub at my lips and cheeks, making sure to remove any hints of Raya's lipstick, but only for the sake of removing Hugo's ammo. Once my face is clean, I grab a few of the chairs from against the side wall to close our circle in a bit tighter. "Okay, okay, I hear you." He's worried I'm too distracted. Maybe I am. Maybe it's what I need.

"With times of war, come stronger acts of devotion," Hugo adds, his words melodizing in a teasing tune.

"Leave him alone," Bette snaps, her back facing us as she organizes papers into piles. "I think it's nice he's finally met someone who can put up with his boring jokes."

"Wow, you too, Bette? Your family has it out for me, don't they?" I ask, adding to their laughter. I enjoy these light moments of being like common people without the thought of war looming over our heads, even if they are at my expense.

"I couldn't help myself," she says. "In all honesty, though,

Hugo is quite jealous of the time you spend with this girl. Maybe she has a friend for him?"

"Enough," Hugo says, flicking his sister's ear. "I don't care what you do with your time."

"You are jealous, aren't you?" I ask, taking back control of this conversation.

"No, but she's making you weak." Hugo's statement isn't another jab. It's the truth. The world of resistance and the one living under authority don't play well together. "Have you considered asking her if she wants to help us? Bette could use another set of hands with the papers. Is she a good typist?"

I wouldn't ask Raya if she'd want involvement with our group as she asked me not to mention the topic in her presence. The idea of what we're doing terrifies her, though she supports the act of rebellion against the Germans. "No. She doesn't know much of what we do."

"You obviously trust her enough to be waiting outside her shop door like a lost dog every night after work, so why not bring it up?"

One of these days, I'll learn not to give Hugo ammo to use against me at his discretion.

"It's something to think about," Hugo says. "You never know, she might surprise you and say she'd like to help."

As the others arrive, one by one, the small cellar fills up and a refreshing chill from the enclosing cement walls dissipates into muggy thick air. It's been almost a year of weekly meetings, but we increased the number of days we met twice over the last six months, making the nights here feel more like an occupation than a voluntary commitment. Everyone looks like they have somewhere else to be, but at the same time, they wouldn't miss a meeting because their devotion to regaining their freedom trumps all else in their lives.

"I have some good news," Hugo says, taking a stance in the middle of the circle. "I've been given some locations to explore for possible access to the tunnels. As you know, the underground passageways lead to every sewer line in the city, which can give us a better opportunity to access roadways we can't easily pass through. We're hopeful this will be a good way to collect counterintelligence without being spotted, and also provide opportunities for sabotage."

"We are only focusing on collecting intelligence," Bette argues. "We aren't taking part in raids."

Hugo drops his head back with frustration. "We've talked about this...if it comes to it, we have to fight, and I'm not sure what other choices we have at this point. Collecting information and distributing it through the city isn't doing enough. We need to take part in the action if we want to make a difference. If we don't start eliminating more Germans, they will soon outnumber the remaining French citizens."

"There are," Bette mumbles.

"Then we give up." Hugo throws his hands in the air.

"Let's take a minute to breathe," I tell them. "Arguing won't get us anywhere. The resistance has grown. There are plenty of us around the city. Damage is being done, but we all want more and we want to see it happen faster. It comes down to the risk we're willing to take. Is that what we're deciding to do?" My question is directed at Hugo because he seems to have taken the reins as the solo leader now.

"We're taking this day by day, just as we always have. I just think we need to be prepared for whatever might come next, because this war isn't ending anytime soon."

There isn't much I can say to disagree. He's right, and we need to be ready if we must fight. If they take anything more from our city, we'll starve and become homeless.

"Anyway," Hugo raises his voice. "Apparently, there are several cafés and shops with access points to the sewers. Some of these shops might be closed, some still open. I assume the ones that are closed have already been ransacked in search of an access point and will be blocked off. Therefore, our best bet would be to find locations with shops and cafés still open for business. The list I have isn't extensive as the research is still in progress, but this will give us a place to start." Hugo slips a folded map out of his back pocket and opens it on the floor by his feet. "I've marked a dozen entrances across the entire city. There are currently fifteen of us in Lions Rebelles, so if we each take one location to gather information over the next couple of days, that would speed up this process. These shops and cafés are most likely privately owned, which means you will need to find the owner and feel out the possibility of them agreeing to allow us access."

I lean forward from my chair to get a closer look at the map, spotting penned asterisks in scattered locations between 6th Arrondissement and the 14th.

"If you see any form of propaganda for the Vichy outside or inside the establishment, it's not worth pursuing," Hugo continues. "With regard to finding the specific location, in most cases there will be a street sewerage cover next to or across from the establishment."

The others are still intently listening to Hugo's lecture but I'm tracing my finger along the streets I'm most familiar with, finding an entrance near Raya's shop. "Do you have a pen?" I ask, interrupting.

Bette reaches over with a pen and a piece of paper. "Write down which location you're taking," she whispers.

I jot down the coordinates on my hand and on the paper from Bette too.

"See something you like?" Hugo asks, peering down at me from over his shoulder.

"I know one of these roads fairly well."

* * *

The long, dark walk home gave me plenty of time to visualize the map coordinates in relation to the proximity of Raya's shop. She likely knows most of the shop owners around her, which may be helpful. Then again, finding a location near Raya could be dangerous if we're found. Maybe I'm getting too deep in this business, preparing for a battle we have so little strength to fight. I made a commitment to Hugo and the others though and there's no stepping back now.

I make a point of walking down Raya's street in search of the sewer holes, but find myself stopping in front of the shop door, wanting to call upstairs just to say hello. I wouldn't knock on the door at this hour because it would startle her, but I told her I would toss a pebble up at her window if I ever stopped by unannounced so she would know it's me out front.

I take a long look in all directions, ensuring there are no German soldiers or officers nearby. It's surprising not to see one, but I don't hesitate to find a pebble on the curb to use.

After tossing the first, I locate another in case she didn't hear it and send another up. A flicker of a light glows behind her curtain and I hear footsteps along the interior steps. The drape in front of the shop window parts from the wall slightly and then the clambering of locks echoes between the door's threshold. She opens the door a crack.

"It's me," I whisper.

"I know, but it's after nine. What are you doing outside?" she whispers back.

"Can I come in?" Raya hasn't invited me up to her flat yet, but I wouldn't either if I was a young woman living alone in this city right now. Although, I do hope she trusts me enough to know I would never make her uncomfortable in any way.

"Now?" she says.

"Yes, I forgot to tell you something earlier. We can stay downstairs in the shop."

She tugs the door open a bit more and reaches out,

wrenching her fist around my wrist to tug me inside. "It's so late. Do you always stay out until this time?" she says while re-locking the door.

I almost forget why I'm out so late, past curfew, and what reason I had to walk down this street, which isn't a direct route home from where I was. The only reason I can focus on now are the lips I desperately want to kiss. "It's becoming difficult to wait until morning to see you," I say, wrapping my hands around her slim waist.

She peers up at me from beneath her thick lashes just before our mouths meet.

After a long minute of hello, she takes a small step back and pinches her pale blue silk robe over her chest. "Your mother must be worried sick."

I'm not sure if Mère has been waiting up for me after I tell her not to, but she hasn't said anything about the hour I do come home, which leads me to believe she's asleep when I do. She's also been asking questions regarding a secret I've been keeping from her, likely speculating if it has something to do with a female companion. I'd rather her be curious about a possible woman in my life than the idea that I'm working with the resistance. She's even stopped asking me where I've been at night, likely hoping I'm making good use of my time so she can someday have the daughter-in-law and grandchildren she not-so-quietly prays for.

"I had to go up to Montmartre tonight."

She tilts her head to the side, glancing at me with wonder at what I'll say next. "To meet with the others?" she says for me, hoping that's all that will come out of my mouth.

"Yes."

With a deep inhale, she drops her gaze, a sign of disappoint-ment, the one I've been desperately avoiding since she asked me not to mention my activity in rebelling against the government. She shakes her head. "I didn't know you were out and about this late. I thought your meetings were short and nearby, and over before curfew. You'll make me worry about you every night. I prefer to think you are home safe, not looking for trouble."

"You sound like my mother," I tease her, sweeping my thumb across her warm cheek. "Speaking of which, I would like to take you to meet her one night this week. You can have dinner with us. What do you say?"

My question seems to distract Raya from thoughts of me roaming the streets after curfew. She smiles and rests her hands against her chest. "I would like that very much. Plus, it would mean one less night that you can be out looking for trouble, right?"

As she stares into my eyes, silently pleading with me to stay away from trouble for just one night, the floorboards above creak and moan, drawing my attention to the ceiling. Usually there's a record playing so the silence highlights any other noise from within the building.

She follows my gesture as if she's wondering where the sound might be coming from since she's down here with me. I consider the thought of a radiator cranking but then I remember we're in the middle of summer. No one has their radiator on now.

"You still live alone, don't you?" I say with a chuckle, trying to make a small joke. I'm here daily. Surely, I would have known otherwise by now.

"Well, yes," she says with hesitation.

The creaking repeats and there is not a doubt in my mind this time that I'm listening to footsteps above my head. "Is someone upstairs with you?" My stomach churns, considering she might have someone else in her life besides me and maybe that's why she hasn't invited me upstairs. "Your brother?" He couldn't have come home now, not with the strict border control. She's told me several times she's asked him to stay put.

"It's—It's not what you think..." she says, her cheeks

reddening among the glow of the lantern she placed on the front counter.

"Another man?" I ask.

She refocuses her stare directly into my eyes. "Another man? Why would you think such a thing? I've told you how much I care about you and what you mean to me. Why would I be doing the same with someone else at the same time?"

She's avoiding all my questions, but at least I don't think there is someone else in her life by her sharp snap of a response.

"Raya, it's clear someone is upstairs. Why won't you tell me who?" The list of possibilities isn't long, and my heart is beating like a hammer, waiting for a response.

"If I tell you who is upstairs, you'll be responsible for a secret you don't want to keep," she explains, taking my hands into hers. "I don't want to put you in that position."

I toss my head back with frustration. "I'm part of the French Resistance. I think I can handle a secret. Unless there's a German upstairs. I can't handle that, so if that's what's going on right now, tell me because I will go right up there and—"

"No, no, no. Calm down," she says, placing her hand on my chest. "I would never allow a German upstairs and if one forced their way in, you would be the first to know." Raya's lips part and her eyes well with tears. "Nicolas," she sighs, "my best friend, Charlette, and her parents are Jewish, and I've taken them in to protect them."

"What? When? You never said—"

"I'm trying to protect them like you're trying to protect us all."

I pull Raya into my chest and wrap my arms around her, feeling her heart racing against my torso. "We need to add some insulation between these floors then," I say. I squeeze my arms around her a little tighter, grateful I took the chance to stop by. "I will help you protect your friends. You can depend on me.

First thing tomorrow morning, I'll see about finding something to soak up more of the sound upstairs."

"I guess we're almost out of secrets now?" she asks.

"I've only withheld because you requested not to know, but if you change your mind—"

Her fists curl into my sides as she peers down, then to the right, clearly debating something internally. Then she lifts her head to focus on my gaze and tightens her shoulders. "I want to know everything," she says. "We're in this together."

TWELVE
RAYA
PRESENT DAY, OCTOBER 1943

Ravensbrück, Germany

I'm not sure how anyone is still alive. I've been here three days and we've been given three small rations of bread, one each morning along with a watery cup of coffee, and then a mug of vegetable stock with turnips, even after working an eleven-hour day yesterday. It's not enough to keep someone going and I don't understand how people here have been surviving this way for more than a year.

After a thirty-minute walk to the textile factory, I make my way down the gloomy brick-walled corridor to the workshop I've been assigned. My seat at one of the long worn wooden tables with unsteady benches awaits me with my supply of needles and threads. I should be opening my shop right now, preparing today's custom orders. My home is in pieces, my present, my past, everything I've ever known is nothing more than shattered glass on the sidewalk now. I let my entire family down.

There seem to be periods where the guards leave throughout the day and the women chat quietly, trying to lighten the mood with old memories, or reminiscing about a book they read years ago. I've kept to myself for the most part. I'm afraid if I begin to talk or trade stories, my strength—or whatever I have left of it—will spill out of me. I would confess my heartbreak and longing for my love, the nightmare of leaving him behind, and the understanding that I may never see what becomes of him. I would tell them how awful I am, how many mistakes I've made, and what they've cost me. Tears would form in my eyes and my breaths would stifle as pain seared through my chest. Then the grief I try to contain within me would spill out all over this table. It isn't fair to them when they must all feel similarly for one reason or another.

"Did you hear what some of the factory girls from Barrack B3 attempted yesterday?" one of the middle-aged women whispers across the table. I've been watching her since yesterday when I arrived at the factory, and she sews faster than anyone else I've seen around me. Her hair is a bit longer than almost everyone else's too.

"Did some of them try to steal extra rations again?" another woman asks.

"No, even better, they purposely jammed up a couple of the ammunition machines, making them unusable for most of the day. They got away with it, from what I heard."

"This is what our lives have come to...waiting around to hear stories about other women stirring up trouble to see if they can get away with not having to do their work. We need more stories about people making a run for it and actually getting out of here."

I glance over at the woman to my right who has piped up. She's been withdrawn like me until now, doing her work and seemingly taking the rest of it all in. I wonder how long she's been here.

"What's your story? You're awfully quiet," the woman who

incited the initial conversation says, tapping her hand across the table toward me.

I look around the room to make sure we aren't being watched by any guards. With my luck, I'd be the one caught talking when we aren't supposed to be. "I arrived only a couple of days ago. I'm still learning the ropes, trying to digest this way of life." My words come out in a mere whisper, but they seem to understand.

"You were with the French Resistance, huh?" the woman continues. Her stare falls to my chest, the red triangle branding me as a criminal for something I would gladly stand behind if it didn't mean I'd end up here, like this.

I shake my head. "No, but that's what I was arrested for."

"You're innocent?" she asks. "How is that possible with all those fresh wounds all over your face and arms? It looks like someone's been trying to get answers from you."

I shrug, touching my numb fingertips to my face, feeling the rigid scabs that have been forming. Someone *was* trying to get answers from me, but they didn't believe my silence. Even with his razor-sharp gaze into my eyes as he delved into deceptive questions, he was blind to my internal wounds and would never understand what a good person would give up to protect someone she loves. "I'm not sure what the word innocent means anymore."

"Most of us are here for similar reasons—a form of resisting, rebelling, whatever they want to call it. The French have had the floors torn out from beneath them and they expect everyone to comply. It's unthinkable."

Most of the women at the table are French except for a few who are Polish but know enough French to join the conversation.

"Did you come here alone?"

"Yes," I tell her, trying to refocus on tailoring this pant leg without jabbing my forefinger for the tenth time in the last hour.

"Did you work before?" The questions don't seem to stop. I bet she knows half of the women in this prison.

"Yes. I own—owned—a leather goods shop."

"That's why you're here," she says, waving her needle and thread around. "We all have experience with sewing in some capacity."

But I wasn't the seamstress. I sold the goods. I suppose I just took the credit for what Charlette did. I've never enjoyed sewing. To me, it's monotonous and tiring, which makes these days feel much longer than necessary.

The other woman is still speaking. "They try to fit people into jobs they should already know how to do, you see. But it's like giving children complicated shapes and telling them to match them up with circles and squares. It doesn't always work out so well."

THIRTEEN

RAYA

LAST YEAR, JULY 1942

Paris, France

Regret has been toying with my head since Nicolas left last night and I slept even less than usual. My mind spins over and over, worrying about everyone and everything while trying to make myself understand that no matter how much concern I drown myself in, I still won't have control over what might become of us. A simple ten-minute walk at night leaves me in distress, knowing that Nicolas was out on these streets after curfew, tempting a German soldier to pluck him from a curb and punish him however they see fit. I told him he could stay, but he said his mother would think the worst if he wasn't home when she wakes in the morning. Again, I'm staring at the ceiling, my gaze burning a hole through the wooden planks. I could have lied to Nicolas about the Levis being here, but there aren't many explanations for noises coming from upstairs when I live alone.

I'm worried Charlette won't be understanding when I tell them that someone else knows of their whereabouts. I can't help feeling I've betrayed them. On the other hand, it's better to have had Nicolas question me about who is upstairs than anyone else who steps foot in the shop, and he's offered to help keep them safe.

My small alarm clock seems frozen in time. Each time I glance over, it reads the same hour and minute, or maybe my mind is playing tricks on me. It's five thirty and I don't know the exact time Nicolas will come by, but I'm sure it will be hours before he will need to leave for work.

I rarely hear the others awake before six, but I need to talk to them, so I pull my robe over my shoulders and secure the silk belt before pulling the sheets and quilt snuggly across my bed. I've kept Nicolas out of my flat to keep Charlette and her parents' existence a secret, but now he'll see my space, where I live, how I live, every detail I might have unknowingly kept to myself throughout the first half of the summer.

I'm not sure whether to make a racket before removing the mirror from the wall to make my way into the hidden room or if I should be quiet to avoid startling them awake. I should have known I wouldn't get further than lifting the mirror before Jacques's head poked through the opening.

"Is everything all right?" he asks breathlessly, panic-stricken.

"Yes, yes, I needed to talk to the three of you. I'm sorry if I've woken anyone."

"Don't apologize, please," he says, backing away from the opening so I can make my way into the space with them.

Charlette and Rose are both sitting upright, leaning against the wall with their quilts pressed to their chests. If I didn't already know they were mother and daughter, I might have thought they were sisters. They look so much alike. People used to say that about Mère and me, too.

"What is it, Raya?" Charlette asks as she sweeps wisps of fallen curls from her face.

I kneel and weave my fingers together over my lap, staring at the green veins pulsating across the top of my hands. "Last night, Nicolas stopped by unannounced. He was on his way home." I'm having trouble looking up, knowing there is worry written across their faces. "He was only here for a few minutes, but he heard the floorboards creaking upstairs. I had told him I live alone."

"Oh no," Charlette says with a long sigh.

"I tried to veer him away from the question, but he thought there was another man here, or worse, a German soldier."

"You told him about us?" Charlette continues.

Her question doesn't seem as full of concern as I would expect. I might be mistaken, but she sounds rather hopeful.

"He is a good man with a heart of gold. His only intention is to protect the innocent people in Paris, and he spends much of his free time trying to assist in—"

"He's part of the resistance," Jacques completes my statement.

I force myself to look up at the three of them, their eyes watery from just waking up, their faces pale from lack of sun exposure, and their mouths all slightly ajar, waiting to hear whatever I say next. "Yes."

"Well then, in my eyes, the man is a hero and deserves the utmost respect," Jacques says.

"Jacques!" Rose snaps at her husband.

"They divide this city into people who are afraid, who agree with the Germans, and the brave. If Raya befriends anyone, I hope he's a brave man. He must trust her enough to confide his secret with her. Therefore, I don't think we have anything to worry about."

"I didn't know you could hear us from downstairs," Charlette says, ignoring the rest of what I said.

"I have a few times, but most patrons wouldn't ask where the noises are coming from, and it's hard to hear when there are more than a couple of people walking around in the shop."

"That's more dangerous than telling Nicolas about us," she says.

"He has offered to come by this morning to find a way to add some extra insulation between the floorboards to mask the sounds."

"He'll be coming up here?" Rose says, leaning forward to grab her robe from the bottom of her quilt.

"How else will he add insulation between the floorboards?" Jacques asks his wife.

"If Raya trusts him, then we should too," Charlette says. "Besides, I've been dying to meet this mysterious gentleman who has kept you blushing long after he's left your side."

My face burns, following her accusation. "Charlette," I say.

"Like it is right now. You see, Mère, there's nothing to worry about because Raya is in love with this man and she has never loved a man, so he must be as wonderful as she says he is."

"Thank you for letting us know and we appreciate the help he's offering. I will do whatever I can to assist with the work," says Jacques.

Rose's expression is contradicting the smile she's trying to force across her lips. "We'll straighten up and get dressed so we're not in his way when he arrives," she says.

There isn't far for them to go, and I wonder if that's the point of her comment.

"Well, okay, I'll—I'll be on the other side of the wall."

As I scoot past Jacques whispers a thank you into my ear. "If you should decide to join the resistance too, I'd like to go with you."

His words swim between my ears as I re-enter my side of the flat. I haven't considered if there are Jewish people active within the resistance, and I wonder if the risk is more or less than the one Nicolas has been taking.

FOURTEEN

NICOLAS

Paris, France

The daylight helps in scanning the area for sewerage covers, but I still don't see one in the general vicinity of where the plot-point was on the map. The two shops on either side of Raya's are both closed and boarded up, but there's a jeweler, a dress shop, and a small pharmacy residing on the same block. The entrance may be beneath any of these places if the map is accurate. None of the establishments will be open for a few hours anyway; and first I need to add insulation to the floorboards above Raya's shop. Hopefully, she's awake.

"Salut, Monsieur Bardot," Monsieur Croix greets me, taking me by surprise as I didn't notice him standing to the side of his newsstand.

"Salut," I say, keeping my salutation short with the hope of avoiding the question of why I'm knocking on the leather shop's door at this hour, or why I will disappear inside for the next two to three hours. I tap lightly against the storefront door, hoping it's loud enough for Raya to hear.

The thought of Croix monitoring what's going on here

didn't cross my mind until right now. I wonder if he's seen any hints of the family Raya is hiding upstairs. I don't think Croix would ever whisper so much as a word if he had noticed something out of the ordinary, but most of us in the area have learned to keep all details about our lives to ourselves just in case. Raya and I disclosing such personal information to each other was along the parallel lines of confessing our love. One must be sure they know who they are talking to, with absolute certainty.

"Back again? You and Raya must be getting along well," Croix says with a proud smirk. "I've noticed you've been spending a lot of time together." He must be staring at my back as I wait for Raya to open the door.

"Oui," I say, grinning as I peer at him over my shoulder.

"Good for you. I wish you both the best of luck."

"Merci, monsieur." I'm not sure why it's taken him so long to ask, since I've been here many mornings on my way to work, but I suppose Croix is busiest at the hour I usually come by and may not always notice me slipping into the shop. Plus, I've also stopped shuffling the newspapers at his stand to avoid any unnecessary attention from the German soldiers as they pass by. I don't want to give them any reason to be down here at all.

I hold my fist up to knock on the door again, but Raya unlatches the locks before my knuckles hit the wood.

"Come in," she says in a hush.

As she shuts the door behind me and re-bolts the door, I place a kiss on her cheek, enticing the adorable smile that always follows our first encounters of the day. "Good morning to you too," she utters.

"What is that delectable aroma?" My stomach grumbles at the scent of something sweet that must be baking upstairs.

"Mini almond cakes. I had just enough ingredients to make a small batch, and when I'm nervous, I bake, so I made them at six this morning." She doesn't have to tell me she's nervous. The pink welts on her neck do the job for her.

"Is everything okay?"

"Yes, I believe so. I talked to my friend and her parents, upstairs—"

"Charlette, you said her name was, right?"

Raya's lips curl to one side, maybe impressed by my memory. "Yes, and her parents are the Levis."

"Are they comfortable with me coming upstairs to see what I can do about blocking some of the sound?"

Raya nods her head before responding verbally. "Jacques said he will help you. He appreciates your offer."

"Wonderful. I'm sure we'll get everything taken care of quickly with the two of us."

Raya takes my hand and leads me to the door at the back corner of the shop and unlocks it with the key she retrieves from her pocket. I'm glad to see she keeps all the doors secure. There is no such thing as being too cautious now.

The stairwell is narrow, dark, and muggy. The handrail wiggles beneath my grip—the screws must need a little tightening.

"I will fix this for you later," I offer, hoping not to offend her.

She turns around, curiosity tugging on her eyebrows. I wiggle the banister again to show her.

"Oh, that's been ready to fall off the wall since my brother tightened it before he left for Zurich two years ago. I've gone up and down these steps so many times, I don't need that old handrail, anyway."

With the hazardous state of the stairwell, I'm unsure what to expect when we reach her flat, but I'm not surprised to find a warm ambiance when I step into the kitchen—the heart of her small space. There's a short hallway on each side, one with two closed doors, and the other side with one. Everything is tidy and in its place. The floorboards whine and thud with each step, making me believe there must be little to nothing between the floor and the ceiling of the shop.

"This is my home," Raya says, seeming embarrassed by this beautiful, comfortable living space.

"It's quite perfect," I tell her. With my curiosity for every detail surrounding me, I nearly fall backward as I watch the mirror on the wall rise and slide to the side before resting on the ground. "What—what is—" I grab a hold of the nearest wall for support, trying to focus on what I know I saw happen.

Raya lets out a giggle as a middle-aged man steps out from the hole in the wall. "Nicolas, this is Jacques, Charlette's father." She turns toward the tall, slender man with short, dark, curly hair, bushy eyebrows, and a thick mustache. "This is Nicolas." Raya gestures to me.

"Thank you for offering to do something so kind for a family of strangers. I can't tell you how much this means to us. Since Raya informed us of your plan earlier this morning, I went through some boxes in the room here and found some holding stacks of newspapers."

"I have some of my parents' clothes and old blankets, too," says Raya.

"Raya," Jacques says, endearingly. "You don't need to use your parents' clothes. I know what those mean to you."

"They would give you the shirt off their back, and you would give them the same," Raya says, pointedly. "Yes?"

Every time I think Raya is going to shatter into pieces, she gains a bit more strength. I walk around the perimeter of the flat, searching for a hint of a loose floorboard so I don't have to do too much damage to her floors. "Do you have a broom?"

"Of course," she responds. "Did you find dirt?"

"I'm Charlette." A young woman climbs out of the wall hole like her father did. "You must be the infamous Nicolas I've heard so, so, so much about. Really, so much." After finding her footing she makes her way over to me with an outstretched hand. "You are exceptionally handsome. Raya wasn't exaggerating." She grips her hand around my biceps and squeezes. "That's accurate too."

"Charlette!" Raya scolds out her name, gritting her teeth.

"I've been hunkering down in a small windowless room for over a month. Forgive me if I've forgotten how to act appropriately around other people," Charlette replies to Raya. "And, no, your flat isn't dirty. I'm sure he has a different use in mind for a broom."

The women are staring at each other with some sort of conviction, but also, they both seem as if they might burst into a fit of laughter.

"Enough, girls. We don't have a lot of time," Jacques says to them as he reaches to the side of the refrigerator and takes out the broom. "Nicolas, there are a few loose floorboards by the back wall and a few behind the breakfast table. We should have enough space on each side to maneuver the materials well enough for decent coverage."

"I'll go get the clothes we can use," Raya says.

"I'll help," Charlette follows.

I'm glad we're all on the same page and have what we need.

"My wife is nervous," Jacques tells me. "She might stay on the other side of the wall, but please don't take any offense."

"Of course not. I understand the difficulties that come along with trust these days," I reply.

Jacques and I begin loosening the floorboards behind the breakfast table, trying to be careful not to bend any nails.

"So, what is it you do for a living?" he asks.

"I'm a journalist for the *Vraie Nouvelle*. It's not the most exciting job these days."

"It's better than no job," he says, reminding me of how fortunate I am.

"Yes, that's true. I am sorry for what you've experienced. It's appalling what the Jewish people are being put through. Our city seems to have ripped at the seams."

"I agree. It's as if we have two choices: think quickly or join the enemy."

"You're absolutely right. If we aren't staying ahead of the Germans, they'll take exactly what they want, and we can't allow that to happen. This is our country. I don't see how anyone thinks differently." Once again I'm rattling off my feelings on a subject I shouldn't be discussing so readily. Although, I imagine any Jewish person would feel the same about what we must do here.

"If you don't mind me asking, are you a member of the... resistance?" Jacques whispers the end of his question as if he doesn't want anyone else in the flat to hear him.

"It's not something I'm supposed to be discussing..."

"I want to join," he says. "How can I be a part of whatever group you're with?"

I'm trying not to act as surprised as I feel because I don't want to show him any form of disrespect, but I don't believe there are many Jewish mixed into the various groups. I could be wrong, and he has every right to fight as I do. "You are welcome to join us, of course, but with all due respect, we're adding insulation between the floors to protect your family. The resistance wouldn't be able to ensure your safety. It's a risk for me walking around the city, making my way to meetings, but it would be much worse for you if we were spotted and questioned."

"To not be sitting here waiting for the Germans to make their next move would give me a great sense of relief. I would do just about anything to fight against this in any way possible."

I can't say I don't understand where he's coming from. He's angry and doesn't want this war to swallow him up, but he has a target on his back as it is and if he wants to keep his family safe, it's something he needs to consider. "I would be lying if I said we didn't need all the people who would consider joining us, especially while we're trying to find access to underground shelter. In good faith, though, I can't suggest this option to you."

* * *

We've made a decent-sized opening in the floorboards and I take a matchbook out of my pocket to hold a light down there to see what we're working with. As suspected, there's nothing but hollow space from one side to the other.

"Nicolas, earlier when we were talking about the resistance, you mentioned something about underground shelter. Do you mind if I ask why?"

"The tunnels are said to be a good location for easy movement and for hiding contraband. Do you happen to know of any nearby openings?"

Jacques groans and pushes himself up from his knees. "Well, you aren't too far away."

"I believe there's an entrance nearby but I'm not sure where to look." He looks in every direction except for where I'm standing. "I'm sure you'll find what you're looking for," he says, taking a handkerchief out of his back pocket and dabbing at the sweat beading along his forehead.

FIFTEEN
RAYA
PRESENT DAY, NOVEMBER 1943

Ravensbrück, Germany

With the few minutes I have before the lights go out for the night, I slip the piece of paper I found on the floor of the textile factory today and the tailor-marking pencil I'm borrowing from the inner lining of my coat. I drape it back over my shoulders for extra warmth as I lay on my stomach between the bunks, the pencil hovering above the top of the soft yellow paper, and close my eyes to focus on what I want to say.

"No, no, where is she?" a woman cries out. "Where is my daughter?"

I open my eyes and peek out from behind the two walls of tiered bunk beds. A woman is climbing up to the top bunk, barefoot, reaching for a person who isn't in the small empty space. Another woman reaches for the mother in distress and tries to calm her.

"What's happening?" I whisper to whoever is within earshot and might respond.

"She's gone," someone mutters.

"How do you know?"

"No!" the woman screams. "She was just a girl."

No one knows. That's the conclusion I come to because there is no response. When someone is missing at this hour, we know.

The number of minutes I'm forced to watch lives dissolving into oblivion each day steal every ounce of hope I cling to. The efforts I make to keep my chin up are becoming worthless. I'm not ignorant to what is happening to us all, but if I allow the thought of an end to steal the last of what's keeping me upright, I would be giving up on myself; I would be giving up on us. All I can do is put up my blinders and find words that will smooth the sword's edge that I lean against all day. If I can convince myself these letters will find a way home, I will never stop writing.

My Dearest,

It's taken me a while, but I was able to find a few more scraps of paper today. I didn't imagine how hard it would be to find. I've been wanting to mail you my letters since I arrived, even knowing that I can never actually send any letters to you through the post. I was warned that each piece of mail that leaves this horrible place is scanned by a soldier. I wouldn't want anyone to know where you live or where you lived, for that matter. I guess I'm not sure where you are now and though I tell myself you're home and safe, there are moments when I have a hard time believing my own thoughts. This isn't what I wanted for us. I hope you know. I imagined a wonderful life, one where we could have picnics in the tulip fields in the countryside, and travel down to the French Riviera in the summertime to swim in the ocean. I have—had —so many dreams for us but for each day longer I remain here, the visions become blurrier and harder to imagine.

If I have any say in the way my life turns out, I will make it through this, for you, for me, for us. I hope you are well and safe. I think about you every waking minute of my day, wondering what you might be thinking about as I write this. I hope it's me. I hope you have enough memories of me to last you a lifetime in case this letter never makes it to you from my hands.

I love and miss you so much it makes my heart feel like it might crumble into millions of pieces.

Take care, my love.

I fold up the note and slip it back into the lining of my coat, wishing to simply place it into an envelope and send it off. I would send many letters if that was the case and those letters would be a call for help—help that may not be possible to find, but at least I could try if it didn't mean jeopardizing someone else's life in exchange for mine. It doesn't matter how many brutalities I've had to bear witness to here, I'm supposed to believe that an innocent life has no purpose. None of our lives have meaning anymore. That's why we're here.

SIXTEEN

RAYA

LAST YEAR, JULY 1942

Paris, France

It isn't long after Nicolas has finished adding the insulation beneath the floorboards of my flat and left for work that I hear a commotion from the Levis on the other side of the wall as I'm getting ready to go downstairs and open the shop for the day. I should keep to myself and mind my business, but the commotion is becoming more of an argument, one the three of them seem to be a part of.

As I finish wrapping up what's left of the mini almond cakes, Charlette grunts as she ambles out of the opening in the wall.

"Is everything okay?" I ask, turning toward her, noticing stained red cheeks.

Charlette's voice deepens and her expression tightens. "No, it's not. After speaking with Nicolas, Papa has told us he wants to join the resistance!"

I feel the need to cycle through her words once more, trying to understand why Jacques would want to say such a thing or why he would have an interest in asking Nicolas about it. "Did your father ask Nicolas if he could join, or did Nicolas suggest the offer to him?" I've never been in a situation when I might have to defend two people I love, but it seems like I'm missing some information.

"My father brought it up. I'm not sure what sparked his idea to ask, though." Charlette presses her hands against her forehead. "My God, Raya, they'd kill him for just attending a meeting. Why would he want to be a part of this? We're already in enough danger as it is."

Jacques is a grown man with the right to decide for himself, and I'm not sure what Charlette would like me to say or do to help.

"I'm sure your father is just angry and wishes there was something more he could be doing, just like the rest of us."

Charlette pulls in a long breath and rests her hands on her chest. "My mother is so enraged right now and the two of them are at each other's throats, arguing right from wrong."

Nothing about this idea sounds safe for any of them, and I'm having trouble understanding Jacques's intention. But if I were him I would be upset about a lot right now. The Germans have pushed most of the Jewish people out of their homes at this point. There is no end in sight, and I'm not sure I could accept the outcome of their progress. As it is, I've considered the idea of helping Nicolas. It's hard to feel like I'm doing anyone much good if I'm not standing up for what's right.

"I understand where you're coming from," I tell Charlette. "I can find out more details tonight when I see Nicolas."

* * *

A slow day. I should have closed the shop by now. I've been doing little aside from staring at the clock. I don't remember the last time I had so little business. I'm not sure we ever have. The only good part of the day was that I didn't hear a peep from upstairs.

I give up the last bit of hope for one more shopper and make my way to the door, which swings open as I reach for the open sign. With my heart jumping up into my throat from shock, I step back as Nicolas rushes inside. "We need to talk." He doesn't wait for me to respond. Instead, he turns away and locks the shop doors himself, then flips the sign and lowers the drapes, one by one, from the door to the end of the front display window.

Something is wrong and I dread asking what that might be, why his hands are trembling as he secures the last drape. It's hard to swallow as I wait for him to say something. My stomach tightens around the hollow hunger pain I have from forgoing lunch after using more ingredients than I normally would for breakfast.

Nicolas wraps his hands around my arms, peering down at me with a firm stare. "Did the insulation help?"

"That's what you're worked up about?" I ask.

"Did it work?" he repeats, his fingertips pressing gently into the backs of my arms.

"I believe so, yes. I didn't hear a sound from upstairs all day, and it was quiet in the shop."

"Good, good." Nicolas releases his grip from my arms and takes a step back, dropping his head into his hand. "While you and Charlette were gathering your parents' clothes this morning,

Jacques—"

"I know," I say, stopping him from having to continue. "His wife and daughter were furious."

Nicolas shakes his head. "I had a feeling you would hear about this at some point today. I did discourage him. It's not safe, especially for him. But that's not what I need to talk to you about."

"Then, what is it?" Again, my pulse escalates, leaving me lightheaded.

"While we were talking, he mentioned that there's a tunnel entrance close by."

Blood rushes to my head and the statement mixes with my hunger and nerves—I might faint. I step back until I hit the front counter and slide down to the wooden floors I still need to sweep.

Nicolas falls to his knees in front of me. "What's wrong?" He takes my face into his warm hands. "Your lips are pale. Raya?" His eyes tell stories, the way they change shapes depending on what he's feeling. When he's worried, his brows curve, encircling his dazzling eyes. I could feel his concern deeply, even if he wasn't to say a word.

"I'm fine," I say through a breath.

"You're fine? I'm quite sure you're not. Is it something I said?" he asks, his voice crackling with worry.

I'm not sure what we have not said today. I shake my head to tell him no, even though his mention of the tunnels doesn't help my current state. Few people know about the entrance beneath the shop, and I made a promise to Papa I would keep it that way. He told me the underground tunnel is this building's greatest asset and it would serve the purpose of protection if ever needed. Papa was always ready for another war or battle to break out. The tunnel was his safety net and he took great care in keeping the hatch greased and the path clear of obstacles in case of emergency. It always seemed like he knew something was coming but didn't know when it would happen. He didn't worry the rest of us much, but I knew when he was over-thinking something. He and Alix have the same tired expression when concealing stress.

"Yes, of course, I'm fine. I am."

"Even though you're fine, would you take a deep breath for

me. Do you have anything to drink down here? Anything with sugar?"

"No."

"What did you have to eat today?"

I blink at him because I don't have the energy to do much else. "I promise you, I'm fine."

"I'm going to be terribly upset with you if you say you are preserving rations after whipping up almond cakes this morning."

"Then you're going to be displeased with me," I mutter.

Frustration weighs down on Nicolas's shoulders as he swings over to my side and sits down with his back against the counter, too. "How are the three of them gaining rations?"

I twist my head to the side, staring up at him through the gaping distance between our seated heights. "I've used Charlette's identification a couple of times, but with so many Jewish people being pushed out of the city, it's becoming too risky, so I've been sharing what I have and purchasing extras where I can."

"Extras?"

I'm not sure I have the strength to explain the details of overpaying bread truck drivers to sneak a few extra loaves into the shop. "It's nothing."

"I'm taking you upstairs and finding something to cook for you. Don't argue. I can't believe you told me you were fine. Not once, but three times." He pulls himself up by the top of the counter and scoops me into his arms. "You must take care of yourself, Raya. I know you are doing everything you can to protect the Levi family, but you can't take care of them if you aren't taking care of yourself first."

Nicolas is a leader, someone who takes charge without concern, and he hasn't done much to hide this empowering attribute. I'm not sure I mind being around someone who has such a strong will. It's quite charming.

"I know," I say, pressing my cheek against his chest.

"Where's the key to get upstairs?"

I lower a hand from around his neck and reach into my dress pocket for the key and attempt to get it into the lock, but my hand is beyond the point of unsteady. Nicolas curls me into his chest tighter, freeing up his hand to take the key and unlock the door. I'm not sure how we'll make it upstairs this way, but I'm not sure I'd make it upstairs any other way right now.

We shuffle around, shimmying into the stairwell. Nicolas locks the door from the inside and continues up the stairs, sideways, somehow. "Does this happen often? You become faint if you skip a meal?"

I try to shrug, but I'm not sure he sensed the movement. "It's happened before. More so in recent weeks."

"Why haven't you told me?" Nicolas nudges my bedroom door open and places me on my bed, then kneels by my side and takes my hand in his. "Raya." He drops his forehead to our tangled hands. "The thought of this happening to you when I'm not here—"

"I'm fine," I say.

"You're not, and I'm not—not while seeing you like this. Raya, I love you—I would do anything to make sure you are okay."

As weak as I am, I manage to glance up at him as he lifts my hand to his lips. "You love me?"

He tilts his head to the side and sweeps my hair behind my ear. "If this isn't love, I'll never know something better than what we have."

A tear falls from my eye and a small smile follows. "I've never had these feelings for anyone before. I'm not sure I knew what love was either but I'm quite sure I know now."

"I want to know all there is to know about you, whatever you haven't told me. We've shared so much, but seeing you like this…I want to be here when you need me."

"It's not a big deal, I promise. I've always had trouble with low blood sugar levels, but I've been able to manage it until—"

"You began sharing your rations with three other people?" He presses his hand to my forehead and sighs. "I'm going to find something for you to eat. Stay put."

After a few minutes of lying down, I stare up through the rippled glass window above my head, confirming that the dizziness is beginning to wane, but I know the rest of the symptoms won't subside until I eat something. I feel well enough to focus on the hushed shouts coming from the Levis' room. They must still be arguing.

Nicolas returns with a glass of cloudy water. "I found spaghetti and a tomato. I can make something from that."

"Why does the water look funny?"

"I added a spoonful of sugar. It will help you feel better after not eating much today."

I push myself upright to take the glass from his hand. "You were worried when you arrived. What's wrong?"

Nicolas takes a seat on the edge of my bed and rests his elbows on his knees. "My group and I have been collaborating in the cellar of a church in Montmartre. One of my comrades informed me today that the Germans have seized the building, blocked it off and are guarding it like hawks. We've agreed to search for an accessible entrance to the underground tunnels and Jacques implied there may be one nearby. Is that true?"

I tap my fingernails against the glass, pausing to think before responding. I've never talked about the tunnels with anyone before. "Yes, they are nearby. You're practically standing a floor above the entrance right now."

"Here?" he asks, pointing toward the ground. "Beneath the shop?"

"Just about," I reply.

He drops his head into his hand and grumbles. "Forget I mentioned the tunnels. I don't want you involved with any of this. I thought maybe you just knew where the opening was. I didn't consider it would be here of all places."

"No, it's okay," I tell him as a thought continues to stir in my head, one that feels as though it would solve most of the problems that developed today.

"It's not okay, Raya," he says firmly, standing up from the bed.

I reach for his hand before he moves away, mistakenly splashing some of the sugar water onto my bed. "Nicolas, listen to me. If Jacques is planning to join you, I would prefer if you all met in the tunnel beneath my shop. It would keep him safer than if he was trailing around the city with you. In fact, I should join too and be of some help." I'm not exactly sure what I'm volunteering to help with, but it's clear by looking outside the window, the days are only getting darker, and this city needs all the help it can get.

"I—I don't know, Raya. I need to think," he says. "I should be watching the pot of water."

The sound of drawers opening and closing, as well as the couple of cabinet doors, reminds me he's not familiar with where anything is in the kitchen. I didn't know he even knew how to cook.

I close my eyes for a few minutes, feeling the effects of the long day followed by my blood sugar dropping, but as soon as the scent of tomato wafts into my bedroom, my stomach gnarls with hunger.

Nicolas returns with his hand reaching out to mine. "Can you make it over to the table? After what happened with the sugar water, it's probably best you don't eat in bed," he says with a grin.

I pull against his hand and find some of my strength has returned as I make my way to my feet and follow him to the table outside of my room. There is one plate with a small pile of spaghetti and a cooked, crushed tomato spilling over the top. "What about you? Aren't you going to have some?"

"I feel you aren't learning a lesson from what happened," he says, leaning his head to the side, looking at me as if I have two heads.

"It doesn't feel right to eat in front of anyone, not when we're all being deprived."

"I ate lunch, and I will have dinner, but I'm not leaving your side until I see you've eaten a meal."

"What if I don't want you to leave my side after that?"

His cheeks brighten with a light pink hue, and he takes a seat at the table across from where I'm sitting. "Eat, Raya."

I do as he says, but only because I am starving, and I know I've set aside leftovers from last night's cabbage and lentil soup for the Levis to eat for their dinner. "I can help you find more food to supplement what you've been sharing with them. Don't ask me where, just agree."

"I thought there were no more secrets?" I ask after I swallow a mouthful.

"It's not my secret. I only have means to take advantage of someone else's secret. The people in my group, we help each other out wherever and whenever possible."

"If I'm going to receive help, in any way, I must do something in return. There has to be something I can do for your group."

"No, I have no intention of pulling you into—this world I'm a part of," he says, slouching his arms onto the table. "I want to keep you safe, but I get the feeling you don't want to keep yourself safe. You just want to keep the Levis safe."

"I can keep them safe, myself safe, and help you if you let me."

"I wasn't aware this topic was up for negotiation?" he says.

"I work in sales," I remind him. "I don't give up easily."

Nicolas leans back in his seat and rests his hands behind his head, taking a moment to stare up at the ceiling as I continue to twirl the spaghetti around my fork, cleaning my plate faster than I normally would in front of him. "This was delicious. Thank you."

"My pleasure," he says, sitting up straight, then leaning forward to place his hand on top of mine. "Listen, I want to talk to the Levi family with you. I think we need to convince Jacques against joining the group. His desire to help would endanger their family and you—even if my group was to meet in the tunnels. I'm happy to keep him updated with communications we receive but he should stay put where he's safe."

I glance toward the mirror that looks like it's never been moved from the wall. "I don't know. They've been arguing. Charlette was bitter and Rose was up in arms with Jacques. I'm not sure any amount of convincing is going to work with either of them, and it doesn't sound like they've come to an agreement yet."

"We can hear you," Charlette shouts. "There's no insulation between the walls."

I didn't think I was speaking too loudly, but maybe since they had become quiet, they were listening in on us.

The mirror swings to the side and the three of them make their way out from the dark opening. Charlette and Rose take the two free seats at the table and Jacques leans against the sink, crossing one foot over the other as he squeezes his hand around his temples.

"I want to know what it is you do when you aren't working," Rose says, her stare hard and cold at Nicolas. I've never heard her speak so sternly to anyone.

Nicolas glances at me for a long second, his mouth ajar. It seems Nicolas is a bit taken aback by Rose's forward question, which I can understand since I made it clear the Levi family was apprehensive about meeting him. I know he didn't ask to be a part of this situation and I feel awful that it's because of me and the help I needed this morning.

With a soft look in his eyes, Nicolas rests his hands on the table, clasping his fingers together. "I understand what you must be thinking about me, and you're justified to be concerned, as we all are." Nicolas pauses as Rose opens her mouth, as if she has something to say. After a measure of silence, Nicolas continues. "With all due respect, Madame Levi, I'm doing what many others in the city are doing. That being, refusal to side with the Vichy government who is giving into almost every single one of Germany's demands. I believe in your right as a Jewish person to have the same privileges as me, a non-Jewish person, and I feel every Parisian deserves to live their life without being suppressed under German regulations."

"Thank you for saying so," Jacques says. "I feel strongly about joining or assisting in some way."

"Jacques!" Rose scolds him. "How many ways must I make myself clear to you. You are putting us all in danger by even considering this foolish idea."

"Then we can just sit here and wait for Hitler to pluck us out of France," Jacques snaps back.

Nicolas takes a deep breath and scratches the side of his face. "Maybe we can find a way that you can help without leaving the building. I agree that it would be dangerous for you to be assisting in any way out on the street."

"What could I do from this building?" Jacques argues.

"I'm not sure, but—"

"Papa, stop," Charlette scolds him. "I apologize for pulling you into this family dispute, Nicolas. It's been a while since we've seen ourselves as equal to anyone who isn't Jewish." Charlette aggressively sweeps off a few crumbs from the table while seemingly trying to remain complacent.

"It's no secret that we are in a desperate time of need without a place to stand in our own country—a country that would once depend on their military to do what still needs to be done. But as you know, we have soldiers being held captive as prisoners of war, and the others have been stripped of their orders. We're being depleted more and more each day, and as my father said before he died, nothing is a sacrifice unless we make a difference, and without sacrifice, it's only a matter of time before we are all kicked out of this country and left without the clothes on our backs," Nicolas says.

His selfless reasoning is something I've questioned several times before tonight, but now it's clear he's trying to live up to his father's dying wish, and I can't think of anything more commendable.

"We should all do what we can," I say firmly while looking into Nicolas's eyes. Though I have no idea what I am in for.

SEVENTEEN

NICOLAS

Paris, France

I've accomplished something that will benefit the Lions Rebelles and thus the people of France, but a new layer of danger has been stacked on my shoulders, knowing I will be escorting fourteen others into the cellar of Raya's shop. Once I inform Hugo, there will be no turning back. He knows little about Raya and nothing about the Levis and while I know his focus is on our revolt, I need to keep the property safe. We can't be the reason something happens to that building. We also have no other available options for places to meet.

The low overbearing pewter clouds feel like a bad omen as I make my way across the city toward the office, hearing rumbles of commotion traveling down each road I pass. The streets have been somber for a good while and unless someone is inciting an act of violence, it's rare to hear much happening on the streets during the day.

The uproar of shouting grows as I come up to the next passing road. I poke my head around the corner, knowing whatever is happening is close by. French police are scattered along the street with German officers peppered between them as they pound on street-level doors, demanding the attention of whoever lives in the row of flats.

I stand back, trying to listen without being seen. Military transport vehicles line the street and it's clear they are performing a raid. Many of the French police have papers in their hands and are the ones shouting violent threats while trying to shove their way in through the locked doors. Some don't seem to have the patience to wait on anyone to open the doors for them as they use bodily force to barge into the buildings.

My mind is full of thick tar, wondering why they've chosen this street, who they are after, and for what purpose. My hands become clammy as I hold myself against the stone wall on the corner, debating whether I should stay to find out what's happening or run in the other direction.

"I'm a journalist. This is my job. I need to know what's happening in our city so I can inform others," I mutter silently to myself. My chest feels as though it might cave in and sweat soaks through my collared shirt.

A list of names echo between the buildings, ranging from several people of a family to a single person.

- Isaac, Edna, Danit, and Paz Berkovic
- Malachy and Talia Greenberg
- Chedva Lehmann
- Elinor and Mira Bakstansky
- Efran, Liam, and Noa Meir
- Hayyim and Karina Wechsler
- Iris Goldman
- Daniella Lieberman
- Jacobe and Dasha Levinstein
- Miryam, Laura, and Roza Schneider
- Fanni Chagall and Shana Benski

They all have Jewish last names. "You're under arrest," I hear repeated by several different voices.

With beads of sweat raining down the sides of my face, I struggle to lean forward to catch another glimpse of what's happening. I've been standing still for minutes but I can't catch my breath and the air is sucked out of my lungs when I see the French police shoving the men, women, and children into the waiting vehicles. Some have a suitcase, others don't.

"There are more on the next block," a police officer shouts as he lifts the top sheet of his papers to study whatever is on the page below. "We'll make our way toward the center of Montparnasse after."

I back away from the corner and turn in the direction I came from, finding the road as quiet and empty as it was on the way here. If I run, I'll look guilty of a crime. My legs are heavy, as if I'm dragging lead weights behind me as I unsteadily tread down the next four blocks toward the leather shop. I turn down the street before Raya's block and make my way to the back of the building. Raya gave me a key to this door yesterday so we wouldn't have to access the tunnel entrance through her shop. Her grandfather built walls to section off the entrance, creating a way into the shop and a way out into the corridor that houses the entrance in a closet between the row of stacked businesses and flats. It's similar to what he did in Raya's flat, which is enabling the Levis to remain hidden.

As I'm fumbling with the second key that leads into the shop, I peer down at my wrist, pleading that it isn't nine o'clock yet. I was going into work early to find Hugo at the bakery, but I spent more time than I should have watching our own people infiltrate innocent Jews with the guidance of German soldiers and officers.

One more door until I can make it up to Raya's flat and my heart feels like it might give out before I can get up those stairs.

As I reach the bottom step, I whisper through a breathy shout, "It's just me, Nicolas. I need to talk to you."

Raya runs toward the top of the steps, dressed and ready for work with a toothbrush in her mouth. Her eyes widen as she takes a better look at me, and I can't imagine what she must see because I feel like I've been running through a swamp.

She pulls the toothbrush from her mouth. "What's wrong? Are you okay?"

I shake my head, trying to catch my breath so I can speak in full sentences. "The—" I take in a few more breaths. "The French police are deporting Jewish people from their homes. It sounds like they're making their way across the city today. We should take the Levis into the tunnels until we find out they're done with this round-up."

Raya drops her toothbrush and clutches her hand around her neck. I know she's been planning for circumstances to arise and formulating plans of how to react if they do, but everything is always different when it isn't happening in real time.

I step to the side and rush to the mirror on the wall, carefully placing it on the ground before charging in through the opening. "You must move right now. The French police and German soldiers are hunting down Jewish people in the city, deporting them to God knows where. They are ravaging houses, going from door to door. You'll be safer in the tunnels today. The Nazis don't yet know where the entrances are," I tell them, watching as they each sit up with ghostly wide eyes, staring at me as if they're listening to an air raid screaming a sound they've never heard before. "We have to hurry. They're heading in this direction. I've seen them."

I make my way back to the kitchen, giving them time to collect their belongings and join us. Shock still frames Raya's face even though this shouldn't be surprising news. We've known the German agenda has been to remove all the Jewish people from Paris. It was only a matter of time before they became more forceful. Knowing doesn't make watching this any easier though.

Charlette is the first to appear. She's in a dingy dress that looks like it's been collecting dust in a corner. Her hair is everywhere, and her face is so pale her veins glow through her skin. She's holding a bundle of clothes in her arms, shaking. Raya is staring at Charlette as if she's forgotten how to speak.

"It's okay. You'll be safe down there. We'll keep them away," I tell her.

Jacques is the next through, helping Rose who's gripping the wall. "How long do we have?" Jacques asks.

"I spotted them about ten blocks from here, near Val-de-Grâce. They appeared to be moving quickly."

Jacques nods with understanding and wraps his arm around his wife whose tears are falling so hard she must not be able to see where she's walking.

"Follow me. I'll make sure you're secure."

Jacques stays behind me, with Rose still in his hold. Raya clutches Charlette's arm and stays close by as we make our way down the stairs. I haven't seen what the tunnel entrance is like or how complicated it might be to get through, but I'm praying we don't run into any trouble.

I close us into the tight closet that we can barely squeeze into together, gathering around the metal floor panel. The lever seems rusted in place but after a minute, I manage to knock it loose and twist it around to unlatch the metal restraint. Jacques leans down beside me and locks his hands under one side of the panel's lip. I take a hold of the other and we pull, fighting against sharp grains that won't give way easily. Once we have it moving in the right direction, the bouncing echo of each slight move sounds as if it is traveling into the depths of hell.

"There are metal rungs that descend all the way to the bottom," Raya says, finally speaking.

Jacques takes the small lantern Rose is holding and heads down first. "Stay close," he says.

"I'll come down when I get word that the raid is over," I say. "Hopefully, it won't be long."

Raya wraps her arms around Charlette's neck. "You'll be okay, I promise. I won't let anything happen to you."

I hate hearing the same words I promised Raya when we first met, knowing it might not be a promise any of us can keep.

"Do you have the almond cakes I wrapped up for you?"

Charlette utters, "Yes," as she peers over at her mother, waiting for her to follow Jacques.

The screeching sound of whistles in the distance interrupts us. It must be them.

"You have to go now," Raya says.

"Thank you," Rose cries out, taking my hand in hers and lifting my fingers to her mouth. "Take care of Raya, please."

"I won't let anything—"

Another whistle blows. This one is louder, closer.

I usher them down the hole, waiting for their heads to disappear beneath the floor before I lower the panel to secure it from the outside. There's a lever on the inside as well, which is comforting to know in case something was to happen to Raya or me.

"Let's get back inside before they come any closer," I tell her.

We move quickly, locking the doors behind us until we make it into the stairwell between her flat and the shop. "If I don't open the front door, they'll be suspicious. It's after nine," Raya says.

I wish she wasn't right.

"I'm staying with you until this is over," I say.

"What about your editor? You said he's awful to you if you're late, never mind if you don't show up."

"It doesn't matter. He doesn't matter. *You* matter."

Mère will be okay. Our flat is on a predominantly Catholic block, close to our church. Anyone of Jewish faith who lived by us left on their own or were given notice to leave months ago.

"The French police don't have a reason to be questioning you. They have lists of people they are looking for and where they live. But it's not worth taking the chance when they seem to make up new laws as they walk." I pull open the drapes and turn the sign around in the glass window of the door and release the locks. Monsieur Croix is in his place, making life seem as usual out there.

But we all know different.

Less than a half hour passes when we watch a convoy of military vehicles crawl down the street at a snail's pace. I wonder if they're already full of Jewish people or empty, ready for more. The familiar garble of chatter I heard this morning travels down the street, muffled from within the shop.

"They're nearby," I tell Raya, who hasn't moved from behind the register since we unlocked the front door. Not one customer has stepped foot inside and, from what she tells me, it's unusual to be quiet at this time of the day.

Within the hour, another convoy rolls down the street, this one stopping. French police spill out from the vehicles, each walking in a different direction.

Again, I watch from a distance, trying to understand how our police can assist in tearing people out of their homes without so much as blinking. I wonder if they are acting upon threat or agreement. No one can be convinced that what they are doing is humane.

"You shouldn't be standing near the door. They may see you," Raya whispers.

No one can hear us from out there but she's still trembling from watching her best friend go into hiding. We've all had the nightmares, but it's easy at the time to say the war will never get to this point, not in this day of age, but here we are, facing the unthinkable behavior that our own are taking part in.

A string of shrieks bellows from outside, a woman pleading for them to leave her behind.

"Ellie. That's Ellie. She used to run the florist shop down the road, but she was forced to close her doors a year ago. She lives across the street with her elderly mother who can't walk," Raya says, still staring from behind the front desk, watching out the door's window as we witness the scene unfold. "She won't be able to move her from the bed."

I close my eyes and fall heavily against the wall to the side of the front door, dreading what will likely happen when they figure out why this woman is screaming. A German soldier screams back at Ellie, telling her to go get her mother or he'll kill them both. I don't want to watch the woman walk back into her building.

When I open my eyes, Raya is staring at me as if she's waiting for something to happen. My stomach tightens with apprehension as I try to swallow against the tightness in my throat. My gaze drifts from Raya's eyes to the stone floors between us. A shot is fired, then another. Two to teach the lesson that disobedience will not be tolerated.

"No," Raya cries out. "No, no. Not that sweet woman. Ellie. Why?" She gasps for air, covering her mouth with her hands as tears bead down her cheeks.

She storms toward the door with an empty look in her eyes, and I catch her before she reaches the doorknob, pulling her back.

"I need to help her," she says.

"They don't leave their targets alive," I utter, pulling her tightly to my chest.

"She—she wa-was trying to-to protect her mother," Raya stutters between ragged breaths.

Monsieur Croix steps away from his newsstand and yanks

on the door, slipping into the shop. "Dear God, I can't watch another minute of what's happening out there," he cries out, removing his fedora and holding it over his chest. "We must do something." He's sincere as he places his hand on my shoulder. "There has to be something, Nicolas."

He knows what I do in my spare time. He's one of only a few people who do since he's allowed me to add leaflets to French newspapers. I look over at Raya, wondering what she must be thinking while listening to this conversation.

"How many of you are there?" she asks, anger seeping into her words.

"Not enough to take down what's in front of the shop right now. We're one small group out of many small groups working together, but apart."

"Does anyone in your group have contact with the Maquis?" Croix knows an awful lot about the resistance for not being a part of it. But even if he wanted to be he must be nearing his late seventies. He's in no condition to fight.

"I think one of the men do, but I'm sure they're already aware of what's going on."

"What if they're not?" Raya asks.

"Give me his name and location. I'll be a carrier pigeon if you can watch the paper stand. I doubt anyone will be coming by today," Croix says.

Raya grabs a notepad from beneath the counter and tears off a sheet of paper and places it down with a pen. "I have an envelope too."

"His name is Hugo. He works at the bread shop next to the *Vraie Nouvelle* office," I tell Monsieur Croix, making my way to the counter to write out a quick note in as few words as I can manage to get a point across.

A lion's brawl, hunger is strong.

8.2430 RdA T.A. IxI * 10

"What does that mean?" Raya asks, watching as I write.

"There's a takedown and raid. Meet at eight at 2430 Rue d'Alesia. Tell All. Meet one at a time every ten minutes. We have a code system setup that I've memorized."

"Won't he need letters to share with the others?" she asks.

"They'll pass it along. We're all behind one person in line and we're each responsible for relaying messages." I fold up the paper and slip it into the envelope then hand it over to Croix.

"I'll be back within the hour," he says.

"Avoid any street where the French police are lined up. And if you see any convoys of military vehicles—stay away," I warn him.

We've spent months talking about how we can take down these forces, but I'm questioning our capabilities and whether we've all been a lot of talk and no action. I don't know if we're ready for what we will face. Maybe I'm the only one thinking that way, or maybe it's because I suddenly feel like I have something important to live for, but if we all feel the same...if we all get scared and drop our will to fight, we'll lose everything. We will all become prisoners of Germany.

Once Croix slips out of the shop, I pull Raya into my arms and hold her head against my chest, wondering why I can't just have her—only her—rather than be here in a world where we need to fight for everything.

Another half hour passes before the convoy leaves the street, which now feels hollow. I know we can't see who was plundered from their homes, but everything seems so still and the quiet is ear-piercingly loud. This isn't a world people have created—this is hell.

EIGHTEEN
RAYA
PRESENT DAY, NOVEMBER 1943

Ravensbrück, Germany

It doesn't matter whether the sun is out, or the clouds are crying tears of pain, we stand in mud, walk through mud, and wear the mud like it's an extra layer of skin until we can take our next shower. The air is becoming dank and bitter. Winter feels like it's already in the air, which seems earlier than usual, but perhaps it's colder up here, north of Berlin, or that's where I've been told we are. I could be anywhere and would have to believe the story because there's no other way to find out unless it's by rumor or gossip. I worry about how we'll fare in the winter temperatures in a measly smock and our coats. Never mind my loafers with soles so thin I can feel every stone I walk over. I can't help but wonder if I'm waiting to die or if the SS are waiting for me to die so they can add another so-called political prisoner to their list of deaths. The urge to fight is all I have left, but thankfully, I don't have the energy to consider the thought of actually putting up a fight. The thought of dying like this, from hunger, cold, and forced labor couldn't be any more degrading. I should be able to live with dignity and pride, but instead I feel like the world is watching my every step, laughing and poking fun as I squint every time mud splatters up my smock.

"Los, los!" The guards shout at us daily throughout our morning walk to the factory and our return to the barracks at night. They tell us to move or go, as if that isn't what we are already doing. We're all moving as fast as we're capable. None of us want to feel this bitter cold or the splashes of mud. The guard is warm in his long coat, boots, and gloves. He feels nothing while shouting at us. Which is why he finds joy out of kicking mud at us while he does so.

Many mornings I stare at the holster on his belt, imagining walking up to him, pulling out the pistol, shooting him, and then myself, so I can die with a warped sense of pride.

NINETEEN

RAYA

LAST YEAR, OCTOBER 1942

Paris, France

"I'm afraid I don't have any work for you today," I tell Charlette. I sit down across from her, on Alix's bed, while she stares at me mindlessly over the sewing machine. We've seen fewer and fewer customers over the last three months. Those horrible couple of days in July when thousands of Parisian Jews were rounded up and deported seemed to be the beginning of a greater decline.

Charlette doesn't seem surprised that I have nothing for her to do. It's hard to tell if she would rather be busy sewing or if she might prefer sitting with her parents behind the false wall. She has never been one to sit in a state of despair for long periods but after they spent two days hiding in the underground tunnels, knowing what was happening all around them, her spark has completely burnt out. We all know there's a strong chance of another roundup of Jewish people at any given time, and that very thought leaves her with a forlorn stare and heavy eyelids. She is no longer the girl I've known most of my life. She may have a slight sense of safety within these walls, but she's a prisoner in them too and it pains me to know there's nothing more I can do for her.

As she stares up toward the foggy window, watching the raindrops rat and tat against the glass, the droplets skating down each square pane, I wonder if this is what it was like for her to watch me after Mère passed away—hopeless, helpless, and lifeless. It's awful to watch someone I love filled with so much misery, especially knowing there's nothing more I can do to help.

"I would give anything to smell the rain," she says. "If I could jump in puddles and catch the falling drops on my tongue, I would feel alive, just for a moment." She has said this to me each time it's rained over the last few months. Charlette was always the girl walking into school with soaked shoes and a dripping dress hem. She was a magnet for puddles and never cared about getting wet. Even as we grew older, I would be the one trying to share my umbrella because she refused to carry one, but she wouldn't stay beneath the cover. She'd start singing and scuffing water off the curb. That love for life is buried inside of her somewhere.

"You don't have to feel bad telling me there isn't any work," she says. "I know it's been less and less each week. Are any customers coming into the shop to browse? Or is it slow most of the day?"

"It's been quiet," I reply.

The word doesn't describe the eeriness of silence I sit through for hours behind the register all day, but it could be worse...I could be sitting in the hidden room. Although I'd have someone else to talk to if I was up there at least.

"I haven't seen or heard Nicolas around much this week. Is everything okay between the two of you?" she asks.

I debate what to say, knowing she will see through a lie or assume I'm withholding information. The Lions Rebelles have been training, preparing, planning, and plotting, but if I tell

Charlette, it will only give her more reason to worry. She understands the point behind the resistance but also thinks the German retaliation will be much worse for everyone in the city. I understand why she thinks that way, and she isn't wrong, but if no one fights back, they will sweep Paris clean of all Parisians. We need to stand strong against their forces, however possible. Still, while Charlette stirs all day, staring at the sewing machine we have no use for, I'm not feeling much better about the risks involved with more and more resistance attacks. Any move against the Germans could result in a deadly citywide battle, and even if it doesn't come to that point, I'm terrified something will happen to Nicolas.

"He's been here most nights but doesn't come up until late, and then he's out and about early in the morning delivering bulletins to other members in the group."

"Oh," she says. "I'm glad everything is going well for the two of you then." Her response feels heavy, but I'm not sure if it's with resentment or concern.

"Me too," I say, studying the changing expressions on her face. "I'm sorry, Charlette. It feels wrong to be discussing the good things in my life when you're not allowed to do much of anything." There are many times when I'm staring into Nicolas's eyes, feeling so much love and contentment when a pang of guilt shoots up my spine, telling me I should be ashamed of myself for embracing the moments of joy.

Charlette stands up from her seat and sits next to me on the bed. "This is what I've been worrying about, aside from whatever trouble my father is getting himself into," she says, leaning her head on my shoulder. The flyaway strands of hair, loose from her curls, tickles my neck and a memory of Mère giggling every time I rested my head on her shoulder with a head of messy hair, relieves me of the anguish that has been building up inside me. "I convinced myself you were trying to keep everything between the two of you quiet so you wouldn't upset me. I know I must give you both a look sometimes that says I wish to have what you have, but I don't mean for it to trouble you or for you to notice what I'm thinking. We know each other a little too well, I guess."

"It's the truth. And you have every right to feel that way. It isn't fair that I'm living some semblance of a life while you're..."

"Being given the freedom of not being arrested like all the other Jews in our city? I don't let a second pass when I don't feel grateful for what you are doing to keep us safe. The look you saw...it was me thinking about how wonderful everything will be someday when this is all over—when I get to experience life with someone I love. It's something for me to look forward to."

I wrap my arms around her shoulders. "We'll both end up with the loves of our lives. I'm sure of it," I tell her.

"Are you two going to get married?" she asks with a school-girl snicker.

"I won't say we haven't talked about it, but I think we'd both rather make that type of plan when there aren't constant worries of air raids and attacks in the streets. I'd want it to be a special memory." It's deflating to know our lives are on hold because of this war, but I keep reminding myself that all good things are worth the wait.

"I can understand that. So are you still...saving yourself for —" she mumbles, lifting her head from my shoulder. Her blushing cheeks must mirror my own.

"Charlette," I say, playfully swatting my hand at her.

"We've always felt the same way, so I was asking if things change when you find that dreamy, charming man you can't keep your hands off of." She fans herself, batting her lashes toward the ceiling while talking like a lovesick woman.

"Yes, I'm still saving myself, for him, when we get married someday," I gush, now needing to fan myself down.

"See, something more to look forward to," she says.

"Precisely," I say, popping up from the bed. "I better open

up the shop in case a customer stumbles in to ask for directions to the nearest train station."

"Maybe today will be better," she says. "Chin up."

* * *

I've spent most of my morning drawing up sale signs highlighting the option to purchase custom gloves, wallets, and belts at a lower price than what we typically offer. I've hung them in the shop windows and now I'm waiting for what used to be a lunchtime rush at high noon.

As I'm beginning to give up hope on the new signage helping attract whoever might be passing on the street, I catch wind of a conversation between a few men outside. The laughter is loud, making my insides tighten, because even though I can't make out the words they're saying, Frenchmen wouldn't dare let out a laugh that boisterous in public right now, which means they likely aren't French.

One of the men steps into view of the door, proving my assumptions to be correct. He's wearing a distinctive olive-green tunic, matching trousers, and a peaked cap secured with a chin strap—the uniform we all avoid. I set my sights on the back of the signs I hung, wishing to snag them down without any of them noticing. I don't want to attract their attention and give them a reason to peruse the shop, but I can't move. I step back to place my hand within reach of the string attached to the second bell. If they come inside, I need to warn the Levis.

Their conversation feels like it's dragging on forever and I feel as if the temperature in the shop is rising by the minute. *Please, keep walking.* I lean forward to peer outside again, this time noticing that Monsieur Croix must have left at some point over the last hour after I hung my signs. He never closes early.

The door handle wriggles. Someone must have rested their hand on it from the outside. *No, no, no.* I wrap my fingers around the string and try to take in a slow breath to calm my nerves. I tug on my sweater, pulling the neckline up a bit higher to hide my all-telling signs of stress. I watch the door, wondering if I'm imagining the handle moving, but then it swings open. The shock doesn't set in until after I've pulled the string, thank goodness.

Three of them, all in the same uniform, step inside and remove their caps. "Guten Nachmittag, Fräulein," they say, one even offering a smile.

I've never before been greeted with any form of congeniality from someone in a German uniform.

"Welcome," I reply, trying to achieve the same level of cheerfulness. I don't want to ask them if there's anything I can help them with. I would normally, but I'm sure they will tell me what it is they are looking for without having to be prompted.

The three tall men walk around in separate directions, holding their wrists firmly behind their backs, with their caps pinched between their gloved fingers. I keep reminding myself to take a breath. Falling faint with them in here doesn't bear thinking about.

"What beautiful craftsmanship," one says to the other.

"Yes, yes, it is," another agrees.

"We must have gloves as warm as these."

Surely, they're able to find gloves in many other places if their unit doesn't already supply what they need. There's no need for them to shop here.

"How much for a pair of these?" He's looking in my direction this time, asking for the price when there's a small tag in front of the display that shows it.

I struggle to figure out the cost with the discount in my head, knowing they'll need the price in Reichsmarks rather than Francs. "The cost is—uh—three marks."

They exchange a look between each other and nod their heads. "I would like a pair."

"Me too."

"Yes, same here."

All three of them would like a pair of custom gloves. All I want is for them to leave.

"Of course," I agree, then pull out my order pad to begin jotting down their information. "I'll need to take down your measurements."

I'm not sure what I said to make them chuckle, but they all share the same amused look.

The man who walked into the shop first, approaches the counter. My neck itches and I know the welts are forming. He's going to notice.

"No need to be nervous, Fräulein."

I try to smile in response, knowing their only intention in this country is to make the natural citizens feel uncomfortable at every opportunity. "What is your name?" I will still call him German tyrant number one in my head, but that might become confusing when they come to collect their orders.

"Gustav Vogel," he says.

I scribble it out and reach beneath the register for my small cloth ruler to take down the measurements of his hand. "May I see your hand please?"

He scratches at his chin, raises a brow, and peers over his shoulder at his comrades. Following a long pause he pinches his lips into a smirk and tugs his glove off. "As you can see, I'm not married," he says.

"Married?" I question, unsure of what he's implying.

He points to his empty ring finger.

I swallow against the lump in my throat, and I'm sure they all heard the struggle of doing so.

I quickly measure the circumference of his hand, the length from his wrist to the tip of his middle finger, the length of each finger along with each circumference, ending with his thumb. I'm able to acquire these measurements within seconds most of the time, but I'm having trouble retaining the numbers from the sight of the ruler to the time the tip of my pen touches the paper. Five minutes is far too long when I've been doing this most of my life.

I would ask for partial payment from any other customer, but I'd rather hope they forget about their orders and don't return. "Äh, Ihre Bestellung...wird ab in, äh, einer Woche ab heute. Ist das in Ordnung?"

"Eine Woche ist in Ordnung," he says, agreeing to the pick-up time of a week from today. "Ich freue mich darauf, Dich wieder zu sehen."

I think he said he looks forward to seeing me again. My stomach cramps with hunger pain and nausea, my body unsure what to feel when all I want is to crawl under the counter and hide. I tell myself to smile so it appears I'm being polite, so he'll move to allow the next tyrant to step up to the counter.

He bows his head of slicked-back blonde hair, a strand falling over the eye he chooses to wink at me before stepping to the side. All I can focus on is the long jagged scar running across his left cheek, curious of how he earned it and if it was through a confrontation with someone who didn't ask for a fight.

If only I was able to breathe properly.

The next two men give me their names and I'm able to take their measurements quicker as I focus on the outcome of them leaving once we're through. The fifteen minutes they've been in the shop feel more like five hours and a cold sweat is forming on the back of my neck, warning me I've gone too long without eating and my blood pressure is irregular.

"Ich wünsche Ihnen eine gute Woche, Fräulein," Gustav the tyrant says upon walking toward the shop door.

I wish you a good week? He thinks I'll have a good time while I'm dreading their return. They must know the infliction of fear they cause people, and they must find enjoyment in it.

When the door closes and their conversation softens as they

move away, I lunge for the door and secure the locks then flip the sign to "closed." I release each of the four window drapes, then fall against the wall beneath the grandfather clock, shaking so hard I lose the strength to hold my head up.

Tears fall, one by one, and my heart throbs from understanding once again how quickly I can be torn apart and rattled. I want to help Nicolas fight for our country, but I can hardly tolerate a fake friendly conversation with a German soldier to sell a product.

They have no hearts. Their brains have been mutilated to think in a way most people can't imagine, and to be face to face with a being so inhumane is like expecting a wild animal in the middle of the jungle not to choose me as their dinner.

Once I'm able to catch my breath and steady my pulse, I push myself up off the ground and ring the bell twice to let the Levis know they are gone. I should have done so minutes earlier.

I forget about the shop, any possibility of customers coming by this afternoon, and lock myself in the stairwell before pulling myself up each step with a firm grip on the wobbly handrail. I told Nicolas he didn't need to fix this because it's always been this way, but I can see now that the nails are giving way from the wall. How many times have I had to pull myself up these steps lately?

Once I make it through the kitchen and into my bedroom, I tear off my heels and toss them against the wall before throwing myself onto my bed to curl up into a ball and let the remainder of tears flood out from my eyes.

A hand rests on my shoulder and I startle from not hearing anything more than the heaviness of my breaths. Rose is sitting on the edge of my bed, running her fingers through my hair like Mère used to do when I was distraught. "My dear, I was so worried about you when we heard the bell ring. Are you okay? Did something happen?"

I shake my head at first and swat at the tears on my cheeks.

Rose hands me a handkerchief from her pocket. "You're okay now."

"There were three of them," I say, trying to regain my composure between each word.

"What did they want?"

"To order gloves," I say with an uncontrollable gasp for air.

"Okay. Did you write up the orders and take down their measurements?"

How is she so calm when I'm a complete wreck?

"Yes, I got all their information. I told them it would take a week from today."

"Maybe Nicolas can find a way to be here with you that day," she suggests.

I think of how he'll react when he knows they were in the shop with me alone today. He'll be mad. We both knew it could happen easily, but before today they haven't had any interest in stepping foot inside. I'm afraid one will attract more.

"Maybe," I say in response.

"Have you eaten something? You're pale."

"Is everything okay?" Charlette calls out from what must be the hole in the wall as her question comes with a shadowy echo.

"I asked you to stay behind the wall," Rose hisses at Charlette.

"She rang the two bells. They left," Charlette argues. "Why are you crying?" She runs to my side and wraps her arms around my elbow. "They didn't hurt you, did they?"

"No, they didn't hurt me."

"You're scared, as anyone would be. You did everything right and they left without a problem," Charlette says, talking as if she was a fly on the wall downstairs.

"One of them seemed to take a liking to me. I wasn't trying to be too friendly, but maybe pretending to be polite gave them the impression that I enjoyed their company. They already have to come back to collect their orders. They're deranged men. I can't even begin to imagine what they might be thinking the next time they walk into the shop."

"Maybe they thought you were German too," she says, flipping a wave of hair off my face.

"They knew I wasn't speaking German well and they found it to be funny."

"This isn't the Raya I know," Rose says. "You are a strong, brave woman who puts herself aside for everyone. You cannot let the fear of these men break apart the person you are. You are better than them, do you understand me? You need to be civil and get them out of your hair like you did today."

I've always been able to convince myself that I'm confident and secure within the life I've been upholding, but today is the first time I've ever questioned the truth of what I'm capable of. I'm not sure I would be able to stand up against any of them if I had to. That's why so many others have left Paris. Maybe it was foolish of me to stay here, thinking I would make it through this.

TWENTY

NICOLAS

Paris, France

Since the French police were forced by the Third Reich and the Vichy government to transport thirteen thousand Jewish citizens of Paris to labor camps and ghettos three months ago, the city is somehow even more desolate than it was before. Jewish people weren't congregating on the streets or going far from their homes, but there's a feeling of emptiness now, knowing that so many flats are either vacant or housing German soldiers. I lie awake at night, wondering how anyone could move into the home of a Jewish family who was forced away without warning, being surrounded by their lifelong memorabilia: a bedroom decorated for a child, or a room shared by a loving couple, a dining table that's hosted thousands of family dinners, a sofa where songs from the radio would soothe someone into a comfortable rest after a long day. A warm, comfortable life that shouldn't have been disrupted for the selfish needs of the heartless souls now manning these streets as if they're protecting something that has been stolen from them. The irony is sickening and unfathomable.

With autumn comes shorter days and it seems most birds have taken off for the south, earlier than usual—intelligent creatures—though they may find themselves having to fly much farther south than ever before if they want to escape this nightmare. Even still, Africa has been pulled into the battles. The wind still blows, but the leaves are falling quickly, and when the winter months set in, there will be complete, utter silence in a city that was once full of life.

Back in June, I was pressed for creativity at the paper, told to remain neutral or speak of other countries' misfortunes. Then we still had a couple of pages dedicated to the arts, classifieds, and the stock market numbers, but now our paper is down to two pages—every article is about the war, not in France, and we report on the closed market for trades, causing a buildup of international troubles. There's nothing left to write about and I'm not sure how our paper is still in business seeing as many others have been forced to shut down. I'm writing what I'm told to write and assisting with some editing. It might not be long before I'm out of a job like half of the others I worked with.

Croix has closed his newsstand early today again, and it seems Raya has closed the shop before five, which is unlike her. Despite the lack of custom, she has stayed true to her business ethics of keeping the shop open through the stated promised hours listed on the front door's window.

Rather than reopen the shop, I turn to go around to the back of the shop where I've been spending many nights underground with the other members of the Lions Rebelles. There's no meeting tonight as Hugo and Bette are in Lyon, collecting supplies for us to inventory tomorrow night, which works out well since Mère has been on my case about bringing Raya home to have dinner with us. Inviting guests over for a meal is a thing of the past as we all only have the bare essentials to feed the number of people in a home. I would have extras before I met Raya, whatever Hugo would give us, but that all goes to the Levi family now for good reason.

The stairwell is darker than usual, making me wonder if Raya doesn't have power in her flat. I take a hold of the railing, finding it looser than it's been and though she's asked me to refrain from fixing it, someone is going to get hurt if I don't take care of it soon. She must have yanked on it today.

I lower my canvas satchel against the wall upon entering her dim lit flat, finding a subtle glow from the setting sun leaking through her bedroom window. She's in bed with the quilt pulled up to her chin, Charlette tucked in snuggly beside her and Rose resting on one of the kitchen table chairs in the corner, knitting what looks to be a shawl.

"Is everything all right?" I ask, directing my question toward Charlette and Rose.

"Nicolas," Charlette speaks out. "We're so glad to see you."

"And you as well, of course," I say, forcing a small smile before redirecting my attention to Raya. "Are you sick?" She looks so pale and unkempt. Before she can answer I place my palm on her forehead, but she's cool against the heated hand I've had in my coat pocket for the last twenty minutes.

"No, I'm fine," she says, forcing a smile. She lifts the covers off her clothed body and lowers her feet to the ground.

"Like you were when you nearly fainted that time because you hadn't eaten anything all day?" I ask with a smirk and a raised brow. She knows I can tell the difference between a real smile and this one. We've talked about it and even made jokes because she still thinks I believe the ones that aren't real. "Why are you in bed?" Raya stays busy unless it's bedtime. If she isn't waiting on customers in the shop, she's working on orders with Charlette, sketching out designs for belts or gloves with charcoal and old newspaper, or baking if she has the proper ingredients. *Lying in bed is for the sick or tired*—that's what she always says when I tell her she should take a rest with everything she's been doing.

Charlette and Rose both stare at Raya with questionable expressions and I can't figure out what I'm missing.

"I can do your hair before you head out," Charlette offers.

Raya combs her fingers through her short locks. She pulls out a couple of pins and tightens the side part to smooth out the hair that was already pulled back. "I'm fine."

"That's the second time you've said you're fine. Once more, and I'll know it's a lie." Another telltale sign of Raya's. The words: *I'm fine* mean she's far from it, but I promised not to speculate unless she describes her mood as fine more than three times in an hour. Then it's fair for me to ask with more demand for the truth she feels the need to conceal.

She smooths out her dress that has gathered slight wrinkles for as long as she must have been lying in bed like this.

"My mother doesn't care about wrinkles," I assure her.

"Well, I do," she says, pulling a sweater from a hook on the side of her wall. Her cheeks are rosy, but in splotches, her eyes are laced with pink veins, and her lips are puffy.

"Why were you crying?" I ask, taking her gently by the arm.

"It was a long day," she says, making sure not to tell me she's fine. Maybe she doesn't want to say anything more in front of Charlette or Rose, but I've also come to see she keeps little from them too. It's become obvious that they have become her family in the time she's been parentless.

"Where is Jacques?" I ask his wife.

She points across to their hiding space. "He's been making notes about something for hours. I'm not quite sure what."

Our plan. He's been organizing a timeline of action to assist some of the other groups with a revolt in the works. He doesn't want Charlette or Rose to know about this, so he's asked me to keep quiet. I haven't told Raya yet either because I know she won't be pleased to hear about our plans of assault. I'm sure she expects everything that is to happen, but without a weapon in her hand, she will fear for the worst as I would too. She'd also feel guilty for not confessing the truth to Charlette and Rose so it's best to stay silent for now.

"Probably regulation reminders for our group," I say.

"That sounds like something he would do," Rose agrees.

"I'm ready," Raya says, slipping on her brown leather Mary-Jane heels.

"You will have her back by nine?" Rose confirms as she does each night that we've left the building after work.

"Yes, madam, and not a moment later," I reply.

"Thank you, and give your mother my best," she says.

I smile and nod because I don't want to say anything more. I haven't told Mère about the Levi family. Mère would have a heart attack if she knew about Raya's living situation, not for the fact that she's hiding a family of Jewish people in her home, but for the danger entailed in it. This is the same reason why Mère knows nothing about the Lions Rebelles either. She's seen enough with what Father went through and I don't feel it's necessary to burden her with unnecessary fear beyond what she already knows is happening outside of our home.

"I'll make sure to let you know when I'm back," Raya says, blowing them each a kiss.

We descend into the stairwell and Raya takes a hold of the railing, listening to it clatter and clank against the wall. I open my mouth to tell her it's getting fixed tomorrow, but she speaks before I can get a word out. "I already know."

"Good. Tomorrow it is."

The sun has dipped beneath the surrounding buildings, leaving a slight flare of orange scraping across the tallest ones in the vicinity. Raya keeps her focus on the ground to avoid the shallow puddles from the rainstorm that passed earlier in the day.

"Are you going to tell me what happened today or am I going to have to beg?" I ask.

She inhales again and seems to hold it in for a long second before releasing the air. "If there are so few Parisians left with the ability to shop in Paris, who do you suspect the customers will become?"

Her words are sharp as if she's angry with me for something I said or did, but I'm not sure what that would be since everything was perfectly fine between us last night when I left.

"My products are too expensive for the economy and rather than close the shop, I decided to hang up discount signs in the windows."

"There's nothing wrong with that," I tell her. I'm aware she's only earning a small percentage above the price of cost and labor, but even a few coins are something compared to nothing.

"German soldiers found the signs intriguing enough to come inside the shop today."

I take her hand, knowing it's been her growing fear since we met. She couldn't understand how she had gotten away without them browsing the store with how long they've been meandering the streets.

"What did they want?" I ask, trying to keep my voice calm so I don't rile her up more.

Raya's gaze falls again, making it look as if she's watching out for more puddles on a flat curb without divots. "Custom-fit gloves."

"You only have what you have in inventory though. That's what you told them, right?" The Germans can't expect anyone who is still in business to have access to extra help, which would include a seamstress in this case.

"They didn't ask to see the inventory. They asked how long it would take before they're ready. I didn't want to say anything that would anger them since they obviously knew the shop is known for custom work."

The rage firing inside of me might have been obvious if she was looking at me, but she can't lift her head, which is likely best for both of us. I take a few breaths, making sure not to squeeze her hand as a hint that there is fury I am trying to suppress. "They'll be coming back then," I say.

"I couldn't think when they were near me. I nearly fainted and did everything possible to remain standing with an unfaltering disposition. The fifteen minutes they were in the shop seemed like hours. I took their measurements and information then sent them on their way."

"Is that all that happened? You seem perturbed, even for the fact that they were in your shop."

Raya lifts her gaze from the ground and peeks up at me through her lashes. "They were chatting in German. It was hard to understand what they were talking about."

She's not telling me something. I can see it in her eyes, the quickness of her blinks. She's scared to tell me what she's leaving out of the story.

"Did they lay a finger on you?" I say, gritting my teeth. I can't help the way I sound. She isn't the reason I'm seething.

"No. They smiled a lot and were friendly. One might have seemed a bit friendlier than the others, but I ignored their foolishness. I would do anything to stop them from coming back to collect their orders. I didn't even charge them today, hoping they might forget to come back."

"There was not much else you could do, I suppose." I wish she had told them there are no custom orders at this time, knowing how terrified she was the one night we were asked for our identification. "When did you tell them their orders would be ready?"

"A week from today."

October 30th—the day before our planned assault. I can blame myself now. If I had told her about the plan to attack, she could have added a day to her timeline and possibly avoided them returning to the shop.

"I'll see if I can be there with you for the day if Paul will let me take time out of the office." I can't see why he won't with so little to do during the day.

Raya nods. We're about to reach my building and I don't want her to be uneasy when we go inside. Mère has a good sense for people's emotions, and she'll ask Raya far more questions than I have, even after only meeting her a few times. She's fond of the girl whom she refers to as my future wife when I'm home.

"What can I do to make you feel better before we go inside?" I ask her.

"I'm sorry if I let you down today."

I tug her hand and pull her back from her attempted step forward. "You did nothing wrong. I understand why you did what you did, and I would have shut down the shop and called it a day too after they left." I assume that's what happened.

"I shouldn't have put those discount signs up. It was asking for a type of trouble I didn't consider when hanging them."

"No one can tell us how to navigate this life we're being forced to live. All we can do is hope we're making the right decisions each day and do what's best for ourselves. That's what you were doing. Don't fault yourself for trying to sustain an income." I slide my finger beneath her chin, forcing her to look up at me. "All I want is to keep you safe and I'll do whatever I can to do so. I love you, ma chérie."

"I love you," she says, sniffling before rising on her toes to kiss my cheek. "I'll let it go so your mother doesn't suspect anything is off." A true smile forms across her lips, though it might be a bit of a struggle to maintain.

I keep a hold of her chin and press my lips to hers, holding my breath to make the moment last long enough for her smile to feel as real as it looks, and mine will follow.

A neighborhood boy flies by on his bicycle and lets out a cat-calling whistle, forcing Raya to pull away and cover her lips. Her eyes are wide and surprised that someone would do such a thing.

"Welcome back to my neighborhood," I say with a chuckle.

Mère greets us both as if we're her long-lost children, even though I was here this morning and it's only been a few weeks since Raya saw her last.

"It's so wonderful to see you again, my dear. You look beautiful as always," Mère says, taking Raya from my hand and guiding her into the kitchen. She can likely smell the vegetable and legume casserole that is no longer a simple meal for Mondays. It's what we eat most nights now.

"Mm, that smells wonderful, Madame Bardot. Thank you for inviting me over tonight. It's so lovely to have a home cooked meal."

Raya cooks every night and does it well, but she knows how important meals are to my mother. It's her way of showing love, which has always been much appreciated throughout my life. I've never gone hungry, that's for sure.

"Anytime you want a home-cooked meal, you come here for dinner with or without Nicolas, you understand?" She's replacing me now. I figured that would happen after meeting Raya once—the daughter she's always longed for.

Raya chuckles in return. "How lovely of you to take me in, your kindness means so much to me," she says, telling Mère all the things she wants to hear, which is why she's beginning to love her more than me. "Allow me to help set the table."

"No, no, you can be my guest and take a seat with my son. I'll bring the bowls out. I'm sure you've had a long day." Though Raya doesn't help with the bowls, she doesn't come out of the kitchen empty-handed. She brings a carafe of water to the table then spots the stack of linen napkins resting in the center and takes them to begin folding each into a fancy decoration.

"It's just us. You don't have to fold the napkins," I tell her.

"We deserve beautifully displayed napkins as much as anyone else," she replies, biting down on the tip of her tongue as she ensures the sides of the fabric align perfectly.

"She's going to replace me with you," I say with a grin and sigh.

"Then fold a napkin and be a good son," Raya lectures me, her dimples deepening in her cheeks.

A good son. In Mère's eyes, a good son wouldn't be planning an assault against the terrorizing Germans soldiers with hope of pushing them out of this country faster than they'd like to go. At least I know Raya will be like the daughter Mère would need if I was to disappear from this world.

TWENTY-ONE

RAYA

Ravensbrück, Germany

I have a new standing position during roll call. We all move around when people die, or new prisoners arrive. Each morning I wish for a better view than the end wall of the barrack and today I'm allowed to see between two barrack buildings. If I blur my eyes, I can convince myself I don't see the electric fence that surrounds the entire camp or the wrought-iron gates that would be impossible to scale. I could make a run for it, find my family on the other side, my old life, one I would give everything up for. It must all be just sitting there without me.

I can picture his eyes, the way he looked at me as if I was the earth and he was the sun. I want those moments back. I need those moments back. I can't live like this.

But even with a chance sighting of a crack in the world I'm confined in, there is nothing beyond the horizon. There is no way out. There has never been a way out, whether cornered by a Nazi or shuttled into an enclosed prison. They get what they want and that's all there is to it.

Roll call seems to last twice as long today, maybe because

the air is so cold and the clouds are low bearing, causing the chill to stick to our exposed skin. As they do most mornings, my knees quiver, fighting to remain locked so I don't collapse from hunger. The bread will do enough to keep me upright but not enough to suppress the never-ending hunger pangs.

The woman who stands beside me each morning, Paulette, taps her knuckles against mine, a gesture only the two of us understand. I reach into my pocket and retrieve a scrap of fabric, small enough to crumple into my fist. She opens her hand beneath mine and I place the fabric inside, concealing it until she folds her fingers over mine, and then I slip my hand away. She shoves the fabric into her pocket. We wait a moment, ensuring no one else has spotted our exchange before she reaches back over and releases four sugar cubes into my hand.

We aren't allowed sugar as it's a rare commodity, but Paulette works in the SS kitchen, serving the guards their meals. She has access to foods we don't and snatches what she can when no one's looking. I would never ask for anything more than sugar, but I know she has several exchange deals with others too. The sugar keeps me from fainting or becoming too weak, which could mean life or death if the wrong guard was to see me keel over. *It would be an opportunity they couldn't pass up, much like when I was alone that one afternoon when I foolishly thought I was a free woman.* She uses the scraps of fabric to stuff a blanket for extra warmth. I'm not sure how many times we've exchanged now, but I feel like it might take more fabric than I could ever give her to stuff her blanket enough to offer the comfort we all desire.

An incoming train arriving outside of the gates releases a whistle that sounds muffled within the foggy clouds, like a piercing cry we're all forced to ignore. It's hard to know if the train is coming or going with people—sometimes it's both. This must be why roll call has been delayed this morning.

We all shuffle from foot to foot, trying to see over each

other's heads for a hint of what's happening, but it's a lengthy wait until we catch a glimpse of a long line of women slinking onto the campgrounds. My heart grows heavy, threatening to plummet to the bottom of my gut, as I watch another group of women unknowingly walk toward their delayed death. They all have a bag or suitcase with them, which is different from what many of us here experienced—we were given no warning before our arrest. The camp is already at capacity and it's hard not to wonder how they will fit us all in. The line seems to go on and on without an end in sight.

TWENTY-TWO
RAYA
LAST YEAR, OCTOBER 1942

Paris, France

The rain is pummeling down outside, cascading in fluid streams off the edge of the door's overhang. The sky is so dark, it feels more like evening than late afternoon. I've lit lanterns around the shop to make up for the lack of sunlight. During days like this, I used to play orchestral records by Tommy Dorsey and Glenn Miller to give the shop a warm embrace. Now I stand in silence, daily, knowing the sad likelihood of anyone with decency walking through the front door.

Nicolas was able to stay with me in the shop until after lunchtime, but his boss demanded he come into the office for the rest of the afternoon to help with the layout for print. The staff at the paper has dwindled to a few only after last week when three more of them were forced to leave, this time for hard labor within German factories. Nicolas managed to escape the demand for all men between the ages of twenty and twenty-three by being just a year older than the requirement. A notice was sent around and hung on every street corner, telling all remaining Parisians in the specified age group to report for duty. There were and are no exceptions.

If the German soldiers return for their custom gloves, I have everything packaged and ready to hand over. I'm mostly concerned about the payment I need to collect, but it's nothing worth fighting over if they feel the need to run away with the gloves. Nicolas said that many of the soldiers who have been stationed here have been redeployed to Northern Africa due to the growing battles there. While most were sent over a week ago, more have left throughout the last week, giving me the slightest bit of hope that the three men who were here have since left the country.

The rain is hypnotizing as I keep my sights set out the window, knowing I won't hear anyone approaching with the splashing pelts of water echoing down the street. My hand isn't far from the doorbell's string even though the three of them have decided to stay put in their room today, knowing the Germans are due to return for their goods. But I still want to give them the warning that they're here if they show up. Standing like this for so long is making me wonder how guards remain still on duty without falling over from exhaustion. I'm not sure I would make a good guard.

For each minute that passes, I tell myself the chance of them not returning goes up. I could close the shop but I'm sure that would infuriate them if they came by during the proper hours, posted clearly on the door. I could take down the hours sign too but with the chance that they took note of it last week, I would be in the same situation of angering them.

* * *

For the last few minutes, I've shifted my stare from the front door to the grandfather clock, counting down the seconds in my head until the hour hand hits the five. I understand this doesn't mean they won't show up tomorrow or the next business day, but I've been so focused on today that a bit of relief is all I want right now.

My heart thuds along with the second hand as I make my way to the front door to flip the sign and secure the top lock. The sign is mid-swing, and my up-stretched arm momentarily masks my view when the door opens with gusto, shoving me out the way. I trip over the thin entryway mat and my fall knocks the wind out of my lungs, stealing a long second of awareness before I look up to find a German in uniform closing the door behind him. Gustav, the leading soldier of the three that were here last week, towers over me with his hands on his hips.

"Are you all right?"

He pushed me over as I was trying to lock up the shop. Why would he care enough to ask?

I rise to my feet and brush the dust from my skirt. "I'm fine," I lie. I wouldn't dare say otherwise. "I was about to close shop, but I have your order ready," I tell him as I make my way around the desk, realizing I never had the chance to ring the warning bell. I reach for the wrapped packages and place them on the counter next to the register. "Here you are."

He takes the center package with his order slip taped to the top and tears off the paper to admire his gloves. I want to look toward the door, hoping that Nicolas might be stepping into the shop at any time. He's usually here a few minutes after five or sometimes right before five depending on the amount of work he has.

"Very nice," Gustav says, complimenting the quality as he slips it onto his hand. "Fits perfectly."

It's obviously going to be a perfect fit since I took down every one of his measurements.

"What do I owe you for the three pairs?"

The price is clearly written on his order slip just as it is on the sign displayed beside the gloves.

"Three marks per pair for a total of nine marks."

With his free bare hand, he scratches his fingers along the side of his jaw as if he's still thinking about what I've said. "What form of payment do you take?"

I believe he's toying with me. We're forced to take Reichsmarks, the German currency. We accept Francs too, but I doubt he has any. "Marks," I respond.

"Anything else?" I don't understand his questions, but he removes his glove and places it on the counter with the other. He steps away, moving toward the front door as if he plans to leave and I'm left baffled at what's happening.

He steps up to the door and secures the lock I was trying to reach when he pushed me over. The blood drains from my face, from my entire body, and I reach my hand over to the counter for support, wishing I had a weapon to defend myself, even though I don't know how to use one. My head shakes, telling him no to whatever it is he plans to do.

"Payments come in many forms these days," he says.

My mind is spinning so fast I can barely make out a word he's saying. I back myself into the wall, knowing there is safety on the other side—the other side that's impossible for me to reach from here. Gustav removes his coat and places it over the top of a belt display while walking toward me, to the opening behind the cash register.

He reaches for his belt, and I wish his only purpose for removing it was to ask for a new one. He smiles and holds a finger to his lips. I spot a pistol in a holster attached to his belt and he reaches for the weapon. I slide down against the wall, holding my hands over my face. I don't want to see how I die. I want to cry and scream, but I'm numb, my throat is too tight to make a sound, and I can hardly breathe. I'm not sure if my heart is racing or if I'm shaking too hard to feel my pulse.

"No, please, no," I cry out.

My feet are pulled out from beneath my squatting position,

forcing me to fall backward, my head hitting the ground. If only it was hard enough to knock me unconscious.

"Non, non," I cry. "Je t'en prie, non."

His cigar-tainted breath fogs against my face, an indication of what's to come. All my strength dissipates as he presses his body against mine, wrangling me like I'm no more than a rag doll. His calloused fingers scrape against my skin as he steals every form of innocence left within me. The pain is insufferable, but nothing compared to the revolting feeling of realizing how powerless I am against him.

Tears skate down my face as he shoves his hand over my mouth, forcing me to smell the scent of new leather mixed with tobacco. The animal-like noises of a wild beast feeding on its prey is all I can hear. I want nothing more than to bite his hand and rip his fingers off with my teeth but I'm positive he'll kill me if I even try to move.

My body shivers beneath a cold sweat covering my forehead and face. I gasp for air, but his other hand moves to my chest, pressing down so hard I can't move or even make a sound. I want to scream, push him off me, and kill him. But my eyes roll into the back of my head and the world around me goes black except for the blurry image of the grandfather clock hanging on the wall. One, two, three, four...I try to count along with the seconds, needing the clock to bring me forward to another time away from now.

* * *

My eyelids flutter open. The shop is quiet, but I'm sprawled on the floor behind the register. Cold air sweeps over tender spots on my legs where my stockings tore. My skirt is bunched up to my thighs and a pain sears up my torso.

I stagger to my knees and struggle to pull myself upright, fearing he might still be in the shop waiting for me to come to. It takes me a long moment to notice the gloves are gone and the bolt on the door is unhinged. The grandfather clock reads twenty-five minutes past five. Nicolas still isn't here. If he had walked in when— Thank goodness he didn't. Gustav would have shot him.

A headache rages around my hairline as I slip out of my shoes and pull my stockings off and circle the store, unsure what to do with them. I use the thin fabric to wipe down my legs and slip my bare feet back into my shoes before burying the tangible evidence into the bottom of the trash bin beneath scraps of paper. I take heavy steps toward the door, quickly securing each of the locks and dropping the drapes across the windows.

All I can do is stand here, still, acknowledging the permanent damage I have been dealt. I would never be able to undo the last half hour of my life, erase the memory of torment or reclaim my purity. A permanent scar will remain on the inside of my eyelids that will never allow me to forget.

My lungs struggle to find a steady deep breath as I make my way toward the stairs. Each step is a reminder of my body refusing to conform to each of his movements.

Before reaching the top, I brush my fingers through my hair, finding a bump where I hit the wall. Every day I'll be forced to think about this. I should have rejected their order, despite knowing that they could have forced me to close my doors. Or worse.

I could have still ended up like this.

I flip on the main light over the kitchen table and walk to the mirror separating my side of the wall from the Levis. I'm whiter than the clouds covering the sky, my eyes are bloodshot and there's a faint red mark to the right of my lips where his fingers dug into my cheek. This isn't me. I can't be her.

The downstairs door opens and closes. My heart thunders in my chest and I amble to the washroom.

He's come back for me. *Please, no, no. Let me be.*

The footsteps thump up the stairs, one after another. Heavy feet, screaming for attention.

I bear my weight against the inside of the washroom door and squeeze my eyes shut, feeling the tug from the painful welt.

"Raya?"

Nicolas. It's after five and he must figure I'm upstairs waiting for him. I wish he had gotten to the shop sooner like he has so many other nights. If he had arrived before closing, this wouldn't have happened.

I fight for air, an inhale deep enough to satisfy my heaving lungs. *I'm fine. I'm fine. I'm fine,* I tell myself. "Just a minute," I force out.

I tear open the drawer beside the sink and fumble to find powder to brush over my cheeks. My hand won't steady as I try to uncap my tube of lipstick and it's a struggle to draw a short straight line along my bottom and top lips.

He can't know.

A courier came on their behalf today and picked up the gloves and left the payment. All the worrying was for nothing.

My ribs ache as I take another deep breath and the pain plunges through me, stretching up and down my back.

I'm okay. I'm okay.

I open the washroom door, finding Nicolas waiting for me just a few steps away. "You scared me. I didn't think you were up here and the shop is closed," he says.

He can't see me well with the one light illuminating the area. "I was—I was dusting. I hadn't cleaned much in the last week and then I got some dust in my eyes and had to come upstairs to wash my face."

"I'm sorry I had to work late. One of our machines jammed and," he holds his arms out to the side, "now, I'm covered in ink."

Why tonight? Why did it have to be tonight of all nights?

He would have been the reason I wasn't attacked. He knew those men were planning to come back today. He knew.

"Ink?" I question, realizing I wasn't paying much attention to the reason he had to work late. There's ink all over his sleeves. "Oh goodness, um—that's a lot of ink." You're covered in ink and I've been assaulted. Nothing will get that that stain off me. I take his arm to assess the stain. "I—I uh—might have something to get that out. Let me go check the washroom."

I'm slow to make my way back into the washroom, not because I don't want to move quicker but because of the pain Gustav inflicted, the soreness is raging stronger with each minute that passes.

"The banister is fixed, by the way. Did you notice?" Nicolas asks, maybe questioning why I seem out of sorts.

"Oh—uh—yes, yes, thank you for doing that. Thank so much," I say.

Nicolas follows me down the short hallway. "Raya, are you okay?"

"Yes, of course, why do you always ask me that? I'm fine," I snap as I rummage through my vanity drawer again.

"Oh—okay. I was—you seem unwell," he says, holding his hands up in defense.

"I'm sorry. I am. I was staring out the door and into the rain all day and it drained my energy."

"Did the soldiers come for their gloves?" Nicolas asks, unbuttoning his white collared shirt so I can help him with the stains.

I continue my search through my cosmetics, unsure of what I'm specifically trying to find for him now. I'm trying harder to avoid eye contact than looking for a solution to his stain. "The soldiers—oh, yes, a courier came on their behalf and picked up the gloves. They left the payment too. I guess all my worrying was for nothing."

"Thank God," he says, letting out a sigh of relief.

"I won't hang any more sale signs in the window. In fact, if I could hang a sign that says, 'No Germans Allowed' I would." This is my fault. Someone might say I asked for this.

"Don't do that. It won't end well, trust me. I've seen a shop try," he says.

I close the drawer and squeeze out between him and the doorway, into the kitchen to take out a soup pot that I place under the faucet.

"I won't have anything to wear home if you soak my shirt," he says. "I didn't even consider removing the ink with hot water." I don't think I have anything else that would take an ink stain out.

"Right. You can borrow one of my father's old shirts." I still have a few in the closet left over from what we didn't use for the insulation.

"It's okay. I figured you were going to blot it with a bit of rubbing alcohol. I can wait until I get home."

"I have rubbing alcohol," I tell him while placing the pot of water on the stovetop.

I head back toward the washroom, but Nicolas snatches my hand before I can go too far. His grip sends a rippling wave of discomfort through my body, and I tear my hand out of his hold, pinning it against my chest beneath my other hand.

"No!" I shout. Why did I say that?

"What's going on with you?" he asks, perplexity straining against his forehead and eyebrows. He points to his cheek. "And did you hurt yourself? Your cheek is red."

I take in a shuddered breath, losing my ability to conceal the despair reeling through me. "You startled me, that's all," I say, touching the stinging mark on my cheek.

"There's something you aren't telling me, isn't there?"

I haven't used this question on him over the last few days that he's been acting distant and lost in his thoughts. I know how much goes through each of our heads daily and it's often too much for anyone to handle.

"Is there something *you* aren't telling me?" I ask in return. "You've been quiet and there have been a few instances when you didn't even hear me talking to you."

"Raya, have I disappointed you in some way?" he asks.

There's nothing wrong between us but if he thinks I'm hiding something, an issue will arise.

"No, no—of course you haven't. I—I just know you've had a lot on your mind, as have I."

His eyes drift past me down the hall. "You're right. We should talk," he says.

My chest becomes cold and my heart seems to drop in my chest as I consider how we went from me concealing my emotions to him having a possible confession. We've been open with each other, hiding little. Perhaps until today.

"What is it?" I ask, forgetting about the rubbing alcohol.

He glances down at my hand, making it known he would like to take it before reaching for me again. When my hand is in his, he leads me over to the chairs around the table and pulls one out for me to sit down. The unforgiving wooden seat causes another wave of pain to surge through me. I bite down on the inside of my cheek to hide the evidence.

He slides a chair out for himself and rests his elbows on the table. "There's going to be an insurgency tomorrow," he says, shocking me with his ice-cold statement. "There are several resistance groups participating and ours is one of them."

His words are crystal clear and before an hour ago, I would have wanted to ask him to stay back and let the others fight but now I want to ask him to show me how to use a weapon so I can join them. "Can I help?"

His eyes grow wide with surprise. "I was not expecting this to be your response, and I don't know if it's a good idea for you to help. It's going to be a bloody battle and there will be weapons—"

"Teach me."

Nicolas lowers his head into his hands and scratches his fingers through his hair. "I don't know, Raya."

"Is Jacques joining you?"

"No, I've convinced him to stay here. It's too dangerous for him to be with us," he answers.

I know, for one, my habit of passing out makes me a hazard to them, but that doesn't take away from my desire to fight. "Well, what if something happens to you?" I ask.

"That's what I want to talk to you about." He takes my hands back into his. "Something is more likely to happen to me if I'm busy worrying about you in that moment."

TWENTY-THREE

NICOLAS
LAST YEAR, OCTOBER 1942

Paris, France

The cool musky air around us picks up the odors of our sweat and nerves as we congregate over dirt-covered stone nearly four floors down from street level. Two dark tunnels veer off from our location and we've taken turns exploring each, finding endless mazes of narrow walkways and a few passageways leading to the sewer line.

The fifteen of us have been preparing for weeks, ready to launch our assault today, but we received word from the head of Maquis to hold until further notice. No one in our immediate links of intelligence knows why. With so many of the German troops sent to Africa, the number of soldiers here in the city has diminished. This would have been the best time to take them down.

"Now what?" I ask Hugo. "We just wait until they give us the go ahead?"

Hugo puts his hands to his hips and shakes his head. The lantern flickers between us, adding a sinister glow to his eyes. "I don't see a reason to waste our efforts. We're ready. So I've devised a plan to take down several high-commanding German officers in an ambush."

"There are only fifteen of us. How are we to take down several commanding officers who will likely be surrounded by security?" I question him.

"Here's what we'll do," Hugo says, lifting the lantern so we can all see his face clearer.

Hugo is typically of sound mind, but with the adrenaline pumping through each one of us, I'm not sure what's about to come out of his mouth.

"Tonight there's a dinner at the hotel on Rue la Perouse. The officers will be loaded, drunk from all the cocktails. I've witnessed them out on the streets after one of these soirees. They can barely balance on two good feet. So—" Hugo holds up a finger to highlight his pause before his big reveal. "Tonight, at eleven, one of us will pull the lever to activate the fire alarm inside the hotel. There will be lots of commotion and cause for concern, but, at last, the officers will spill out onto the street as the building evacuates. We'll have to be right on our targets as civilians will be in the mix, but I'm certain the officers will be easy to spot."

"Hugo," I say with a sigh, "there could be far more of them than we can take on, whether they're drunk or not. It won't take long before more are called to the scene."

"I was just getting to that part," Hugo replies, holding his finger to his lips. "Anyway, we'll take cover behind parked cars. Once there are a group of officers outside, we'll attack for as long as we can until the first hint of a siren rises in the distance. That's when we'll need to run, all of us in different directions, to take cover from retaliation. If we can take down a handful of high commanding officers, we'll have made a dent in our progress."

"Do you know for sure this hotel has an alarm?" I ask, glancing around at the dark shadows of hungry eyes, sensing they feel the same way I do. No one else is eager to ask questions, but I won't just jump in without knowing all the answers to every question I have first.

"Yes, it's in the lobby of the hotel beneath the grand stairwell, surrounded by tall plants. Once the alarm is pulled, we wait opposite the hotel. The officers will exit through the front doors, and we light them up."

"You're going to have to pull the alarm since you're familiar with the location."

"Very well. I can do that," he says.

My heart thunders as I envision the plan, imagining it working out so brilliantly. Other than a few minor one- or two-person attacks, we haven't taken part in much of the heavy action.

"I've already spoken to another couple of the groups and they'll be joining us. With more of us, we can cover each side of the building just in case they leave another way. Half of us will meet around Myron T. Herrick's statue at a quarter before the hour. The others will meet at the corner of Rue la Perouse. Everyone here will be meeting at the statue."

"If one of us gets caught?" I add, asking the one question no one wants to know the answer to.

"We can risk losing more of us. We all know we're on our own in this battle and we live and die along those terms."

I can't wrap my head around that part. I couldn't leave someone who has been fighting next to me behind.

"Get some rest. It's going to be a late night," Hugo says as his parting words.

* * *

Since I believe Raya isn't too happy with my plea for her to stay in the shop rather than accompany us, it's best to check up on her to see how she's doing. The shop is quiet and empty, as it usually is these days. Raya is standing in her typical spot, jotting down notes by the cash register. When I secure the back door behind me, she jumps, letting out a scream.

"Oh mon Dieu!" she shouts. "You can't sneak up on me like that, don't you understand?" I come through the back door almost daily and I didn't mean to startle or frighten her.

"I'm sorry, ma chérie."

She huffs. "Shouldn't you be on your way to—"

"Shh," I hush her. She doesn't need to be yelling anything out even if we're in the shop alone. The walls have ears in this city. "No, no, we were told to hold off, but we have a plan for something a bit smaller this evening."

"Can I join you then?" she asks, her eyebrow arching as she scribbles what must be nonsense. No one can have a conversation and continue writing something different at the same time. At least, I couldn't do that.

If she's angry with me for not agreeing to her participating in the fight, then maybe I shouldn't be making these decisions for her. I didn't give her any say in what I decide to do so I can see why she might be frustrated with me.

"I won't say yes, but I shouldn't tell you what to do. I gave you my reasons last night but if those aren't good enough, then you are your own woman and should decide based on what you think is best for you."

Raya drops her pen and embraces her arms around her torso. "Then, I'm coming with you."

All I can do is stare at her, wishing she wouldn't be so determined to experience something no one should have to go through. I haven't considered what I might feel if I end up killing a German, whether it will haunt me for the rest of my life. I'm not sure I'm capable of pulling a trigger when aiming at a man's head. I do know if we're caught and unprepared to fight, we'll all go down, regardless of whether they're drunk or sober.

I walk closer to Raya, noticing a small welt on her cheek. It wasn't nearly as prominent yesterday. I reach across the desk to touch her face and she turns away from me. "What happened? This isn't from being startled when I walked in last night."

She touches her fingertips to her cheek. She seems to know exactly where to place her hand on her face. "What do you mean?"

"The welt. Where did it come from?"

"Oh, this, I was tired this morning when I opened the medicine cabinet in the bathroom. I forgot to close it before I reached down to clean my face over the sink."

"This morning?" I ask, feeling like I must have been imagining the red mark on her face last night.

"Yes, I was up early."

"I can get you some ice," I offer.

"No, no. I'm fine."

And there is part one of what I assume to be a lie forming.

"Since I'm not going to work today, is there anything I can help with around the shop?"

"I'm taking down inventory, then I'll be drawing up new signs for pricing that includes the German Reichsmark. The less I have to speak to—"

"What? No, don't comply with their demands to use German currency in our country."

"It's not our country anymore. Surely, you've seen the bulletins."

"Are you expecting more of them to be shopping here?" I ask, curious as to why she's suddenly so complicit in helping them.

She shrugs. "How should I know what they have planned? If the three who purchased gloves begin to talk to the others, I can assume I might end up with more customers, right?"

"No, we should be doing whatever we can to dissuade them from coming inside, Raya. We don't want their business."

"We?" she asks. "This is my shop, and without customers I won't have the means to keep the business running."

I don't understand where this change of thought is coming from. Yesterday, she was terrified of the three soldiers coming into the shop to pick up their order. "Then, I'm not sure I understand why you are so eager to help with the attack tonight," I whisper.

Raya takes a deep breath, her shoulders rising with obvious tension. "I am doing what I can to avoid conversing with them if they are to come into the shop. There is nothing I can do to keep them out unless I hang an explicit sign on the door that says, 'Germans are not welcome,' which would entice them to make themselves so. They don't play the same way we do, Nicolas. Don't you see that? If we don't fool them into thinking we're scared and compliant with their regulations, they gain more confidence and control with the thought that they can do whatever they want without consequence. I refuse to put a target on my shop door, especially while I'm protecting—" She points toward the ceiling.

"Okay, okay, I understand. You're in a difficult situation without many options." I still don't think it's reason enough to create new price tags that include the Reichsmark next to the Franc. There's a fine line between being agreeable and giving in.

She pushes the notepad she's been writing in across the counter. "If you'd like to help, you can count the inventory. The products are all listed out on the left side. I'll start working on the signs."

There's a part of me that doesn't want to help. The price signs are a bad idea. "You know, I forgot to hand something in at work yesterday and Paul will be on my case about it with me being out of work all day. I'm going to run down there."

Raya finally looks up at me, making eye contact for the first time since I questioned the welt on her cheek. "You're leaving?"

The way her eyes shimmer, along with the croak in her voice, breaks my heart. "I won't be gone too long." Long enough that she can spend a bit more time thinking about the pricing signs while working on the inventory update.

"Oh, okay."

"Will you be alright?" I ask, worried I'm troubling her.

"I'm fine."

* * *

My heart has been racing for the last two hours, depleting me of the energy I desperately need to get through this night. I'm sweating through my dark clothes and my hands aren't steady with an assault rifle locked between my fingers.

Each quiet, dark road seems twice as long as it was, and my thoughts have been on nothing other than a German soldier or the police turning a corner and finding us trying to blend in with the opaque shadows of each building. We can hardly see where we're stepping, when a curb ends, or if there's something to trip over.

I shouldn't have agreed to this. I wanted to join the resistance because being complacent isn't an option, but fighting—combat—this isn't what I had mind. After Father died, Mère made me promise her I would never enlist in the army. I gave her my word. She told me he would not have wanted that life for me and she couldn't lose another loved one to acts of war. However, I feel as though Father would have handed me a rifle today then sent me on my way, telling me to take out as many enemies as possible. He fought to prevent the Germans capturing French territory. He always said this wasn't over, but I thought it was just his anger speaking. We can't let them win. This is what Father would be doing.

Raya's breaths are ragged and heavy behind me. I wonder if she is doing this for my sake or, if not, what else could be moti-

vating her to take action at this level. The darkness brewing
within her is sudden and fierce, and I don't understand where it
came from, but I've learned well enough that when she sets her
mind to something, nothing and no one can get in the way.

"Where are we stopping?" Raya whispers over my shoulder.

"One more block up ahead at the Myron T. Herrick statue."

The silence finds the rubble and small twigs crunching and
snapping beneath our feet. I scan both sides of the street and up
through the center of the buildings we're between. I don't want
to miss a lurking set of eyes watching us. I can't see too far up
the building with how dark it is, but the feeling of being
watched like mice running toward a trap gnaws at my stomach.

* * *

There's little conversation between our group, just a plan in our
heads of where we are to go at what exact minute. Then we will
wait for our target and pull our triggers faster than they can.

Raya doesn't seem as nervous as I would expect her to be,
especially while holding an MP-40 submachine gun—or any
gun—for the first time in her life. Instead, she looks confident
and comfortable with her decision to be here, expecting the
unexpected.

"Do you remember everything I showed you earlier on how
to hold and reload?" I whisper.

"Yes," she says peering down at the weapon pinned
between her arm and side. "To reload, I insert the magazine,
pull back the bolt, then pull the trigger."

"What about your aim?"

She huffs through a stammering breath. "I've got it. I
remember everything you said. Don't worry."

I ignore her statement and repeat what I told her earlier, for
my own sanity. "Until the target is in the center of your view,
don't pull the trigger. Stay behind a wall while reloading the

magazines, and keep your body concealed as much as possible while shooting. If you panic, move behind the wall, and don't start up again until you've regained your confidence." I taught her a lot in a short amount of time, and she was acting a bit sour while we were going over it all. She has me worried but maybe she'll feel better after this is over with.

"Okay," she says, her eyes wide and assuring.

"Stay near me if you can," I tell her as we cross the street, heading in our assigned direction to one of the four corners that faces the hotel. We will spread out when we arrive. Hugo is pulling the fire alarm inside since he's the only one who knows exactly where it's located. It should be loud enough for us to hear from the outside of the building.

Once we reach the statue, I peer at my watch, struggling to see the time in the gloom.

Within seconds, the muffled fire alarm clatters like a school bell, chiming in a pattern, repetitively.

"Get down, get down," I tell everyone. "Take cover behind the cars and wait until you spot the targets."

A minute passes then the front doors open, releasing a louder ring to float through the air. I grab Raya's arm and pull her next to me behind a Volkswagen. The larger vehicles are closer to the front doors and I'm not bringing her up that far.

I'm out of breath even though we've been fairly still for the last couple of minutes. I can hear my pulse drumming in my head and throbbing throughout every limb of my body. I try to avoid swallowing too hard, knowing it might be louder than the blood pumping through my veins. The front doors of the hotel swing back and forth, releasing small groups of people each time, most of whom are civilians.

Several long moments pass before there is a loud commotion of babble, laughter, and hollering. It's clear the officers are as intoxicated as we hoped. We discussed waiting until a group of them had gathered outside before pulling the first trigger.

Now, each second feels like a long minute and I'm not sure if I'm waiting for my gut to tell me to fire or if I'm waiting until someone else fires first.

I glance over at Raya once more before we start something I know we can't undo later. She's focused intently on the front door and the crowd, her eyes zoned in on the target as if she was born to be present in this very moment. I wish I had what looks to be an ounce of her confidence.

I'm not sure why I'm shaking to my core right now. This is what we need—this is for us and our country, our freedom, and rights. This is for Father who sacrificed his body for this country. It's for everything.

Men in brown uniforms pile out of the doors, creating a larger gathering than I expected.

"Ready?" Raya asks.

I hold my hand out in front of her, an instinctive move I can't explain. "Wait." I'm still not sure why we're waiting. We shouldn't be. We should all be firing our weapons right now.

Upon my hesitation, the first shots fire, and more follow. The street lights up like fireworks around a smoke pit. People are screaming and I can't tell if they are civilians, our people, or German officers—a scream is a scream no matter the language.

"Let's go. Why are we waiting?" Raya asks. There is no worry in her voice despite so much chaos around us.

"No," I tell her. "It's a bloodbath."

She pushes my arm away and moves to the next car to retake her aim, ignoring my words as if I don't know what I'm saying. Adrenaline must be pumping through her veins. My knees shake as I make my way over to her and I feel like a coward. As I reset my sights on the cluster of chaos, I spot a uniformed body drop. Blood pools out from the back of his head onto the street. His eyes are open, staring into the sky. He's dead.

Bullets are flying in every direction, making it clear the

officers are retaliating. I'm having trouble spotting moving uniforms and I have to keep blinking to clear my vision. I'm not sure if Raya has fired her weapon but her finger is curled around the trigger, her fingertip turning white against the pressure she's maintaining. I'm not even sure if I've fired mine.

What's wrong with me? I can't get myself together.

"Nicolas, behind you!" Raya shouts.

The barrel of a rifle is pointed in our direction and it's all the motivation I need to pull Raya to her feet and push her forward, shielding her body with mine. I pull her in front of a car, far too close to the action, but out of sight from whoever was aiming for us. I push her beneath the car, her rifle clattering against the road as she moves. I slide in next to her and wrap my arms over her to protect her in any way I can. I put us in this situation. I shouldn't have told her I was doing this tonight. It would have been safer for us both.

A soldier creeps by the car, holding out his weapon, ready to fire when he spots us. He spins around, searching in every direction and my heart is beating in my throat. Raya whimpers and I'm forced to place my hand over her mouth, feeling her tears fall over the side of my knuckles. The soldier moves on, checking out the next narrow alley adjacent to this road.

"We need to move, roll out and run. Okay?"

She nods her head within my hold, and I release her, following as closely behind her as I can. We remain crouched as we make a run for the statue, moving out of visibility from the hotel. Sirens hum in the distance, which means more backup has been called in for the Germans.

"Ruée!" Hugo's voice is a stake to my chest.

"Hugo." I stop and turn to see where he's yelling from.

Raya joins me, keeping her weapon pointed at the scene before we're completely out of sight. I don't see Hugo. We're not supposed to go back for another for the sake of salvaging the lives of those who will fight to recoup this country into the right hands.

"Come on, come on, we need to go," I say. "He'll be okay."

She doesn't move or loosen the grip of her finger.

"Raya."

"Wait," she snaps in a whisper. "He must be here," she mutters.

"No, Hugo isn't over there. We need to go." I'm not sure she even knows what Hugo looks like as she's only heard stories about him from me.

"Not Hugo," she replies calmly.

"Who?" I ask.

She whips her head around as if I pulled her out of some kind of trance.

"Who are you looking for?"

She stares into my eyes for what seems like a minute too long and I notice that she releases the rifle from her grip and stands up. "I don't know," she says as more tears form in her eyes.

"Let's go," I tell her, wrapping my hand around her arm and pulling. "We can't go back to your flat right now. We don't know who has their eyes on us."

She tugs away from my grip but remains by my side as we run as far away from the center of the city as we can before we need to catch our breath. We continue to sprint without a destination and I'm not sure where we can run where there won't be soldiers speculating if we were a part of the incitements, especially with visible weapons on us. We need to hide and wait this out.

"This way." I lead us toward the newspaper's building, pulling out the key to the back door.

My lungs burn as the sight of my office rises above the horizon and my legs each feel like they weigh more than my entire body. When we are secured inside the metal door of the building I drop to the ground on my knees and wrap my arms around the back of my head. How did I get here? To this place I never wanted to be?

Raya kneels beside me and wraps her arms around my back. "It's okay. We're okay."

I shake my head. "I'm not. I'm worthless. I couldn't do a thing out there except freeze up and stare at those murderers."

Raya places her hand on the back of my head. "Look at me," she says.

I lift my head, my temples pulsating and my eyes burning. "I'm a coward."

"A coward is someone who kills because they can't get their way. A coward takes what they want because they can't have it any other way. You are not a coward. You are anything but that." She scoots in front of me and places her warm hands on my cheeks. "We're okay." Her arms loop around the back of my neck and I fall weak into her hold as she touches her lips to mine. "We're okay. As long as we have each other, nothing else matters."

I nod to agree silently because if I open my mouth to talk, I'm not sure what will come out. But a few minutes later I say, "I don't know what happened. I froze."

"I did too," she says. "Three Germans stopped in front of my sights. I couldn't pull the trigger. They're torturing people every day and we don't have what it takes to retaliate."

"You're too good for that," I mutter.

"We both are," she says.

"I should have my head examined for even telling you what we'd planned on doing."

"Nicolas," she says, giving me a look like my words are stealing something from her, something she wants to take back and hold tightly to herself. I'm suddenly afraid I'm causing her life's destruction, and I wish I had seen it sooner.

TWENTY-FOUR

RAYA

Ravensbrück, Germany

The sound of our feet crunching against a thin sheet of ice left from last night's snow adds a layer of static around the thoughts that swim around in my head like fish in a small tank, going back and forth all day. The mud beneath the ice is frozen and unforgiving, sending slivers of cold up through the centers of my soles. I would do anything for a pair of boots. The walk to the textile factory takes us past every row of white stone barracks then up to the camp's encasing brick wall that separates us from the Schwedtsee Lake. The last leg of our trek is through a barren field with a line of trees wallowing over our heads like a tunnel, eventually dumping us at the foreboding bar-crossed windowed factory where we spend all our daylight hours. The distance has become unbearable in the mornings and even worse, eleven hours later, on the way back to the barracks in the evening after sunset. What may be less than a kilometer takes us nearly three-quarters of an hour with how slow we move.

I've never been much of a complainer, more of a problem

solver, and if I did have something irking me, I would keep it to myself, which has come in handy while being here. There is no one to express my agony to because we all feel the same. Sometimes I allow myself to wallow along the walk, enduring the pity I feel for myself, but other times, I stare up at the trees peeking over the tall walls and imagine they are the same trees that stretch out of the gates along the Luxemburg Gardens. Until now, I never wondered how the trees on the inside of the gates might feel, only being able to watch the world walk past them each day.

Gunshots fire in the distance and my heart palpates in response. My stomach caves in and I press my fists against my chest while searching in every vacant direction for where the blasts are coming from. More shots are fired and this time I can tell the rumbles are growing from behind us at the barracks. A low hum of questions arises between the line of women in front of and behind me.

"Keep moving," the guard shouts, his words landing on my cheek through a hot fog, waving us forward to continue moving as he blows his whistle to accompany his command. The stale scent of tobacco singes the inside of my nose and I see Gustav's face in front of me, snarling. My heart pounds tirelessly, weakening my muscles as I fight to push the image out of my mind.

"What's happening?" one of the women asks. I would never ask a guard a question. Their answers are not anything anyone wants to hear and that's only if they choose to respond at all.

"French women like many of you—the resistance leaders— have finally been convicted for their crimes of infiltration and obstruction of the Vichy French government and the Third Reich. Execution is their punishment. We plan to find all of those who were vices of political corruption." The guard snickers and blows his whistle again. They live to instill the feeling of uncertainty when it comes to taking our next breath. I wish I didn't fall into their brainwashing trap, but they mean what they say, if they say anything before their actions. Not even a warning seems fit for those they plan to plunder from. What they want, they get, and if we argue, the consequence will be far worse than a simple shot to the head.

I'm quite sure I'll never step foot outside of these gates or reunite with my love. I may never know what became of Charlette and will never have the chance to tell Alix he was right—I should have gone with him. For not listening to his plea, I will be the one who leaves him alone in this world without a family. Alix must be distraught, having gone so long without a response to the letters I'm sure he's continued to send me. I fear he'll be foolish and set out to find me, breaking through country barriers, possibly finding himself in more trouble than I'm in. I wish I could tell him to stay where he is and not worry, but he would do the exact opposite if he knew for certain where I was.

Every decision I have made over the last few years, while seemingly selfless at the time, has led me here, and though this is my punishment, the ones I love will suffer the greatest. The leather shop was a place I treated as a person, a part of my family, the souls of my parents, and for that, I have given up everything else for the sake of offering others more than I can give. I couldn't even protect Charlette and her parents, despite my promise. I made so many promises. I've broken them all and it was never my intention.

For the remainder of our walk, gunshots continue to fire into the air and each pop feels like a fist pounding against my chest, knowing the only crime these women committed was being braver than others and standing up for the rights of every French person.

TWENTY-FIVE

RAYA
LAST YEAR, DECEMBER 1942

Paris, France

While sitting on the edge of my bed, tapping my hands on my knees, I stare at the open jewelry box housing a still ballerina on top of my bureau and wonder how so many years have passed since my tenth birthday when Mère gave me the beloved gift. Of course, it holds very little jewelry these days. I also wonder why Nicolas has stopped visiting me before work in the mornings. It's as if he knows about the something that I'm currently in denial about.

The last few weeks, he's said he's been too busy, which doesn't make much sense since he said there's hardly anything to write about and even less to publish in the paper. My assumption is that he's avoiding me, or maybe I pushed him away with my behavior. I don't want to be touched. I don't want to be held. I don't want him breathing too close to me and I can't tell him why. I wish the memories of Gustav would go away, but I fear more than anything that I will have to live with them for the rest of my life, torturously alone.

Nicolas and I see each other at night but not for too long

since he has many meetings in the tunnels. The Germans are on the hunt for the resistance groups who took part in the ambush last month, so he said they need to make sure they are prepared to face them at any given moment. I've decided to stay upstairs during the meetings, feeling guilty for the stress I must have added the night in front of the hotel. But retaliation was all I had on my mind.

If he knew the truth of what I've been through, I'm not sure if it would push us further apart or close the gap growing between us. Worse, if my appointment confirms my fears I will lose him and I don't want that. I want a say in what happens with us, but that's been taken from me. I love him. He's my one, the only one out there for me, but as the seconds carry me closer to the top of the hour, I feel him slipping away. In my heart, I must already know the truth.

With one look outside the window, I can see the blustery chill is creeping in for the season, so I lift my wool coat from the rack behind my bedroom door and slip my feet into my oxfords, tightening the laces before heading out of the flat. There's a stillness upstairs, which offers me relief, as I've been worried about the cold seeping in through the walls where they are, but they haven't complained, and if they were cold and uncomfortable I believe I would hear them moving around more than they are.

I didn't want to have to explain my whereabouts to anyone this morning anyway, so it works out for the best that they're still asleep and Nicolas didn't show up.

A pre-wrapped slice of bread is on the kitchen table where I left it last night, knowing I wouldn't sit down to eat before leaving. I slip it into my pocket and head out of the building through the back entrance, avoiding Monsieur Croix who will be asking why I'm not opening the shop on time and where I'm going. Privacy seems to be a rare possession for me lately.

As expected, the wind is lowering the air's temperature by several degrees, and I wish I had taken a scarf with me. I pull my gloves out of my pocket, slip them on, and wrap my arms around my torso as I stay close to the storefronts while making my way down the seven long blocks against the growing wind.

I notice two German soldiers walking on the opposite side of the street and my heart bucks as I stare toward the cobblestone walkway, praying silently they don't spot me and request my papers. They search for weakness in a pair of eyes, along with the slim frame of someone they can take down easily. I wonder if now there is a target on my back to tell the others I won't fight back. I wish I had been able to retaliate, save myself somehow. But I was frozen, helpless beneath his weight.

My thoughts seem to carry me past the soldiers and I am out of sight when I turn the corner toward the small brick building nestled in behind a few old overhanging trees. In front of the building's main entrance, a tornado of leaves dances in a spiral pattern, lightly fluttering across the stone.

I struggle to fill my lungs as I walk through the small lobby, peeling off my gloves while taking in the worn pale-yellow color of the walls, disliking the contrast between them and the dark rickety old floors as I always have. Fumes of rubbing alcohol fill the air and I approach the front desk, feeling every muscle in my body tense for the second time this week. "Good morning, I'm Raya Pascal. I have a nine-fifteen appointment."

The woman behind the front desk stares at me for a long minute, almost as if she's trying to read the thoughts brewing in my head. "Welcome back. If you could have a seat," she says, pointing to the few wooden chairs against the wall behind me, "we won't keep you waiting long."

As I'm choosing which of the three identical chairs to sit in, the door next to the front desk opens. "Madame Pascal, we can take you back now," the woman from the front desk says. She must be working the job of two people here, which isn't surprising.

"Mademoiselle," I say, correcting her again for the second time this week.

"Oh, that's right...I apologize. Follow me, please."

The many times I've been here over the years, before this week, the lobby was crowded, and the hallway doors were always closed. Now they're all open and empty. The woman stops in front of an open door and waves her arm to the right, gesturing for me to walk inside. "It will be another minute or so. Make yourself comfortable."

"Thank you," I say, watching her reach for the door, her wool suit jacket tugging away from her wrists as she closes me into a tight space, alone with my unstable mind. I pull the upholstered gray-blue and pink-blossom patterned chair away from the chestnut desk. I shrug out of my coat and fold it neatly to drape over my lap then rest my purse on top of the pile as I sink into the seat. The walls are bare but there are a few framed photographs on the desk I can only see the backs of.

When the door opens, I clench my hands together, feeling my ears burn with apprehension.

"Good morning, Raya," Dr. Aubert says. "What a treat to see you twice in one week."

I'm not sure this is as much of a treat for me as it might be for him.

"I assume you only called me back in for one reason," I say, staring at my unpolished nails. I couldn't force a smile even if I tried. A call to come back into an office can only mean bad news.

"Well, I suppose that depends on the type of news you're hoping for," he says, taking his seat across from me while simultaneously placing a yellow folder, one that matches the walls in the lobby, on top of the desk.

"The kind of news where there is no news," I say, the sound of my voice faltering with the last word of my statement.

Dr. Aubert folds his hands over the yellow folder and

straightens his shoulders. "I see. Well, the test came back positive. Raya, I can confirm that you are pregnant."

My lungs give out. I can't breathe. My body is a slate of stone, cold, lonely, paralyzed from the effects of the world around me. "No," I whisper. As if I haven't taken a breath in minutes, I gasp for air to fill my lungs and I clutch the collar of my blouse. "I can't." I heave, in and out, as a wave of dizziness spins my brain like a top.

"Raya," Dr. Aubert utters my name. "I'll get you some water." He stands from his seat and scurries out of his office, returning just a few seconds later. He holds the cup above my lap, waiting for me to take it from him.

But I can't lift my arms. Hot tears burn the backs of my eyes before spilling out and down my cheeks. I can't see my future. It's all dark. This can't be happening.

"Raya, I need you to take a deep breath for me," Dr. Aubert says. "In, and out." He shows me how to breathe properly as if I've forgotten how to instinctively keep myself alive.

Oxygen won't help me now.

My body breaks free of the internal restraint, and I lift my coat off my lap, preparing to slip it over my shoulders. My forehead feels like it's melting over my eyebrows as I continue to stare straight through the wall behind the doctor's desk.

"I can't," I say again, pushing myself to my feet, praying my knees lock well enough to keep me upright.

Dr. Aubert swallows hard. "Uh—Raya, have you spoken about this possibility with the—the—uh—father of the child?" His question comes out hoarse, forcing him to clear his throat.

My heart lurches against my chest like a slamming door. "That man will never know," I mutter.

Dr. Aubert places the cup of water on his desk and returns to his seat. He puts his palms over the folder. "Without knowing much of your personal life, I just want to say that it's common for a father not to be ready for such a commitment until they see their child for the first time. If you're worried that he might not be ready—"

My eyes blur behind the film of tears and heat rages through my cheeks, "Dr. Aubert, your thoughts are misguided." I press my lips together and clench my jaw, trying to contain the sobs lurching up my throat. I cover my mouth as if I can physically contain my agony.

"I shouldn't have said anything. I apologize," he says, dropping his gaze to his desk. "It's—It's just that I'm unable to offer you any other options—it wouldn't end well for either of us, as I'm sure you're aware."

Because ending a pregnancy could result in capital punishment, despite the nature of the situation.

I shake my head. "I under—understand." I fold my arms over my chest and pinch my fingernails into the flesh of my arms.

"Switzerland might be an option to consider. I could give you the name—"

Alix is in Switzerland. I was meant to stay with him, by his side. Maybe he didn't need me but I needed him. I tried to do what was best for him, it's all I wanted. Why am I being punished for trying to do right by him?

"I couldn't get to Switzerland." I know Alix has tried to come home several times, it was impossible.

"I will write you a note for a different reason. It could help you cross the border."

"I couldn't afford that but thank you for your offer," I say, reaching my shaking hand into my purse for a handkerchief.

Dr. Aubert opens his desk drawer and retrieves a paper brochure and slides it across his desk. "Here are some tips that might help you throughout the duration of your pregnancy. I'll want to see you again in about two months unless you experience any unusual side effects or pains before then." He doesn't make eye contact with me as he recites what must be his usual mantra following a positive pregnancy test.

I take the brochure from his desk and fold it in half to place inside my purse. "Okay."

I want to tell him this wasn't my choice and that I was saving myself for marriage to ensure something like this didn't happen before I was ready, but that option was taken away from me, leaving me to face a life I'm not sure I can manage on my own, but telling him such a thing wouldn't do either of us any good. I'm sure it's not difficult to assume.

* * *

I've lost track of time when I return to my flat. The shop is still closed and I'm not sure I have the will to open it today.

"Raya?" Charlette calls out, my name hitching in her throat. I forgot she didn't know I'd left or didn't open the shop. She's working on the couple of repairs we've gotten over the last week.

I toss my coat onto my bed and make my way down the short hallway to Alix's bedroom where Charlette's working. "Sorry, I didn't mean to startle you."

"I was making sure it was you," she says, curling a smile to one side. "Why are you up here and not in the shop?" I don't normally come upstairs during the day because I would need to lock up first.

"I had an appointment this morning. I thought I mentioned it..." I know I haven't said a word. She only knows I went the other day because I was experiencing dizzy spells, even after eating. I wanted to make sure my blood sugar levels were okay, but after a thread of questions Dr. Aubert asked me, my thoughts shifted to another possibility, one I didn't want to fathom.

Charlette lifts her foot off the pressure pedal of the sewing machine and rests her arms over the top. "You had an appointment a few days ago," she says. "Is everything okay?"

"I'm fin—"

"No," Charlette says. "Don't try that on me."

"Try what?" I ask.

"'I'm fine,'" she mocks me. "Do you know that Nicolas told me that he has a rule about not asking you what's truly wrong unless you say you're fine three times in one conversation?"

"What do you mean?" I ask, trying not to feel the emotional pull in my chest upon hearing his name while I'm juggling so many other thoughts.

"I think he knows you're lying the first time you say it, but he tries not to pressure you into confessing what's wrong until you're good and ready, and by the third 'I'm fine,' he considers you to be good and ready. He thinks it's adorable, which is why he told me, but you should assume he knows."

I can't help but laugh, knowing that sounds like something Nicolas would say and think. Of course, I'm not sure that matters anymore. Even if I didn't want to receive the news I did until I was married, I'm not sure about anything with us.

"He's been distant," I tell her.

"I've noticed," she says. "I think we all deal with our surroundings at different times in different ways. I'm not sure I would assume it has something to do with you." She's only saying that because friends try to make each other feel better. "Now, what was the appointment for?"

I try to swallow against my dry throat and end up coughing instead then press my hand against my chest. "There's no easy way to say this," I begin.

"Is it your blood sugar levels? There are ways to make it better. I know for a fact."

I shake my head to say no. "I'm—I'm..." I take in a shallow gulp of air and look into her eyes like I did on the first day we became friends, the day I told her my father died. "I'm pregnant."

"Oh dear," she says, standing up behind the sewing machine and coming around to wrap her arms around me and hold me tight. "I didn't know you and Nicolas—is that why he's been distant?"

A sob erupts in my throat. I cover my hand over my mouth and rest my head on her shoulder. "No, that's not why he's been distant," I cry out. "We haven't—I mean, he's not the father."

Charlette's grip loosens and she takes a step back, almost as if she needs space to breathe. "What do you mean?"

My face burns and my head throbs as tears continue to stream down the sides of my nose. "One of the German soldiers came into the shop last month to pick up the order of gloves... He locked us in the store and..."

"No, no, no," Charlette says, holding her hand over her mouth to match mine. Her eyes fill with tears and her skin becomes a deep shade of red. "Raya."

"I didn't want to talk about it. I thought if I didn't say anything, the memory—the horror of that day—would go away, but now I know I'll never forget." The words coming out of my mouth are so awful, I can't believe they are mine.

"You should have told me," she says, gritting her teeth.

"I know," I peep.

She throws her arms back around me and pulls me over to the bed, sitting us both down. "Nicolas doesn't know either, does he?"

"No, he'd try to kill him and then..."

"I understand."

"He can't find out, Charlette. He must already sense something has come between us and that's why he hasn't been acting like himself. No matter if I tell him or not, the outcome will be the same, and to know that..." I gulp. "My heart is broken. It's broken so badly it hurts to breathe."

TWENTY-SIX

NICOLAS

Paris, France

There are times when I forget who I am, why I'm standing in a particular spot, what I've been doing that led me to this point and place, and where I'll go from here. I should know these answers, but it's like a fog rolls in and blankets my thoughts, leaving me to stare mindlessly into the distance until I can reconnect my pieces. I haven't slept in days. I've been searching every corner of this city for Hugo. All of us were accounted for after last month's mission. We all escaped unscathed, which is more than I can say for the German commanders who piled out into the street that night. We made a dent, but it wasn't enough. All it did was light a flame in a box of dynamite.

Hugo hasn't shown up for a meeting in two and a half weeks, and neither has Bette. I've waited for him outside of his family's bread shop every morning, hoping someone would turn on the lights, but the shop has remained dark. At night, I've thrown small stones at the windows above the shop, hoping someone would come to the door. I've seen a flicker of a light and the subtle movement of a swinging curtain, but no one will come downstairs to talk to me.

I've been standing behind the newspaper's office and the bread shop for hours, waiting for someone to go in or out of that door. Hugo wouldn't abandon ship like this, which means something's wrong. I'm cold to the bone and my ears feel as if they might snap off every time a gust of wind whips me in the face.

I consider going back into the office, but I keep telling myself to wait another few minutes. As I'm tugging at the collar of my coat to cover more of my neck, I spot the door to the bread shop crack open, or maybe I'm imagining it after staring for so long. With a couple of quiet steps in the direction of the door, I wait to see if it will open more.

A head pops out and Bette spots me. Her eyes close and I'm sure she sighs before stepping out. "What are you doing here?" she calls in a loud whisper.

I hold my hands out to the side. "Do you have any idea how worried was when neither of you showed up to the meetings? Where have you been? Where's Hugo?" My questions come one after another like rapid fire as I approach her.

The wind whooshes at her hair and coat and she wraps her arms around her torso to withstand the cold temperatures. "You shouldn't be here," she says.

"I work next door. Have you forgotten?"

"No," she says, her hazelnut-brown wavy hair falling back into its natural state over her shoulders. She looks around as if she's anxious for what she might find in this back alley lined with dumpsters and dozens of pigeons pecking around. I'm close enough for her to continue whispering and hear what she has to say. "He's been captured."

The words ring in my ears like the faint sound that muffles everything else after a gunshot is fired. "How—what, how do you know?" My breaths quicken, the proof being the puffs of fog rolling out of my mouth.

"I watched," she says, gritting her teeth and clenching her eyes. "There was a roundup of Jewish people by military vehicles. He noticed someone waving for help from the back of the wagon. We heard cries and pleas. Hugo snapped and told me to leave, to hide. I begged him not to do whatever he was about to do but he didn't stop. He shot two of the four German drivers before he was restrained. I don't know where they took him or if he's even still—" Bette inhales sharply, forcing a face of unnecessary bravery. "My parents won't talk, eat, and hardly move. They're devastated and terrified, as am I."

My mouth becomes so dry I'm not sure I can form a word on my tongue and my head swells with pain. Why would he do something like this by himself, without any backup? I pull Bette into my arms, feeling her quiver against me. I'm not sure how much Bette knows about what the Germans do to any member of the resistance if they're caught, but it's best if she doesn't. I, on the other hand, find it too easy to imagine what Hugo might be going through or has gone through—the stories we've heard— I wish they were just tales of a nightmare someone experienced. But considering the rest of us are still alive and well, means he didn't give up any information. He's either their prisoner or dead. "He shouldn't have—"

"You don't have to tell me. You know Hugo...there's no talking him down when he has his mind set on something."

"He is a man of his own mind," I agree.

"All we can do is pray for him."

"Of course," I say, nearly biting off my tongue to keep myself composed for her sake.

"I won't be joining any more meetings."

"I understand. But listen, Bette, if you hear anything of his whereabouts, you need to tell me what you know because if I can do anything to help him, I will." Most likely, she won't find much out. There isn't a public list of prisoners who are being integrated or deported, but I feel helpless not knowing where to even look for him, as I'm sure she and her parents are feeling too.

"I will. Please be safe and take care of yourself," she says, dropping her head, her hair falling to the side of her face as she hurries back toward the shop.

The fog floating around in my head clears for a moment, making room for every possible emotion to flood through me at once. I must do something. There has to be a way to find him.

Before the fog resettles, I make a beeline toward Raya's shop. I have to talk to her. I've been so preoccupied searching for Hugo, hiding the fact that he's missing, and trying to keep the group moving forward with our next set of plans, we haven't had much time together.

When I arrive at the shop, I find the "closed" sign still hanging in the glass window between the drape she keeps lowered at night. Raya has never opened the shop late in the time I've known her. The sweat soaking through my clothes from my overactive nerves and jolt across the district stings against the cold air and turns to ice as I run for the back door, digging into my pocket for the key. My hand trembles uncontrollably as I try to get the key into the lock. I wrap my opposite hand around the doorknob and press against the metal until the key slips into the hole. I barrel up the stairs, thankful to hear voices rather than silence.

"Raya?" I call out, peeking into her bedroom first but finding nothing but her perfectly made bed.

She steps out of Alix's bedroom, perplexity illuminating her face. "What are you doing here?"

"Hugo's been captured," I blurt out before I even ask why she hasn't opened the shop. All I know is I see her standing in one piece and I can't control myself from exhaling my pain as I reach for her, needing her.

She complies but with what feels like reluctance. "Nicolas," she says, "what do you mean he's been captured? We all made it out. There hasn't been a mission since, has there?"

I try to catch my breath that I've managed to forget about needing for the last twenty minutes. "He went on his own. I don't know. I—I'm not sure why he would—he was caught after taking down two soldiers. I had been looking for him, but instead, found Bette. She told me."

Raya draws me in closer and wraps her arms around my body. "I'm so sorry," she says. "I didn't know that's what you've been so busy doing. I would have helped you look for him."

With a step backward to pull myself together, I lean against the wall and rest my head back. "I have a bad feeling." I pulse my shirt away from my sweat-covered chest, needing more air. "I think they've killed him by now. They wouldn't spare him after killing two soldiers. They've taken lives for far less."

She doesn't respond, just takes my free hand, and holds it between hers. The silence is a form of agreement with my thoughts. Where she might typically be optimistic in dire situations, she'd know not to give me false hope too.

Charlette slips out of Alix's bedroom. I didn't consider the thought that she was in there. "Pardon me," she says, shimmying behind Raya to head for the hole in the wall. "I wasn't listening to anything you said."

When Charlette is out of sight, Raya leads me to the kitchen table and slides out a chair for me. I take a seat and rest my arms on the table.

"You are all getting in deep," she says, "and I understand the feeling. I also know you aren't going to rest until you have answers, which worries me more than anything." Raya places her hands on top of my arms, stroking her thumb back and forth across my hot skin. "They won't hesitate to do the same thing to you. There is only one of you."

"I won't find him," I say. "I may never know where he is, if he is...All I know is I'm not sure how much more I can take and continue peacefully passing these masochists without engaging. None of them deserve the air they're breathing." Rage boils my blood and the desire to go hunt down every Nazi in this city is making me feel like I'm losing the ability to control myself.

"I know, but you do deserve to breathe that air, and it would take less than one wrong move to endanger yourself."

"I know," I tell her, "you're right. I'm sorry for being so distant lately. I haven't been able to think straight while wondering what happened to him."

"I understand," she says, lifting her hands off my arms and pulling them onto her lap. "I've been distant too."

I've been so consumed with Hugo that I'd convinced myself Raya was dealing with the aftermath of the raid. The guilt for taking her along with me is still eating me up inside and it's been easier to avoid the topic than to rehash that nightmare. "I noticed, but being at the forefront of an assault, watching what we did, then running for our lives after, it can haunt people."

"It isn't because of the raid," she says, her gaze following her hands to her lap.

I want to tell her to just tell me what's going on because I don't have it in me to beg. I just need to know. Everything with her takes time though and if I push too hard, she'll pull away. "Does it have something to do with the shop? Is that why it isn't open right now?"

"I had a doctor's appointment this morning." Her cheeks burn red, and she squeezes her hands together so tightly her fingers become white.

"Another one? You went the other day. You said your blood sugar level was okay."

"It is—but, I'm pregnant."

Her words crash through my head as a sense of puzzlement disorients me. "That's imposs—" Without a second thought, I push myself and the chair away from the table, distancing myself from her.

"It's not what you think..." she says, sniffling. Her chin quivers and her dimples deepen as she fights the urge to cry, but nevertheless, tears break free from her eyes. "Please, believe me."

I stand and wrench my hands around the back of my neck, feeling the searing heat rise within my body. My stomach burns and acid rises in my throat. How could she do this? Why? She's the one who wanted to wait until we were married. I never argued. I've respected her in every way possible. "What am I supposed to think?" I croak out. "Raya, I know the baby isn't mine, so whose is it?" As if my heart didn't already feel like it has shattered into a million pieces today, she's been disloyal to me. The one person I was positive I could trust and count on has betrayed me. The thought of her doing something like that never crossed my mind, not once. Not Raya. She wouldn't do that to me.

But she did.

She can't even look at me. Her gaze, full of heavy tears, is frozen as she stares toward her lap, still squeezing her hands together as tightly as she can. "I love you," she says. "I love you so much. I never wanted things to turn out this way."

"No, you don't love me. How can you say that? I trusted you, Raya. I thought we were going to spend the rest of our lives together." My throat tightens and tears find my eyes too, bringing me to an emotional state I rarely share with anyone. I sniffle and take in as much air as I can. "I've already seen so much of what life can do to a person—knowing my father killed himself because I wasn't enough of a reason to live. He killed himself, Raya. It was his decision to die, and he left me with his scars, with his unfinished business." I gasp, trying to catch my breath. "I've endured that godawful pain for years, but this—" I swallow hard against my swollen throat, shaking my head at her. "But this...I put my everything into what we have together. The instant I laid eyes on you, I knew you were different—someone I couldn't walk past. I just knew. It looks like I can't even trust my own gut anymore. That lies to me too."

"Please—" she cries out. "I need you to understand something. Please. Just—wait."

"Who is he?" I grunt through gritted teeth.

She inhales sharply and holds her breath, her eyes bulging as web veins streak across the whites of her irises.

"Well? Spit it out!"

"I can't," she cries.

She has torn my heart out and she can't tell me the damn truth.

"Never mind," I say, curling my fists by my sides. "I don't want to know. Good luck to the two of you." I can't get myself to face her. It's best if I leave before I say something I might regret.

"Nicolas, no, no, please don't go, please...I'm begging you to stay. I can't be without you. I can't live without you. I need you."

"How could you say any of this after you betrayed me? I wanted to ask you to marry me, and I wanted us to have a family together. I wanted to have children with you. I could picture us with a baby, but not like this. It doesn't even matter, does it? No, you know what—" I hold up my hand because I don't want to know. "I don't want an answer. Goodbye, Raya. God, I wish things could have been different. I do." I jog down the stairwell and fly out the back door before I have to endure another word from her.

TWENTY-SEVEN
RAYA
LAST YEAR, DECEMBER 1942

Paris, France

I've never imagined one could feel so hollow and lifeless when carrying a life. With the slamming of the back door downstairs sealing the end to what I thought would be a forever with Nicolas, my body shakes as a heavy weight pushes my shoulders down, making it hard to move across the kitchen to my bedroom. My feet drag and scuffle across the floor until I reach the windowsill in my room and rest the side of my head on top of my crossed arms. Through a steady stream of tears, I peer out over the skyline, the rooftops with smoking chimneys, and snowflakes falling solemnly over the dried leaves layered along the awning just below my window. If the rooftops were another world, I could run away, hop from building to building and forget about the world below. Still, the trouble will remain within me, and I don't know how to accept what will become of my future.

I climb into bed, pull the covers up to my chin and curl onto my side, wishing someone could tell me that everything will be okay. I don't see how anything could be right now.

If only Mère or Papa could give me advice; I would do anything to hear what they would say.

Without them here I must listen to my instincts, and my gut says if Nicolas were to know the truth, he would take revenge and get hurt or worse, and I cannot let that happen.

My face burns as tears continue to skate across my nose and onto my pillow. How will I love a child I was forced to have, one that will be associated with the horrors of that day a couple of months ago? How could I blame a child who had no say in the matter? Nausea rolls through me like a tidal wave, and I curl my knees up closer to my chest, wishing this pain and discomfort would subside.

I don't want my life to be like this. I don't want to be a lonely woman, raising a child alone. It's not how I pictured my life. And how can I do this on my own while keeping everyone around me safe?

TWENTY-EIGHT
RAYA
PRESENT DAY, DECEMBER 1943

Ravensbrück, Germany

The pile of pants I have hemmed today is stacked in four tall piles in an open crate behind my bench. Two guards have been moving from table to table within the textile factory this morning, inspecting every woman's uniform rather than the work she's doing. By the questioning looks in everyone's eyes, it seems no one knows what they're looking for or why. The guards glance at each number written across the badge on our chests, then peer back to their clipboards, over and over, eventually reaching our table. My heart flutters as hard as it's capable when one of the guards approaches me. He holds his pen above his paper and looks back at my number once more before grasping my wrist, my fingers pinching around a needle with thread.

"I found her," he shouts, claiming me as some sort of prize.

I push back my chair, forcing space between us. *Please, leave me alone. Don't touch me. Don't hurt me.* "There must be some mistake. I haven't done anything..." the words pour out of my mouth, defense against an unknown accusation—the most common type here.

"The glovemaker?" the other guard replies.

"Ja, Raya Pascal of Pascal Maroquinerie," the man holding my wrist says. "Wonderful, come with us." He pulls me away from the table. From the women who I've been working beside for months, with the exception of those who have unfortunately perished from starvation or illness. These are the faces I've come to recognize here and are my only form of comfort aside from the few women in the surrounding wooden bunks. They pull me out of the room and down the dismal hall to a smaller one with a sewing machine and stacks of leather. The guard thrusts me toward the chair at the machine and shoves a notepad against my chest. "Measurements and names. Make the gloves and pin the paper to the completed pair. Understood?"

"Yes," I respond, thumbing through the pages in the notepad. There appears to be hundreds.

"This is where you will work now. You produce quality gloves, and you will receive an extra ration of food every other day."

All I can wonder is if this is my ticket to staying alive or to endless days of slave labor.

TWENTY-NINE

RAYA

Paris, France

Three years feels like a lifetime ago, when I was standing in this exact place in the kitchen, handing Alix his acceptance letter to the University of Zurich. Now, I'm holding a letter from him, with what I assume to be a response to my last letter telling him I was pregnant. I didn't add details, for the same reason I forfeited my relationship with Nicolas three months ago. If I told Alix the truth, he'd find a way to come home, and would either get himself killed in the process or killed hunting down Gustav once he arrived. Charlette, Rose, and Jacques are the only ones who know how this happened. They promised to keep the information from Nicolas for the sake of his safety.

No matter what I do right for everyone else, nothing ever seems to be what's best for me. But isn't that the promise I made to Mère before she passed away? I told her I would step into her shoes and take care of everyone around me just the way she always had. I didn't know how difficult of a promise that would eventually become.

I open the letter and rest my hand on top of the growing bulge of my belly.

My dearest sister,

I'm going to kill whoever did this to you. Let that be known, first and foremost. I assume you would have told me if you decided to marry a man while I was out of the country. Therefore, I'm left questioning the details. Perhaps you've forgotten that I know you better than anyone else in the world, which includes your beliefs, morals, and values. While yours might be different from others, I'm sure about what is important to you, and having a child out of wedlock tells me there is more to this story. I would like to request that you come to Switzerland and stay with me for a bit. I'm sharing a flat with two students and we can make space for you.

Furthermore, I'm aware of the growing disaster our country is becoming, and to know you are still amid the war in all its rage gives me much to ponder before I go to sleep every night. As I mentioned in my last several letters to you, I'm uncomfortable with you staying in Paris. Our family's shop is not as important as your well-being. Please, Raya, listen to me for once, and come to Zurich. I'm quite sure your doctor would write a letter on your behalf stating the importance of you being with family during a time when you need someone to depend on. That will make traveling across the border much easier for you.

I love you dearly, sister, and the thought of you going through this without a husband is devastating me. Perhaps I misunderstood your letter and there is someone in your life that is standing beside you through this time, but my gut tells me you're alone right now.

Please take my suggestion into consideration. I know Mère

and Papa would want me to do whatever I could to take care of
you now. Let me know as soon as possible what you plan to do.
   Stay safe, sister.

With love,

Alix

I re-fold the letter and return it to the envelope, scolding myself
for not forming a lie so that he didn't suspect something was as
wrong, but I couldn't bear the thought of lying to my only living
flesh and blood. The answer is simple: there's no way I can
travel to Zurich even if I could be sure I'd make it across the
border. I don't have the funds to do so. The shop would have to
close, and of course, Charlette and her parents would be left
here alone. I couldn't abandon them.

   Alix is yet another person I'm forced to disappoint. I peer
down at my stomach and run my hand over the protrusion. I
don't know what I will tell my child when he or she is old
enough to ask why they don't have a father, or whether I will
choose to lie or not. I worry for the life he or she will have to
face either way. I've questioned the thought of giving the baby
up for adoption, but as soon as I imagined myself handing a
baby over to a stranger after spending nine months with them
growing inside of me, it seems impossible. The more weeks that
pass, the easier it becomes to tell myself that this baby is coming
into my life for a reason I may never understand, but that they
deserve a fair chance at a good life.

   "We're all brought together for unexplainable reasons, but
for all that counts and matters, you are mine, and mine alone.
There will be no trace of evil in your blood, and you will love as
you are loved, and know nothing less, my sweetheart," I whisper, hoping I'm being listened to. I have convinced myself that if

I tell the baby these strong words every single day, it will have to be the truth.

Nothing has changed within my heart; I long for Nicolas every day. There have been so many times I have kept myself from chasing him down to tell him I was not willingly unfaithful to him, nor would I have ever been, but I worry more for his well-being that accompanies the truth than the damage being inflicted on my heart.

With a glance at the wall clock, I take another sip of water from my glass and head back downstairs to finish out the workday. A lunchtime break has become a necessity and I've found it helpful to rest my feet for a half hour each afternoon. Of course, I still find it to be a pain to lock up and unlock the shop within one hour, but I know I have to take care of myself in order to take care of the baby.

I only wish being closed for the lunchtime hour meant I could avoid the newest form of customers I've inherited over the last few months. It seems Gustav and his comrades shared word of how wonderful their gloves are, and now I have German soldiers frolicking through the shop on a regular basis, placing their custom orders. I can only be thankful for the fact that the others have been leaving a monetary form of payment, which Charlette needs for Jacques, who still acquires extra rations from Nicolas. It's hard knowing they still see each other on a regular basis, and I haven't so much as spotted Nicolas. I miss him so much. I would do anything to see him. He truly did love me—it was clear by the way he smiled at me, the way he'd tilt his head to the left, just so, before leaning in to kiss me with an "I love you" whispered between my lips.

Five minutes don't pass before the shop fills with a group of soldiers. I've been ready for them lately, with my hand on the string to pull the bell, making sure the Levis know we're among unwanted company.

As usual, I close myself into the corner behind the counter, using two display racks of wallets to keep anyone from assuming I'm available for their entertainment purposes. I'm no less fearful of every one of them who steps into the shop. In fact, the same cold sweat strikes down the center of my spine every time that door opens.

Today, there's an extra measure of horror when I recognize one of the soldiers. Gustav. The urge to vomit hits me hard, so hard I reach for the trash bin, worried about being a spectacle. It's the first time he's had the nerve to step foot back into this shop, and it shouldn't be a surprise that he does so with a grin as he chats with his fellow soldiers, telling them how amazing the gloves will be for them too.

I glance down, noticing my stomach and the fact that it's becoming harder to hide, but my dark sweater will do the trick for now. I hold it together and remain still behind the register that conceals most of my body, praying Gustav leaves quietly and without any passing words.

Ice run through my bones the longer he remains within close quarters and I see flashes of his gritting teeth while he was hovering over me, piercing his manicured nails into my arms and then against my face as he used every ounce of his strength to satisfy his urge. A wave of dizziness shrouds my entire body and I reach for the chair I placed behind the counter so I can rest my feet when the shop is empty. I hold myself up by the seat's back, hoping it's enough to keep me upright. *Leave. Leave. Get out of here. Go. Please, God, don't let him hurt me again.*

My gaze fixates on the grandfather clock, wondering how long these men could possibly need to decide whether they want custom-made gloves. It's as if they're using the shop as a gathering spot rather than a place to do business. The extra time spent chatting among each other gives Gustav several opportunities to glance over, and each time I can feel his hands on me, his callouses scraping against my skin. I keep my stare set on the clock, needing to avoid eye contact. I loved that clock. It was

Papa's, given to him by his father. He told me someday it would become mine and that way, I too, *"would never miss a moment of this wonderful life."*

When I look at that clock now, I count how many times I breathe in and out within a minute, telling myself I'm still alive and survived an attack, thinking about the seconds advancing, taking me along with the time—pulling me away from the current situation.

"Nice to see you again, miss." His voice, familiar and like a serrated knife slicing down the center of my back, causes a tightening in my womb, a sensation that would concern me if I hadn't experienced it before now. The doctor assured me that the feeling is the body's way of preparing for labor. They'll become more prevalent as time progresses. It's become clear that stress can induce the reaction, though.

"Hello," I reply, simply, hoping he will take the hint that I don't intend to engage in conversation with him.

He admires me from head to toe, and I will myself to remain calm. In truth, I'm not sure what I'll do if he makes another attempt to attack me. He will find out I'm pregnant and only God knows what will happen then.

The door chimes again, another person entering the shop. This is the most people I've had inside in years and the last type of people I want here.

The tall display of wallets closing me in behind the front desk lifts from the ground and moves to the side. I clench my hands over my chest, backing up toward the wall, trying to tell myself nothing can happen while there are so many people here.

Shock strikes a nerve when I come to learn that the man closing himself into the small space with me is Nicolas.

"What are you doing here?" I ask, breathlessly.

Gustav studies Nicolas for a long second and turns to walk

away, back to his comrades enjoying their conversation among the leather goods.

"I have a delivery," he says, which could mean anything. He places his arm around me and makes a show of placing a kiss on my cheek. The warmth of his lips feels like a full body embrace, one I have longed for since the day he walked out on me. "When I walked by, I caught a glimpse of how full the shop was," he whispers in my ear.

"Thank you," I utter through a hush. "Thank you."

"Kann ich jemandem helfen, etwas zu finden?" Nicolas speaks up, pointedly offering to help anyone find what they're looking for.

They ignore him at first, but within the next few minutes of our elongated silence, they form a line at the front desk, waiting for me to take down their sizes and contact information. Nicolas remains next to me, helping by scribing the sizes as I call them out. A half hour passes by the time I'm able to get the last of them, including Gustav, out the door.

I believe in my heart Nicolas has saved me from the horrors of what could have been. "Could we talk?" I've been praying for the chance to ask him this one question for what has seemed like forever. I'm not sure what I would follow the question with, but I don't want him to leave again.

He stares into my eyes, and for a moment I think he might agree but his gaze travels down my torso, finding the swollen belly I was desperately trying to hide from the Nazis. His eyes widen with surprise, maybe trying to comprehend how much can change in a few months.

"I—I don't think it's a good idea, but—Raya, is—whoever you—whoever the father is, has he been around to help you?" The pain written along his face is evident and for Nicolas to struggle with words is all telling.

I wish I had something better to say if not the truth, but I love him far too much to strike a match and set him free on a hunt after Gustav. He will end up like Hugo, wherever that may be. "No, there is no one else in my life."

"But at one point, there was someone else other than me. You can't deny this fact. There's just no one way around it."

I close my eyes, wishing I could change all of this with a simple response. "No. You have always been the only one."

"Well, clearly that isn't the case," he says, gesturing to my stomach. "This doesn't just happen."

"No, it doesn't," I agree, wishing he could consider that this may not have been my decision, and I am simply choosing not to tell him any more for the sake of protecting him.

"Then how? How did it happen?"

The ticks and tocks from the clock grow louder, reminding me of the one sound I tried to focus on during the long minutes I thought I was going to die. I close my eyes and place my hands on my stomach. *It was against my will.* "It—" my breath shutters. "It just happened."

"Raya," he says, his voice so low it sounds like a growl. "Did someone hurt you?"

I open my eyes and look up into his, anger staining his face red. Can he read the truth in me? Would he believe it over the words I speak?

"Well? Tell me, Raya. I'll hunt the bastard down and—"

Just as I knew he would. "No," I say, the word so short, quickly spoken, and filled with an eternity of lies.

"Thank God," he says, exhaling a ragged breath. "I didn't think you would consider keeping something of that nature from me. I'm grateful that wasn't the case. Very grateful. And I'll hate myself for saying this later, but I still love you more than anything in this world. That will never change. Regardless of my feelings, you should find the father of your child and make him do what's right. You deserve that much."

"That won't happen," I cry out. "Ever."

"Why?" He shrugs and twists away so he doesn't have to keep looking at me.

"It just won't. I love you, no one else. I will always only love you, no matter what you want to believe."

"You speak in riddles, Raya. None of this makes any sense. You won't give me any real answers, and I can't just stand here and accept that. I'm sure you can understand where I'm coming from."

"I do understand," I utter, knowing this heartbreak is going to be present for the rest of my life.

"I need to go. Take care of yourself. And the baby," Nicolas says, moving the display of wallets to the side so he can step out from behind the desk.

"Wait..." I don't know how many times I can ask him to wait before he'll stop turning around to see why I'm stopping him, but it isn't this time. Perhaps he does it without thinking first. "How did you know the soldiers were in the shop today?" I ask.

He drops his hands into his pockets and drops his head. "I can't be with you, but I won't let anything happen to you, not on my watch. I guess I was just at the right place at the right time today."

"Will I see you again soon?"

"This," he says pointing between the two of us, "it hurts too much to say yes."

I wonder how often he strolls by the shop, if he checks on me daily without my knowing, if he thinks about me as much as I think about him every day. Like a deep root buried beneath soil, love doesn't just die, it finds another path, to grow around whatever obstacle is in the way.

THIRTY

NICOLAS

SIX MONTHS AGO, JULY 1943

Paris, France

I can't quite figure out what it is about a war that makes everyone involved lie to the ones they love, whether for the purpose of protection or for keeping secrets. Sometimes both, I suppose. Each morning before I leave for what I'm still lightly referring to as work, Mère leaves me with a slap on the back of my head as I walk out the door of our flat. "Make things right with Raya," she scolds me. "Don't let her go. She's your one. You must listen to me, son. You must. I know things you don't know. Age is wisdom and you are a fool to ignore your mother."

I haven't had the heart to tell Mère Raya's pregnant with someone else's child. I'm not sure she would be sending me out the door with the same lecture if she knew what I know. Because she adored Raya so greatly, I don't have the heart to taint Mère's perception of her. It's painful to listen to Mère's words, to believe them, but still know I must live a life without the woman I was sure I'd spend the rest of it with. I've told Mère the choice wasn't mine to end things, but for that reason she holds me accountable for ruining what we had. She tells me to fight for Raya, to win her back, and to woo her, which is embarrassing advice from a mother to a son. I wish I could simply get over what has taken place, but I'm afraid that isn't possible when someone else must have their claim over the life growing inside of her. I wish the story was different and sometimes I wish I didn't still love her so much, but I'm not sure that will ever change. Love seems to be a permanent fixture in a person's life, no matter how long it lasts or doesn't. Love makes a man do foolish things like still checking on the woman who no longer belongs to him.

No matter how often I walk by the shop to quietly peek in on Raya, I've never seen a single soul by her side except for the day I spotted the group of soldiers loitering there. From what I can tell, the orders have slowed down since the weather is becoming warmer, but I'm sure it's only a matter of time before they find another reason to pay her a visit.

For now, it gives me comfort to know she's carrying on and not in danger. If that's all I can have when it comes to her, I'll take that over the alternative.

As if the city streets are laughing at my simple thoughts, a swarm of German soldiers crowd the way, more than there have been recently. More deportation vehicles are seen regularly, and it appears Jewish people in great masses are being plucked from their homes. I thought most of them had already been taken, but I was apparently wrong in thinking so. It concerns me to know how dangerous it is to be hiding Jewish people, both for the Levi family and Raya. I would do the same if I was her, but it feels like we're being boxed in here.

"Salut, Monsieur Bardot," Monsieur Croix greets me, lifting his beret away from the fine threads of white hair matted across his bald head. "I haven't seen you in a while. I hope everything is okay?"

"Salut," I reply, inconspicuously peering toward Raya's shop. The drapes are still hanging over the windows and the closed sign is on display. I check my wristwatch even though I know it's nearly ten in the morning. "Of course. Everything is just fine." I've been avoiding his questions anytime he sees me, questioning what happened between Raya and me.

"I guess she isn't opening the shop this week," Croix says with a shrug. "I can't say I blame her. The only people who go in and out of there are those nasty soldiers. They're just vile." He cringes and shakes off the thought. "In any case, I hope all is well with her. Is it?"

"Yes, yes, of course," I lie, knowing there's no way I could know if she's all right.

I hadn't been by the shop since last week. When I do walk by, I peek in to make sure she's there, feel my heart shred into pieces again, and then move on with my day. There are days I can't get myself to walk by, knowing how much I will hurt after, which has been the case this week.

I should mind my own business and continue with what I have to do, which consists of printing leaflets at the office when Paul takes his frequent smoke breaks throughout the morning. He never believed in going outside to enjoy a cigarette before, but now he seems to do it several times a day. Maybe he's searching for some sort of news on the street that he can use to actually print the paper.

"Have a good day, Monsieur Croix," I say as I continue between Raya's shop and the newsstand.

"Same to you, my good man."

As I reach the corner where a side street intersects the road, I take a sharp left and make my way around to the back of the building. I unlock the doors and let myself in, knowing there is a real chance I could be instantly sorry for entering Raya's building without being invited. I haven't let myself up into her flat since the day she informed me of the pregnancy, but I won't be able to continue with my day unless I know she is okay upstairs, even if that means she's with the man who stole her away from me.

The flat is dark apart from the faint sunlight pouring in through Raya's bedroom window. I poke my head into Alix's bedroom, spotting no sign of Charlette either.

The hallway mirror is hung in place to conceal the hole in the wall and my nerves fray as I consider what might have happened here. As bad as it is that I've let myself into Raya's flat, I'm taking things a step further by removing the mirror from the wall so I can get into the hidden space to check on the Levis.

Not a sound greets my presence as I crouch through the opening, but when I poke my head into the space, I spot the three of them huddling in a corner, shaking with fear as to who has been walking through the flat, or so I assume.

A gasp of relief finds each of them. "You scared us half to death," Jacques says. "What are you doing up here?"

"The shop was closed and I was worried something happened. Where's Raya?"

Charlette glances at her father then at Rose. "Raya went into preterm labor. She's at the hospital."

"Who's with her?" I demand an answer rather than asking casually.

Rose pats Charlette on the shoulder and nods at her, giving her a silent nudge to move toward me. While Charlette is blocking my view of Jacques, the look of concern on Rose's face is quite clear.

"Let's go to another room," Charlette says.

I back out of the opening, allowing Charlette to follow me. She pulls me down the hallway and into Alix's room.

"What's the meaning of this?" I ask her, my pulse quickening, stealing my energy to even stand up straight.

"No one is with Raya," she says.

"What about the man who—"

Charlette wraps her hands around the back of her neck and

peers between us, shaking her head as if she's having an internal battle of some sort. "Nicolas, there is no one else."

"Immaculate conception isn't quite on the table for discussion," I argue.

Charlette lifts her head and reaches for my shoulders. "That wasn't what I was suggesting."

"I understand you are her dearest, closest friend and you won't do anything to jeopardize her privacy, but I've been left in the dark for months and months, not understanding what it is I supposedly don't understand, or how I could come to any conclusion with the number of secrets being kept."

Charlette's face scrunches with pain and conflict. "I don't know what to do, Nicolas. I'm protecting both of you by not saying anything. I can tell you that much, but anything more than that—"

"Protecting me?" I ask, cutting her off. "Wait, wait, what—what could you be protecting me from? What does that even mean, Charlette?" The words boil in my chest and escape like the steam from a hot kettle.

Charlette places her hand over her mouth, her eyes growing rounder with concern. "I've already said too much."

"No," I shout. "No, you haven't said enough. You need to tell me what's going on right now. I can't—Charlette, dammit, tell me whatever it is that hasn't been said. I don't need protection. I need the truth." My rage shouldn't be directed at Charlette, it should be with myself, for assuming Raya lied to me and doing nothing to find out otherwise. It all comes down to protection. Of course it does. All Raya can do in life is protect everyone but herself. I should have known better. I should have seen through her lie.

"Nicolas, shh," she tries to calm me through a stuttering hush.

I drop to my knees, unable to keep myself upright, and wrap my arms around the back of my head. "Charlette," I cry out.

"Someone did this to her, didn't they?" Agony strikes every one of my nerves like bolts of electricity. I don't need the confirmation. Charlette's eyes say it all, the sickening pain of knowing someone you love is hurting so much and there's nothing you can do to take that away.

Charlette gulps the air and lowers herself to her knees as well, wrapping her arms around my neck.

"How could I let this happen?" I say.

"You didn't do this. This isn't your fault," she whimpers.

"This is all my fault!" I shout before sobs explode out of my chest. "I left her all alone when all she needed was love. What kind of monster am I? How could I be so ignorant?"

"Stop it, Nicolas. Just stop," she grunts. "This isn't helping her or anyone else. She purposely kept this from you so you wouldn't go after—"

"Who?" I ask, trying to catch my breath. "Who did this?" I lift my head to stare Charlette square in the eyes. "Tell me. It was a damn Nazi, wasn't it? It was one of them." Everything around me takes on a faint red hue and I can't see straight. Charlette is talking and I'm not digesting her words.

"Nicolas," she says, grabbing my face. "Stop. Yes, it was one of them, and it was against her will."

My body bucks against the stabbing pain and I rest my forehead on her shoulder, crying so hard I think I might vomit. I clench my arms around my waist. "Oh my God. What did I do?"

Charlette's hands grip my shoulders, forcing me to pull up my head. Tears fall from her golden-brown eyes and her cheeks burn as she places her hand over her mouth again. "You," she says, her breath hitching in her throat. "You. Can't. Blame. Yourself. You can't."

"She was afraid I'd get myself killed if I knew," I confirm my thoughts out loud.

Charlette still won't offer a single word, but the tears continue to fall in a steady stream down her cheeks.

"Who is he? You need to tell me, Charlette."

"I don't know," she cries out. "I promise you; I don't know which of them it was."

"What hospital is Raya at?"

"Saint Anne's, I believe, unless she was taken elsewhere. I don't know. I don't know anything. She went into labor almost a month early. We don't know how she's doing."

"When did she go into labor?"

"Monday," she says.

"I have to go," I huff, standing up and wrangling my fingers through the sides of my hair. My beret falls off my head and the urge to scream at the top of my lungs is so forceful, I hold my breath and bite my tongue until I taste blood.

"Where are you going?"

"To find Raya."

"Please, Nicolas, you can't tell her I alluded to—"

"The truth?" I snap.

Charlette takes a hold of my arm and presses her fingernails into my skin. "Please. She'll never forgive me if I cause you to be reckless."

"I need to go," I say, pulling my arm out of her grip, feeling her nails scratch along my skin. "Go back to the other side of the wall. The animals are sniffing out the streets, hunting Jewish people again. You aren't safe on this side of the flat. Do you understand?"

"Yes," she whispers.

I leave with fury, adrenaline making my legs move faster than I would normally walk down these streets. My office is on the way to Saint Anne's, I'll tell Paul to take fewer smoke breaks today and get the work done himself.

The swarm of Nazis parading around the shop flashes through my mind repeatedly during my walk, debating if it was one of them or if this happened elsewhere. Raya doesn't go far, I know that much, but this could have happened anywhere. She didn't even tell me when it happened. Now I know why she looked like something had crawled into her soul and shrouded her with darkness for the weeks leading up to when she told me she was pregnant. She was attacked and tormented, and I wasn't there for her. She must have been in agony, and I didn't recognize this. How could she hide something so detrimental? It must have been rotting her brain and she just kept moving forward. I should have believed her when she said she loved me, and I was the only one. She was telling me the truth, not trying to cover up a mistake. I'm the one who made the mistake. It was me and I should be the one paying the price for that, not her.

I will find out which one of those bastards did this to her and I will make him pay dearly for what he did. A slow, torturous death is what he will beg for when I'm through with him.

The newspaper's office doors are in sight when I hear my name called from behind a nearby building. I circle around, searching for whoever is trying to get my attention and finally spot Bette along the side of the bakery, peeking around the corner. I haven't seen or heard from her in all this time, not since she told me what happened to Hugo, even though I work right beside her family's shop.

I stop short in my tracks and pivot in her direction, stalking over to her with what must look like wrath, though it isn't intended toward her. I should ask her how she's doing, seeing as she's grieving the likely loss of her brother. But instead I growl, "What is it? I don't have time to talk right now. I have somewhere I have to be."

Bette blinks but otherwise doesn't react to my tone. "I received a memo from an unknown source telling me that Hugo is being held captive in Lyon in an underground German prison. The location is coded at the bottom of the memo. It could be a trap."

"Do you have the memo on you?" I ask, leaning my hand against the brick wall for support.

Bette reaches into her sweater pocket and pulls out the small paper. I unfold it and smooth it out, trying to focus on the unrecognizable handwriting—the writing of what appears to be a young child with how illegible it is. The code though—this code could have only come from Hugo. It's more than a location. "Can I hold on to this?"

"Are you going to help him?"

How could she think I wouldn't?

"Yes, yes, I will," I say, wishing I could avoid the desolate plea swimming through her eyes. "I'll get to him as fast as I can. I'll do whatever I can." I just need to get to Raya first. Please God, just give me time. That's all I need.

THIRTY-ONE

RAYA

Ravensbrück, Germany

I have skimmed some of the blank pages at the back of the notepad the guards left with me to fill their custom glove orders, keeping them for myself to write more notes at night before bed. It's what I look forward to most each day. Though my hand shakes furiously while trying to write, I imagine the feeling of warmth, telling myself my coat is a thick wool blanket and I'm resting on top of a bed of feathers. It hurts to push away my questions of what a human body can withstand when it comes to the cold. I never know how much more I can handle. Each night is unforgiving and my body aches from my muscles contracting and tightening over and over to instinctually sustain some warmth within my frail, boney body. I could freeze to death. Women here have. I'm not sure what makes them different from me or how I've managed to wake up each morning. I'm terrified I won't wake up tomorrow, knowing these letters I write won't have a chance of finding their way home.

My Dearest,

The weather is continuing to decline by the day. The cold air feels trapped like we're inside a glass snow globe. I have a glass snow globe, one hidden in a crate in the closet of Alix's bedroom. I want you to have it, it can be a connection between us, something you can look at when you want to think of me and know I'm on the other side watching between the falling flakes of snow.

For the last two weeks I have been put to work, sewing custom orders of leather gloves for the Nazis. The understanding of their popularity is underwhelming though I remember once daydreaming about these remarkable gloves becoming a fashion statement in Paris, everyone in the city waiting in line for their tailored pair. I could never imagine this would be the case instead. I can't take pride in knowing I've created a product so desired that only the Nazis favor them. I've already considered the thought of adding itching powder into the lining of the gloves. I wouldn't have access to such an absurd thing, but the thought brings a small smile to my face.

I wish I knew how you were getting on. If you're safe and healthy. I would do anything to know that you're okay because it would give me hope and motivation to keep pushing through this quicksand that feels like it's swallowing me up. If I have you to fight for, I know I can make it.

I miss you so very much and love you more than I could ever put into words.

Take care, my love.

I tuck the letter into the lining of my coat, along with the others, and pull the heavy wool around my back for comfort.

I wish I didn't need to sleep. If I never had to close my eyes again, I might be grateful. My days are filled with scenes I once could only imagine as nightmares; and my nights are filled with my mind replaying those scenes over and over again. To be starved, beaten, degraded, exhausted, and worked till we're useless is our daily life. To watch someone die or be murdered in front of me is common. And each time I watch a person die, a part of me perishes too.

Why couldn't it be him instead? Gustav and his beady eyes.

I see my hands around his neck, squeezing so tightly his face pales, his lips turn blue. He tries to lift his arms to fight but doesn't have the strength as he chokes on the remaining air exiting his lungs. I watch his body expel his soul, leaving behind a lifeless stare in exchange for my innocence.

I wouldn't be innocent, though. A man would be dead, and I would be the murderer.

I'm left thinking about the night I held a rifle in my hands, ready to take down the very kind of people holding me prisoner here, but no matter what I told myself that night, I couldn't pull the trigger. Even if I had spotted Gustav, I couldn't be like him or the rest of them, which has, in turn, brought me to this place —hell. This prison camp is a holding ground for all those who didn't have a trigger to pull or couldn't get themselves to end another person's life—for the innocent.

The door to the barrack opens and a few women amble in, one limping. All of them are disheveled and before the door closes behind the last woman, the dim light from outdoors glows over them, highlighting a familiar look upon their faces. They're hollow inside and their bodies are objects used for satisfaction in the night because the SS guards don't have enough already. It took me a while to realize how lucky I am to be working in a factory rather than a brothel.

I ask myself over and over why these men would need to take from us in that way too. But I've come to a jeering realization.

I reach out from the edge of my bunk and sweep my hand across the head of the first woman walking down the row of beds. She startles in her step but stops and glances up at me, life vacant from what little I can see of her eyes.

"No one will ever love them, desire them, or willingly stand before them knowing what they've done. They will forever go without the one thing most people desire more than anything—to be wanted. It's their lifelong sentence for what they've done to you," I whisper.

The woman takes my hand and presses it against her tear-streaked cheek. "Bless you and your wise words."

The other two women take my hand as they walk by and squeeze it gently. "You are right," the last woman says. "To live in sin—there's no worse punishment."

Her words, a mere response to mine, make me wonder why I'm still alive. I haven't sinned, yet I'm serving what feels like a life sentence, and I'm not sure what purpose there is to continue like this.

My Dearest,

The weather is continuing to decline by the day. The cold air feels trapped like we're inside a glass snow globe. I have a glass snow globe, one hidden in a crate in the closet of Alix's bedroom. I want you to have it, it can be a connection between us, something you can look at when you want to think of me and know I'm on the other side watching between the falling flakes of snow.

For the last two weeks I have been put to work, sewing custom orders of leather gloves for the Nazis. The understanding of their popularity is underwhelming though I remember once daydreaming about these remarkable gloves becoming a fashion statement in Paris, everyone in the city waiting in line for their tailored pair. I could never imagine this would be the case instead. I can't take pride in knowing I've created a product so desired that only the Nazis favor them. I've already considered the thought of adding itching powder into the lining of the gloves. I wouldn't have access to such an absurd thing, but the thought brings a small smile to my face.

I wish I knew how you were getting on. If you're safe and healthy. I would do anything to know that you're okay because it would give me hope and motivation to keep pushing through this quicksand that feels like it's swallowing me up. If I have you to fight for, I know I can make it.

I miss you so very much and love you more than I could ever put into words.

Take care, my love.

I tuck the letter into the lining of my coat, along with the others, and pull the heavy wool around my back for comfort.

I wish I didn't need to sleep. If I never had to close my eyes again, I might be grateful. My days are filled with scenes I once could only imagine as nightmares; and my nights are filled with my mind replaying those scenes over and over again. To be starved, beaten, degraded, exhausted, and worked till we're useless is our daily life. To watch someone die or be murdered in front of me is common. And each time I watch a person die, a part of me perishes too.

Why couldn't it be him instead? Gustav and his beady eyes.

I see my hands around his neck, squeezing so tightly his face pales, his lips turn blue. He tries to lift his arms to fight but doesn't have the strength as he chokes on the remaining air exiting his lungs. I watch his body expel his soul, leaving behind a lifeless stare in exchange for my innocence.

I wouldn't be innocent, though. A man would be dead, and I would be the murderer.

I'm left thinking about the night I held a rifle in my hands, ready to take down the very kind of people holding me prisoner here, but no matter what I told myself that night, I couldn't pull the trigger. Even if I had spotted Gustav, I couldn't be like him or the rest of them, which has, in turn, brought me to this place —hell. This prison camp is a holding ground for all those who didn't have a trigger to pull or couldn't get themselves to end another person's life—for the innocent.

The door to the barrack opens and a few women amble in, one limping. All of them are disheveled and before the door closes behind the last woman, the dim light from outdoors glows over them, highlighting a familiar look upon their faces. They're hollow inside and their bodies are objects used for satisfaction in the night because the SS guards don't have enough already. It took me a while to realize how lucky I am to be working in a factory rather than a brothel.

I ask myself over and over why these men would need to take from us in that way too. But I've come to a jeering realization.

I reach out from the edge of my bunk and sweep my hand across the head of the first woman walking down the row of beds. She startles in her step but stops and glances up at me, life vacant from what little I can see of her eyes.

"No one will ever love them, desire them, or willingly stand before them knowing what they've done. They will forever go without the one thing most people desire more than anything— to be wanted. It's their lifelong sentence for what they've done to you," I whisper.

The woman takes my hand and presses it against her tear-streaked cheek. "Bless you and your wise words."

The other two women take my hand as they walk by and squeeze it gently. "You are right," the last woman says. "To live in sin—there's no worse punishment."

Her words, a mere response to mine, make me wonder why I'm still alive. I haven't sinned, yet I'm serving what feels like a life sentence, and I'm not sure what purpose there is to continue like this.

THIRTY-TWO

RAYA

Paris, France

When I walked in through the hospital doors last week, I was a different person and that person would have been sure that people, no matter who they are or what they are going through, remain the same throughout the entirety of their lives. I was wrong.

Inconceivable measures of love and patience are all I feel now as I stare down at the blonde peach fuzz sprouting out of baby Amalia's head. She hasn't a care in the world, peacefully asleep, wrapped in a blanket held tightly against my chest. She knows of no evil and for as long as I can protect her from learning anything but the meaning of happiness, I will do whatever it takes.

Resting is easy while soothed by her steady quiet breaths. I haven't ever heard a more beautiful sound.

An unfamiliar type of tapping on the door alarms me and I shoot my gaze toward the opening. My chest tightens and air catches in my throat. Nicolas is standing beneath the door's threshold. He removes his beret and holds his hands behind his back, staring at me with what look like tears in his eyes.

"How—what are you—how did you know I was here? Why are you—"

He holds his finger up to his lips and closes his eyes, then makes his way to my side. Nicolas leans over me and places a kiss on my forehead and immediately touches the thin blanket wrapped around Amalia. He tugs carefully at the hem to get a better look at her face. His jaw quivers and a muffled whimper escapes his throat.

"Nicolas," I say, finding myself breathless just trying to speak his name. "Why—"

"You can tell me to leave, and I will," he utters through a quiet cry. "I just needed to know you were okay."

The anguish swimming through his eyes makes my throat tighten and my pulse race. "We're both doing fine." My words come out in a whisper.

"If I had known," he begins, but stops to stare up at the ceiling, muttering something to himself. "Raya, I would never have left you."

"You know," I state, not having to wonder how seeing as he still has keys to my flat and access to Charlette. She promised me she would never say a word.

"You should have told me."

I sniffle and shake my head. "I was protecting you."

He inhales sharply and covers his hand over his mouth. "No, no. Raya, no. What about you? When have you ever put yourself first?"

All I can do is stare at him, curious about what thoughts might be going through his head and if my worries will have been for good reason. "I did put myself first. I knew I couldn't live with myself if I lost you, even if that meant I couldn't be with you."

Nicolas drops his knees by my side and places a hand on Amalia. "She's beautiful, perfect. She's everything you are."

"She is," I concede, staring at her cupid-bow lips, parted just slightly in the shape of an o.

"Raya, I'm going to make things right. I will do whatever it takes, and I promise I will not go on a hunt for the—" He breathes heavily and swallows hard. "For the person who hurt you. I just want to take care of you and—"

"Amalia," I peep, "like my mère."

A faint smile unfurls across Nicolas's lips. "That's wonderful." He sweeps the tip of his thumb across Amalia's cheek and his smile grows wider. "How much longer will you be in the hospital?"

"Another day or two."

He glances around the room. "Do you think they have a spare chair? I'll stay with you."

"Don't be ridiculous. You can't sleep on a chair for two nights. The nurses here have been great. I'm in good hands."

He nods and glances toward the door. "I'm not leaving you, Raya. I'll stay right here on my knees if I must."

Nicolas unbuttons his vest and slips it off to place it on the edge of the bed. At the same instant, a slip of paper flies out from his pocket and lands beside my hand.

"What's this?" I ask, turning the paper over, finding letters and symbols that don't make any sense to me.

He takes the paper from my hands and drops it into his pants pocket. "Bette caught me while I was on my way to find you. She received a message from Hugo, or someone on behalf of Hugo. He's alive. She asked me if I could help find him."

"He's alive?" I croak. I had wondered what became of him but with everything that happened between Nicolas and I, I wouldn't know if anything had changed.

"I only know he's been held as a prisoner in Lyon."

"You aren't going to look for him?" Instead, he's here trying to tell me he will sleep on the floor of this hospital room.

"I need to be here right now." I can sense the struggle within his words. "There's no saying if I'll be able to find Hugo."

"He's like a brother to you. You can't choose sitting here with me over possibly saving his life." There I go again, putting others first. It's who I am, and I can't live any other way. I won't be the reason someone doesn't get the chance to be saved.

"I can try to find someone else to go after him," he says, taking my hand within his.

"Nicolas, I'm fine. We're fine."

"Don't say you're fine. You can't ever tell me you're fine again." There's no humor to be found within his demand, and I understand why.

"We're under good care here so if you can help Hugo, you should. The trip to Lyon isn't too long and if you find him, I'm sure you'll be back soon."

"I'll make sure I'm back before you're released from the hospital, but Raya, I'm not going unless—"

"I won't let you stay here." The words float out of my mouth on their own accord. I wish I could just be a selfish person today. I also won't ask how dangerous this might be because I don't want to know the answer.

* * *

Three days have come and gone. The nurses allowed me to stay an extra day following the questions of why the father hasn't shown up to bring us home yet. I wish I had a good answer for them, but even if Nicolas was the father, I don't know where he is and he didn't come back for me like he said. I imagine his trip wasn't as simple as he hoped it might be.

I'm in a wheelchair at the front doors of the hospital,

waiting for a cab to pick us up and take us home. The nurses said it could take a while as cabs are hard to come by these days since the Germans control most modes of transportation.

The sun is warm and comforting after being stuck inside for so many days, but I pull the blanket up over Amalia's head to protect her fair skin. "Here we are," one of my favorite nurses says, pointing toward a cab rolling along the curb.

"Thank you for all you've done for us," I say, knowing how challenging it is to be working for the citizens of this city—both the ones who belong and the ones who don't.

"We'll miss you and Amalia, but I know you'll take wonderful care of her. I wish you the best of luck," she says, fetching the back door of the cab before returning to my side.

I'm only mildly sore but afraid to stand from a rolling chair even with the brakes secured. I'm unsteady on my feet with all the weight I had been carrying around. With Amalia snug in my arms, the nurse places her hands behind my arms and assists me into the back seat of the cab. Once I'm settled, she returns once more with my bag and places it beside me on the seat. She wishes us well with two words that I'm not sure anyone has considered altering since the German occupation began.

"Happy life."

A flutter of both excitement and nerves quakes through me as the cab pulls away from the curb. We're on our own now, her and me against the world.

"Pascal Maroquinerie?" the driver confirms.

"Oui, merci."

In my dreams over the last week, the Germans had miracu-lously disappeared. Never again would we see them parading up and down our city streets in their green and brown uniforms. A dream is all it was. With that dream came visions of friends and family waiting for me upon arriving home with a bundle of joy, Nicolas by my side, perhaps, a feeling of completeness. Then I realized this life is no longer about my dream, it's about

Amalia's, and all she knows and desires is me. I'm enough for her, so surely she will always be enough for me too.

The cab reeks of stale cigar smoke and sweet liquor, making me wonder who might have been sitting in this seat last night. With our curfew still intact, I'm sure it was a German soldier enjoying his life the way we once did. I can only imagine what this driver has witnessed over the last two years. I don't envy him for that.

"If you could pull off to the right between these two blocks, that would be perfect," I tell him. I'd rather go in around the back way than draw attention to myself at the storefront where Monsieur Croix will likely be waiting. That man has asked me more questions than everyone else combined. He's sure Amalia belongs to Nicolas, but has also asked where Nicolas has been far too many times to still believe I was carrying his child.

"Oui, madame."

I won't bother correcting him to mademoiselle. There's no purpose other than to call attention to my evident shortcomings.

The driver kindly jumps out of his seat to help me out of the vehicle, gently placing my bag over my shoulder so I can keep a firm grip on Amalia. I reach into my pocket and retrieve a handful of Francs and drop them in the driver's hand. "Merci beaucoup."

I may only be a week into motherhood but if there's anything important I've learned so far, it's to keep everything I might need in an accessible pocket.

Climbing the stairs proves to be a bit painful and I'm grateful for a sturdy railing to hold on to as I make my way up the steps. As if Amalia knows we've arrived home, she lets out a loud wail of a cry likely wanting her next meal. I place my bag on the kitchen table and pull out a chair.

"Raya?" Charlette's voice peeps from around the corner.

I'm sure she wouldn't have taken a chance on coming into this side of the flat if she hadn't heard Amalia's announcing cry.

"We're home," I say, trying to find a comfortable position on a hard chair.

The three of them climb out of the hole in the wall and tiptoe over to me as if I'm holding a thin piece of glass. I suppose that's how I feel while carrying her around too.

Charlette reaches out to Amalia, who has taken a moment to catch her breath from crying. "Oh my goodness..."

"This is Amalia, the little girl who couldn't wait until she was ready to come out," I say, grinning at her perfect face.

"Oh, Raya, she's beautiful, and I love the name, Amalia—just like your mother—that's wonderful," Rose says, stroking the side of her finger along her cheek. "Mazel tov, sweetheart."

"Well," Jacques says, clearing his throat, his sign of discomfort in a situation he isn't sure about being a part of. "She's certainly got her mother's nose and blonde hair." He takes a long look at Amalia and a faint smile touches his lips before the next set of questions arrive. "Where is Nicolas?"

Rose elbows her husband in the stomach. "Jacques," she scolds him.

Of course, neither of them knows what became of our rendezvous.

"He went to find you."

"Father," Charlette follows. "Enough."

"Why did you tell him what I didn't want him to know?" I ask Charlette, keeping my stare on Amalia's face to keep me calm.

Charlette grabs my arms and pulls me closer to her. "I would never do anything to hurt you. You know that. He came here, worried about you, and I told you had gone into preterm labor. Then he started asking if the baby's father was with you. I said no, he won't be. I'm not sure what it was about my statement that made a light bulb go off in his head, but he asked me if someone did this to you...When I didn't answer right away, he questioned if it was a Nazi."

My breath catches in my throat. Charlette may be bad at keeping secrets but she's a worse liar. "What did you say? Please don't tell me you confessed about who it was?"

"I didn't have the chance to. It was as if he could see the truth on my face. Before I knew it, he was running out to find you. Please, please don't be cross with me. I—"

"I understand. We spoke. He's apologized, but I'm not sure what for since this was my decision. Right now he's in Lyon looking for his friend who had gone missing. He found out he's alive. I made him go even after he insisted he'd stay by my side."

Rose and Jacques share a look I wish I didn't notice.

"That sounds dangerous," Charlette utters.

"He'll be fine, I'm sure, and I have plenty to keep my mind occupied in the meantime."

Charlette forces a smile across her lips. "Of course you do." She shifts her gaze to Amalia. "Could I hold her?"

I put her in Charlette's arms and she stares at her with adoration as she sways from side to side, cooing at her. "I'm your aunt Charlette, and I'm going to give you everything you could ask for," she utters.

Rose rolls her eyes and chuckles. "Wait until she asks for a chateau in the south of France."

"If that's what she wants, that's what she'll get," Charlette says, speaking in a low babble of elongated words.

"Where will you be feeding her, dear?" Rose asks.

"Mazel tov, Raya. She's a darling little girl," Jacques says, nodding with one last quick smile before turning around to go back to his room.

"Here, I suppose," I say, looking at the chair I'm sitting on.

"You still have that upholstered chair in the corner of Alix's bedroom, don't you?"

I almost forgot about that chair. It was Mère's favorite, and I couldn't bear to part with it after she passed away, but the memories associated with it also made the pain of missing her worse so it became a foundation for scraps of leather. I'm not sure when I last saw even a sliver of the fabric with the amount of leather that's stacked up. The chair has been in Alix's room since he was born. That's where she fed him, read to him, sang him lullabies and snuggled with me as she rocked him to sleep.

"I'll go clean it off and push it out here so you have a comfortable place to sit when you're feeding her. You won't be able to sit in this hard chair all the time," says Rose.

"Does Alix know about Amalia?" Charlette asks.

"He doesn't know she's been born. I receive letters from him so often and I reply with lies so I don't risk him worrying too much."

"Maybe it would be best if he came home," she says. "He can finish school in a year. It wouldn't be the end of the world. We both know he would take care of you."

"No, absolutely not. I won't interfere with his life. He deserves to have a proper uninterrupted education." As the words slip out of my mouth, I realize Charlette was denied that opportunity. Jewish people haven't been welcomed in most universities.

"We all deserve a fair chance at life, Raya, even you."

I rest my elbows on the table with the urge to place my head down and close my eyes for a minute. The nurses were helpful with his nighttime feedings, but Amalia likes to eat a lot and I haven't gotten much sleep in the last week.

With everything Charlette has said over the last few minutes, the only thing I can focus on is her thought of Nicolas doing something dangerous. I've refused to acknowledge this realization over the last three days. What if something has happened to him?

THIRTY-THREE

NICOLAS

Lyon, France

I've been in the countryside outside Lyon for almost two-and-a-half weeks. This was not my intention. I should have been back home by now, taking care of Raya and Amalia. I told her I'd be back before she left the hospital, and again, I've let her down.

The information Bette had given me about Hugo wasn't much and I didn't know I would be joining up with another resistance group at the location coded on the note. Nor was I aware that this group has been preparing for a raid to rescue several prisoners of war, Hugo being just one of them.

The meeting location took me nearly a day to find after venturing up and down hundreds of steps within the interconnected medieval passageways, stairwells, and courtyards that connect various streets and buildings to make up the structure of Traboules. Each unmarked, narrow wooden or metal doorway leads to a different maze of interwoven paths surrounded by walls of stone or brick and wrought iron balconies then conjoined by ornately carved archways.

The group is hidden well within a dark tunnel of stone

enclosures, and I've quickly accepted that it's in my best interest to have someone familiar with the area overseeing the plans for the rescue mission.

Eighteen of us have been sleeping within the dark corridors for the last two and a half weeks, training and preparing for the right time to attack. Each day we've had to stand down due to a variety of reasons, whether the number of Gestapo guarding the target was too risky for us to attack or if there were other officials in the area tending to meetings. The situation must be in our favor for us to take down the outdoor guards and any Gestapo inside the building, surrounding the prisoners.

It's musky and warm between the dirt-covered enclosure where we wait for our morning briefing, and I'm praying today is the day we can go in and rescue our people.

"It's going to be today," Franco says, sweeping a small pile of dirt into a small pyramid between his legs. He's from outside of the Lyon resistance too, summoned here for a similar reason—to assist in rescuing a member of his group. As many days as we've spent together, I still don't know too much about the guy, but he's been the only one I've been exchanging words with.

"Did you hear something?" I ask, leaning my heavy head back against the stone wall just as all the others who are beside us or across the way.

"I overheard some of the others talking earlier."

For every minute longer we sit here, our people are coming closer to their death. The one thing I do know is that there are at least eight members of the French resistance in this one location and they're being interrogated daily. Assumptions have been made that more than thirty of them have already been hanged or executed, but the people remaining must be worth something to the Gestapo guarding the prison built within the cellar of a condemned school building around the corner from our location.

With so much time to wait for action, my mind revolves

around Raya as I struggle between feelings of remorse for what happened to her and outrage against whoever did it. Each day I've spent here, I've regretted leaving her, but I would feel regret for abandoning Hugo too. I'm terrified of Raya going back to her flat, wondering if the man who assaulted her knows where to find her. I'm not even sure if he's found her again since the original time. I should have asked her more questions, but it wasn't the right time, not when she had just given birth. I can't even imagine what must be going through her head when she looks at the innocent baby or how she will forget how she came to be. I'm not sure I would be able to be as strong.

"Listen up, everyone," Antoine, the man leading the group, says as he walks around the bend in the wall to face those of us sitting across from each other. "Today, we attack. At ten this morning." He peers down at his watch. "One hour from now, we are breaking up into three groups, Alpha, Bravo, and Charlie." Antoine lifts a rolled map and unravels it for us to all see. "There are two blocks between the exit of our current passageway and the school. There are two main doors in use, one in the front and one in the back. Group Alpha will take down the guards in the front on the riverside, and Bravo will do the same for the back entrance. Alpha will move up through the three floors, clearing each room before returning to street level. Bravo will sweep the street level and move down to the basement to clear the way for group Charlie to storm in the front and find a clear pathway down the steps, to the right, and into the farthest room at the edge of the building where the prisoners are being held. Charlie's objective is to rescue the prisoners and extract them from the building then move them next door into the West Side entrance of the church where we'll meet back before discreetly making our way back in through Traboules."

He has circles and lines mapping out which group will

travel where but no one knows which group they're going to be assigned to.

"Alpha, after you clear the upper levels of the building, return to the front entrance where everyone is to exit to keep guard for any incoming Gestapo. Take down any one of them in sight to keep the path clear for Charlie, who will go when given the clear from both Alpha and Bravo. Bravo, you'll then sandwich Charlie to keep them surrounded since they likely won't be able to use their weapons once they have the prisoners in hand."

"How many Gestapo are assumed to be in and around the building at this time?" I ask.

"The number is variable, but we are estimating twelve to fifteen at this hour."

"We're going head-to-head and saving prisoners at the same time. I don't see what could go wrong," Franco mutters.

We all need to stay positive if we want any chance of accomplishing this mission today. "We're ready to take them on. They've captured our people and our country. We're doing something about it," I hiss back to him, hoping Antoine doesn't hear us talking while he is.

"We have MP 18 submachine guns and Mauser pistols for everyone here. Charlie will also be supplied with bolt cutters to break through the chains that are likely restraining the prisoners. We'll distribute the ammo you'll need as well."

"If one of us goes down?" I'm not sure why I'm always the one asking this question.

"If you're dead, you're dead. If you're injured too badly to move, play dead and we'll do what we can to retrieve you once the fight is through."

Just as cold as Hugo put it but in different words. I'm here to help him because I can't get myself to leave someone for dead, not someone I care about.

Antoine continues. "I'll call off names assigned to each of the three groups now so listen carefully."

* * *

Charlie. I should have assumed I would be responsible for retrieving the prisoners. I'm sure that's why I was called here by whoever found out Hugo was one of them.

The six of us are against a stone wall beneath the entrance of the bridge that crosses over the Saône River, splitting the city in half. Our location is directly across the street from the front doors of the school, but we're concealed until we're given the clear, twice, to go. The other five men look how I feel, green, pale, and covered in sweat. I doubt they have much more training with weapons than I do. Most resistance members aren't formally trained in a military setting. I need to make it through this. I have to get back to Raya.

The sun is blaring down over the bridge, drawing a sharp dark shadow against the narrow coverage we have. I should be furious with Hugo for throwing himself into a situation he likely knew he couldn't get out of on his own. We're a group and a team for a reason. Regardless, I understand what anger can do to a person—what it's done to me, the mistakes I've made that have hurt others.

Rounds are firing from within the building, and we've heard the scampering of local citizens run across the bridge toward the other side of the city for safety. My heart pelts like their running footsteps, never slowing, not even to catch their breath. Sweat is streaming down the sides of my face, stinging my eyes from the dirt caked across my forehead. The wait feels like an eternity as I imagine the other two groups clearing each room they enter, wondering how many rooms they have to get through or how many minutes it's been since we discreetly made our way down here beneath the bridge.

"It's taking a while," one of the others says.

"Shh," another hisses.

I try to take in a deep breath, knowing I won't be able to once we're flagged to go.

"Clear for Alpha!" The shout is mild and muffled but loud enough for us to hear, thankfully.

"Shouldn't be long now," I whisper. I said it more for myself than the others. I continue to focus on taking deep breaths while counting the seconds to occupy myself while we wait.

"Clear for Bravo!"

I'm the first to jolt and run up the ramp to the side of the bridge, jumping over the shallow end of the stone holding wall to save time and get through the doors. Bravo is waiting for us just inside and three of them run in front of me, leading the way to the basement.

The inside of the building is twice as hot as the outside and the air is so stale it's hard to breathe. My stomach twists into knots, tightening so hard my body feels like a slate of steel. We run together, like sardines trapped in a tin, bound to be knocked over or tripped if we skip a beat. We're stepping over the bodies of dead Gestapo and I wish that would give me the slightest bit of peace but there is an endless supply of German soldiers and police ready to kill whoever stands in their way or threatens their plan of domination.

My legs cramp and my chest aches as we make our way down the end of a short corridor. I can't see over one of the taller men ahead until we spill into the open space where half-naked people are chained to the walls, hanging by their wrists, appearing lifeless at best. It is as if animals have ravaged their bodies through hunger, I can't imagine how any of them will survive this, if any of us do. The smell of urine, sewerage, and mildew strikes me with a wave of nausea as I spot piles of bile in the corners of the room. My eyes tear from the pungency and I struggle to scan the area in search for Hugo.

I didn't consider the thought of Hugo not being here at the end of all this. If someone confused him for another person when Bette was notified, or if he was no longer alive. These people all need to be saved, regardless, but I came here to help him. The others are scattering around the room, tending to the people who look like they may still be alive, or at least that's how it appears.

Once I'm across the large open space, I spot a head of strawberry blonde curls, standing out against the others who neither have curly nor orange hues to their hair. Hugo's hair dangles over his forehead, his face parallel to the ground as his arms are each restrained by a thick chain secured to the cement wall behind him. While terrified to face the truth of whether he's alive or dead, I mindlessly run to his side, noticing lacerations all over his pale body. I drop my hand on his back, thankful it's warm to the touch.

"It's Nicolas, can you hear me?" I call out to him as I unclip the bolt cutters from my belt. Once the metal splits, his left arm falls, and I know I'm going to need to catch him upon cutting through the other chain.

I work from beneath him, his chest resting on my back as I struggle to center the cutter in a chain link to get a clean cut. It doesn't take long before Hugo's body falls heavily onto my back, and I fight to keep my balance while resecuring the bolt cutter to my belt. By the weight of his body there's no way he's conscious, and I'm grateful we're more or less the same size so I can swing him over my shoulder to get him out of here.

Others are moving at the same pace, carrying prisoners' bodies in every which way. Some of the prisoners seem more alert now and can stumble with assistance.

More gunshots fire from down the hallway. We could be getting blocked in and who knows how many more Gestapo have shown up. I have one arm holding Hugo up over my shoulder and my other hand on my sidearm. The shots continue and because of the echo in the corridor, I can't tell what direction they come from. We all continue moving at the pace we would be moving if we didn't hear fighting in the distance. All we can hope is that everything is going according to plan and no one is blocking the exit.

By the time we reach the center crossway between the corridors, ammo is flying toward us and panic strikes every one of my nerves at once as I duck and try to keep Hugo covered at the same time. People ahead of me are going down and my blood turns cold as I force myself to keep pushing forward. I don't see where we're being ambushed from, and I might as well be walking through a maze of mirrors with how blind I feel to every passing corner.

"Hang in there, brother, I'm doing what I can to get us out of here. Just hang on," I grunt.

I make it to the stairwell that leads toward sunlight pouring through an open door. There are two guys in front of me carrying people and the chance of hope in this dire situation is firing through me as my muscles ignite, burning through my skin as I push harder to get up the steps while holding up Hugo's body weight.

The sunlight bares its sharp claws of heat over us once we step outside. Shouts of German surround us and another wave of rounds fire above our heads. I spot others from our group blasting the Gestapo but those of us carrying prisoners are in their firing line too.

"Run!" someone shouts, but I don't know who the shout is directed at when we're all under fire. I keep my sights forward, moving toward the church on the next block.

"Halt!" a soldier screams.

A sting and burn singes through my body, followed by another, and I stiffen, knowing I've been hit. I question whether my heart is beating, if I'm lifeless and still capable of lifting my sidearm before twisting it over my bloody shoulder to fire at whoever is shooting at me, but the Gestapo aiming his rifle toward me is hit by someone else, and he drops to his knees then falls flat onto his face.

I can't give up. "Keep moving, son. You're better than me. You always have been." Father's voice rings through my ears. I'm not better, and I'm not nearly as brave. He knows this. "Run. Just run." I haven't heard his voice in more than a dozen years but I remember it so clearly now.

I take a sharp turn away from the church, remembering the ramp leading to the underside of the bridge. I'm not sure how much farther I can go. The feeling in my legs disappears and a cold sweat coats my limbs as I fall into a warm puddle of welcoming water. "I'm sorry, Hugo. I tried."

I blink, noticing the sky split in half between dark and light. Then Raya's hand brushes along the side of my cheek, her palm smelling like fresh rose petals. I nuzzle against her warm touch, trying to reach for her with my heavy hands.

"Stay with me, Nicolas. Don't let go," she pleads.

THIRTY-FOUR
RAYA
PRESENT DAY, MARCH 1944

Ravensbrück, Germany

"The construction is done," Paulette whispers, walking by my bunk, weaving in and out of resting bodies on the ground as I'm trying to find a semi-comfortable position to settle down between the others leaning against me, trying to fall asleep.

"What do you mean?" I reply before she moves too far away. Her bunk is down the row with at least twenty others between us.

"They're going to start gassing people. I heard guards talking while they were picking up their lunches. That building they've had prisoners working on, it's a gas chamber, and they're going to start using it to kill prisoners. One wrong step now and all they have to do is lock us in the chamber."

Gassing people. They've been deporting prisoners to other locations, but I'd have to be blind not to notice the overcrowding issue here. People are sleeping on the floors, covering every free square of space.

"What is she talking about?" Mabel, my bunkmate on the

left, asks, her body shivering against mine. She's also from France, and a member of one of the resistance groups in Lyon.

"I'm sure it's just another way to scare us into doing what they want," I explain, but I'm saying what I'm sure she'd rather hear than assume. I don't blame those who depend on the use of denial. Each person has to find a way to keep their mind in one piece if there is any hope of surviving the odds here.

"Do you think they're going to kill all of us now?" Mabel asks. She doesn't typically ask me many questions, but I hear her asking others, needing validation for the answers we all already assume and would rather not acknowledge.

I push myself up a bit and use the back of my fingernail to scratch a line into one of the planks of wood I'm lying on. Each line tracks the number of days I've been here. I've managed to keep myself alive for ninety-three days. I refuse to give any more thought to Mabel's question.

"No. Like I said, I think they're using it as a way to scare us into doing what they want."

I should only hope I run out of space to make lines and that I'll be strong enough to last that long, but for each line I draw, it means I've made it through another day, which is no easy feat with as many deaths as we witness. I can't help but wonder if the numbers inked on our arms has any correlation with our fate, or if the number of days I'm counting will relate in any way someday.

The irony of thinking about Mère explaining her under-standing of a Bible Psalm with regard to death: that everyone is born with a number and when their number is up, it's our predetermined time to go. Her explanation gave me relief after Papa passed away, but when she died later, nothing made sense anymore. Why would God want Alix and I to be left alone? Now, I wish I knew to ask her what would happen if we were assigned different numbers, if people could be cruel enough to take the power of God into their own hands and determine another person's fate. What happens to the number we were born with?

THIRTY-FIVE
RAYA

FOUR MONTHS AGO, AUGUST 1943

Paris, France

I've been sleeping in the enclosure with the Levis since I returned home from the hospital because of the windows rattling in the flat with each low flying war plane or nearby air raid. Amalia wakes up if I blink too hard, never mind the war growing more vicious outside by the day.

The weight on my shoulders keeps me awake most nights anyway, so instead of staring at the ceiling in my bedroom, I'm staring at the wooden roof planks angling over my head. Sometimes I believe I can see right through them up into the night's sky and watch the planes flying over us but then I'll imagine one dropping a missile and realize it's best to remain in this reality with my biggest concern being where and how to acquire more food. As it is, I've been stealing from outdoor markets—something I would have never dreamed of doing unless it meant the difference between starving or staying alive. The shop is still open, but the income has been poor over the summer, only now picking up with German consumers preparing to place orders for the upcoming colder months. All the while, I must continue to protect the Levis at all costs, knowing if they are caught, we will all pay a consequence, including Amalia.

Then there's Nicolas, who has been missing for over two weeks. Or maybe he isn't missing. He's had time to consider the thought of being with a woman who is raising a little girl that doesn't belong to him; worse, he could see her as a product of the enemy. It might only be a maternal instinct to see past the truth of genetics and to believe a person will turn out the way in which they're raised. I can't expect anyone else to understand my faith in this precious child.

"You need to get some sleep. She'll be up soon enough to eat, and you aren't taking care of yourself, Raya," Rose scolds me under her breath.

I slap my hand against my chest, startled. I wasn't aware she was also awake.

The more I think about needing sleep, the less capable I am of doing so. Something in this war must give. We can't continue living like this forever but there is still no end in sight. Even Alix has tried to come home several times, despite my plea for him to stay put, and he can't get through the borders between Switzerland and France. His misery is my own. I know he's worried, but aside from sending him letters, there's nothing more I can do than assure him I'm okay, even if my statement isn't an indefinite guarantee that I'll remain this way.

* * *

Amalia only woke up once last night and though I could have taken advantage of the extra sleep, I didn't. This poor child is going to be able to tell people she's been running this leather shop since she was a few weeks old. She's been with me daily, secured to my body by a neatly tied sheet, content unless hungry or wet. I can't leave her upstairs with the Levis with how much she cries if she's not near me. The insulation does well enough to conceal footsteps but I'm not sure about a wailing scream from a brand-new set of lungs. At least she's given me something to focus on during the quiet hours in the shop, but as expected, each day leading toward the end of summer brings along more Germans to place their order for custom gloves. Charlette and I have been taking care of custom orders and repairs after the shop closes and Rose takes the opportunity to cuddle with Amalia in Mère's chair.

We've stopped ringing the bell upstairs because it's become too risky, deciding it's safest if they stay concealed in case someone was to ever break through the back door and make their way upstairs. There are few Jewish people left in this city and those who remain are here by similar means as the Levi family.

Four orders for gloves in an hour today is the most I've sold since last April. The Germans aren't as chummy as they were. I'm not sure what's changed, but they all seem more miserable and irate these days. I can't help but wonder how many of them don't want to be here, away from their families in Germany. But then I immediately scold myself. Any German who takes part in this crusade is undeserving of a personal thought from me. Plus the more anguished they seem, the less they speak to me, which is preferable.

The chimes alert again and again today, and I've stopped glancing over at the door with curiosity for who is coming inside. I have little hope of Nicolas appearing out of thin air and less hope of an average Parisian shopping like they would before the German occupation.

"Ah, a little baby now. I had no idea."

The words slowly translate in my tired mind as I piece them together. Someone commenting on a young infant and having no idea. The odd comment strikes my attention and I peer up, finding my worst nightmare has returned once again. I wonder if he's been in here other times that I haven't noticed. With their eyes shadowed by the lids of their caps, dressed in similar uniforms, they can all appear the same.

I choose not to respond with the hope that he will turn around and walk away. Amalia is awake and her head is turning side to side, probably wondering why my heart is punching her in the chest so hard and fast.

"You're not married."

He points out this burning fact, which is seemingly obvious by a bare ring finger even though no one has been able to comfortably afford jewelry here in the last couple of years. A ring shouldn't be the only symbol of whether someone is taken. To him, though, he's already made it clear that he takes what he wants.

"I am married," I lie. I wish I was married to the man I so badly wanted to marry.

"Beautiful baby. Does your husband have blue eyes too?"

Why does he care if my husband has blue eyes? What does it matter to him?

Gustav the mongrel reaches toward Amalia and I flinch, turning my side to him. "Please don't touch her." To say please to a German makes me want to choke, but a polite statement of do not touch my child should be enough to make him step back.

"How old is the baby girl?"

Lie. Lie to him.

"Two months old." Now he can go on and assume he defiled a pregnant woman to add to his list of vulgar merits.

Gustav reaches out once more, quicker than I can move, and tickles Amalia's back through the sheet. "It was nice to meet you." He escalates the pitch of his voice, talking to Amalia as if he was a squeaky child.

God, please leave the shop.

An hour of hell is what I'm left with as Gustav and his cronies meander around, purchasing nothing but touching everything. The instant he leaves, I lock the doors and close the drapes. I can't have Amalia here anymore. Not now. I know what that man is thinking. I can feel it in my bones. I will die before allowing him to lay a hand on Amalia again. Not once more.

With frazzled thoughts, I take Amalia upstairs and through the flat then move the mirror to the side. I poke my head in, finding the three of them occupied with the same mundane hobbies they've become accustomed to while I'm working downstairs—knitting, reading the same book over and over, or writing letters they can't send.

"I just wanted to let you know I'm running an errand and I'll be back in a bit."

Charlette makes her way across the pitch-angled room, forcing me to back up. "Where are you going? You've been on your feet all day with Amalia. You must stop pushing yourself like this."

"I need to visit Nicolas's mother to see if she's heard from him. I also need to ask her if she'll watch Amalia during the hours I'm working. I have no other choice. That Nazi—he came back into the shop today and was asking questions about Amalia. I can't risk him ever being near her again."

When Rose overhears part of the conversation between Charlette and me, she makes her way to us with a look of concern growing across her face. "Where are you going?"

"To visit Nicolas's mother. I need to—I won't be gone long. There's nothing to worry about. They live less than ten minutes away."

"Dear, that's not a good idea, not with Amalia. You shouldn't have her out on the streets with all those awful soldiers lurking around."

"That's exactly why I must go."

I wrap Amalia up to conceal her as much as I can before making the ten-minute walk across the district. My mind bounces between worry for where Nicolas might be, or if he's avoiding me, to the awful thought of having to leave Amalia for the hours I work every day. But I can't risk Gustav spotting her again.

I knock on the front door of Nicolas's flat, wishing and not wishing he'd answer the door.

"Nicolas?" I hear his mère call out, and I'm not sure if she's asking whether he's out here or if she's trying to get his attention from within the flat. I pray it's the latter.

The door opens and Madame Bardot is clutching a shawl over her chest, her eyes full of worry and hope, the hope fades as fast as the door opens. "Raya?" She's as surprised as I would assume since it's been months since I've last seen her. She studies me for a moment and at the same time I wonder what she must know or think of me now. "A baby?"

"Yes. This is Amalia," I say, trying to keep my voice upbeat to veer away from the other emotions she must be feeling.

"Dear God. Is Nicolas the father?" She crosses her hand across her chest in prayer.

"No, madame."

"This is why my Nicolas has been heartbroken and won't listen to me when I told him to make things right with you. I thought you were different. How could he make things right with you when you've sinned? And how dare you come to my door today? What is it that you need, money or something of that nature? Surely you must know we don't have anything to spare, the same as the rest of the people in this city. Consequences are a burden to pay, Raya, and unfortunately, you must learn this the hard way."

I thought I was becoming numb to the pain of being mislabeled as a sinner, but I was wrong. "I'm not here to ask anything of you. I'm only trying to find Nicolas. It's urgent that I speak with him."

Madame Bardot drops her head into her hand, her white strands of hair cascading to the sides of her face. "For the love of

God. Nicolas hasn't been home in over two-in-a-half weeks. I'm not sure where he's run off to now, but he isn't here and I'm very worried about my son. Besides, if he was, I wouldn't think you deserve his time after what you've done." She scrutinizes me with the worry she must feel for Nicolas, but with an additional layer of resentment she must have for me.

"My situation is not what it seems," I try to explain, reaching for Madame Bardot's arm.

She tears her arm away from my loose grip and takes a step back, creating more distance between us. She pushes the hair away from her face and narrows her eyes at me. "How could you do this? I thought you two were destined to be together. I could see you in our future. I had dreamt of you for him."

"I want the same," I say. "If you could allow me to explain, you would understand I'm telling you the truth."

"Not now, no, you've ruined any chance of being with my son—if he's even all right. Dear God. I can't worry about you right now. Can't you think of anyone else?" Words have never hurt so much, knowing all I've ever done is put everyone before myself—even now, I just want to make sure Amalia is safe even though it pains me to think about leaving her.

"Please, Madame Bardot, I didn't ask for this," I cry out, realizing I'm talking about my daughter who is innocently sleeping soundly against my chest. "Please, if you would listen, you would see this is a misunderstanding. May I come in for a moment?"

"Most women don't ask for a child out of wedlock. It happens when you make foolish decisions," she says. "This is going to be the one and only time I'm going to ask you to step away from my front door. Leave Nicolas alone, and take care of yourself and...your daughter, Raya." The last glance she gives me is one full of grief and turmoil.

Sobs assault my chest while Madame Bardot closes the door in my face as if I was nothing more than a pesky salesman. I want to scream against the wooden fixture and tell her every detail of what happened to me, but doing so would call for attention I certainly don't want.

How do I tell someone I was attacked, raped, and impregnated by a Nazi and expect them to look at me as if I'm not some form of damaged property that now belongs to the Germans? No matter what decision I make, or what I tell people, I will never be seen as pure or anything more than a walking sin.

THIRTY-SIX

NICOLAS

Paris, France

Wet stone scrapes the backs of my hands and I open and close my eyes several times, feeling an ache in my cheek from resting against the wall of coarse bricks as the rising water wades around me. There's silence around us and I'm not sure how long I've been lying here in the river's overflow, but I try to push myself up, feeling a sharp tear along my left hip and shoulder. The pain anchors my body to the wet ditch, but I know I have to move. I need to get up.

The sound of garbled words bouncing over a puddle encourages me to push through the pain, remembering I'm the one who is supposed to be saving Hugo right now. He needs me.

He's on his back, his hand over his chest and his head resting on sludgy grass.

"It's okay. Don't worry. I'm going to get us out of here," I grunt.

Our luck has run dry, and we have two options ahead of us: risk the train in blood-soaked attire, me with the attire, and

Hugo without a shirt, or we could flag down a Frenchman who might be willing to drive us all the way back to Paris before I bleed out. The thought of these options brings me to my knees as I search over the holding wall that has kept us somewhat hidden, finding no one in the distance—no one alive, at least. The others must have assumed we were gone.

We must wait until nightfall to continue in the condition we're in. I tear off my shirt, rip it in half and make two tourniquets to stop the bleeding from my shoulder and hip. With a bit of time to come up with a plan, I'm left with nothing other than praying for a miracle.

After the sun sets, I scavenge the area for clothing off dead bodies and weapons from both the French and Germans, all victims of today's battle. Hugo is still quiet and not saying much. He seems confused and disconnected from his mind, making me speculate why the Germans were even keeping him around. I'm glad they did for my selfish reason of wanting to save him, but he's in no condition to offer anyone insight and I don't know how long he's been this way.

He manages to drag his feet, thankfully, so I don't have to carry him as we make our way toward the train station. I flag down every French vehicle passing by, pleading for a ride with a promise of nothing in return. Unless someone decides to have mercy on us, our last stop will likely be on the train itself, when we're spotted by Germans who can easily assume what we've been up to by the looks of us.

"Do you gentlemen need a lift?" A man pulls up beside us.

Someone is having mercy on us and I'm not sure why. Maybe I'm imagining this older man staring at us with empathy as the moon glows off the hood of his car and shines dimly against us.

"Where are you heading?"

"Paris," I utter.

"Part of the resistance?" he questions, keeping his voice

down, quieter than the motor of his car.

I nod, knowing I have nothing to lose at this point. He greeted us in French, he's in a French vehicle, and he wouldn't have pulled over at the sight of us if he didn't intend to offer us help.

"Get in. I'll take you gentlemen home. As a veteran of the French military who fought in the First World War, may God have mercy on us all," he says as I help Hugo into his seat.

"My father fought in the first war too. Lieutenant Bardot of Paris. He was part of the 8th Army division during the Detachment of Lorraine but was injured before the end of the war."

"Lieutenant Bardot," the man repeats as if he's searching for a memory. He chuckles softly. "I remember hearing about him. I was in the 10th Army division but joined up with the 8th after the armistice as part of the occupation of Rhineland." The man takes a minute to gather his thoughts and it's hard to comprehend that he could have known my father. "Yeah, a lot of the men spoke of Bardot. He was quite the war hero from what I recall."

"He didn't think so, monsieur."

"No one who witnesses combat ever does, son."

I think it's been three or four days since the man who spared our lives with a ride out of Lyon dropped us back in Paris. Despite feeling as though I was treading along the edge of death by the time I made my way to our front door, Mère chose to spare my life and kill me with kindness instead of a frying pan, but she had some choice words for me too.

The pain has been so unbearable that I've been sleeping more than I've been awake. I've asked Mère to find Raya as it's been three weeks since I told her I'd come back for her. Of course Mère fought me on the subject, telling me to stay away from her after what she did. I tried to explain everything, but she won't listen or let me talk. She talks over me and walks out of the room before I can form a full sentence. As soon as I have the strength to make her listen, I will.

"We need to change the bandages," Mère says, sitting on the edge of my bed for what feels like the fifth time today. She adjusts the pillow behind my back and the mere stretching of my skin makes me wince still. The pain is relentless.

"Mère, it can wait. I want to rest," I tell her.

"No, it can't wait. I need to make sure you don't end up with an infection."

Part of me wonders if she's changing my bandages more often than I think is necessary to remind me of the pain once every few hours as a punishment for "putting myself in danger," as she's been not so mildly suggesting. I know she'd be more furious if my reason was for anything other than trying to rescue Hugo. Still, she knows now what we've been up to, and I wouldn't be surprised if she tries to hold me hostage in our home until the war ends.

I have no intention of going back in for more battles, not now, which makes me feel like Father would be ashamed of the man I've become—giving up, much like he did at the end despite accomplishing more than most people can say.

Mère dropped the two bullets into a glass jar and placed it by my bedside as a reminder. "Every woman became well-versed with first aid care during World War I," she's told me several times. That, and I should be lucky she knew how to extract the two bullets I was hit with. Thankfully, due to the distant range from which I was hit, the bullets didn't embed too far into my flesh, and she was able to extract them both with a set of tweezers.

"Hold still," she says, unwrapping the tight bandage from my shoulder first.

The pain causes a heaviness in my head, pinning me to my

pillow. Once she finishes wrapping me up with clean bandages, she scoops up the pile of bloody gauze and huffs.

"Mère, could you please help me find Raya? I must talk to her."

"Nicolas, please. You have far more to worry about than her feelings. I'm not having this discussion again."

She leaves my bedroom with the mess of bloody gauze, giving me the quiet I need to focus on nothing more than the closed curtains of my window. This must have been what Father felt like all that time, sitting and waiting for whatever was going to come next—something no one could ever know. What a miserable way to live.

"Ouis, ouis, je viens," Mère shouts.

I'm not sure who she's talking to but only a few seconds pass before the sound of the front door's rusting hinges squeak.

"I thought I told you not to come back again."

"S'il te plaît, Madame Bardot. It's been three weeks since I've seen him and I'm so worried. I just need to know if he's okay?"

The woman's words carry through the flat and my ears perk up when I identify the voice.

"No, you must go."

"Have you heard from Nicolas yet? Could you at least tell me that much?"

"Back away from the door, dear," Mère says.

"Mère?" I try to holler but my voice hardly carries.

"Is that him?" she asks.

I suppose it was loud enough to hear at the front door.

"This is not a good time," Mère continues.

With the pain of a million knives stabbing me all at once, I push myself upright, knowing I will likely start bleeding again, but I need to get to the door. "Mère, please," I call out as I stumble and drag my heavy weight around the corner.

"Oh mon Dieu, Nicolas. Get back into bed before you start

bleeding again," Mère scolds me.

"Bleeding again?" Raya repeats. I spot her brushing by Mère, forcing her way into the flat, her face becoming pale when she spots me. "Nicolas..." She gasps and holds her hand up to her mouth but continues toward me, slowly and with concern.

"I'm fine," I tell her, smirking at the use of her signature response.

"You are anything but fine. What happened?"

"It's a long story, but Hugo is home and alive."

The corners of her lips sulk, her chin tremors but she steps in closer.

"Raya, I don't think it's best that you are here," Mère continues to argue because she refuses to listen to me when I try to explain that Raya has done nothing wrong.

As Raya approaches me, I spot a baby's bonnet poking out of a pouch attached to the front of her body.

I reach my right arm out for her, needing to wrap her into the side of me that doesn't ache with every breath. "I'm sorry," I say, resting my chin on the top of her head. "I wanted to be back when I said I would. I know I let you down again."

"Again?" Mère snaps. "You have done nothing wrong, Nicolas!"

"I already know what lengths you go through for the ones you love," Raya points out, words I can't argue with. "But I was terrified something happened to you, and it did."

Mère has her arms crossed and a brow lifted to a point, fury illuminating her eyes.

"Mère, Raya and I need to talk. You don't need to be so cross. There is always more to a story than one might assume. I know that now."

"You should be resting, Nicolas. If you start bleeding again, it's not going to be good."

"I will be fine, Mère. Come with me," I tell Raya, catching a glimpse of a little button nose and long lashes resting across plump cheeks. "Amalia is even more beautiful since the last time I was with her." I hate that it pains me to say so, knowing the science behind her existence, but a baby didn't ask for the history she was born with. I understand that. "Just like her mother." I place my hand on the top of her bonnet covered head. She's so small even in comparison to the arch of my palm.

Mère's bedroom door closes with anger but I take a deep breath. "She'll come around."

Raya doesn't say much about Mère's reaction, almost as if she was expecting the response. I take her hand and lead her into my bedroom and close the door. When I reach for the chair tucked under my writing desk, Raya places her hand over my arm. "Get back into bed," she says, pulling the chair out on her own.

I move slow while easing back down onto the bed, trying to hide the agony shredding through me but once I find a position I can breathe through, I glance back over at Raya, watching her stroke Amalia's back in slow circular patterns. "I would have been by your side," I tell her.

"You would have hunted down every Nazi in this city until you were satisfied that you'd caught the right man."

She isn't wrong. I'm not sure I would have been able to accept what had happened to her and let it go like she's had to.

"Do you know who he is?" I ask.

Raya drops her gaze to focus her attention on Amalia. "I know he's a horrible excuse for a human being. I know he deserves to be the one in pain, or dead. A name won't do either of us any good and I'd rather it disappears from my memory, if you wouldn't mind."

I won't push her. It's clear she makes decisions based on the safety of everyone around her rather than herself, and it's something I should understand well. "Has he seen you since Amalia was born?"

"Yes, that's why I came here a few days ago. I was hoping your mère might have heard from you and that she would help me protect Amalia. However, she seems to despise me for hurting you and won't listen to anything I have to say. I know she was worried about you too, but I didn't tell her I knew where you were. I figured you wouldn't want her to know."

Mère never mentioned a word that Raya had stopped by unless I was too focused on the pain to acknowledge her.

"I appreciate your discretion. Unfortunately, she knows just about everything now except for what truly happened to you. I'm so sorry. I will talk to Mère and explain everything to her, but if you think Amalia is unsafe at the shop that means you are too."

"What choice do I have? I can't survive on stealing food. I could get caught and—"

The hell she's going through isn't fair. None of us know anything of fairness anymore. "Of course. Amalia can stay here while you're working, but we need to figure out a way to keep you safe in that place with the Nazis coming and going all the time."

I'll be laid up in bed for a while anyway so if Mère doesn't come around to the idea as quickly as I need her to, I will take on the responsibility of caring for Amalia. I'm not sure I'd even have a job to go back to if I wanted one. I'm sure Paul has forgotten about me by now after not showing up to work for so long. I'm not sure the paper is even still printing, but when I'm up to it, I'll pay him a visit and explain everything.

"She can stay with you during the work hours?" Raya asks, letting the rest of my statement fall to the side.

"Yes, but open my desk drawer," I say. "This is the condition."

She pulls open the wide drawer, fighting against the uneven wooden frame to get it to budge. "A pistol?"

"I have others. You need to keep that on you in case anyone

ever tries to hurt you again. If you'll do that for me, I'll keep her safe while you're working."

Raya stares at the gun as if she's never seen one before even though I distinctly remember the night she was ready to take out a group of German officers. I suppose I know why she had that urge now. "We must always be prepared to protect ourselves."

"Okay," she agrees.

"May I hold her?" I ask.

Raya's dimples deepen in her cheeks and a blush blooms across her nose and beneath her eyes. "Are you sure her weight won't cause you pain?"

"The right side of my body is all intact. We'll be okay," I tell her.

Raya coos at Amalia as she gently pulls her out of the bound fabric embracing the two of them together. I notice she's dressed in a pale yellow sundress with a pattern of white daises and a small white blanket draped over her shoulder as Raya stands up from the chair and carries her over to me. She places her tiny body in the crook of my right arm. She's warm and smells like powder. It doesn't take her long to squirm around and make herself more comfortable as she places the side of her face on my chest with her hand fisted up beside her nose. Her eyes flutter closed as she lets out a deep sigh.

My heart aches or maybe it doesn't ache—it's a feeling I can't describe. The urge to hold her closer and kiss the top of her head leads me to do just that and I undoubtedly love this little girl for no other reason than everything inside of me saying so.

"She looks smitten in your arm," Raya says.

"Shh," I tell her. "She's trying to take a nap."

"She takes a lot of naps," she whispers back, glowing with a sense of pride.

Mère opens my door, but with less heat this time. When she

spots me with Amalia in my arm, she places her hands over her heart.

"Raya," Mère says with a rasp. I notice her eyes are stained red and her cheeks are flush. "I've been so worried and upset about Nicolas that I didn't understand what he meant when he said you hadn't done anything wrong. It just hit me like a sack of flour—you weren't unfaithful at all, were you?" Mère keeps her voice to a soft hum, speaking directly to Raya.

Raya folds her hands on top of her lap and drops her gaze. "No, madame."

"You were trying to tell me so too, weren't you? I wouldn't listen. I saw what I saw and couldn't think of anything past my assumption."

"All the time leading up to having her, I only wanted to keep Nicolas safe. If he knew what happened—"

"He'd end up like this," she says, rolling her eyes at me as she shoves her hand out in my direction.

"Or worse. I couldn't bear the thought of being the cause."

"Unlike Hugo," she says with a sigh.

"Mère, not now," I tell her.

"I told you boys to keep your good senses and stay away from the war. But no, you can't listen. You never listen. Raya, boys never listen to their mothers so I'm going to pray for us all that this sweet little girl will be easier on us than Nicolas."

Raya laughs at Mère's frustration, which incites Mère to laugh too. "Oh, dear, I am sorry for closing the door on you. What an awful world we live in...it's hard to see beauty through the troubled skies sometimes, I suppose."

"Mère, Raya needs somewhere safe for Amalia to be during the day while she keeps the shop open. There are too many Germans soldiers and police going in and out of the building and the man who—Amalia shouldn't be there. Neither should Raya, but..."

"A person who has income is in no position to turn it away

right now. I understand," Mère says. "Amalia is welcome to stay here, but I do wish you didn't have to face your own danger every day, dear."

"Don't we all?" Raya asks.

I'm glad she chose to leave out the part where I'm forcing her to carry a weapon to work every day now. I'm not sure Mère would be too fond of the idea.

"May I?" Mère asks Raya.

"I'm holding her," I say.

Mère ignores me as I figured she would and scoops Amalia out of my arms, wrapping her in the blanket, and props her over her shoulder before walking right back out of the room as if she belongs to her.

Raya seems relieved and content. "To be clear, I don't expect anything from you. It wouldn't be fair to ask you—"

"Like I told you, before I even knew the truth, I will always love you, and Amalia too. Nothing else matters to me but your safety and hers. Do you understand?"

Raya kneels by my side and takes my hand in hers. "I sat awake every single night since I returned home from the hospital, worried out of my mind that something had happened to you. I tried so hard to convince myself you were okay and even considered that you may have changed your mind about us, knowing where Amalia came from. Of course, that just made everything worse because I can't imagine a world without you. The last nine months only grew harder by the day but I vowed to do the right thing by you and for that, the emotional pain I went through...I've never experienced something so awful."

I reach my hand over to her silky cheek and curl my fingers behind her ear. I forget about my injuries as I reach for her lips, but with a quiet groan rumbling in the back of my throat, Raya closes the gap, reconnecting us to the way we were always meant to be.

THIRTY-SEVEN

RAYA

Paris, France

The daytime hours without Amalia secured to my chest feel longer than they ever have before, but it gives me comfort to know she's safer at Nicolas's flat than she is here with soldiers prancing in and out of the shop daily, but it makes the walk go by quicker at the end of the day when I'm on my way to pick her up.

With the shop secured, I leave through the back door, finding the entrance to the underground hatch closet unsecured. I poke my head in, finding the hatch locked. I knew the Lions Rebelles continued to use the entrance for their group meetings even after Nicolas and I were apart. I didn't want to tell him to find another place to go, knowing they had been safe down there. The next place might not have been as safe. I never witnessed anyone coming or going, especially since it was so late at night, but I assume someone must have forgotten to lock the door when they left from the last meeting. It's been gusty out today too.

"Oh, I'm sorry, that was my fault," a man says, carrying a

stack of papers between his arm and side. "Louis," he says, reaching out to shake my hand, "I think we met a while back. You're an acquaintance of Nicolas Bardot, right?"

I met the entire group a few times before deciding I couldn't continue to be a part of their missions, but most of the men looked the same because of the way they wear their beret caps curving over their brute stares. "Yes, I believe so, but it's been a while since I've seen any of you."

"I'm Margot's brother. It seems we're all related or connected in some way I guess," he says with laughter. "Anyway, how is Nicolas doing? Is he healing well? We've all been worried about him."

"He's on the mend," I say.

"I'm glad to hear. Are you planning to see him soon?"

"Yes," I say, keeping my answer short as I don't recognize this man as well as I wish I did.

"Would you mind bringing him one of these leaflets? I know he wants to stay in the loop of what's going on," Louis asks. "I'm sure he'd like one."

I adjust my purse over my shoulder, keeping it clutched tightly in my hand. I'm not getting involved with any of this business anymore. "I don't think that's a good idea." I don't want to get caught carrying any of their leaflets around.

He takes a step back and places his hand on his chest. "Of course. I'm sorry. I shouldn't have asked—I understand and I'm sure like the rest of us, you want him to focus on getting better. I'm sorry for disturbing you, mademoiselle. I was about to bring them downstairs to hand out to the others for distribution, but I heard the back door to your shop rattling and ran in case you were someone else. Bad timing, I guess."

"No need to apologize," I say, peering around to make sure no one is witnessing this unnecessary exchange outside the building. "Thank you for being mindful. Be careful about leaving the door open behind you. It's important to keep it always locked," I tell him.

"I won't let it happen again. My apologies." I didn't mean to make the man so nervous, but he's stuttering, and his hands are trembling. Some of the papers pinched between his arm fall and I drop my bag to the ground and scurry to scoop up the leaflets before they blow away. "Gosh, I'm having a rough time today. I've been late to arrive everywhere I need to be." He rushes to pick up a couple more that flew behind me.

"We all have days like that sometimes, I guess." I lift my bag back up and sling it over my shoulder. "Good luck with everything," I say, nodding before walking off as he closes himself into the hatch closet.

From what Nicolas has told me, everyone in the group is paranoid, especially with what happened to Hugo and what Nicolas had to do to save him, but the requests for action are picking up, more and more each day as the calls for attacks are occurring regularly as they continue to try and push the Germans away.

I hate that Nicolas is injured, but knowing he's recovering well and quicker than I expected makes me curious to know how long it will be before he rejoins the fight. I wish I didn't have to think about it but what good are any of us doing if we aren't trying to get our lives back. If I didn't have Amalia, I might have changed my mind several more times about helping the Lions Rebelles. I was terrified after the one raid, but I shouldn't expect all the other members of the resistance to be fighting on my behalf if I'm capable of joining them.

As I enter Nicolas's building, the silence out front strikes me as odd. There have usually been children still playing outside and occupants gathering when I arrive. The Germans aren't down in this small district as often as they are everywhere else, and it has been nice to know there are still a couple of locations they don't seem to care about.

I knock on the front door, being greeted almost immediately by Nicolas with Amalia cradled upright within the fold of his right arm. "Mère is back!" he coos to Amalia. Amalia smiles and presses her fists up to her mouth. "How was your day, ma chérie?" Nicolas asks before placing a kiss on each of my cheeks, then a longer one on my lips, allowing me to feel his smile grow across his cheeks.

"Long, tiring, and German, but it's over now and I'm here," I say, placing my bag down and reaching my arms out for Amalia. I could have the worst day in the world, but as soon as my baby is in my arms, I can forget about everything else. "How was your day?"

"Well, Amalia had five wet nappies, drank every last bit of milk you left, and took two good naps," Madam Bardot says, stepping into the small living area from around the corner. She has a load of laundry held between her hands with a stack of clean, dry diaper cloths piled on top. I feel terrible that she's been adding the diapers to her laundry, but she insisted and gives me fresh nappy cloths to take home with me each night.

"I could have told her, Mère," Nicolas replies.

"You would have told her that you listened to records for hours while playing peek-a-boo with her toy lion and told her three stories and laid her down beside you for a nap while you jotted down notes for your next article," she laments.

"Well, you left those important parts out of her daily roundup, didn't you?" Nicolas argues with a grin.

"I'm thankful she's in such wonderful hands here," I say.

"Where did you get this?" Nicolas asks, pulling a paper out of my bag.

I recognize the back of the leaflet that Louis was bringing down to the others. "Oh, how did that get in there?" I question out loud, tracing my fingers up and down Amalia's back. "I almost forgot to mention that I ran into Louis, one of the gentlemen from your group, when I was leaving. I guess he was

delivering a stack of leaflets to the others downstairs, but I startled him, and some fell. One must have drifted into my open
bag."

"Just now before you came here?" Nicolas questions.
"Hmm. Well, Louis has always been clumsy, but he's good at
acquiring materials during the day. He's taken over from Bette
since she left the group. I wasn't sure you ever met. Did you?"

"The name sounds familiar, but everyone blended into one
another those few times I met them. He also left the hatch
closet door open when he thought I might have been someone
else, but I told him it must remain closed at all times. I think I
scared him enough that there's nothing for you to worry about."

"Mind if I keep this?" Nicolas asks, folding the paper and
slipping it into his pocket before I can answer him.

I wouldn't tell him no, but I would rather keep our conversations about the resistance to a minimum, especially with Amalia
in the picture now. "I don't want that to make you crazy with
thoughts," I warn.

"I don't have full range of mobility with my arm yet. You
have nothing to worry about. I'm still as good as worthless."

As if Amalia understood what Nicolas said, her lips pucker
into a pout and her chest heaves with a warning of an incoming
cry. I rock her from side to side, hoping to calm her down before
we head home for the night. "You upset her," I say, teasing
Nicolas. "You aren't worthless to us."

Nicolas leans toward us and lightly pinches Amalia's nose
between his first two fingers. "You know what I mean," he
explains. "Can you stay for a bit tonight?"

Most nights, I stay for a while so I can spend time with
Nicolas before I head out to make it home in time before
curfew, but because of the number of times I've stayed out over
the past week, I've gotten Charlette and I behind on the orders
that have been stacking up. The Germans have added wallets
and belts to their list of custom needs. We're busy with the

worst customers, but I've padded the time, so they don't query if I'm receiving help from someone who they haven't witnessed in the shop. Even still, I'll be working longer hours at night for the next few days to catch up. I would much rather be here.

"I want to, but I've been putting aside work that must get done. If I don't get through a good amount tonight, I'll end up getting behind on the orders, which will aggravate the impatient patrons." The sarcasm oozes through each of my words.

"I understand. Could I at least walk you home?"

I tilt my head to the side, giving Nicolas the same surly scowl that I've given him each time he's asked the same question. "You shouldn't be walking that far, not yet. If you're in pain after a couple of blocks, you should take it slow and build up your strength before you put yourself back into a mess of pain by walking such a far distance when it's not necessary."

"You're worse than Mère some days, you know that?"

"She's experienced in taking care of her brother and she's a mother now—a smart one you should listen to," Madame Bardot says with a smirk as she folds an undershirt that she's taken out of the laundry basket.

"We will be fine, and I'll return first thing in the morning with this little ham," I say, tickling Amalia's tummy, coercing the giggle I live to hear.

Nicolas sighs and lifts my bag, then hands me the second bag already packed up with Amalia's belongings. He stacks them both on my shoulder and kisses Amalia's head before opening the door.

"Goodnight, Madame Bardot. I'll see you in the morning. Thank you for everything," I say.

"Goodnight, dear. As always, my pleasure, and be safe."

Nicolas closes us out into the corridor. "I want us to live together. I don't want to say goodbye to you anymore. I spend all day thinking about this—about you, and I want to get married and have a life together despite the nature of everything surrounding us. I know it won't be an easy process with how challenging the Vichy government is making everything, but I want to make this happen, Raya."

The topic has come up a few times now, but never with so much determination behind his words. I've become complacent with the thought of knowing we will have a life together but I think we've both been waiting for the war to end first so we can celebrate without the many rules and regulations in place. He's even told me he has a ring for me for when we're ready.

When I look outside each day, there is nothing I see that tells me this war is coming to an end anytime soon and to wait for this unknown day is becoming more of a fantasy than a reality. "Okay," I agree, my heart pounding with joy and excitement as I try not to bounce Amalia around too much. If she wasn't in my arms, I'd forget about Nicolas's injuries and jump into his, which would likely make him yelp, so it's best that I'm holding Amalia. "I don't want to wait any longer either."

"You mean it?" Nicolas asks, his gaze wide and full of hope and eagerness. "I'll figure out how to get Alix home so he's with us too. I'll find a way. I mean it."

Alix. I would do anything to have my brother by my side, his blessing, him home with me.

He palms his hands around my cheeks and pulls me in, kissing me, loving me as much as I love him. Amalia reaches up between us and pokes our chins, likely wondering what we're doing above her head.

"I'll work everything out," Nicolas says, pulling away for a breath. "I'll make it special, so special we'll forget there is a war in the background of our life. I promise you. I promise you everything you both deserve, forever and ever."

THIRTY-EIGHT

NICOLAS
THREE MONTHS AGO, OCTOBER 1943

Paris, France

The feeling of intoxication is overwhelming as I make my way back inside, trying to maintain a straight face so Mère doesn't question why I'm as giddy as I feel inside. I'll need to find a way to let her know that I'll be living with Raya. After all, she has her own place, and she can't leave the Levis alone upstairs. Mère won't like the topic of me moving out, even if it is only a few blocks down the road.

"Is everything all right?" Mère asks, staring at me with a questioning eye.

"Of course," I answer, sounding breathless—because I am.

"What's that's sticking out of your pocket?" she asks, spotting the leaflet I shoved in there.

I glance down and push it down deeper into my pocket. "Oh, it's nothing. It fell out of Raya's bag. She asked me to toss it away. It's a newspaper advertisement."

"You need to get off your feet. You've been up, walking around for over an hour," she scolds me.

At least she'll be content knowing I'll still be scolded when I move in with Raya. "Okay, okay, Mère."

I close myself into the bedroom, inhaling the scent of baby powder left behind by Amalia. I hate that she goes home at night too. I've gotten so used to having her around all day that everything seems too quiet when they leave for the night.

Once I hoist my legs up on my bed, fighting against the heaviness that still thrives through my left side, I pull out the folded leaflet from my pocket, curious to see what the Lions Rebelles are planning next. It's hard not to feel like I'm wasting away here, unable to participate in the group Hugo and I both started, but at least he's back on his feet and back to attending the meetings. He's not ready to enter any raids yet, or so he said when he visited the other day.

I scan the front of the paper, finding a framed text box of German words. My eyes widen, and my breath catches in my throat, knowing we would never send out a leaflet with any German writing.

DIES IST EINE WARNUNG, DASS ES KEINE WEITEREN ANGRIFFE DES FRANZÖSISCHEN WIDERSTANDS GEBEN WIRD. DIE ZEIT IST ABGELAUFEN. ALLE GEWALTTATEN WERDEN NACH DEUTSCHEM RECHT MIT DEM TOD BESTRAFT.

My heart plummets into the pit of my stomach as I translate the German, reading:

THIS IS AN ALERT THAT THERE SHALL BE NO FURTHER ATTACKS BY THE FRENCH RESISTANCE. TIME HAS RUN OUT. ALL ACTS OF VIOLENCE WILL BE PUNISHABLE BY DEATH IN ACCORDANCE WITH GERMAN LAW.

I keel forward, wrenching my arm around my stomach. This

isn't one of our leaflets. Whoever Raya was speaking to wasn't Louis, it must have been a damn German spy dressed as a Frenchman. They must have been trying to confirm suspicions of the sewer entrance being utilized by a resistance group.

I need to stop her from going home. It's a set up.

I force my legs off the bed and grab my coat before limping off toward the front door.

"Where are you going?" Mère shouts after me before I close the door without giving her an answer that she will fight me on. "Nicolas!"

My mind moves faster than my body and the dread riveting through me is stronger than my ability to move at a fast enough pace. If I could shout her name at the top of my lungs, I could only hope she'd somehow hear me, but she wouldn't be the only one. I'd be causing a disturbance in a city that doesn't belong to us. They've caught us in a trap.

THIRTY-NINE
RAYA
THREE MONTHS AGO, OCTOBER 1943

Paris, France

My mind must be playing tricks on me. There hasn't been any rain all week but the sidewalk in front of the shop looks slick.

The closer I get, the easier it is to confirm that I could only wish there had been rain this week. The glass windows to the shop are shattered and the front door is ajar.

Charlette. No.

I run around to the back, praying the door is still locked even though I know it doesn't mean anything since everything can be reached from the front. The door is locked. I pray they only robbed the shop. They'd have no reason to look beyond the goods.

I struggle to get the key in the door. *Please, please, let the Levis be okay. Please.*

I let the door sit open for a moment, listening to the surrounding space and for noises upstairs, but there is only silence everywhere. I lock myself into the stairwell, check the door of the shop and find it still locked and untampered with. I make my way up half of the steps, listening again for a hint of any movement. I'm up high enough to see the mirror is still hanging on the wall upstairs. If the Levis were found, they wouldn't replace the mirror; they would have ransacked my flat. But everything is still in its place.

By the time I make my way to the mirror, my knees threaten to give out and I cannot fall, not with Amalia in my arms. The mirror vibrates against the wall as I lift it from the hooks and move it to the side. It takes less than a few seconds to see that the Levis are gone. *No, no.* Where would they have gone? There is nowhere for them to go.

Sirens blare in the distance, and I feel like I'm spinning in circles trying to understand what's happening right now. I press Amalia's head to my chest, covering her exposed ear from the piercing sounds growing outside. "I don't know what's happening, darling."

Thuds and clanging bangs of metal echo around the building and I can't tell where the sound is coming from, but I know it's closing in on me.

A fist charges against one of the two doors downstairs and my pulse replies with a louder beat, echoing through my body. I peer down at Amalia, staring at her as if I can embrace her with a feeling of protection. *I will always take care of you, always, no matter what,* I think to myself.

"Aufmachen!" a German soldier shouts, demanding that I open the door.

I'm lightheaded as I spin around, debating whether I can hide or if it's too late for that. They may have been watching and waiting for me. I spot the straw basket lined with a plush blanket, where Amalia sleeps at night when I'm in this room with the Levis. My chest feels like it's tearing open as I place her down, trying to smile and coo at her like I do before I lay her down to go to sleep at night. I lift the basket and place it behind a stack of wooden crates. "I'll be right back, darling, please rest your eyes. Mère will come right back for you. I promise." I crouch down beside her, leaving a kiss on her forehead. "I love you, my sweet girl. I'll be right back."

Another round of pounding against the back door makes the portraits on the wall rattle and it hard to hang the mirror up over the hole.

I must seem unaffected. I've done nothing wrong. The Levis aren't here. It's only Amalia and me, or me if they don't know any better. With an attempt to pull in a deep breath, I tighten my coat over my chest while unlocking the door to crack it open. "Ja?" I question the German standing in front of me.

"Identification," the Gestapo snaps.

I struggle to keep my hand steady as I pull it out of my coat pocket and hand it to the man, who nods upon reading my name. "You are under arrest for collaborating with the French resistance," he says.

I stare into the man's insipid glare as he doesn't seem to be able to make eye contact. "No," I snap, affirming my objection. "No." They have no proof that I've taken part in anything they're accusing me of. I've been too busy caring for a baby and running a shop.

The German shoves the door open fully and beside him is Louis. My mouth falls open as I come to realize Louis is in a Gestapo uniform now. He wasn't a member of the Lions Rebelles and I'm sure his name isn't Louis. He tricked me into giving him information and I've set myself up to be arrested for complying with the resistance. I should have known better than to talk to anyone. What have I done? How could I have been so stupid?

"Give us access to the tunnel immediately," the man who called himself Louis says, shoving his hand out for me to hand over a key, I assume.

There's no way I can do that. I would get all the Lions Rebelles killed. I shake my head, knowing it might mean they are free to do whatever they plan to do to me. "I don't have a key," I cry out.

"You own the property, which includes the tunnel entrance. Surely, you have one of the keys," he says, gritting his teeth. "You said it is important to always keep the door locked, didn't you?"

"No. I don't have access."

"She's lying," he says. "We'll find the key ourselves then."

Amalia. They'll find her if they're looking for something as small as a key.

"Empty your pockets."

They pull the lining of my pockets out from my jacket, finding nothing as I left everything upstairs. But the key isn't in the flat at all. I keep one hidden in the wall behind the grandfather clock in the shop. Even if they find it, they may be able open the hatch but once they reach the bottom, there is only a bit of space to move around before a locked gate keeps them from accessing any other area.

"I wouldn't keep a key on me or in the building. It's dangerous to have. You are making a mistake thinking I have access. I don't," I shout. "Let me go!"

"You've already confirmed you are aware of the group that meets down here. There is no sense in lying."

The two soldiers yank me outside and pull my hands behind my back and secure them with a tightly knotted rope before pushing me toward their vehicle. "This is a mistake," I shout, knowing they won't listen to a word I say, regardless of whether I speak German or not.

I can't leave Amalia. I need to go back for her. Sweat bleeds through my clothes as I force myself to keep my gaze set ahead rather than looking behind me toward my flat. If I look in that direction, they will assume there is something I've left behind. My baby.

"Please let me go," I beg once more before I find myself

sliding across a cold metal floor on the bed of their covered truck. I can't breathe as I rebound from the thud of falling to my side and try to lunge for the opening, but the gate shuts and I'm caged like a stray animal, scratching my nails against the metal as tears flood down my face.

Amalia. My baby. What if they find her? What if they don't? What will happen to her? My God, please, please, don't let this happen to me. I've done nothing wrong. Nothing.

FORTY

NICOLAS

Paris, France

The stitching pain, like a blade against flesh, is all I can focus on before spotting a crime scene of shattered glass out in front of Pascal Maroquinerie. I wanted to be wrong, but their games are tactless, and there is no such thing as a battle when it comes to the Nazis. It's one life over another and they have the means to protect their own.

My body stiffens, the pain numbs as I let myself into the unlocked shop, finding it destroyed from corner to corner. Every handmade product is gone, the shelves torn from the walls, the cash register upside down in the middle of the floor, empty.

The heaviness bearing on my chest makes me want to tear my skin off to get more air, but it won't help. I limp to the back door, nearly paralyzed with terror as I reach for the knob, finding it still locked. Relief should come instantly but it doesn't. I'm not sure Raya even made it home, never mind the chance of her being in one piece upstairs.

I shove my hand into my pocket, retrieving the key I thankfully still have. I step into the stairwell and close the door behind me, wishing I had chosen to look right, up the steps, first for that last bit of hope. But I peered to my left, finding the back shop door ajar. I shut the door and lock it, knowing how likely it is to be too late for locks, but I do so anyway and bolt up the stairs, ignoring the tearing sensation in my hip as I push through the internal agony that has nothing on the dread filling my body like a thick tar.

"Raya?" I call out, keeping my voice to a moderate volume. After poking my head in every room, finding each intact, but quiet, I stare at the mirror, wondering if it did what it was intended to do—distract. I lift it from the nails and place it down gently against the wall before making my way in through the hole. I shove my hand back into my pocket, this time looking for a match to light up the dark space. A click and scratch before the slight illumination glows in front of me. I step in toward the bedding set up for the Levis, finding it all untouched. I spot Raya's bedding that she's been using to sleep here with Amalia so she isn't awoken by the air raids, but the cradled basket is missing.

They got away. Can I convince myself that they all got away?

With another match lit, I walk the perimeter, confirming no one is up here. I'm not sure what form of hope to grasp at. If the Levis are gone, they could have been found. Jacques...he was the loose end between the Lion Rebelles and the lone fact that Raya was hiding a family of Jewish people in her flat.

I circle around within the dark space without a clue as to where to go from here, where to begin looking for them. I feel my way over to the wall's opening and lift my left leg like it's an anchor to get through to the other side.

While ducking to make my way out, a peep, as quiet as a mouse, pricks my ear. A shuffling follows and I turn around, listening for more noise. Another peep, this one longer, louder and a warning sound before a full-out cry begins. *Amalia.* I light another match and trip myself going back through the hole, dragging my knees across the floor as I hold out the flickering flame. Before the stick disintegrates into my hand, I spot the sight of a wicker basket. I'm down to only a few matches as I light another, moving in the direction I saw what I hope not to be an illusion. The match remains burning until my fingers sweep against the rigid tight weave of silky straw. A cry follows the darkness with a halo of smoke left behind as a reminder of where the light was just shining. I reach my hands into the basket, feeling the small, warm body. Another whimper and a cry. I would recognize Amalia's cry anywhere in any crowd among hundreds of people. It's gentle, but fierce; not a growl, but a purr.

I hold her against my chest, knowing without a doubt it's her, without having to see a single strand of hair. I push myself up to my feet, arching forward to avoid hitting my head against the angled ceiling and again, feel my way around for the hole in the wall. I groan louder than Amalia as I step through the opening again but with the light from the stairwell, her blue eyes glisten with despair. "Where's Mère?" I ask her, knowing she can't respond. "Where is she, darling?" I try to hold back the tears threatening to pour from my eyes.

Raya would never leave her behind. She's gone. My love. My everything. Please, don't take her from me, God. Please. I gasp, trying to catch my short breaths.

I re-wrap Amalia in her blanket and hold her firmly against my chest as I stagger down the steps. Neither the front of the shop nor the back is safe, but I have to assume there will be less of a chance for someone watching me leave this building if I go out the back. "It's okay, darling. It's okay, shh," I say, soothing her when I can't manage to calm myself.

Not a soul is in sight, which affirms to me that the Gestapo came and took what they wanted. Raya had time to hide

Amalia. There isn't a doubt in my mind that they have her held captive.

"I'm so sorry, my sweet girl," I tell her. "This is my fault. I should be taken, not her." I don't know why I'm whispering these words to Amalia but she needs to know Raya would never abandon her.

I take every side alley back to my building, wishing I could go faster, but I can only move at the pace my body will allow. I don't know how I'm safely inside, about to walk into my flat with Amalia but Raya is gone. This isn't right.

Mère is still standing where I left her, staring at me with unwavering horror watering out from beneath her lashes. "Where is Raya?"

I try to get the words out, but short breaths are all I can manage as my lungs threaten to fall flat. "She's—" I heave for whatever air I can take in. "She's gone. She—she—she wasn't—wasn't home." Despairing groans thrust through my chest as if I'm releasing trapped steam from a piece of old machinery.

I try to speak, but a bellowed, "Why?" comes out instead. I take a heavy step forward and Mère jolts toward me to take Amalia out of my arms. "What—what—Mère—what do I do?" I moan.

She has Amalia in one arm and her opposite hand cupping her mouth as tears skate down her cheeks too. "Do you think the Germans have her?" she whispers between breaths.

"Yes, I'm sure of it," I reply. "She doesn't deserve this. I must find her."

"Where?" Mère asks me.

Her question isn't intended to be obvious and straightforward, but it is and there is no answer to her question because the answer is anywhere. She could be anywhere.

FORTY-ONE

RAYA

THREE MONTHS AGO, OCTOBER 1943

Paris, France

The road is unforgiving beneath these horrible tires and each bump is a slap against the face as my cheek rests on the floor of this filthy vehicle. I don't know if they captured the Levis too. Maybe that's why they are taking me away. I was hiding them, which is considered treason. But they didn't mention a word about them, only the resistance.

My short breaths continue to come and go, causing me to see colorful spots around me within the darkness of the vehicle. I can't faint. I must stay alert and convince them this was all a mistake.

When the truck stops and the back gate opens, I'm pulled across the metal floor and blinded by a bag tugged down over my head.

They've moved me into a building and the chair they've tossed me onto feels like an old school chair, cold and metal. The bag lifts from my head, exposing a large room with cement walls, bright lights dangling from the ceiling, and the smell of body odor mixed with blood and sewage. Several soldiers, stationary like statues, stare at me as if I'm the cornucopia they're all about to fight over. Except, the man standing directly in front of me will win over all the others because he has a pistol pointing toward the center of my forehead. The man who has already taken so much from me isn't satisfied yet.

"Where is the baby?"

I still have control. This fight isn't over.

"What baby?"

Gustav narrows his eyes, intimidating me with his monstrous stare I have nightmares about whenever I close my eyes. "The baby you had with you in the shop," he says, speaking with a kinder inflection as if that will get me to say more than I already have.

"That wasn't my baby. I was watching her for a friend."

Gustav's nostrils flare as he takes a stiff step toward me but lowers his pistol. "My memory is quite sharp, and I'm sure I recall you referring to her as your child when you asked me not to touch her."

I hardly remember what I was saying that day and there's a strong chance I did say what he's accusing me of. Rather than respond, I concentrate on keeping my eyes open like stones, refusing to blink or give any inclination that he has any effect over me.

"Who is the father of that baby?"

My heart is pounding so hard my rib cage feels like its punching bag. "I don't know his name."

"Either you're a witless prostitute, or it is more important to keep the father's name protected. Which is it?"

"Neither," I respond, gritting my teeth so hard they ache.

Gustav pivots on his heels and takes a few steps away from me before pivoting again. "How were you assisting the resistance below your shop?" His question is far too calm for me to assume he's only casually asking the question.

"I was not helping the resistance. I was running a shop,

serving German soldiers with their orders of custom leather goods, as you know."

He moves so fast his body becomes a blur and my head feels as if it detaches when he backhands me across the face. The sting searing down the back of my throat and up to the top of my head.

"Who runs the resistance group in the tunnels beneath your shop?" Again, Gustav lifts the pistol to my head.

I stare at him, forcing eye contact. Speaking will only make this worse so I don't. I could give him an answer and he would still kill me, or I could keep quiet and be killed but know there is still a chance Nicolas will remain safe and somehow find Amalia. He's my only hope.

Gustav releases the safety on the pistol, and I close my eyes, waiting for him to decide my fate.

FORTY-TWO

NICOLAS

Paris, France

"Nicolas," Mère shouts from the kitchen. "Would you please go to the store for the rations today? The rain is coming down so heavily this afternoon."

I've been nothing more than a hollow person, grieving, pacing, writing, and caring for Amalia—Amalia only. I only leave her side when I meet up with Hugo late into the night as he helps me try to track down Raya—where she could have been taken, and if we can obtain intelligence from anyone inside the prison camps.

All these months later, I still don't have a clue if she's alive or dead. I refuse to accept the possibility of the former thought. Therefore, my search will continue until we have run out of resources. Even then, I won't stop. I'm trying my hardest to remain safe for the sake of Amalia, knowing that she could lose me too if I'm not careful. I hate having to choose between going to the ends of the earth to find Raya and staying complacent, here, and in sight for this sweet child who deserves her mère.

She's almost a year old and she's babbling words. I've taught her to say Mère or Mè-me as she pronounces it, but she doesn't understand what it means. She doesn't know Raya and I'm jealous that she doesn't have to live with the constant heart-break of missing her like I do.

"Nicolas, did you hear me?"

"Yes, Mère. I'll go. I'll go."

"The store on the corner is closed. You'll have to go to the one on the east side of Montparnasse." I run my hand down the side of my face, listening to Mère go on and on before she steps into my bedroom. "How many times have I told you that Amalia needs to do something other than watch you write. She's a baby. She shouldn't be assisting you in writing your articles."

My articles, the ones that are mostly all stored in my desk drawer. Paul had to let me go from my desk job after I was injured. However, he still allows me to submit articles that he can choose from and pay a small fee per word for the ones he likes. But it's rare that he takes more than two in a week.

"She's content and playing with the rattle I made her. I don't see a problem," I argue.

"Just because you are holding her does not mean she is content. She needs to crawl around and explore. That's how babies learn, Nicolas." Mère takes Amalia off my lap and carries her out of the room.

I drop my pen and push my chair away from my desk, dreading the walk to the store in the rain. The wet weather brings about a stiffness to my shoulder and hip, but enough to be a nuisance rather than hindering.

I take my raincoat out of my closet and take the umbrella out from the tall porcelain stand by the front door. The ration book is on the side pedestal, and I tuck it into my pocket before stepping out the door.

The rain slows to a drizzle once I make my way onto the main street and the clouds hush across the sky, giving me hope that the rain might stop altogether soon. I don't often walk in this direction, avoiding the leather shop and the reminder of what I came to find and lose. I've only gone back twice, both in the same week Raya was taken. I wanted to clean up the glass in front of the shop and board up the windows. I'm not sure I did a great job with the condition I was in, but it was better than leaving the shop in shambles and inviting stray people in from the street that may find a way upstairs into her flat. I suppose I wouldn't be surprised if the Germans have already done so. They steal every habitable location they can for housing.

I'm relieved to see the wood boards still in place and the door closed. It will be a miracle if it's still locked, as I left it. I reach for the doorknob and find it stiff. I should be heading to the line at the store, knowing it will be wrapping around the corner as usual, but while I'm here, I should see if I can find the address I've needed. I searched the flat those other two times, but I couldn't bear the heartache of going through her things as if she was dead and never coming back for them.

I search my pocket for the key; I keep it on me at all times in case I need it, for whatever reason, and let myself into the empty shop. I straightened up a bit too and placed the register beneath the counter so it couldn't be spotted easily if someone was able to look through the cracks of the boarded windows. There's nothing inside it, but a cash register would be tempting to anyone right now.

I make my way through the shop to the back door and head up the stairs. The smell of old dust reminds me how long it's been since I've walked up these steps or back down with Amalia in my arms.

No one has moved in and claimed the place to be their own. That, itself, is a miracle. I didn't search through the kitchen drawers last time and it didn't dawn on me until after I left that she might put letters or other important information in one of those. She doesn't have a writing desk like I do so I suppose there are only so many places to store things, and there was nothing helpful in her bureau or in Alix's closet.

I sweep my hand over the top of the empty refrigerator, touching nothing but dust. Raya liked to have everything in a place, whatever place she decided that would be, but usually not out in the open. The drawers are next. The first holds silverware, which I should have remembered. The next one holds cooking utensils and then the small panel that looks like it should be a drawer but likely isn't, is all that's left. I wedge my fingers under the protruding panel and tug, finding it to indeed be a small drawer. My shoulders fall forward as I find a stack of letters. Please let this be what I need.

I've called many operators and searched through various directories, looking for Alix Pascal in Switzerland, but for the life of me, I couldn't recall what school he was enrolled in or in what city. She might have only mentioned it once.

I remove the stack of letters, finding the first one addressed to Raya with a return address to Alix. Thank God. I press the envelope to my chest, wishing I could ingest the slight amount of relief this gives me.

I slip the letter into my pocket and head toward the stairs to leave but the mirror in the hallway catches my attention, the reflection from the few rays of sun breaking through the clouds and into the rippled glass window of Raya's bedroom hit the face of my watch and then the mirror.

A creak moans and I feel the plank of wood I'm standing on nudge.

It could be anyone or anything, but I need to know if someone is on the other side of that wall.

I remove the mirror and step through, startled by large gasps. Then I consider the possibility of suddenly seeing ghosts for the first time in my life, but Charlette's arms swing around my neck before I can wonder for much longer.

"I thought you were taken when Raya was," I say, trying to catch my breath that I somehow lost over the last thirty seconds.

Charlette pulls away and shakes her head. "When we heard the shop being broken into and glass smashing, we made a run for it by climbing through Raya's bedroom window. Thankfully the awning above us overlapped with the one beneath her window and we managed to make it up to the rooftop where we hid between the chimneys. There was so much activity coming and going behind the building that we had no choice but to wait it out. I was hoping we could get down into the tunnels, but it seemed like there were eyes everywhere and we didn't know why. We stayed put up there, flat on our backs for several days, before we attempted going back inside. We had no idea where Raya went or if she left because she thought we were gone."

I'm not sure I want to know how they've been surviving all this time but whatever they have managed to feed themselves with hasn't been much by the emaciated figures hunched over in front of me.

"If Raya was taken..." Charlette cries out, "where —where is..."

I swallow hard, trying to find my words as I peek over my shoulder into the corner where I found her. "She left Amalia in the wicker basket up here. She must have known they were coming. There was a German spy, posing as one of the men in our resistance, and he handed her a leaflet. I found it but realized too late that she was heading home to a trap. I couldn't get to her in time."

Rose drops her gaze, her facial muscles strain and the glow from the gas lamp in the center of the floor highlights the rosy hued webbing across her cheeks. "You have Amalia?"

"Yes, she is at my home with my mère. She sent me to pick up food and the store closest to us closed so I had to come this way and wanted to check in on the flat while I was down here."

"That poor child," Jacques says.

"What about Raya?" Rose asks him. "God only knows where she is right now or if she's alive. Do you think they took her in connection with the resistance?"

I nod, confirming her thoughts match mine. "Yes."

"All she did was try to protect and help everyone. That's all that poor girl did, and after losing everything already—her parents, and Alix leaving the country. She still put herself last."

Rose's words feel like a fishhook to my gut. "I can do whatever possible to help keep you safe here. After dark, I will find a way to bring you some food and supplies. I will check on you as often as I can and help you with whatever you need."

"Nicolas," Rose questions my offer. "We couldn't ask that of you..."

"You're not asking. I'm telling you, like Raya would have done. I'm going to collect the rations for my mother. I'll be back here after nightfall."

Ravensbrück, Germany

There isn't a cloud in the sky and the sun is radiating over us all. If I stare at the dirt between the holes covering the tips of my shoes to the splitting seams of the woman's shoes in front of me, I can trick myself into thinking it's sand from a beach. Even before the war, it had been years since I'd been to the beach in Marseille, but I can remember the way the sand filtered between my toes and the sound of waves crashing into the shore. I could leave behind the thought of Alix playing catch with his friends, kicking up sand into my face while I tried to get a bit of sun, but even that memory would outweigh anything I've experienced here.

A weapon fires in the distance, another execution with more likely to follow while we wait for roll call. Waves crashing against the shore. Not a bullet searing through a skull. A light breeze blows the sand up to my knees, not dirt riddled with runoff fecal matter and other bodily fluids.

A woman two rows up from me falls forward, her face smashing into the ground, and dirt pelts us all as she lands harder than a sack of potatoes. A melody of muffled gasps grows from us all as we lunge forward to help her to her feet.

I'm no longer at the beach. I'm far from there. And we're holding a woman upright to appear as if she's standing on her own even though she's completely unconscious. Her skin is blotchy, red, and white, her lips have no color, but she weighs less than an older child and she's easy to hold up with so many of us grabbing onto to her.

Another shot is fired. It's a rifle not a wave. The sun beats down on us like we're standing in front of an open oven with licking flames reaching for each of us. The guards see us all. They know someone has already fallen unconscious from dehydration, heat, dread, and panic as we stand here waiting for God knows what every morning. She'll just be another notch on their score sheet.

The middle of July did not spring up on me like it has in every other year of my life. It was more like a slow race, one where we couldn't use our arms or legs to move us from one point to the next. Time seems to stand still when embracing the depths of hell. It's so hot. I'm not sure if I know the exact date as there have been nights I have forgotten to scratch a line into the wood of my bunk. But I wouldn't forget Amalia's birthday, her first birthday—a year of firsts I've missed.

I would have made her an almond cake with buttercream frosting. She'd be in a sundress and her hair might be long enough to style. She'd be giggling and smiling with every gift I had for her. Alix would have her hoisted up on his tall shoulders, parading her around like a proud uncle as Nicolas and I would sit and take in the moments flying by too fast to hold on to.

I try to force myself to believe she's safe, even after the long nine months I've been held captive here. I wonder if Nicolas or Alix have any clue where I am, if they're looking for me, or if they think something else happened. I don't want to consider what could have happened to them during this time apart.

"Are you sleeping at roll call?" a guard shouts. "Open your eyes, rodent!"

"She's overheated," one of the other women says. "She needs water."

"Aw, she's overheated, ja?" He tsks his tongue against the roof of his mouth three times before lifting his pistol and shooting the woman in the head.

Blood sprays over each of us, much like the dirt from the pressure of her hard fall.

I glance down and wish more than anything I could tell myself I'm covered in red paint.

FORTY-FOUR

NICOLAS

Paris, France

Before I open my eyes each morning, I imagine Raya is sleeping beside me. I keep fresh lavender in a vase on my nightstand to fool myself into believing she's here with me.

"Pa—pa—pa."

"Amalia, don't you ever want to sleep in, baby girl?"

"No, no."

A shriek follows as it does every morning. She knows precisely how to wake me up and get me out of bed. I twist my head, finding her standing in the small crib I built for her, bouncing up and down on the thin mattress. A mess of blonde curls is flying through the air and a smile awaits me. All I can do is smile in return. She's made the hardest of days tolerable and I'm not sure what I would do without her, which brings me guilt, knowing Raya is without her.

I amble out of bed and lift her out of her crib. She kicks her feet until she can reach my neck, then claws onto me like a little monkey, resting her head on my shoulder.

When I feel her heart beating against mine, my soul cries.

We're free from the Germans now and life might even return to something we could consider normal someday, but there is still a war in our country and Raya—I can only believe she's not dead because she hasn't appeared on a list of deceased citizens of Paris.

"We need to get dressed and have some breakfast then we're going to see Uncle Alix and bring Aunt Charlette some food. Is that okay, darling?"

"No, Pa," she says shaking her head against my shoulder.

"We need to learn how to stay quiet once in a while too, ma bébé."

"No, no."

"Is that my beautiful grandbaby I hear?" Mère shouts from the kitchen.

"And your beautiful son," I jest.

Mère storms into my room and snatches Amalia from my arms. "You can fetch your own breakfast," she says, scrunching her nose at Amalia with a smile.

It's endearing to hear Mère refer to Amalia as her grandbaby, but the word is like a knife to my chest every single time. The last thing I said to Raya was that I wanted us to be a family. At least she knew that much. I still want that, and I can't give up on that dream. In my heart, I feel as if she's somewhere just on the other side of where I can't see. In the meantime, though, I feel like I'm stealing Raya's life rather than saving part of her world. Despite searching for her in every possible direction, there isn't a trace of her existence anywhere. It's as if she disappeared off the face of the earth.

FORTY-FIVE

RAYA

Ravensbrück, Germany

A rattle in my lungs woke me several times last night and my throat burns like I've swallowed a rusty nail. I've caught more common colds here than I'd like to count but this is a bit different. I'm not sure my body can fight off whatever is running its course through me. It's been nearly a week and it's taking everything I have to keep myself upright as my head feels like a goldfish bowl.

"Take this," a woman says, dropping her hand into my coat pocket as I hover over the long narrow wooden table in the center of the barrack.

"What is it?" I ask, my voice hoarse and weak.

"Mint leaves. Drop one in your coffee water or soup broth. It will help your cough." I glance up at the woman and my eyes deceive me into thinking she looks just like Mère. The woman places her hand on my head and smiles kindly. "Take care of yourself. You've come this far."

"Thank you," I utter. The woman continues past me and when I twist my head to watch her walk away, I don't see where she went. I would think I'm imagining things if I didn't feel the mint leaves resting in the bottom of my coat pocket.

So many of the others have died from illnesses and I wish I could have asked them ahead of time what they experienced just before they took their last breath. I think I want to know, but I'm not ready to go yet. I'm scared of death, the unknown, but I'm also not sure I will be released from this prison alive. The guards are doing everything they can to get rid of people, but they aren't moving very fast, or so it seems.

"Did anyone else see the group of women leaving?" one of the younger inmates calls out. "I don't mean on a train. They were walked out of the camp, following a guard."

"Where could they be taking them?" another woman asks.

"Maybe they're setting them free because there are too many of us to handle."

If I could laugh, I might. We all know they would kill us before setting anyone free.

"I wish I was walking with them," the first young woman says.

"Don't wish for something that could be far worse than what we're currently experiencing," someone shouts at her. "It's either this type of suffering or death. There is nothing else. They've made that very clear to us."

I'm not sure what to think, but I can understand both sides of the argument. Leaving the camp would give us a chance to escape, but only if we were to have enough energy to run from a healthy guard watching our every move.

I stare down at my hands, the shape of the bones in my fingers. I never realized how much fat fingers contained, and I didn't think my bones were so narrow and frail looking without the fat surrounding them. I've seen skeletons and my hands look the same but covered in thin, pale skin. My arms are similar, but I keep them covered with the sleeves of my coat and I prefer to avoid staring down at my ankles that make me wonder how they're holding up my body at all. There's hardly anything left of me. Soon there will be nothing. I imagine one day I just won't wake up and I wonder if I will know I have died or if that will just be the end, like a blank piece of paper with no words or explanation—nothingness.

FORTY-SIX

NICOLAS

Paris, France

Six months ago, the relentless, unforgiving French resistance accomplished the unthinkable. While it was without my assistance, help I desperately wanted to offer, we forced Germany to forfeit their occupation in our country. Our city and country, though still in shambles, is turning a corner toward brighter horizons a bit more each day. The war isn't over for Europe, but there is hope among Germany's weaknesses.

We are all becoming stronger, filling our mouths with more food, and venturing out into the streets again, slowly and with caution, but seeking the new day with eagerness.

I have not seen the light of this new time because there will be no such thing until I locate Raya, whether alive or dead, I will find her before I rest.

"Nicolas, where are you taking Amalia in this brittle weather?"

"I need to submit my articles to Paul." The last thing I want to be doing these days is writing daily updates for the paper or working at all. The war updates are crucial to the public and the income is keeping us fed. It's hard to acknowledge that no matter how hard I work or how much effort I put forth toward the newspaper, I will likely never be able to publish the only information I will ever need—that the love of my life and Amalia's mother is alive and free from whatever hell she must be living within.

"And then?" Mère asks. "The French headquarters again?"

"One of these days, they will have an updated list of prisoner names with their locations."

Mère gives me a look, the same look she unknowingly shares when I spout off hope for something that seems impossible to acquire. She won't argue but I feel the doubt she suppresses inside. She lowers herself to her knees and opens her arms for Amalia to give her a hug. Amalia looks like a ball of fluff dressed in the thick winter clothes Mère has knitted for her as she makes her way into Mère's arms and gives her a pinching squeeze before returning to my side.

"Amalia could stay with me."

"I'm aware," I respond, tying a scarf around my neck. I rarely go anywhere without Amalia. It would be easier to leave her with Mère, but I hate being away from her for too long. We need each other.

* * *

I knock on the back door of Raya's flat, hoping the sound carries up the stairwell. Less than a minute passes when I hear footsteps jetting down the stairs and the door opens wide.

"Nicolas, it's early," Alix says, his face pale and eyes bloodshot. He takes Amalia from my arms and wraps her into a tight embrace.

"I have some errands to run but your phone call sounded urgent. I didn't want to wait any longer," I tell him.

I'm thankful I received the phone call before Mère did last

night. She would have asked Alix a hundred questions if she'd heard the tone of his voice, but we don't share news over the phone lines still. Alix returned home shortly after France was liberated in August. I had sent him a letter last spring after locating his information within the flat and informed him about Raya and Amalia. We conversed back and forth for months until he was finally able to make his way home from Zurich.

Since being back, he's been on the prowl for Raya alongside me. He's also been seeking information about the man who assaulted Raya, doing what she had asked me not to do. I pleaded with him to respect her wishes, but he told me this was on him and not me. I worry that's what his phone call was about last night.

"I found him. The Nazi, Gustav Vogel. Charlette said he had been a paying customer and I was able to go through the order slips she had filed away and match up the dates and times."

I wish I didn't have to know his name. I wish Raya didn't have to know his name.

"Alix, whatever it is you're—"

"No, no," he says, pacing back and forth between the bottom of the stairwell and the open door between us as Amalia pinches her fingers around the stubble over his top lip.

"You won't find him. We both know this. And if you do find him, then what?"

Alix places his hand over Amalia's ear and holds her head gently against his chest. "I will kill him."

"You won't," I tell him. "You aren't a killer. You won't do that. You understand?"

Alix shakes his head and all I can do is pray he won't be able to find this Nazi. "He stole Raya's life. He will pay."

"I stole her life. I was part of the resistance. She was in the wrong place at the wrong time and was tricked into a confession by a German spy. It's my fault, Alix. You should hate me." The words of truth never come out any easier and not a day goes by where I don't blame myself for what happened to Raya.

"Don't take the blame away from that man," Alix snaps, but in a whisper so as not to scare Amalia. "We will find Raya, and then I will find him."

There is no use in arguing with him. He won't rest until she is found and until there is retribution for what has happened to her. I understand, but there's no saying we'll find her, and that's the hardest part to comprehend.

"You're going to be a teacher. That's what she wanted for you. You know this, right?" I say.

"I can't be a teacher without defending right from wrong," he responds.

FORTY-SEVEN

RAYA

Ravensbrück, Germany

"Get up. Get up at once. Move, move, move!" In the eighteen months that I've been subjected to life here in Ravensbrück, like an abused barnyard animal, never have I been awoken like this. Every day has been the same, like a ripple in time, repeating over and over and over, never to falter unless I've been ill, making every minute of the day worse than any other day. Until now.

My eyes flash open and I gulp the stale air, panic-stricken to hear shouting demands in what must be the middle of the night with how dark it is in the barrack. The bunk platform rumbles and shakes as everyone struggles to follow the demands. There isn't enough space for us to all move at once, but we try so none of us are the one caught being the slowest.

The overcrowding issues in Ravensbrück that have been consistently growing by the day mean it's nearly impossible to get from one side of the barrack to the other without stepping on someone or tripping. Chaos in the dark is something none of us can manage in our current conditions of delirium, fatigue, and being beaten to the bone.

"Move, you rats!"

Like the cattle car transport to the camp, we're all pinned together, moving as if in one solid unit, trying to funnel our way out the door into the cold night air. I pull my coat tightly over my chest, trying to block the wind from slapping against my neck.

More SS guards appear, swarming us from each side as prisoners unload from the surrounding barracks too.

Many of us are shoved into one another, trying to remain steady on our feet, and it isn't long until we're sleighing forward through the thin coating of icy snow mixed with mud. It's hard to see what direction we're traveling once we're out of the main courtyard.

As we walk, moans of misery, groans of distress, and whimpers from torment sound like a haunting melody, something I would expect to hear when approaching the gates of death. The guards don't tell us anything, where we're going, why we're going, or what's the purpose of us marching in four rows down the snow-covered path in the middle of the night. They've proven to incite terror and pain for the sake of their pleasure, so beyond that objective, there isn't much else to assume. The cold air bites and sticks to us like sap with the low-bearing clouds hovering overhead. My ears crackle and pop and my nose is leaking like a faucet, leaving my face raw and chapped.

I want my legs to move on their own accord, trying not to focus on the burden of life pushing me down along with the gravitational force. I stare at the woman's bare neck in front of me, the scars in thick lines diagonally across her neck. I speculate if they are left behind from burns or a punishment of flogging.

Though I've been more silent than the others, I've heard more stories than I could retain and to assume an injury is one thing or another unthinkable one is useless. The guards come up with new forms of punishment daily as if they are trying to outdo each other with their creative ways of abuse.

The longer I stare at the scar on the woman's neck, the less present I feel. Visions of Amalia, Nicolas, Madame Bardot, Alix, Charlette, Rose and Jacques, and even Monsieur Croix, remind me of the life I was so lucky to experience.

The thud of a body against the stale ground vibrates through my feet. We all crash into each other's backs, forced to stop walking.

It's becoming clear that they plan to march us into the ground, but for a reason I'm not sure any of us understand when they've had no trouble executing and gassing the others.

"Keep going!" the leading SS guard shouts, shoving the women in front to move faster than they're capable of. "Move, move, move!"

The wind hurtles toward us like a wrecking ball, threatening to take down all of the prisoners with one swing. Debris from the dirt spins around us, flying into our eyes, making the challenge of keeping up with the person in front of us more difficult. My head must be swaying from side to side as each step has an effect on the trees, pulling and pushing them toward us in every direction. The world in front of me is like a curved mirror, distorting everything in its reflection and promising to be no better ahead.

* * *

"Have a nice day, monsieur," I say, handing the man his receipt for the belt he had us emboss.

"Merci," he says. "Good day—"

From the corner of my eye, a curtain falls, but when I turn to question why, I find Mère flat on the ground, clutching her chest, struggling to get herself back up.

"Mère, Mère, what happened? Are you okay? Did you hit your head?" I cry out. "Help, someone please help!" No one comes to help. I'm not sure if anyone can hear me until Alix finds us and drops to his knees on the other side of Mère's body.

"Mère, what's wrong?" he bellows.

"I—I don't know," she says, her voice hoarse. She continues to clutch her chest, her fist so tight her knuckles become pale.

"We need to find a doctor," I tell Alix, trying to push myself up from my knees. Mère reaches for my hand and holds me in place.

"My beautiful children, please listen to me," Mère sighs then follows with three short breaths. "I believe there is something else waiting for us once we've accomplished our predetermined expectations in this lifetime." Mère swallows hard and takes another couple short breaths. "I don't know why we are born or why we die, but I know there is an answer greater than anything we could ever conjure." She reaches up to touch both of our faces as her eyes stop moving, stop seeing...just—stop.

"Mère," I shout, shaking her shoulders as she lies stiff on the ground behind the front desk. Customers are now circling around us, watching, wondering what is happening, as we are. But like Mère's eyes, everyone around us seems frozen, their feet stuck to the ground. Time is still. Alix and I look at one another, unblinking with terror lacing our eyes with red veins. And in silence, we share the same sense of grief and understanding that we are now parentless. Alix is still a child, and I'm only seventeen, barely an adult who has already lost everything. In a split second, the world changes, shifts, moves around a lifeless body, and then life continues to whatever comes next.

* * *

Night and day have both come many times as we continue to walk through heavily settled woods without carved paths, smooth terrain, or an end in sight. We've eaten so little, even less than the usual daily allotment we've been surviving off, and dozens of women have fallen and been left behind. I keep questioning how I'm still upright, why my body has chosen to comply with these inhumane conditions. I wasn't designed for this—none of us were. I'm unsure how far we have walked, but not a person outside of the familiar prisoners has passed by. We're in the middle of nowhere, walking deeper into an abyss of cold, relentless conditions.

My vision is blurry, and my toes have been numb for what seems like days, but as long as there is someone in front of me, I focus on following in her steps, as I'm sure the person behind me is doing.

Flashes of light ping against my eyes as the sensation of tiny nails scratch down the center of my spine. I hope my legs know to keep moving.

Merely a second passes before we're moving again, and though the noise of our asynchronous steps along the crunchy snow are all I can mostly hear, it doesn't drown out the shrieks from ahead or the gunshot blast that follows. The guards don't speak out the rules, they show us by example.

Now we all know, if we fall, we die.

FORTY-EIGHT

NICOLAS

Paris, France

Not a day has passed since the Red Cross sent a medical unit down the street that I haven't waited in line to check for any new information regarding Raya. I'm not the only person seeking help for a reconnection, and all we can do is continue to ask, continue to wait, and continue to pray. I'm not sure if my hope is still intact or if it's something I've convinced myself I still have deep inside of me, but there will not come a day when I tell Amalia I stopped looking for her mother.

"Monsieur Bardot, it's late for you this morning," a nurse behind the reception booth says with a smile.

They always greet everyone with a smile, and yet, I'm not sure I remember how to do something so simple.

"Is there an updated list?" I ask, failing to greet the woman who has graciously searched through lists for me morning after morning since she has been working this shift.

"There is, but I haven't gone through it yet." Even if she had gone through it, I'm not sure Raya's name would stand out among the thousands of incoming names of displaced and deceased people. She lifts the catalog of names from beneath her table and sets it down heavily in front of me, flipping over the thick cover page exposing rows of alphabetically listed names.

I lift the stack of pages in handfuls before making it to the surnames that begin with the letter P and start at the top of the first column, dragging my finger slowly down the page until I have to turn to the next side. I wouldn't have ever thought there were so many last names that started with a P and then an A but there are more and more every day.

After five pages of the first two letters of Pascal, I reach the surname, slowing my search to glance at the next column over to scan the first names.

Another page turn makes my stomach hurt as it always does, but then the blood in my body rushes through my veins, my pulse zings like a speeding motor and I press my finger down over her name. My Raya's name. Raya Pasqual of Paris.

"She's—she's on the list," I heave, talking to the nurse who is assisting someone else at the same time.

The nurse doesn't respond as I slide my finger across the page to the status column. When I reach the box, I focus on the scripted writing, reading the words over and over as if I've forgotten how to connect letters to form sounds.

Status:
Injured/critical care

Location:
In transit for Hôpital de la Salpêtrière, Paris

Date of Last Update:
15th of May 1945

"She's alive, she's alive—this is her; do you see? It says she's alive, here in Paris," I shout, spinning in circles as the catalog of names fans through the air.

The nurse folds her hands over her heart, her smile still in place. "God bless you, monsieur. I wish you the best of luck."

"Merci beaucoup, thank you, thank you," I say, running out of breath.

I don't remember the last time I've run this fast, but the stretch of my legs feels incredible against each bounce in my steps. I'm moving so fast, my tears are sweeping across my face and running down my ears. How long has it been? How long have I been wondering if she's alive? How long have I refused to give up on her?

The hospital is surrounded by people, inside and outside, the crowds, visitors, and patients are in every movable spot, but I weave in and out of people until I find the registration desk, panting out Raya's name with hope that they understand I need to know where she is.

The woman with tired eyes behind the desk opens the registry and I wish to lean over the counter and help her move faster. I'm sure she's been doing nothing other than searching for patient names, but I can't wait any longer.

I didn't notice I was tapping my fingers on the counter until the woman glances up at my hands. I flatten them, forcing myself to stand still and wait. "She's on the fourth floor in room 415. Are you family?"

"Yes, yes, she's my future wife. Thank you, thank you, madame."

"Monsieur," she calls out.

But I don't have time for more questions. I've waited long enough. I weave through more and more people, searching for the back stairwell, hoping to find a quicker way upstairs. Every path is jammed with people, and the minutes it takes me to approach the fourth floor feel like an eternity has passed. My lungs burn as I try to catch my wind while still trudging forward, hating to stop and look at the number on the doors I'm passing, but needing to know the layout to find her room.

I end up circling around the entire unit, finding her room close to the opposite end of where I entered. There are several people in the room, but I would recognize my beautiful love anywhere and in any condition. She's asleep, peaceful, and I allow my tears to flow now before she wakes. I take in every detail of her face, the scars and marks she didn't have before, the faint freckles I remember so clearly, I could redraw the pattern on paper without being near her. Her cheeks are narrow beneath her prominent facial bones and she's pale, so pale, but still so lovely. Her hair is shorter, curling beneath the backs of her ears, but she's here. Her chest moves up and down as it should, telling me she's breathing. I fall to my knees and take her limp hand into mine.

"Ma chérie," I whisper.

I watch her eyes, waiting for movement and an inclination that she hears my voice. The reaction is delayed but her lashes flutter slightly. Her eyes move beneath her lids and like a butterfly emerging from a cocoon, she uses every ounce of energy she has to open her eyes, batting them again and again in search for clarity.

Then she finds me, twisting her head gently to the side. "Nic—" she whispers.

"I'm here. I've got you. You're going to be okay. Amalia is safe and at home with Mère." I'm sure I must be overloading her with so much to say, but it's everything she needs to hear.

"Ama—" she utters, trying to speak.

"Yes, our little girl, our daughter."

The flesh above her eyebrows puckers and the tip of her nose burns crimson. "Our daughter?" A hint of sound fills her breathy words, and I can see my girl coming back to me.

"She's incredible, Raya. She's perfect in every way."

Her chin shudders and her fingers squeeze around my

hand. "I didn't know if you would ever find her. I didn't know if I made the right—"

"Shh," I say, trying to calm her. "You are so brave and strong. You don't have to question anything." I lift her hand up to my lips, wishing I could recognize the sharp contours of her hands, but I know she's inside and that's all I care about. "We're going to get you better and then I'm taking you home."

Her lips curl into a glower and her cheeks redden like the tip of her nose. "I thought I had died. I wanted to die so many times, but..."

"You didn't."

FORTY-NINE

RAYA

Paris, France

I wanted to go home as soon as I heard Nicolas's voice. I didn't know I was in France, let alone Paris. The world had been spinning around me in dizzying circles for weeks since the Soviets took a detour in their path and ran into the group of women who had made it through the unforgiving trek we had been traveling from Ravensbrück. Like scared children in a dark room at night, the SS guards leading the trail took off in opposite directions, abandoning us, their prisoners, in the woods with a promise of returning to kill the rest of us. They tried to force us to hide behind rocks and in ditches as the sounds of a troop's heavy thudding steps grew closer. The SS guards' parting words to us were: "You will be killed by whoever finds you first, whether them or us." I questioned why we should hide if we were undoubtedly closing in on the end of our journeys. Rather than hide, I stood in the unmarked path we were on and didn't move. I was giving up and though the sound was a part of my imagination, I could hear the ticking of my beloved grandfather clock, each click dragging along with slower pauses in between, reaching an end I had to come to terms with.

Time was up.

I closed my eyes as the blurry sight of soldiers approached us and Amalia's face was all I could see. "I'm so sorry, my darling," I whispered into the wind.

A soldier took me by the arm, shouting at his comrades but I couldn't understand what he was saying. He scooped me up as if I was a dead body that he had to clear off a walking path but didn't drop me into the brush like I thought he would. Instead, I was taken to a vehicle and covered with blankets. Warmth spider-webbed up limbs, slowly and painfully as my nerves sparked a fight.

The thought of being rescued didn't play through my head, not once until I was placed on a cot and caught a glimpse of doctors in white coats. I began to wonder if this new place, the warmth of a sheet, a cot filled with cotton, a thin pillow, was death—life beyond the hell I tried to survive. I didn't imagine Nicolas would be in this place, waiting for me, but Mère once told me there was something better to find us after life, and that's what this feels like to me.

The doctors have called my situation cases of confusion, disorientation, disassociation, delirium due to brutal abuse in inhumane living conditions. They've said there were others like me who survived only by a miracle—those who fought through the cruel weathering elements while starving throughout the duration of a coordinated death march accompanying a plan to lead us astray, away from the Soviets heading toward us. The SS guards did whatever they could to prevent us from being rescued, but then they became cowards and ran when their plans went awry.

I still don't understand how we were found if we were off the map and untraceable. It doesn't make sense. Nothing in my life makes sense now. I keep asking the doctors and nurses if I'm here because I didn't survive. No one seems to understand my question or maybe I'm not asking them with the proper words.

Throughout the last three weeks, I've been transported to two different medical facilities that have tended to my wounds and reintroduced nutrients and supplements to my body. The world around me still feels like it's moving too fast for me to step back into and take part of and I'm not sure I'll ever be ready, but the doctors think it's okay for Nicolas to take me home now.

* * *

"Watch your step," he says as he helps me into a cab, placing his hand above my head and his other arm around my back as if I need padding around me to ensure I remain in one piece. Am I that fragile? Will I always be?

Nicolas meets me on the other side of the cab and slides in beside me, taking my hand within his, holding me tightly. I recognize the touch of his fingers, the warmth of his skin, but they feel foreign against mine and that part doesn't make sense in my head.

I glance at him, finding him staring longingly at me with a soft smile resting on his face. He hasn't asked me many questions, which is good because I don't know many answers, but having him beside me is enough, it's something I didn't think I'd feel again—it's warm and it's home to me, even here in a cab.

He keeps speaking about Amalia and I can only picture the baby I left behind over a year and a half ago. I can't imagine what she must look like now, how big she is, what she's like. She must not know me. I'll be a stranger to my child, but I will take that over her never finding out who I was. It's hard to comprehend that he has been raising her all this time without question, without hostility for the conception of her being. He keeps calling her our daughter and I've never heard anything more beautiful in my life. To love without condition isn't something everyone is capable of. In fact, I was sure no one was capable of such a thing after witnessing the things I've seen, but where the deficit of love has been, it's all the proof I need to regain some hope in society as we journey toward a better life where evil is a deficit so grand it's unrecognizable to the innocent.

I peer out the window, watching the city skate by us, wishing I could easily recognize the roads we're traveling, but nothing looks the way I remember. Buildings are missing, roads are gone, there is rubble in piles along the sides of the streets, but there are people walking, smiling, talking, eating, living.

"We're going to my home for now. Yours is still there for when you're ready, but Mère has been cooking and storing food for you all week and it's best for us to get you back on your feet before you decide what you want to do next."

I look back at Nicolas, feeling the confusion tug at my forehead. "What do you mean?"

"I mean, your life is what you choose it to be, where you want it to be, and with who."

"You and Amalia. That's all I need."

Nicolas smiles, his charming bright grin I remember admiring so much when we first met. "Then that's what you'll have, forever, without question."

The cab pulls up to a curb, stopping and waiting for payment. Nicolas drops some coins into his hand and rushes out of his side to meet me at mine, helping me out. The memory of walking up the steps to his building and flat reminds me of the day I left, so easily and free as if there was nothing to worry about when I had everything to worry about.

He was the one in physical pain, hurt, unable to do the things he wanted to do, but now it's me who can't move fast or stand for too long. It will be a while before I regain the muscle and body fat that I need to feel whole again.

Nicolas unlocks the front door and swings it open, allowing me to walk in first. My nerves fray and I'm hesitant to step inside, back into my former life to face a world I left behind. Nicolas places his hand on my back and gently urges me forward. My small steps comply, enough to allow him to close the door behind us. The living space still looks the same as it did when I was here last. The smell of garlic and other rich spices fills the air and it's like slipping into a warm bath full of bubbles. Euphoria.

Madame Bardot steps around the corner, tears in her eyes, a sullen look tugging at her lips, and her finger wrapped in a little hand that belongs to the most exquisite little girl I've ever laid my eyes on.

Madame Bardot kneels beside her and whispers into her ear, "Mère is back. She's here now."

Amalia peers up at Madam Bardot with her big blue eyes, and two blonde coiled pigtails, curious, then glances over to Nicolas with the same look. She runs across the room, her little dress swiveling around her waist as she catches Nicolas's leg between her arms while she pauses to stare up at me.

I don't want to scare her or act too quickly. "I don't know if you remember me," I say. "But I'm your mère and I have loved you so much every single day of your life."

It's hard to know what she understands at two years old, but she lifts her arms up toward me and I'm taken aback by her ease. Nicolas lifts her up and keeps a handle of her as Amalia wraps her arms around my neck. She rests her head on my shoulder as if it's something she remembers doing, which doesn't seem as though it should be possible.

"Yes, my sweetheart. I'm your mère."

"Me-me," she replies. "Me-me."

Nicolas beams with pride, releasing a soft chuckle. "We're still working on our Rs."

"She can call me Me-me. She can call me whatever she

would like." I wrap my arms around her, recalling the warmth from her chest against mine. Her golden blonde hair sweeps against my face like strands of silk, and I nuzzle my cheek over her head, catching sight of the way Nicolas is looking at her. Pride. Like a father would see his daughter—with pride.

"Come, let's get you comfortable." Madame Bardot pats the cushions of the sofa, inviting me over.

Nicolas lifts Amalia off my chest and carries her over to the sofa, waiting for me to settle down before resting her on my lap.

Madame Bardot layers a blanket around my shoulders and places a kiss on my forehead, holding her lips in place for a long moment. "Thank God you're okay. Thank God," she says softly.

I want to ask Nicolas if he ever heard from the Levis again after I was taken, but I don't want to sound ungrateful for what I've already regained. I pray they made it through everything for whatever they endured, and I hope to find them again someday but for now, I'm blessed.

"What's going through your mind?" Nicolas asks, sitting beside me.

"A lot," I say, running my fingers through Amalia's hair as she plays with the buttons on my shirt.

He twists on the sofa and turns toward the kitchen, where the sound of multiple footsteps echoes between the small galley space. I turn to see who Nicolas is looking at since Madame Bardot is on my other side.

Charlette, a healthy Charlette, her hair in long dark curls, her cheeks plump and rosy, in a casual sky-blue day dress walks toward me. Her lips press together tightly, and I can hear her swallow against the thick of her throat as she comes closer.

Again, I question life after death. Is that what this is?

"Charlette?" Her name doesn't form with sound, only air.

Nicolas stands up from my side, gesturing for Charlette to take his seat.

"You're okay?" I say to her.

"Thanks to Nicolas," she says. "He's taken care of us, me, and my parents, kept food on our table, checked on us nightly. We didn't know what had happened to you. When the shop was broken into, we made our way out of your bedroom window and up to the rooftop where we hid for days until it was safe to return inside. It was months before Nicolas found us, unaware that we were still there after everything that had happened to the building. We survived by rationing the remaining cans of food we had managed to set aside, with your help, of course, but without a way to acquire more, we ate less and less each day. We didn't know how much longer we could make the remnants last. We're so thankful for him. We're alive because of him."

I search between Nicolas and Charlette, trying to wrap my head around everything she's saying. "How?"

"None of that matters," Nicolas says.

"Where are your parents?" I ask, hoping they're okay too.

"Mère and my father have been helping with the reconstruction of our former building so we can move back into our home soon too. They didn't want to inundate you today with everything else you're coming home to, but they would like to see you as soon as you're up to it," she says, circling her hand across Amalia's back.

I feel as if there is a glass window between us and we're speaking different languages even though I can understand them perfectly well. I don't feel like I'm sitting here, alive. My entire life is unfolding, a page at a time, as I try to match up the past with the present. Life before the war feels so long ago that I could call it another lifetime. It only makes sense that it was in fact another lifetime.

Charlette carefully places her arm behind my neck and embraces me with such a gentle touch it seems she's afraid she might hurt me.

"I didn't think I'd ever see you again," I say.

"We're all together as we should be." Charlette sweeps her hand across the scars on my cheek. "Everyone you love is still here."

"What about Alix?" I ask.

EPILOGUE

ALIX, PRESENT DAY, NOVEMBER 1946

Paris, France

A girl's dream should never be based on what she can do for everyone else around her because there comes a time when there is no more time, and no one can repay her for each selfless deed.

I knew when she stopped writing to me that something had happened, and I had no way to find out where she was or if she was okay—the girl who was forced to become a woman at seventeen and take care of her orphan brother in exchange for a life she was on the brink of beginning.

For almost two years, I scorned myself for not trying harder to get across the border between Switzerland and France before it was too late. I should have read between the lines in her letters and assumed she was in trouble when she told me she was pregnant. I didn't try hard enough to protect her, and I should have. I was selfish and followed my dream and escaped a reality so horrific I don't always understand the words describing the atrocities many survived or didn't.

After Germany's occupation ended in France, I received a

letter from Nicolas, a man I knew little about other than the fact that he and my sister were close friends. Raya wasn't one to share intimate details of her life through letters. I would only know her truths by standing in front of her and watching her cheeks turn different shades of red when asking certain questions.

When I learned that Raya was missing as I had been fearing, I was still stuck in Switzerland, unable to cross the border no matter how hard I tried. No one was coming in or going out and it wasn't until the Germans forfeited their occupation with France that I had hope of making it home sooner rather than later.

The war ended for France in August last year, but nothing was fixed overnight. Everything took time, so much time that I didn't have the patience to deal with it when my sister was still missing somewhere. I was doing everything I could to search for her from Switzerland and then continued to do the same when I finally arrived back home. Information wasn't being released about victims of the Holocaust or prisoners of the camps, the deaths of anyone, and we had to wait until those lists began to form. With each prison camp's liberation, a new list would slowly formulate, and we would check for her name day after day.

It's hard to admit I was losing hope after so many of the camps had been liberated and we still had no update about her whereabouts. I stopped going to the Red Cross with Nicolas on a daily basis, unable to face the letdown and heartache every single day. Instead, I focused on the family shop, trying to put it back together in a semblance of the way it once was, knowing that if Raya was to make it home to us, she would have her memories still intact. We grew up in this shop, it was our life and it's all we had left with Mère and Papa dead. Raya had held on to it so tightly, refusing to give up on it as if it was a member of our family, the tie to our family that kept us all together.

When I learned Raya was alive and coming back to us, it was my job as her brother to ensure she would come home to a life she wouldn't have to dread, to remove any threats that could impact her well-being. It didn't take me as long as I suspected it might, but I found Gustav Vogel's name among the list of detained war criminals following the status of "executed" as the period of his sentence. I was relieved that I didn't have to hunt him down and kill him with my bare hands because I would have if he had still been alive.

Raya can move on in her life, knowing she won't ever have to see that man again, and it's the very least I can do to relieve her of the suffering she's endured, but it's a start.

*　*　*

1950

"Alix, I need another order pad. Can you take down the sizes from those gentlemen by the door?"

"I'm already on it, sister." She must not be able to see me standing in front of the gentleman with my ruler out. Everyone in this shop is elated to be here, eagerly waiting for their custom classic French leather gloves. Even those who are outside on the street are bright-eyed as they chat around the newsstand while Monsieur Croix appears to entertain them all.

"Thank you," she shouts.

My days of teaching are ahead of me, but for now, it's Raya's turn to live out her dream and I'm not going anywhere until I see it through. I vividly remember the day she had reflections of stars in her eyes, standing beneath the lively Parisian sky with her hands up in the air telling me that someday she was going to be known all over France for her classic French leather gloves. That moment reeled through me over and over for the years she was missing, knowing I didn't do anything to help her accomplish this sooner.

"Monsieur Faure? Is there a Monsieur Faure? I have your order ready," Amalia hollers from the back of the shop. My niece, a spitting image of my dear sister, at the ripe old age of seven has become the top saleswoman of our family's leather shop.

"Right here, chérie," a man calls out.

Amalia runs to the man and hands him his ribbon-tied box, then curtseys. "I do hope you enjoy your custom French leather gloves, monsieur."

"My goodness, what a fine young lady you are. I hope your mère knows how lucky she is to have you. That woman is something else—the strongest of all the women I know, and you know where she gets that from, sweetheart?"

"No, monsieur, where?" Amalia asks with a tilt to her head.

"Your grandparents. They would be remarkably proud of you and your family for continuing this shop's grand legacy."

"Monsieur Faure," Raya calls out as she makes her way across the shop toward him and Amalia. "How lovely to see you."

"Where's the old man?" Monsieur Faure asks her. "I need to have a talk with him about one of his articles I read last week."

Nicolas has a desk set up in the back of the shop where he spends the day writing articles to sell to various newspapers around the city. Most of them have offered him permanent jobs, but he's found great luck being sought after for his words. A smart man knows what he's worth, and Nicolas won't let his family out of his sight. If I could handpick a husband for my sister, there is no one else in the world I would choose but him.

"Who are you calling an old man, and what does that make you, monsieur?" Nicolas announces his rebuttal, standing from his desk in the back corner.

"I didn't see you back there," Monsieur Faure responds with a hearty chuckle, "and to answer your question, I do believe I am considered older than dinosaurs now, which means there isn't a name dedicated to my kind."

Nicolas shares a laugh with the man who has been a long-time family customer and shakes his hand. "I wanted to ask you where you came up with the inspiration for that article published in...what...four newspapers last week? The Glove-maker's Daughter – that was the title, right?"

Nicolas studies the man for a moment, trying not to grin. "Monsieur, as you know, inspiration derives from life experiences and I've come to learn that the most valuable gift a man could ever receive is—well," Nicolas peers over at Raya then down at Amalia with so much love it's impossible to describe in any other way than Nicolas has managed to do so. "Well, the most valuable gift anyone could ever receive is something that is made with love, cared for with nothing but the finest qualities, keeps the cold away, and encompasses everything he touches with warmth—giving an unsuspecting person everything they never knew they needed."

A LETTER FROM SHARI

Dear Reader,

Thank you for choosing *The Glovemaker's Daughter*. If you'd like to keep up to date with all my latest releases, just sign up at the website link below.

www.bookouture.com/shari-j-ryan

As a lover of history and storytelling, I enjoy learning about the past—especially World War II. The Holocaust is a subject dear to my heart. I grew up listening to stories from my grandmother, a Holocaust survivor. To honor her and the rest of my family who endured life during World War II, I'm fortunate for the opportunity to honor my family's experiences.

I hope you found the book engaging and worthwhile. If you enjoyed the book, I would be grateful if you left a review. Feedback from readers always assists me in improving my craft. You'll also be helping new readers to discover my works for the first time!

The greatest pleasure in the publishing process comes from connecting with readers like yourself! Please reach out through any of these means: Facebook page, Twitter, Instagram, or my website.

Can't wait to hear your thoughts! Thank you for reading!
Xoxo
Shari

KEEP IN TOUCH WITH SHARI

www.sharijryan.com

 facebook.com/authorsharijryan

 twitter.com/sharijryan

 instagram.com/authorsharijryan

ACKNOWLEDGEMENTS

I want to thank Bookouture for being an incredible publishing house. Your kindness, generosity, and compassion are something I value deeply throughout each publication. It's an honor to be a part of such an excellent team.

Lucy, it's been a joy to work with you. Your insights, edits, and advice are so inspiring to me. I'm so thankful for the opportunity to collaborate with you.

Linda, thank you for everything—for motivating me to progress and stay true to myself. Our friendship is so dear, and I don't know what I'd do without you in my life.

Tracey, Gabby, Elaine—thank you for always being by my side with your feedback and honesty. Your friendship means so much to me; I wouldn't even know where to start without all of you.

Thank you to every amazing blogger and reader out there—being surrounded by this community has impacted my life in ways I could never have expected. You're all truly supportive and encouraging; I'm incredibly grateful for this chance at living out my dream!

Lori, my amazing little sister—thank you for being my number one reader and my best friend in all the world. I love you!

My family—Mom, Dad, Mark, Ev, and Papa—thank you for always reminding me I can accomplish anything I set my mind to. Knowing how much you care and believe in me keeps me pushing forward. Love you all!

Bryce and Brayden—my incredible boys, you may not realize how much you both inspire me, but knowing how excited you get for each one of my releases fills my heart with so much joy. I can't wait for the two of you to feel the same about your own passions someday. I love you both dearly!

Josh, before sending off any manuscript, I take a moment to appreciate the unending support you give me. Though we often talk about fictional characters, you believe in them just as much as I do. Your faith in me encourages my efforts day after day. I love you very much!

Milton Keynes UK
Ingram Content Group UK Ltd.
UKHW011835041023
429950UK00004B/187